THE
AUTUMN
SPRINGS
RETIREMENT
HOME
MASSACRE

ALSO BY
PHILIP FRACASSI

NOVELS
The Third Rule of Time Travel
Boys in the Valley
Gothic
A Child Alone with Strangers
Don't Let Them Get You Down

STORY COLLECTIONS
No One Is Safe!
Beneath a Pale Sky
Behold the Void

NOVELLAS
Commodore
Shiloh
Sacculina

FOR CHILDREN
The Boy with the Blue Rose Heart

POEMS
Tomorrow's Gone

PHILIP FRACASSI

THE AUTUMN SPRINGS RETIREMENT HOME MASSACRE

NIGHTFIRE

TOR PUBLISHING GROUP
NEW YORK

THE AUTUMN SPRINGS RETIREMENT HOME MASSACRE

A Nightfire Book
Published by Tom Doherty Associates / Tor Publishing Group
120 Broadway
New York, NY 10271

www.torpublishinggroup.com

Nightfire™ is a trademark of Macmillan Publishing Group, LLC.

EU Representative: Macmillan Publishers Ireland Ltd, 1st Floor, The Liffey Trust Centre, 117–126 Sheriff Street Upper, Dublin 1, DO1 YC43

The Library of Congress Cataloging-in-Publication Data is available upon request.

ISBN 978-1-250-87906-6 (hardcover)
ISBN 978-1-250-87907-3 (ebook)

Our books may be purchased in bulk for specialty retail/wholesale, literacy, corporate/premium, educational, and subscription box use. Please contact MacmillanSpecialMarkets@macmillan.com.

First Edition: 2025

Printed in the United States of America

10 9 8 7 6 5 4 3 2 1

FOR **MOM** AND **DAD**,

WITH LOVE AND REMEMBRANCE.

ONE

MOVIE NIGHT

1

Rose has seen better movies.

Not that she doesn't enjoy something artistic, mind you. But this?

This was goddamned depressing, is what this was.

Who the hell shows a bunch of old folks a movie about Death?

But that's Gopi for you. A retired film director whose personal crusade is to educate the residents of Autumn Springs on the great films of the past. Even the artsy black-and-white ones.

Our own personal Criterion curator.

Still, she has to admit she enjoys these little productions of his. Tonight's movie, *The Seventh Seal,* had been interesting, if a smidge on the slow side. But her friend put a lot of work into his presentation, and the folks who showed up seemed to enjoy it well enough. And even though the private theater (located in the Autumn Springs Community Center) is small—only about forty seats—it's full every time he puts on a viewing. Heck, these last few months, folks had to RSVP via email just to secure their spots. And if they didn't show they were banned from future RSVPing. And no one, not even Rose, wanted that.

Miller leans in close.

"I think a good portion of the audience is asleep," he mumbles, and Rose smells the peppermint on his breath, a ghostly remnant from the cellophane-wrapped candies he always carries in his sport coat pocket.

Rose glances around and does indeed notice a few nodding heads. She also notes that Angela Forrest is sitting with Owen Duffield, grinning like a schoolgirl. The two of them are probably holding hands down at seat level so as not to make a spectacle. Rose smiles, happy that they've found love so late in life.

Many don't.

Many don't want to.

Rose considers herself the latter, a fact she has to remind Beauregard Mason Miller—he of the peppermint-scented breath—of every few weeks, it seems.

"Now that we've all experienced Ingmar Bergman's masterpiece," Gopi says, standing before them like an old professor, his thick spectacles and tweed sport coat completing the impression, "I'd like to open the room to questions. Obviously, there's a lot to unpack here, and I'm happy to answer as best I can."

Rose sits up, feeling mischievous. "Why would Death bother playing a game of chess?" she says. "Our book club just finished *The Book Thief*, and it says that 'Death waits for no man', and I think that sounds about right." She glances quickly around the room. "Present company excluded, of course."

There's a murmur of laughter from the others, and even Gopi smiles at Rose, his bushy gray, Hercule Poirot–style mustache—tipped up with a little wax at the ends—rising as he shows off dazzling white teeth. "An excellent question, Ms. DuBois," he says with a wink. "Most believe that the chess game is Death's way of proving there is no free will when it comes to dying, that no number of games played will ever jeopardize his mission, because fate must always win out over free will. Much like playing bridge against the Pickfords," he adds, causing another round of good-natured laughter from the group.

Mary Reynolds (who is sweet on Gopi, Rose thinks) raises her hand and asks about the significance of chess being Bergman's choice.

"Why not cards? Or cribbage?" she asks playfully.

"Ah!" Gopi replies, delighted to have a softball lobbed his way. "Good question. For one, many great thinkers consider chess a perfect metaphor for our daily lives, each move on the board being a symbolic representation of our free will. In chess, a good player plans ahead. They sacrifice when needed and strategize every decision." He pauses, scans the room somberly. "And sometimes there are consequences to those decisions, and those consequences are not always obvious, right? Because they're not necessarily things that occur right away, but often well into the future . . . too many moves ahead for us to see plainly."

The room is quiet for a moment. Rose thinks about what Gopi has said and finds herself wondering if Miller knows how to play chess and, if so, perhaps he would teach her.

"For Bergman, however," Gopi continues, smiling once more, "the idea came from a work of art. Let me tell you about a famous painting by Swedish artist Albertus Pictor, which inspired Bergman's decision to have a knight challenge Death to a game. . . ."

2

When the Q&A is over, everyone makes their way out of the Community Center, most residents eager to get home and settle in for the night. A small group, however, gathers in the small courtyard at the rear of the building, where they stop to chat with friends or share lengthy goodbyes.

As Rose and Miller step into the biting autumn air, she shivers and pulls her wool cardigan more tightly around her shoulders.

"Allow me, please," Miller says, and removes his sport coat.

"Miller, I don't—"

"I insist."

He settles the coat over her shoulders, and Rose has to admit that the heavy coat—along with whatever body heat it retains—abolishes the chill that had clawed at her back when they first stepped into the night.

"Fine, fine . . ." she says. "Now, I'd like to get home and have some hot tea, unless you want to socialize, in which case I'll say thank you and good night."

Miller chuckles and lightly touches her elbow, leading them toward the Greenview Apartments where they both live, along with twenty-four other souls.

Rose *likes* Miller—likes him very much—but wishes he could leave it there and not always be trying to court her with some foolishness. She is done with love. She'd been married, raised a daughter (who in turn raised her own beautiful son), and cares little for the complex bindings of a relationship or the aromatic allure of romance.

A former high school English teacher (retired for nearly a decade), Rose DuBois was born and raised in Brooklyn, New York, and had spent her entire life in the city before finally moving north to live out her days at Autumn Springs. Now she wants nothing more than a peaceful existence from here on out, free of attachments or drama or confusion or heartache, and she most certainly wants nothing to do with silly romances or the entanglements of men.

From the day she'd moved here, however—five years ago now—Beauregard Mason Miller had been an instant and constant companion: a funny, objectively handsome man who she appreciates spending time with. But he's also a man she's happy to leave at the doorstep so she can enjoy her peace and quiet: her books, her private space, her delightfully large bed, and her independence.

Rose wants no ties. No pets, no plants, and *no* boyfriends.

To her consternation, however, as they walk down the lit path toward home, she finds herself sparing a sidelong glance his direction, more curious than usual about the man who'd been her best friend since arriving at her new home.

Beauregard Mason Miller ("just Miller" he'd said that first day, the moving boxes still unpacked in her undecorated living room) is a tall man with a shaggy head of hair, a dimpled chin, and big, strong hands. He'd been a professor at Columbia College for more than forty years before finally retiring at the age of seventy-six, just a couple years younger than Rose herself is now. He's good at cards, terrible at technology, and near impossible to upset, or even irritate. He has a savage sweet tooth (though where the calories go on his lean frame she has no idea) and enjoys detective shows (an entertainment he and Rose immediately bonded over, she herself being a junkie for a good crime story). He knows everything there is to know about ancient history, especially the rise and fall of the Roman Empire, which was his specialty at Columbia. He is warm and kind and gentle, and Rose supposes that she does love him in a way. . . .

But not enough to give up her autonomy.

Or her bed.

She'd been through too much, and grown too old, to let a man crimp her lifestyle now. If she ever finds herself desperately lonely, perhaps she'll get a goldfish. Or a canary. Something small. Something *easy*.

Miller glances over at her, a smile curling his lips. Rose shakes her head brusquely and turns her eyes back to the path, slightly embarrassed at having been caught staring. Instead, she focuses on the ground, studies the ridiculous colored-tape lines running beneath their feet: The yellow line leads to the Community Center. Green to the Greenview Apartments. Blue to the Seaview Apartments. There is a red line as well, which takes one straight to the Medical Center—a large, square, concrete bunker of a building most residents try to ignore as best they can.

The Medical Center is where you went to live when it was deemed you could no longer take care of yourself. It's where you went to see a doctor, to get treatment, checkups, or prescriptions.

It's also where you went to die.

Five years I've been here, Rose thinks as they walk through the night. *Five years . . . and how many more to go? Ten? Twenty?*

Feeling a wave of melancholy (and blaming the strange movie for getting her moody in the first place), Rose looks up toward the night sky, wishing the spray of stars would do something to lift her spirits, make her feel *good* about where she is in life, where she lives, the person she's become.

My forever home, she thinks, and fights off a surge of nauseating depression that piggybacks atop the knowledge that this place—from now until the day she dies—will be the last, and only, home she'll ever know.

The Autumn Springs Retirement Home is less of a "home" and more of a campus. It isn't the largest, or most modern, retirement facility in upstate New York, but it's well maintained and well staffed, just nice enough for those who had diligently saved their pennies over the course of their lives to afford a comfortable—if not glamorous—way of life for their sunset years.

The bulk of the complex is separated into three large brick buildings: the main building, four stories high—and through which visitors and residents exit and enter the campus—is the Community

Center. In addition to the theater Rose and Miller just left behind, the building also houses several large activity rooms, multiple classrooms (with rotating curriculums), a relatively up-to-date library, an outdated gym, an indoor pool, and the administration offices. The large front lobby includes a grand piano (rarely played), a reception desk, and a set of glass double doors leading to the parking lot and—beyond that—the greater world: a world the residents of Autumn Springs have, for the most part, left behind.

Directly behind the Community Center, just across a small concrete courtyard, sits a large dining hall, one that boasts a restaurant-sized kitchen and a diverse menu for breakfast, lunch, and dinner. Nightly specials are always a surprise, and residents take their three meals a day there almost exclusively.

Stretching out to either side of the Community Center are two narrow brick buildings, each only two stories. If one entered the main lobby from the parking lot, the building to the left would be the Greenview Apartments, and the building to the right the Seaview Apartments, supposedly named as such because it rests a few hundred feet closer to the Atlantic Ocean than its partner (as the coastline is more than one hundred and fifty miles away, the "Seaview" branding is more whimsical, or possibly ironic, than literal).

A dense, state-protected forest horseshoes the campus's surrounding grounds, which are spacious, if a bit rustic. There's a trailhead of sorts (not state certified) at the foot of the trees that is wide enough for a wheelchair, followed by a flat dirt trail that never swells wider than a few feet. The trail tunnels through nature, leading to a small meadow and an old, boarded-up well. Although the forest path is rarely used by residents, the rear grounds behind the apartments also boast a lovely asphalt walking path—complete with a weathered gazebo—cutting through what is colloquially referred to as the "back lawn."

To the east of the campus lies the broad, bubbling Seminole Creek, one of many natural springs in the region (and what gives Autumn Springs its moniker) that draw visiting grandchildren like a piper's song. The land to the west of Greenview, however, is far less opulent, consisting primarily of a straw-grass clearing carpeted with hearty pachysandra and low brush. Other highlights include the sad brown cage of a forgotten community garden and a rather uneven, weed-spotted tennis court.

All of which, more or less, comprises the bulk of what the Autumn Springs geography has to offer.

Still, for most residents, it's enough. There is always something going on in the Community Center for folks to enjoy, and the campus is large enough that, on most days, you can get in a nice walk (if it isn't too cold outside). There are regular shuttles into town where one can day-shop or dine out, and regular group outings to museums, baseball games, and other activities. Some residents still have their cars, of course, but most hardly use them given the convenience of the shuttles.

That said, there are a couple things about the Autumn Springs Retirement Home that Rose, if she's being honest, doesn't much care for.

The first is having to live next to the CSX freight train line, which normally pulls anywhere from twenty to fifty cars, chugging and rumbling past on tracks that lie just outside the main parking lot and the west section of the back lawn, no more than a hundred yards from the brick walls of the Greenview Apartments. The massive train burrows past at sixty-plus miles per hour, wheezing a dense trail of black smoke into the air (and waking up every living thing for half a mile or more) as it winds its way north, toward Albany and beyond.

The nerve-frying *bing, bing, bing* of the crossing signal isn't so bad, since it only occurs twice a day during the week and once on Saturday evening—at 8 PM sharp—but the deep grumbling of the massive engine and the ensuing lumbering trail of cargo cars sets Rose's teeth on edge (usually right around the time she's settling down for sleep), only to repeat itself again early in the morning, right at 7 AM on the weekdays. Since her apartment is at the western-most part of the building, and therefore nearest the tracks, she has it much worse than the others. But what can she do? She'd requested a different apartment just weeks after arriving, but every time someone dies (or "leaves," if using the local parlance) a new face moves in, claiming they'd secured rights to the apartment many years prior.

Simply put, it's something she'll just have to live with.

Even worse than the train, however, is the creepy, abandoned building settled at the rear of the back lawn, the one residents and staff refer to as the "old asylum"; a decrepit, hundred-year-old structure hunched along the forest's tree line, ugly and lifeless as an eyeless, concrete corpse. The long, single-story building has a moss-covered A-frame roof and milky-brown walls. The windows are boarded over and the metal doors securely locked, so there's no chance one might mistakenly wander into its decaying interior. It's an eyesore that gives most residents—Rose included—the heebie-jeebies, since it's where they used to house folks who were dying or mentally ill, cleanly separated from the other, healthy, residents.

Some, of course, have suggested that the old building might be haunted.

The old asylum had, to date, escaped the demolition axe due to the fact (if rumors were true) that some great Union general had died there during the Civil War. Regardless of its historical significance (or lack thereof), every year or so there is renewed talk of tearing the decaying building down to the ground but, since the expense outweighed the benefits, it stolidly remains, a ghost of the past pigheadedly refusing to push itself into the afterlife.

Much like the residents themselves.

3

"What did you two think of the movie?"

Rose startles, broken from her thoughts, and notices Angela Forrest walking at her side, neat round glasses reflecting the pathway's halogen lamps, a white puffy jacket making her look like a giant marshmallow with legs.

"Good evening, Angela," Miller says, nodding.

"Hello, Miller," Angela replies, but her eyes stay on Rose. She shuffles closer as they walk, slides a hand beneath Rose's arm. "Can I call you tomorrow, Rose?" she asks in a hushed voice. "I need some friendly advice."

Rose smiles, knowing what Angela really needs is a girlfriend to chatterbox with about the new man in her life. "Of course, hon. Why don't we have lunch?" She gives a little wink and lowers her own voice to match Angela's conspiratorial whisper. "Just us girls."

Angela snickers and nods. "Yes, yes please."

Miller, sensing the moment, hangs back a few feet from the women as they cling to one another, murmuring happily as two birds on a branch. A few moments later they reach the entrance of the Greenview building, and Miller dashes ahead to hold the door for the women as they breeze past.

The heated air of the lobby is a luxury on his chilled skin as he follows them inside, happy to be home.

When they reach the elevators, Rose gives Angela a quick hug. "I'll call you in the morning and we'll make a plan for lunch."

"Lovely," Angela says, her round face cherubic with its cold-reddened cheeks, her wide, bright eyes glittering behind bifocal glasses. "You have my number."

"Of course . . ."

"Goodnight, Angela," Miller adds, pressing the button to call the elevator.

"Goodnight, Miller. Goodnight, goodnight," she says cheerily, waving them off as she walks down the west hallway toward her apartment.

The elevator creaks and, after some minor coughs and groans, the doors shuffle wearily open. Miller and Rose step inside, and Miller hits the button for the second floor. "I take solace every day knowing this old elevator will kick the bucket before I do," he huffs, rubbing the cold out of his arms.

"Here," Rose says, and shrugs off his sport coat. "I'm fine now."

"Was hoping you'd hold on to it," he says glumly, but with a twinkle in his eye. "You could wear it around, let folks know we're going steady."

"We're doing no such thing," Rose says, lifting her chin.

Miller chuckles as the elevator creaks and whines its way upward.

"Faster to take the damn stairs," he says.

"Don't be a grouch."

The elevator finally bumps to a stop and the two friends step into the quiet, carpeted foyer of the second-floor apartments.

"May I see you home?"

"You may not," Rose says, and pats his forearm. "Thank you for the movie."

Miller nods, smiles. "May I kiss your cheek goodnight?"

Rose exhales dramatically, hating the heat that rushes to her cheeks. She cranes her neck, tilts one warmed cheek toward him.

Miller bends down and pecks her lightly.

"Goodnight, Miller."

"Goodnight, Rose. Enjoy your lunch with Angela," he says. "Oh, there's a new show I heard about, a good detective series with Liam Neeson as Marlowe. You want to watch it tomorrow night?"

"We'll see," Rose says, feeling childish in the cozy light of the foyer, still blushing from the man's light kiss on her cheek. *Like a butterfly landing then taking off again,* she thinks, then chides herself for foolishness.

"Good enough." Miller tips the brim of an invisible hat and

walks toward the east wing, his tall, lanky body moving effortlessly, almost gracefully. For a moment, Rose watches him.

That man, I swear . . .

Rose hears voices rise through the elevator shaft, the grind of the car's gears as it is called downward once again. *More folks returning from the movie.*

Not wanting to do any more socializing this particular evening, she hustles down the west hallway, eager to be back inside her small apartment so she can make a pot of tea, wash her face, put on some comfy clothes, and settle in with a book.

As she nears her door at the end of the corridor, however, the elevator *dings* from behind. She turns back to see a small group exit, laughing and speaking in loud, enthusiastic voices. She recognizes Vic Roberts and Sandra Freeman, who everyone knows have been screwing on and off for the last year, even though they both deny it. Mickey Lake is with them as well, towering over the others; he's built like a damned lumberjack, but Rose likes the man—he's sweet and quiet, if physically intimidating. A gentle giant who once played professional football, if the rumors are true.

It's Mickey who catches her eye from the foyer and gives a small wave. She waves back, and a couple others turn to look, spotting her.

Damn.

"Rosie!" Sandra Freeman yells, giving her a big, silly wave. "Come on over; we're having a nightcap."

Rose smiles politely and puts her key into the door. "Not tonight, I'm afraid. But thank you. Have fun." She twists and pushes before anything more can be said and feels silly for yelling down the hallway so late at night. *You'd think we were in high school.*

She enters her apartment and closes the door behind her. The lamp by her reading chair is on, as is the stove light in the white-tiled kitchen.

For a moment, she allows herself to rest against the door, taking in her small living room, the tidy kitchen, the doorway leading to the bedroom beyond.

Her eight hundred-square-foot life.

Surprisingly, she finds herself saddened by the sudden vacuum of quiet, by the tidiness of it all. By the emptiness of it all.

She debates going back down the hallway, knocking on Sandra's door, and having that nightcap after all. A warm brandy, perhaps. Or a glass of red wine.

Instead, Rose shakes off the melancholy and heads for the kitchen to put on a pot of water, thinking of Miller kissing her cheek—that warm tickle of a butterfly landing and then flying away.

4

Angela is tired but excited.

And, truth be told, a smidge shaken.

That horrid movie, she thinks, climbing slowly into bed, her face greased with Oil of Olay, her glasses set neatly on the nightstand beside her. *Still, it was nice to hold hands with Owen.*

The sheets are pleasantly cool against her feet, the thick cotton nightgown soft on her skin. She sighs contentedly, wonders if it's silly of her to dream of things like marriage. She's eighty-two years old, after all, and Owen a rabbit's whisker over eighty. They're no spring chickens, not anymore.

But she *likes* the idea of having a companion—a *real* companion—in her August years. Someone to share a bed with, to wake up with, to go on shopping trips and vacations with. Someone to kiss and hug and hold hands with.

She wonders if he's a good cook. She'd never thought to ask, but that *might* just be the icing on the cake. He's already handsome, and fit, and seems eager for small adventures, things fitting to their age. Maybe a trip? Or a cruise?

Well, goodnight, sweet Owen, she thinks, letting go of her whimsical daydreams with a smile, and reaches for the bedside light.

The room falls into darkness.

The wind whispers softly outside her curtained window, which, when uncovered, offers a view of the back lawn—a flat clearing walled off in the distance by an army of tall, dark trees. She would prefer to be on the other side of the building, so that her window faced the lighted path instead of the unlit clearing (which sometimes gave her the late-night willies), but perhaps one day she could move in with Owen, who has a lovely second-story apartment in the Seaview . . .

Creeaak.

Beneath the covers, Angela goes still.

She stops breathing, stops thinking.

Her blood turns to ice.

Something . . . something in the other room . . .

Moved.

Now she hears more sounds in the dark. Sounds like . . . the shuffling of clothes?

And then—

Creeaak.

Was that the living room's closet door?

Feeling like a scared, silly little girl, Angela defiantly pushes herself up on one elbow and turns to look across the bedroom, glaring at the door.

And there, framed in the open doorway, is a shadow darker than the night.

A person.

Standing there. Watching her.

"Hello?" she says, voice choked with fear.

Terror, alive and ice-cold, crawls into Angela's bed, snakes beneath her fluffy cream nightgown and settles itself atop her body like a slinking, hairless cat.

"What do you want?" she whimpers, lips trembling. She debates reaching for her glasses so she can see better, but she's too afraid to move, too afraid to do anything that might make that person in the doorway become more *real*, shatter the threadbare illusion that this could all be a dream, a horrible nightmare.

Then the figure—clad all in black, Angela is certain—walks quickly toward her.

"Oh, God!" she yells and, with a sudden burst of energy—of *bravery*—her survival instincts kick in and she rips away the sheets, throws her legs from the bed. She has no weapon—no stray scissors or knitting needles, not even a dulled letter opener—but she thinks if she can get to the front door, pull it open and scream for help, perhaps this intruder will run. Perhaps they'll leave her alone.

This is what she thinks. This is what she desperately *hopes*.

But as she gains her feet, a fist grips the front of her nightgown and a ghastly black mask stares down at her, only inches from her face.

"Leave me alone!" she screams, and slaps weakly at the intruder's head.

There's a laugh—a strange, horrible chuckle from beneath that fabric—and then Angela is pushed away. *Hard.* She falls backward into the nightstand, the edge of which digs sharply into her hip. The bedside lamp crashes to the floor, along with her glasses and the well-worn paperback she'd borrowed from the library, an old Fannie Flagg book she'd read several times over.

She catches her balance but is immediately grabbed once more, this time by the neck, where a strong gloved hand *squeezes,* harder and harder, until her throat is forced closed. Her tongue juts from her gaping mouth as her breath and voice are stolen away, her trachea slowly crushed. She gags, tries desperately to pull away, but the intruder simply spins her around like a doll and shoves her across the room, toward the open door.

Stumbling, she smacks into the doorframe and hears—actually *hears*—something *snap* in her hip, as if a precocious child had pulled the trigger of a loaded cap gun. She falls hard to the ground, pain shooting through her side like fire.

The front door! her mind screams. Angela immediately begins crawling away from the devil in her room, this would-be murderer. But the pain is too much, and her throat burns horribly. She tries to call out but realizes that something is very *wrong.* Something inside her neck has been badly broken, damaged to such an extent that she can hardly breathe, much less cry for help.

Even worse, based on the searing pain and the way the bone is shifting down there, she knows that her hip is truly broken, oh yes, as certain as death and taxes. Her legs, meanwhile, have gone numb, powerless.

Realizing that it's useless, Angela stops her feeble attempt at escape and rolls slowly, painfully onto her back, desperately trying to pull in oxygen as she wheezes on the floor like a broken doll. With growing horror, she watches as the masked killer approaches slowly, almost casually, from the bedroom, head cocked, as if studying her with curiosity.

I don't want to die, she thinks, her mind wild with panic and fear. *Please, God, I don't . . .*

And then she remembers.

How *stupid* she'd been! Why hadn't she thought of it before?

Ever since her eightieth birthday, Angela has worn a Medical Alert device around her neck. It's tasteful—a simple black square with a button in the middle—and she'd attached it to a heavy silver chain that she thought quite pretty.

She'd never had to use it and wouldn't have it at all if her granddaughter hadn't insisted (even if it was more for the girl's peace of mind than her elderly grandmother's).

But she could use it now. All she had to do was press the damn button and emergency services would be sent—sent right away!

As the dark figure steps closer, Angela digs her fingers beneath the neckline of her gown, reaching . . . reaching . . .

That strange laughter comes once again: a high-pitched, muffled chuckle from the killer who has invaded her home, from the one who is now dropping to a knee in front of her, a single gloved hand thrust forward, as if proposing.

Even in the dark, and even without her glasses, Angela sees the familiar silver necklace in the killer's fist, the onyx rectangle of the Medical Alert device swinging back-and-forth from the chain like a pendulum . . . a hypnotist's charm.

Tears run down her face as she stares at the chain, at her last gasp of salvation.

Well, that's it then, she thinks sadly.

That's it.

Even so, hating to be defeated so easily, and refusing to simply give up, Angela rolls onto her belly once more and crawls, inch-by-inch, toward the front door, which might as well be a million miles away.

After a few feet, however, her broken hip is screaming in agony, and her throat is all but completely closed, restricting her breath to nothing but short, raspy, painful gasps.

Broken windpipe, maybe, she thinks, sickened by the taste of blood on her tongue.

Her tired heart is pounding—*pounding, pounding*—in her chest. Going fast, much too fast, and thumping so loud that it creates a dull, rhythmic drumbeat in her ears.

But still she crawls.

Only when a pair of heavy-looking black combat boots step into her path does she accept defeat. As if relieved that she can finally give up—finally give in—Angela sighs and lets her forehead drop to the floor to rest lightly against the cool, brittle carpet.

She is resigned to whatever comes next. All the fight has been beaten out of her, and all the years of her life have been whittled down to this strange end. This impossible murder.

Owen . . . she thinks. *My sweet Owen. Perhaps in the next—*

The killer raises one thick-soled boot high above Angela's prone body, then stomps it down onto the back of the old woman's frail neck, snapping three vertebrae as if they were nothing more than dried-out chicken bones, thereby abruptly ending Angela Forrest's long, joy-filled life.

TWO

MADAME HARDY

1

Rose calls her friend early the next morning, and since Angela has never bothered with a cell phone, or even an answering machine for her landline, she lets it ring a dozen times before giving up.

Rose thinks it odd, but not necessarily worrisome.

When she calls back again an hour later, after her midmorning routine of coffee and a crossword puzzle, she still doesn't get an answer.

Now she starts to worry.

Getting hastily dressed, she leaves her apartment and takes the stairs down to the first floor (down being an easier task than up these days, and Rose likes to get her steps in where she can) and walks past the other apartments to reach Angela's front door.

She knocks. Waits. Knocks again.

Then—worry turning to fear—she calls out her friend's name. Again, and again.

"Angela, please answer. It's Rose!" she calls. "Angela, can—"

"Something wrong?"

Rose turns in surprise to see a neighbor sticking their white-headed noggin out of the next doorway, staring at her with wide, wet eyes. She doesn't know the man's name (one can't know everyone, even if they tried) and for a moment considers smiling with mild embarrassment, turning around, and going back home.

But she doesn't.

Instead, she shakes her head at the man and says, "Yes, I think there might be."

"I heard some strange noises last night," the man says as he steps from his apartment, his white T-shirt baggy on his bony frame; brown, smooth-kneed corduroy pants held up by frayed red suspenders. "But didn't think much of it because it stopped right away."

Rose feels the slightest chill, as if a goose had stepped on her grave, perhaps even shuffled a two-step, given the cold pit expanding in her stomach. "What kind of strange noises?"

The man shrugs his bony shoulders, shakes his head. "Hard to say. Thumping, I guess. Lots of thumping." He looks at Angela's door with drooping, vacant eyes. "Didn't think much of it, at the time." He clears his throat, eyes focusing on Rose once more. "I'm Henry Barber, by the way."

"Rose," she says, with a polite nod.

"Yes, I know," he says, then reddens. "I don't get out much."

Rose doesn't know how to respond to that, so she stays quiet on the subject, her mind thinking instead about the noises Henry mentioned.

Thumping. Lots of thumping.

"Anyway," Henry continues. "What do you suppose we should do? Call someone?"

"Would you mind?" Rose is frightened at hearing the urgency—the *fear*—in her own voice. "Henry, would you call the office and tell them something's wrong?"

"Of course, of course," he replies, and walks briskly back into his apartment.

Ten minutes later, the administrator himself, Jerry Blackwell, is there, along with a nurse from the Medical Center. He pulls a jumble of keys from his pocket as he approaches Henry and (a now borderline frantic) Rose. A few other residents have since appeared in the hallway, grave faces carved with concern.

"Hello, Ms. DuBois," the administrator says as he approaches.

"Hello, Mr. Blackwell."

Rose likes Mr. Blackwell. He's a tall man with sandy hair who reminds her of Robert Redford (if the light hits him just right). He always wears a suit, and she's never seen him without a tie and collar (even the time the fire alarms had gone off in the middle of the night and everyone had been forced to shuffle outside; even then, at two-thirty in the morning on a warm summer night, he'd pulled up in his black Lexus sedan and stepped out looking like he'd just left a business meeting). He was born in London—having moved to the States as a child—and still retains just enough accent to present a comforting, polished tone when he speaks. He is kind to the residents and always quick to fix something that needs fixing. Even better, he never makes anyone feel like they're a bother, or being silly, or paranoid. He takes every request, every complaint—and every resident—seriously.

And so when Henry had informed him that Angela Forrest in Greenview 14 wasn't answering her door, he'd arrived quickly and without question.

Now Rose just hopes it isn't for naught.

"I called and called, and I knocked . . . but she's—"

"I understand," Blackwell says, and pounds his fist on the door so loudly that Rose flinches.

"Mrs. Forrest?" he yells, not bothering to lean on decorum.

Now even more residents are opening doors, the hallway slowly filling with folks trying to see what all the ruckus is about.

To find out who died.

After a few more door poundings and a good amount of yelling Angela's name, the administrator shoves a key into the lock, twists his wrist, and pushes open the apartment door.

"Stay here, please," he says, directing his request to Rose. Then he turns to the young woman behind him. "Nurse?"

The nurse nods and, together, they go inside, leaving Rose to watch from the doorway.

"Mrs. Forrest?" the administrator calls out to the empty living room.

His voice is different now. Wary.

The nurse moves to an open window, one that faces the green of the back lawn, and slides it firmly shut. Rose watches as Mr. Blackwell and the nurse finish giving a cursory look around the small living space, then disappear into the bedroom.

Which is when Rose hears—hears quite clearly, all the way from the apartment's front door—the nurse say the words she'd dreaded from the twelfth ring of her first phone call early that morning, just before her coffee and crossword.

"Oh no."

2

"A horrible accident," Miller says.

Rose grunts noncommittally. Miller raises his eyebrows.

"Something on your mind, Rose?"

It's late in the day for lunch, nearly two o'clock, and the dining hall clientele is sparse. Miller had eaten a late breakfast, and the news about Angela spoiled any appetite he may have had for an afternoon bite. Rose called him with the news a few hours ago and, after getting details from Mr. Blackwell (what scant information he was able to offer), they'd all held vigil in the Greenview foyer while the medical team came and took Angela away on a stretcher, her small body covered in a heavy white sheet. They all knew she'd be taken to the Medical Center until next of kin was notified, then transported to either the local morgue in the Med Center's basement, or elsewhere if need be, possibly to be buried near family or deceased loved ones.

No one, to Miller's knowledge, wept at the news. Not because they weren't sad—even devastated—by the loss of Angela Forrest, but because they're *old*.

The residents of Autumn Springs are of an age where death simply isn't the tragedy it once was. It isn't sneaking up on anybody—it isn't a thief in the night snatching away your struggling spirit while it desperately clings to life.

And it sure as hell isn't a surprise.

At Autumn Springs, death is hunkered in every shadow of every room. It hovers in the high corners like a giant spider, stands at your bedside and watches you sleep, or sits congenially across the table while you sip your morning coffee, or your evening brandy.

And then, when it's time, death simply taps you on the shoulder, whispers softly in your ear, and slips its icy hand into yours.

For the residents of Autumn Springs Retirement Home, death isn't a horror movie. It's an inevitability.

Sometimes, it's even a comfort.

Sometimes, it's a friend.

"I'm sorry, but I don't buy a word of it," Rose says, stabbing her fork into a Caesar salad like she's trying to kill it. "Not a damn word."

"Don't believe what, exactly?" Miller says placidly, not wanting to provoke Rose, but curious to know what's causing her misgivings. Rose drops her fork to the table, where it clatters, then folds her arms across her chest. She leans back into her chair with a heavy sigh.

"Frankly, I don't even know," she says. "You must think I'm a fool."

Miller takes another long sip of his coffee, smacks his lips. It's hot and strong, just how he likes it. "Not even a little bit. You've an instinct for such things."

Rose looks at him—really *looks* at him—dark eyes blazing, her expression teetering somewhere between angry and amused. "Don't you patronize me, Beauregard."

"No ma'am," he says, setting the cup down. "I'm serious, Rose. You have a sixth sense when things aren't right. And you're good at deduction. Like how you always know the way those crime movies will end and who the killer is." He taps his nose and smiles. "You got a nose for it."

Rose scoffs. "That's me. A black Angela Lansbury."

Miller laughs, debates a refill. "Anyway, it's sad. She was a sweet lady."

But Rose seems to barely hear him. Her eyes go distant, as if her thoughts have drifted off, her mind working a puzzle far away. It's a look Miller knows well, and he keeps quiet so as to let her think things through.

"How the hell could a slip and fall do so much damage to a person?" she says finally. "And what was Angela doing taking a bath at nine o'clock at night?"

Miller tilts his head, offers a playful smile. "You don't like a late-night bath? Candles and a glass of wine? A good book?"

Rose shakes her head. "You've seen too many movies, hon."

"That's true," he says with a chuckle, and lifts his empty cup toward the dining hall's sole waiter.

"You don't need more coffee," Rose scolds, but without much enthusiasm. "It's past two o'clock."

Miller waves a dismissive hand. "You do you. I'll do me."

Rose laughs and leans forward. She pushes her plate away and folds her arms atop the table. "I'm serious, though, Miller. It's awfully strange."

"I agree, Rose. I do. But consider Occam's razor. A slip and fall is the simplest solution. And if there's no other logical reason for those injuries, then it must be what happened. Sure, it's strange, but not unheard of."

"I suppose," Rose agrees, albeit half-heartedly. "Still, I want to find that nurse. That little thing who went into the apartment with Mr. Blackwell. I've never seen her before . . . I don't know her name, anyway. But I'd like to ask her about what she saw."

"Now you *do* sound like Angela Lansbury . . . oh, good."

The waiter arrives with a carafe of hot coffee and fills Miller's mug.

"Thank you, Scott."

"Of course." He turns to Rose. "Anything else for you, ma'am?"

"No, darling, I'm good," Rose says distractedly.

The waiter leaves, and Miller continues. "Okay, let's see what's what," he says, pouring a little cream into his cup. "The bathtub is full of water. Angela is found, well . . . naked, yes?"

Rose nods. "That's what I heard. Millie Strong says that she heard from one of the cleaning staff, who spoke with one of the orderlies at the Medical Center, who'd said that the body didn't have a stitch of clothing on it, and that Angela's neck was badly broken and her hip fractured."

Miller clears his throat. "Okay, let's sidestep how and why that information came to pass and focus on facts."

"Go on."

"Full bathtub. Angela undressed, getting ready for a bath. She . . . what? Slips on a wet spot on the tiles. Maybe she'd been slapping at the water to check the temperature and some splashes out onto the floor. She goes ass over teakettle, slams her neck on the side of the tub . . . and crack. The hip . . ." He shrugs. "Hitting the floor would do it."

"It's tidy, I'll give you that."

Miller's gaze stays on Rose. His smile slightly fading.

"But."

Rose shakes her head. "It was something I saw on Mr. Blackwell's face when he walked out of that room. My goodness, Miller, that young man has seen more death than most, right? But just then, he looked . . ."

"What?"

Rose looks up, her expression somber as a grave.

"Scared," she says. "Miller, that man looked scared as hell."

3

Rose is still considering the possibilities of what may—or may not—have happened in Angela Forrest's apartment when she notices the dining room doors open to let in a cool gust of wind, along with three of the strangest residents of Autumn Springs. Or, in Rose's opinion, three of the strangest people she's ever encountered *anywhere*.

The trifecta of women who enter the dining room together are sisters. And while the Baxter sisters aren't identical triplets, they do look an awful lot alike. Disconcertingly so, if one were to ask Rose.

"What are those old hens doing here?" Miller asks under his breath, but manages to smile and nod when the eldest sister, Bridget, glances toward their table.

"Having lunch, I suppose," Rose says, but can't help wondering if it's something more than that, such as a good old-fashioned gossip hunt.

"They must have run out of batwing soup," Miller says with a laugh.

The three women—all dressed in layered shades of black, all peaking at five-foot-two, and all adorned with poofy, black-dyed hair—slow their progression. Having turned their full attention toward Rose and Miller's table, they quickly huddle together like witches by a cauldron.

"Oh, boy. This can't be good," Miller mumbles, turning back to Rose. "Maybe we should—"

"Too late," Rose says, and puts on a genial smile.

Bridget, Betsie, and Barbara Baxter (commonly known to the residents of Autumn Springs as the Three B's), make their way toward Rose and Miller. Wide, sharp grins slice through their pale faces.

"Good afternoon, you two," Bridget says. "Late lunch or early dinner?"

"Late lunch," Miller says. "How are you ladies doing today?"

"We heard about Angela," Betsie interjects, ignoring Miller's small talk. "Horrible."

"Just horrible," Barbara tuts. "A terrible accident."

All three women shake their heads in despair, but Rose can see the remnants of wry grins hidden beneath those painted lips and powdered cheeks, the thrill of a suspicious, violent death arousing their dark sensibilities.

Rumor has it that the Three B's are witches, which makes for good, if lighthearted, teasing from the other residents (a rumor Rose finds hard to argue with, since the three women offer little that would dispute such a claim).

The Baxter sisters live in the same one-bedroom apartment—albeit one of the larger floor plans offered in either of the two resident buildings. They keep mainly to themselves, but that doesn't keep neighbors from the occasional complaint of strange smells and sounds coming from their unit. Rhythmic chanting, for one, and odd, sudden shrieks of pain (or joy) were not uncommon. Others who live nearby speak of an almost constant smell of smoke, or sulfur, despite the sisters having never once triggered the incredibly sensitive smoke alarms.

Some residents have even made mention of bizarre *animal* noises coming from the Baxter apartment. When Rose once asked a pale-faced Ginny Gavin, who lives right next door to the Three B's in Seaview 7, what *kind* of animal she'd heard in the night, Ginny had simply widened her eyes and replied: "Something big."

Having known the sisters since they'd first moved in over three years ago, Rose has never had much interest in their strangeness or in seeking out the odd stories told about them. For the most part, she'd found them relatively harmless, if a little unsettling. Now, however, she wonders if perhaps they're not quite as harmless as she believes.

Witches or no, Rose thinks, watching them hover over their lunch table, *these three are worth keeping an eye on.*

Part of Rose knows she's likely being paranoid—and for no good reason at that—but no matter how hard she tries to shake it, she has a bad feeling in her gut about what happened to Angela, even if she can't quite put her finger on why.

Experience, perhaps. Sure, she's had her share of slip and falls, that much is certain. Maybe even more than most. But when she thinks about her dead friend's body lying in the Morgue, hip broken, neck broken . . . something feels decidedly *wrong*.

Given the veracity with which the three sisters are burrowing into the mud for kernels of gossip, like starved chickens in a barnyard, she wonders if she's the only one who might feel that way.

"It's very sad," Miller says, pulling Rose's attention back to the conversation.

"You were close, weren't you?" Bridget asks, focusing on Rose, a mask of empathetic sorrow on her face. "You and Angela?"

Rose nods. "We were. She was a very sweet, very generous person."

"Have you heard any more, you know . . . details?" Barbara asks, the corner of her lips curling despite her best efforts.

"Ladies, I don't think this is the time," Miller interjects calmly. "We're all still in a bit of shock, and I think we, and Rose especially, need to process the loss."

"Shock?" Betsie says with a roll of her eyes, then cackles before putting a hand over her mouth to stifle it. "Sorry, Miller. But she wasn't exactly hit by a bus."

"What my sister is saying," Bridget adds quickly, "is that these things can happen at our age. If we're not careful, I mean. Accidents and what-not."

"I once knew a woman who died getting out of bed," Barbara says, her long bony fingers working a ball of black yarn from which two silver knitting needles protrude like antennae. "They said the bedsheet caught her ankle as she stepped away and she fell face-first into a bedroom window, broke the glass on impact, and impaled herself on a particularly long shard. Here, I think, by the jugular."

Barbara tilts her chin upward and points at the soft, wrinkled flesh of her throat.

"Ladies," Miller pleads. "Please, I don't think Rose needs to hear about any more death or tragedy right now."

"I'm fine," Rose snaps, suddenly angry—angry at the world for taking her friend, angry at these damn witches for their coarse manners and ugly thoughts. And yes, angry at Miller for thinking she needs protection or someone to speak for her. "But I *am* sorry to be rude. There's something I need to do. So, if you'll all excuse me."

Rose stands, and Miller begins to rise with her. "I'll speak to you later, Beauregard," she says sharply, and walks brusquely away from the table.

Miller's eyes widen slightly, but he nods and settles back into his chair, shoulders heavy.

By the time Rose reaches the entry, her quick flare of anger has dropped to a low heat, and she finds herself fighting off a pang of remorse at her abrupt departure. She turns back and sees the sisters making themselves at home at Miller's table, who looks tangibly miserable as he takes another sip of coffee, which has probably gone cold.

I'll make it up to him, she thinks, then pushes out the door, eager to obtain more details—and some answers—about what happened to her friend.

4

As Rose follows the red tape line toward the Medical Center, she isn't sure what she's going to do, or what she expects to find out. But Angela had been a good friend—she was kindhearted and loving, and they'd made killer bridge partners. Yes, even against the dreaded Pickfords. Rose feels she owes it to her old friend to . . .

To what, exactly?

Rose doesn't know.

Investigate?

Care?

If nothing else, Rose needs to know, for her own peace of mind, that what happened to Angela was indeed an accident. That somebody—as unthinkable as it sounds—hadn't *hurt* the poor woman.

There's a small, dark voice in Rose's mind, one she doesn't think she'll ever be rid of. It's the same voice that's been living in her head for thirty years (a constant companion since her marriage), and one that sounds an awful lot like her dead husband. It's a voice that skulks in the dark crevices of her subconscious, a dark whisperer that does its very best to corrupt every happy thought or good feeling that surfaces, that keeps her on the defensive, that keeps her *wary*, that fills her with uncertainty, and fear.

Of course, sometimes the dark voice is right about a thing or two, and those are the times Rose hates it the most.

Right now, that voice is whispering into her ear that maybe—just maybe—Owen Duffield has something to do with all of this.

Sure, she's known Owen as long as she's known Angela—since the day she moved into Autumn Springs. They weren't a couple then, of course. That's recent. Owen was still married for one thing, his wife of thirty years dying later that same year.

And how did Susan Duffield die, anyway? the voice wants to know. *Was it really natural causes . . . or does Owen have a history of losing those he loves?*

"Bullshit," Rose mumbles as she walks, breath frosting the early-evening air. Susan Duffield died because she'd been suffering from congestive heart failure for years, and her sweet little ticker finally succumbed to its inevitable fate. *People get old. Bodies get old,* Rose thinks to herself. *Not everything is a mystery novel.*

And yet . . . she can't help but wonder about Owen. When Angela came to her last night, asking to talk, Rose had assumed it was standard girl talk of the *should I* or *shouldn't I* variety. At the time, she'd thought Angela seemed so happy.

But when she lets the memory play through her mind one more time, she wonders if there's something else there.

Something she was hiding.

Fear, perhaps.

Maybe they'd had a lovers quarrel, the dark voice says. *Maybe Owen pushed her too hard and she fell and her little frail neck snapped like a goddamn toothpick and he set up the bathroom angle to cover his tracks and—*

"Enough, enough . . ." Rose mutters, giving her head a little shake, hoping to jostle the intrusive voice out of her ear and back to its little cave in the back of her subconscious. She also pushes Owen Duffield out of her mind (at least for the moment) and focuses on the task at hand.

She has questions, and she'd very much like a few answers.

Rose continues down the path, still following the silly red tape (as if she couldn't find the building without a trail of breadcrumbs). She says hello to a couple she doesn't recognize as they pass, watches as they head toward the Seaview building. She wonders if their place is quiet when the train rumbles by and feels a stab of envy she doesn't try too hard to squash.

Adjacent to the path outside the Medical Center sits a small koi pond, partially covered in lily pads, a few wooden benches set around its neatly trimmed grass perimeter. Surrounding the tidy clearing are hedges of Madame Hardy rose bushes, the kind that bloom in lush whites and pinks during the spring and summer months, and stand as scraggly green sentinels in the winter.

But those harsh winters are necessary, Rose knows, in order for the flowers to fully bloom in the summer months. Madame Hardy roses need that winter chill if they are to burst back to life beneath warm sunshine.

As she studies the bushes—their green leaves already beginning to absorb the upcoming months of brittle cold—she thinks again about Beauregard, and about her own inner flower, the one twined with thorns of the past . . . and wonders if there might perhaps be one summer left in her winter-trapped heart.

"Hello, Rose," a man says from a nearby bench, startling her.

Rose steps past a large clump of bushes to see her friend Tatum Bird sitting peacefully near the pond. He's wearing blue jeans and clean, white sneakers, an old brown Carhartt jacket and a beaten-to-hell Yankees cap. Rose takes a step in his direction, glances once toward the Medical Center, then decides it can wait a few minutes more.

"Hello, Tatum," Rose says, giving the man her warmest smile as she steps carefully through the damp grass toward the bench, where she sits comfortably next to him. "Nice to see you this afternoon."

"Have you seen Jack?" Tatum asks, his eyes on the sky, hands dug deep into his coat pockets.

"Actually, I think I have," Rose says, putting a hand on Tatum's forearm. "I believe he was sleeping on the back lawn."

Tatum nods, mollified. "He's a good boy."

"He is, indeed," Rose says. "A lovely dog. You're very lucky to have him."

They sit in companionable silence for a moment, then Tatum points to a nearby bush. "The butterflies are pretty today," he says.

Rose glances over, sees a pair of gold-winged butterflies dancing around one of the dying blooms. "That they are. I guess they're not all hibernating yet."

"No . . . not yet. But getting there," Tatum says, shoving his hand back into the warmth of his pocket. "I want to go home," he says without inflection. A statement of fact.

Rose pats his arm. "I know, baby, I know. Maybe when Jack comes back you can go home together. How's that sound?"

Tatum looks at Rose and smiles. "Sounds good, Rose. That sounds really good."

Like many other residents, Tatum Bird now lives in the Medical Center full-time, needing around-the-clock care. He suffers from dementia and has already survived strokes on two different occasions. But unlike some others getting full-time care, Tatum is universally docile. He's never angry or violent. He's never tried to hurt himself or any of the nurses or doctors. As far as Rose knows, he's never needed restraints of any kind. In fact, the medical staff all but dotes on him because he's one of the tame ones.

One of the *easy* ones.

His dog, Jack—a beautiful, chocolate-furred Labrador retriever who Rose has seen pictures of a few times over the years—has been dead for decades. Ever since Tatum's second stroke, however, he's been obsessed with the dog, stubbornly searching for him from morning to night. Every day he'll stroll outside to look for his old friend, never straying too far, and invariably ending up on this very same bench by the pond, watching the koi and butterflies, hoping Jack will soon return.

"Tatum, honey, I've got to be moving along. Are you okay? Are you hungry? Want me to have someone come out here and sit with you?"

The staff gives Tatum a lot of free rein since they know his nature and, more likely than not, where they can find him. Rose just hopes he never gets it in his head to stray too far. She hates the idea of him getting lost in the surrounding forest, or stumbling down the hill toward the creek, or—God forbid—going anywhere near the train tracks. More than once he's wandered into one of the apartment buildings and knocked on a door, wondering if that particular resident had seen Jack. All the residents knew Tatum by now, and on most of those occasions he would be invited inside to sit down for a coffee or a Diet Coke, and usually the homeowner would put in a call to the Medical Center, just to let them know where the man was.

He was harmless, and sweet, and heartbreaking.

"I'm okay, Rose," he says clearly.

She is genuinely impressed—and more than a little touched—that Tatum always seems to remember her name, despite the rotting in his brain. She imagines his mind as a constant thunderstorm, complete with boiling gray clouds where the occasional spark of lightning flashes brightly—a rare coherent thought—before being swallowed by the maelstrom once more. How her name survives inside the squalling, tempestuous world of his mind she couldn't possibly guess. During one of Rose's routine checkups, a nurse had commented on it, saying that Rose's was the one name Tatum always seemed to recall, that he would often tell others how much he enjoyed sitting with her by the pond.

"I'm sure it has something to do with all those rose bushes," Rose said at the time, slightly embarrassed. "How could he possibly forget?"

The nurse had laughed and agreed it was a strong possibility, even if they both knew better, knew that kindness could be its own miracle, and that a friendship could often hold anchor in a storm, even one that raged so savagely.

"I'll see you later, Tatum," Rose says, standing, anxious to see what she can discover from the medical staff. "Or shall I walk you home?"

"I better wait for Jack," he says quietly.

"Okay, but don't wait too long," Rose says. "He'll come back. He always does, right? He always comes home."

Tatum nods, stares meaningfully into the distance and says nothing.

Rose bends down and kisses the top of his Yankees cap, then walks away.

As she approaches the squat, two-story building, a small, illogical part of her glances left and right as she goes, wondering if she might just see a flash of brown fur, running hell-bent toward the pond.

5

The Medical Center's lobby is brightly lit, the interior more modern than the other buildings on the Autumn Springs campus. The floor is faux hardwood instead of carpet, the lights clinically white—lacking the warmth of the foyers and hallways Rose is used to. Directly before the entrance is a large reception desk that is manned twenty-four hours a day, seven days a week. Rose notices two nurses and a doctor in there now, all of them busy typing at computers or flipping through file cabinets.

They look like extras on a TV show.

Just past reception, and to the left, are closed double doors that lead to the hospice care residents. To the right, two more closed doors lead to a series of apartments for residents needing full-time care—those who need their meals prepared for them and often ask for help to get around—but are otherwise healthy. Straight ahead past the desk is a white-walled hallway, where folks who live in the apartments get monthly checkups or meet with a doctor to consult about this or that minor ailment. Next to the hallway is a bank of elevators, which either takes one up one floor or down to the basement.

The basement, which is identified on a wall-stuck placard simply as STORAGE, is more commonly known by staff and residents as the Morgue—an air-conditioned, industrial space where bodies are regularly held while awaiting transport to the city morgue or, more commonly, a funeral home.

If one were to travel up one floor they'd reach more medical offices, physical therapy rooms, and a boardroom that Rose has never been inside of but had once seen while attending therapy for a strained calf muscle.

Despite its polished interior and sterile facilities, the Medical Center is by no means a hospital. Doctors only visit the Center twice a week to attend appointments, and there are no X-ray or surgery rooms, but it serves admirably as a convenient stopgap for residents who either require immediate emergency care—at least until an ambulance arrives and they're transferred to a real hospital—or folks who require basic maintenance on a day-to-day basis and around-the-clock care, such as Tatum Bird.

In between the dead and the needful, of course, are the dying.

The hospice wing is a melancholy place: temporary housing where residents are taken to be made "comfortable" as they wait for the end. When they finally pass on, there's very little muss, very little fuss. Just a quick trip down to Storage while they wait for a ride to their final resting place. For the most part, Rose doubts the police even bother sending anyone out to verify cause of death anymore. Most likely they just rubber-stamp whatever cause the hospice nurse gives them over the phone—usually heart failure, organ failure, or aneurysm.

In other words, *old age.*

Sometimes, if rarely, family will come visit those who've passed—spend a few quiet minutes in the hospice room before going on with the rest of their day—which in turn leads residents to gossip about so-and-so having a son or a daughter no one knew about. Most family members, it seems, only visit at the end, as if feeling the moral need to say goodbye to someone they've likely ignored for years.

A chill runs up Rose's spine at the thought. She tries to fathom the horror, the despair, of having that kind of a relationship with her daughter. What if Sybil wasn't the loving, caring daughter she is? What if, like these other poor souls, her daughter only came to visit Rose at the end, when it was too late to have a proper talk or a meaningful goodbye? What if they never spent time together, never went into town for lunch or some shopping? What would those last visits be like if Rose was heavily drugged or on a ventilator, breathing her last?

She can only imagine the pain of it—of seeing her child, or her grandchild, when it was much too late. When their lives together were over . . .

With an effort, Rose pushes the selfish, melancholy thoughts away, hating the rise of bitterness in her heart at the way some elderly folks are treated by those they'd raised: the very ones they'd sacrificed so much for. Their children had lives, too, of course, but that often seemed to take precedence over caring about those who missed them, who loved them. Who *made* them.

Regardless of her fears and biases, the despair pervading the Medical Center is much worse, and borderline palpable. The truth is that none of the residents enjoy spending time there, regardless of the conveniences. Despite the prevalent stink of bleach, the place reeks of pain and death. It made Rose think of the old asylum out by the trees—that nasty, decrepit building this modern one had replaced. She couldn't help but imagine the horror of being wheeled out there, perhaps against your will, perhaps strapped to a gurney, drugged and restrained, only to wake up in that foul place—a building huddled like a filthy secret near the dark woods—trapped to the end of your days in the sticky palm of the tall trees' sky-reaching fingers, as if you were a sick dog dragged out to the shed to be put down. She—

"Can I help you?"

Rose snaps free from her gloomy thoughts, her attention drawn back to the reception desk where both nurses and the doctor are now staring, stoic as surgeons, directly at her. "Hello," Rose says, taking a step closer, trying and failing to conjure a smile.

"Do you have an appointment?" the nurse sitting at the computer asks. Meanwhile, the doctor—the one Rose doesn't recognize, and who looks younger than her own daughter—has seemingly grown bored and steps out from behind the desk. Rose strains to see the name stitched onto his white coat but can't make it out.

"Excuse me? Doctor?" Rose says, ignoring the harried, and slightly annoyed, look of the woman at the computer.

The young doctor punches the elevator button—going up—and partially turns back, eyebrows raised.

"I was curious if you're new here. It's just . . . I haven't seen you before." Rose gives a light laugh, trying to ease the strange, growing tension in the lobby. "I thought I knew everyone."

The doctor smiles warmly and approaches her. She notes his tall, muscular build, his large brown eyes and thick hair that, in her opinion, is a bit on the long side for a man in his profession.

Looks like he stepped out of the 1980s, she thinks, but extends her hand when he offers his, reflects his smile with one of her own.

"I'm Doctor Kincaid," he says. "Matthew Kincaid."

"I'm Rose DuBois," she replies. "Pleasure."

"Nice to meet you, Rose." Behind him, the elevator dings and the doors slide open, but Kincaid's dark eyes stay locked on her, as if nothing in the world could possibly be more important. "I'm only here Tuesday and Thursday afternoons; my primary practice is located about a half hour away, near Kingston." His eyes narrow thoughtfully, studying her. "What brings you in, Rose?"

"Oh, I'm fine," she says, waving a hand. "Fit as a fiddle. But a friend of mine passed away this morning, and I was curious about the circumstances."

Kincaid nods, furrows his brow in thought. "I'm so sorry. Yeah, I heard about that. I wasn't here when they brought her in, but . . . slip and fall, right?"

"That's what I understand," Rose says. "Sorry, I don't mean to be rude, but you didn't say . . . *are* you new here?"

Kincaid laughs, his teeth perfect and bright white. "Oh, sorry. Yes, I've only started recently. I'm replacing Doctor Withers."

Rose frowns. Dolores Withers had been Rose's doctor the entire five years she'd been at Autumn Springs. A lovely woman, who was older, sure, but not of retirement age. "Strange, she didn't say anything."

Kincaid glances over at the sole remaining nurse, the other having slipped away to do her rounds. "It happened fast," he says, lowering his voice. "Her mother fell very ill, and Dolores . . . sorry, Dr. Withers, moved down to Florida to be with her. I was brought in just last week. When did you last meet with her? I'm assuming she was your GP? Or were you seeing Dr. Brighton, who comes in on Fridays?"

Rose takes all this in, wondering why her doctor would leave and not tell her, even if it was relatively sudden. "No, it was Dolores," she says. "Anyway, let's see . . . I think I last saw her back in January. I'd needed a refill on my Prilosec. I suffer from reflux."

Kincaid nods, suddenly more serious.

Shifting into doctor mode, Rose thinks.

"I see. Well, Rose, since it's been almost a year, I'd love for you to make an appointment with Nurse Cooper over there. Let's get you in for a full checkup and start a fresh chart, okay? Maybe there's something else we can do for that reflux."

"Sure, thank you. I'll go see her right now."

"Wonderful. Nice to meet you, Rose."

"You as well."

As Kincaid goes back to the elevator, Rose approaches the large, strong-looking woman sitting at the computer.

"Hello," Rose says, still trying to figure out a way to extract some information from one of these people. "I didn't catch your name."

"I didn't offer it," the nurse says, but smiles gamely, as if to wash away the bitterness of her reply. "I'm kidding. I'm Annie, Annie Cooper. And what's your name, sweetie?"

Rose didn't like being called "sweetie." Not by a man, not by anyone. She also didn't care for similar, equally demeaning, terms of endearment young folks have used when addressing her, as if she were a child. A nurse in Brooklyn had once called her "precious." Rose had wanted to bite her goddamn ear off.

One of the many things she'd learned over the years, however, was that being old made you childlike in the eyes of many people, especially those who were responsible for your care. *I suppose it's what happens when they've seen us at our worst,* she thinks. *Brains muddled, frail as newborns, needy as toddlers.*

Nurse Cooper stares at Rose patiently, wide-eyed and waiting, as if she'd given Rose a complex problem and was curious whether the old bird could figure out the answer.

I'm quite sure you overheard me say my name to the young doctor just a minute ago, Rose thinks sourly, but suppresses a grimace. "Rose DuBois."

Before the patronizing nurse can start throwing dates and times at her, Rose leans in and lowers her voice. "Nurse Cooper, I'm hoping you can help me. I'm looking for the nurse who was on site when they found my friend this morning. She's a young woman with short, almost boyish, black hair. I'm assuming she came back here with the body?"

To Rose's surprise, Nurse Cooper's face softens, her mask of tortured patience turning magically into one of genuine compassion, and Rose notices that the woman is younger than she'd first thought, and pretty in her own way. "I'm sorry for your loss, Rose," the nurse says. "Let's see . . . I believe the nurse on duty this morning was Mindy Jarvis. I mean, it was her and someone else, but I think it was Mindy who went over there to . . . to see the body."

"I see," Rose says, thrilled to be making some progress. "And could I speak with Nurse Jarvis? See, the woman, Angela, was a close friend, and I would like to ask about . . . well, about how she was found. It's not morbid curiosity, I assure you, but I just need to understand—"

Nurse Cooper nods. "You need closure."

"Yes," Rose replies, almost too enthusiastically. "Closure."

Nurse Cooper blows out a breath. "Well, Mindy is doing her rounds right now, likely visiting someone in the apartments." The nurse cups her hand over her mouth and lowers her voice, as if imparting some great secret. "We make lots of house calls."

"Of course, I'm aware. Tell you what," Rose says, noting the row of visitor chairs along the far wall. "Let's make that doctor appointment, and then, if it's okay, I'll just sit over there and wait until she comes back."

The nurse's eyes dart to the chairs, then to Rose. "You sure? It might be a while."

Rose pats the cool surface of the desk. "Well, if I get bored, maybe I'll go sit with Mr. Bird out there by the pond. Keep him company."

For the first time since their meeting, Nurse Cooper's smile touches her eyes. "Isn't he sweet?"

Rose smiles back. "As sugar."

6

Miller makes his way home, exhausted from having spent the last half hour chatting with the Baxter sisters, who he thinks of as mostly harmless, even if they are completely batshit. He taps the button for the elevator, waits dourly for the sad, creaky old thing to make its way the twenty feet to pick him up.

He feels bad for upsetting Rose. He knew he'd stepped in it by defending her to the sisters—Rose was nothing if not fiercely independent—and understands why she walked off the way she did. He loves her fiery nature; he just wishes he wasn't on the receiving end quite so often.

Dumbass, he thinks, chiding himself. *That woman doesn't need you, old man. She doesn't need anyone or anything. Stop trying to be her husband and just try being her friend. If her heart opens, it opens.*

Just as he's debating whether he should try calling her that afternoon to make amends, a door opens down the hall to his right, and a woman steps into the hallway.

"Miller!"

Confused, he turns to see Maureen Stapleton standing in the open doorway of unit 9, wearing her usual outfit of blue jeans, sneakers, and a fuzzy sweater. Her dark hair is done up sloppily (but purposely so, he thinks) atop her head; her brown eyes are wide and—if he's being honest with himself—striking. At one point in her life, Maureen had been a model and had even taken a stab at acting for a while ("mostly off-off-Broadway," she liked to say). Regardless, she was a knockout of a woman, more beautiful at seventy-eight than most women were in their prime.

Right now, however, she isn't wearing her patented smile or burning through him with her effortlessly flirtatious, come-hither eyes.

Right now she looks scared.

"Hello, Maureen," he says, giving a little wave.

She takes a few steps closer, then spins back to hold the door, making sure she doesn't lock herself out.

The elevator grinds to a stop, dings loudly in the near-empty lobby. The doors creak open, ready to accept whatever sacrifice is willing to step inside the car's gaping mouth, but the woman in the hallway has Miller's attention, so he pauses, lets the disappointed doors slide shut.

Looking relieved that he didn't disappear into the elevator, Maureen gives him a hint of that smile—the one that had once sold perfume and designer clothes from the flat glossy pages of *Vogue* and *Vanity Fair.*

"Will you . . ." she starts, then looks around the hallway, as if making sure they're alone. "I'm sorry to ask, but would you mind coming in for a moment?"

Miller thinks about this for a beat, surprised at the request. Sure, he and Maureen are friendly, but he wouldn't consider them friends. As he ponders the invitation, he finds himself thinking about Rose; thinks about how many times she's told him she wasn't interested in romance, or in a relationship.

Miller blushes at the stray thought. *She ain't asking you in for a quickie, jackass. You're acting like a child. So stop being a creep and go help the woman. She probably wants you to reach a pot off a high shelf or some such nonsense.*

"Of course," he says politely, and walks toward the apartment.

Maureen smiles gratefully and holds the door open as Miller steps inside, wondering what in the world she could possibly want.

Inside the apartment, Miller looks around, takes a quick inventory. He notes right away how tidy her home is, and how lavishly furnished. The carpet is plush, off-white, and freshly vacuumed. A leather white sectional faces a wall-mounted, flat-screen television. The room's other pieces—from a comfortable-looking Eames lounge chair to the glass-top coffee table—are decidedly midcentury in style, but fresh and new, as if she'd plucked them straight from the pages of a Herman Miller catalogue.

"Nice place," he says, wondering if he should remove his shoes before stepping onto the pristine carpet.

"Thanks," she says offhandedly, running a hand through her (attractively tousled) black hair. She gestures toward a tidy bar cart stacked with various bottles of liquor. "You want a drink? It's happy hour somewhere, am I right?"

Miller shakes his head. "I'm good, thank you. What did you want to show me, Maureen?" he says politely, but also wanting to make it clear this isn't a social call. Miller doesn't like the idea of being fooled, or taken advantage of, and if Maureen brought him in here to help with something, then that's what he's here to do. Not play childish games of flirt and innuendo.

Maureen's pretty face falls for a beat, and she nods. "Okay. Can you come in here for a second?"

Miller's eyebrows rise as Maureen moves toward a short hallway he knows—having become familiar with the handful of layouts that Autumn Springs apartments offer—leads straight to the bedroom.

Sensing his apprehension, Maureen laughs lightly. "Not trying to seduce you, Miller. If I was doing that . . . well, trust me when I say you'd know it."

"I—"

"Look, let me just show you, okay? Please."

Miller nods, hearing Rose's voice in his head: *Silly schoolboy.*

He almost smiles at the thought of Rose watching his awkward dance with Maureen Stapleton—he'd be hearing about it for weeks, and rightly so—but then clears his throat and walks toward his host. "Understood. Let's take a look."

In the bedroom, Maureen stops at the lone window facing the back lawn. "Here," she says, pointing to the window. "He was right here. Staring into my room."

Miller shuffles to the window, glances outside. From her bedroom he can see the gazebo and beyond that the heavy wall of trees. A hand-holding couple walk along the winding path that cuts through the vast back lawn like a ribbon. "*Who* was here?"

Maureen shrugs. "Some fucking creep, that's who. A man in a ski mask. I was getting ready for bed, and had just come out of the bathroom, when I saw him staring into my room. He was so close to the glass his breath fogged the window."

Miller looks at the open curtains, then leans forward to see the short drop to the grass outside—no more than five feet down. "A man in a mask?" he says, turning to look at her.

"That's right. And me half-naked in just my pajamas . . . which are very revealing," she adds.

Miller fights off a blush, as well as the images popping into his imagination.

"So . . . a Peeping Tom?"

Maureen crosses her arms, shrugs. "Fuck if I know. But I screamed, then ran back into the bathroom. I put on a robe and peeked back out, but he was gone."

"Did you call anyone? Administration? They could have sent someone out."

She shakes her head. "No. I didn't want the hassle, I guess. I mean, seriously, what are they gonna do? But that's why I wanted to show you, because I figured if you believed me, you could help me sort of spread the word. People trust you. They'll believe you. I'm . . . you know, not all that well-liked around here. I think the others would just think I was trying to get attention."

Miller nods, finding it hard to argue with her logic. Maureen *does* have a reputation for the dramatic, and because of her looks, her somewhat flirtatious nature, and her flare for clothes and accessories, most folks already treat her with a bit of suspicion. Standing in her bedroom, seeing the obvious fear in her eyes, Miller realizes that he's one of those people, and feels a pang of guilt about it.

"I'll let folks know to keep a lookout," he says. "Do it in such a way that it doesn't cause a panic."

To his surprise, Maureen steps forward quickly and hugs him.

"Thank you!" she says, squeezing her body against his. "I'm so relieved, honestly."

"That's okay," he says, patting her on the back. "I'm sorry it happened to you."

Maureen releases him, takes a step back, smiles up at him—an alluring flush in her cheeks makes him immediately uncomfortable.

"There's one more thing I want to show you," she says, and takes him by the hand.

He doesn't resist.

7

After sitting for fifteen minutes in the too-bright, cheerless, sterilized waiting room of the Medical Center, Rose decides to move herself back outside to wait on the nurse's return.

It's a warm afternoon for October—the sun is out in full force and the breeze is slight, so she doesn't mind relaxing with Tatum for a bit and enjoying the day. She certainly has no other plans, other than perhaps watching a show with Miller that evening.

Sitting by the pond, she does her best to keep up a conversation with Tatum but, because of his dementia, the poor man's thoughts are like a time-traveling merry-go-round. His conversation consists primarily of fragmented memories—things that happened to him forty or more years ago, recounted as if they'd just occurred that morning. Tatum's other favorite topics include requests for her to help find his deceased dog, his desire to go back home (a common refrain), and something about a lost Yankees hat, which she patiently reminds him is sitting atop his head.

"Oh, that's right," he says, pawing at the cap for a moment before giving her a million-dollar smile that breaks her heart.

Just as she is thinking about giving up and getting Tatum safely back to his room, the front door of the Med Center opens and the young nurse she'd seen that morning walks out. She spots Rose right away and gives her a little wave, which Rose reciprocates.

The nurse steps up to the bench, a good-natured smile on her face. Her short, choppy black hair makes her look like a child (which she pretty much is, at least in Rose's view). "Hey there, you two," she says in a perky, but noticeably raspy, voice.

Must have been a colicky baby, Rose thinks automatically, having had a few students over the years who had similar traits. A voice like that was usually caused by a disease during their developing years or, more often than not, from screaming their heads off as babies, primarily ones whose intestinal tracts were still developing post-birth. Sometimes, of course, it was just the way God had made them.

"I'm Mindy," the nurse continues. "Hope I'm not interrupting." She gives Rose a little wink, and Rose finds herself liking the young woman off the bat.

"Hello, Mindy. I'm Rose, and you know Tatum, of course." Rose takes a moment to study the nurse, who is dressed in scrubs and white New Balance walking shoes, a frayed cardigan pulled over her small frame. She's short, but not petite, with bright, active eyes and a smile that likely gets her a free drink or two at the bar. "And no, you're not interrupting. We were just taking in the beautiful day . . . but I think it might be time to get Tatum back home. He's been out here a while, and it'll start cooling off soon."

"Sounds good," Mindy says cheerfully, turning to Tatum. "Whaddya think, big guy? Should Rose and I walk you home?"

"I'm waiting for Jack," Tatum says, absently scratching at one thigh. "Who are you?"

Mindy laughs kindly and bends down to look Tatum in the eye, puts a hand gently on his shoulder. "I'm Mindy, remember? We talk about the Yankees all the time."

Tatum's eyes light up. "Rose found my hat!" he says, tapping his cap.

"That Rose is something else," Mindy says, then slips a hand beneath one of his arms. "Come on, hot stuff, we're gonna get you home and get you some dinner."

Together, they walk back toward the Medical Center, Mindy with an arm through Tatum's and Rose tagging along at the nurse's side.

"So, you had some questions for me?" Mindy asks, glancing at Rose.

"I saw you this morning, you might recall," Rose says. "I'm friends with Angela Forrest, the one you found."

Mindy nods. "Yeah, of course. I'm so sorry."

"Thank you."

"And I remember you, sure. You were by the door when we went in. Man . . ." Mindy shakes her head. "It was honestly pretty horrible."

"I'm sure it was," Rose says, her mind working to find the right questions, the right path that will lead toward the information she's looking for. "Of course, you must see quite a few dead bodies, given where you work. The hospice alone . . ."

Mindy gives Rose a sidelong glance, brows slightly furrowed. "I guess . . . but you make it sound like I work on death row. It's not like the people who live here are dropping like flies, Rose."

"Oh, I didn't mean—"

"In fact, if I'm being honest, that was only the second death I've had to personally deal with," Mindy says, pulling Tatum gently along by an elbow. "So, no, I don't see a lot of dead bodies, as you put it."

Rose gives an embarrassed smile. "Of course, I don't mean to be crass." Rose sighs. "I'm trying to come to a point, and I'm afraid I'm being clumsy about it."

Mindy nods, and her guarded expression drifts away. "My grandfather used to always say: If you got a picture to show me, show me the picture. Don't paint it for me with watercolors."

Rose laughs. "Quite a unique aphorism. Was he an artist?"

Mindy shrugs. "I don't recall. But you're right; he was a unique guy. Anyway, I guess it's a long-winded way of saying: If you got something to say, just say it."

"Well then, let me ask it this way," Rose says. "You saw Angela's body, her injuries. Did they seem . . . I don't know . . . consistent with someone who'd slipped on a tile floor?"

"Sorry. I'm a bit lost, Rose," Mindy replies, her tone unreadable.

"It's just . . . I heard she was hurt pretty bad. A broken hip, a broken neck—"

Mindy looks at her quizzically. Almost warily. "How do you know this? And, not to be a jerk, but what business is it of yours?"

Rose gives a nervous chuckle, knowing she's on the precipice of being rude, but she also knows this might be her only chance to talk with the nurse so candidly, so she pushes forward. "To be frank, I wondered if it seemed like an accident."

Mindy stops walking, bringing Tatum to a stop with her. She looks at Rose directly for a moment, as if studying her. "I'm not sure what you're asking."

"Well, I—"

"Did you see the body, Rose?" the nurse asks, accusation interwoven into her tone. "Did someone—"

"No! No, of course not," Rose says, suddenly flustered, her confidence slipping for a moment, as if she'd stepped on a patch of ice but recovered before falling. "Nurse Jarvis, I'm sure you know how it is around here . . . there's an active grapevine at Autumn Springs. And let's just say word of mouth is that Angela looked pretty banged up. Abnormally so, one might say."

Mindy squints at her, and Rose doesn't see a child there anymore. She sees a woman. A *suspicious* woman. "I don't think I can get into details, Rose. If you're concerned, you should speak with Mr. Blackwell. He was there, too."

"I suppose I will, but I thought I'd ask you first. Mr. Blackwell isn't medically trained, you see."

Mindy nods, turns away, and continues moving them all down the path. "I guess."

"So . . . will you tell me what *you* think? Just your opinion, nothing more. Between us ladies, of course."

"Secrets between us girls, huh?" Mindy offers a little smirk. "Yeah, okay. My opinion is that Angela died from a bad fall, Rose. Older folks have fragile bones, no offense, and dropping onto the side of a tub with a little speed and the right angle . . ." She shrugs. "Snap crackle pop, you know?"

Rose feels a wave of disgust climb up her throat, a little dismayed by the young woman's crude description . . . but she's also relieved to hear her opinion that it really was just a freak accident. *Poor Angela.*

"So you don't think . . . it sounds silly, but you don't think maybe someone hurt her? One of the other residents, perhaps? Maybe an angry boyfriend?"

Mindy laughs. "C'mon, Rose. Who'd want to hurt Angela? Or any of you?"

Rose nods. "Of course, you're right."

Tatum stops to study a nearby cluster of flowers, mumbling about needing to water them, and Mindy lets out a mildly impatient breath. Regardless, Rose decides to push her luck. "Just one more question."

Mindy gets Tatum moving again, and the quick flash of annoyance seems to have dissipated. "Sure, why not."

"Was there a window left open, by chance? Did you happen to notice?"

Mindy scoffs, shakes her head. "Jesus, Rose, I'm not a detective. I just work here, you know?"

"Okay, but do you recall?"

"No, Rose, I don't recall," the nurse says, annoyance creeping back into her tone. "I'm sure they were all closed. It was pretty cold last night."

"I see," Rose says, deep in thought. "Well, thanks anyway."

"Sure thing. Sorry I couldn't be more help."

As they reach the Med Center entrance, Rose steps forward to hold the door open for the nurse and Tatum. "That's okay, you've helped quite a bit, actually."

"I'm glad. Sorry if I'm a bit snappy, I've been on since five a.m. Hey, you want to come sit with Tatum for a bit? You're welcome to stay and hang out, but based on the smell I'll need to clean him up first."

"No, no," Rose stammers, suddenly flummoxed, and still holding the door as the nurse walks Tatum into the lobby. "Thank you for your time and for being so candid."

Mindy smiles at her. "No problem. But remember, this is between us, okay?"

Rose nods. "I'll take it to my grave."

Mindy laughs as Rose lets the door handle go. "Dark," she hears the young woman say as the door shushes closed between them. "I dig it."

8

Later that night, Rose invites Miller over to watch the new crime series he's been so worked up about. Partly because she wants to watch the show with her friend, and partly as an apology for walking out on him earlier that day. To help make amends, she opens a bottle of wine and bakes her famous lemon bars, which are still cooling when he arrives.

"Smells wonderful," he says, a silly grin spreading on his face as he enters holding a quart of Häagen-Dazs chocolate ice cream. "I come bearing gifts."

"I hope you've had dinner—"

"I have, I have, thank you," he says, patting his stomach, which is still flatter than Rose would like, worried the man doesn't eat enough.

"Good," she says. "Because we're going straight to dessert. I have lemon bars and wine. A nice, chilled bottle of Chardonnay that will pair nicely, I think. And now it seems we have chocolate ice cream for a second course."

He smiles. "My sweet tooth weeps with anticipation."

The show is on-demand through Netflix, so they don't have to hustle to the television. Instead, they chat in the small kitchen, Miller sipping wine and picking off small pieces of the warm lemon bars while Rose pulls out small plates and napkins.

"I saw Maureen Stapleton today," he says, pulling off a paper towel to clean his powder-coated fingers. "She was upset."

Rose sets the plates on the countertop, then turns to look at him. "About what?"

Miller shrugs, but his expression is suddenly grim. "She says someone's been coming to her bedroom window at night. Watching her from the back lawn. She got a glimpse of the guy before he ducked and ran. Scared the hell out of her."

Rose crosses her arms. "Did she tell Mr. Blackwell?"

Miller shakes his head. "She doesn't want folks to think she's gone off the deep end or vying for attention. So she confided in me."

"Why you?" Rose says, fighting to keep the scratching claws of illogical jealousy at bay as she sets a lemon bar on each of their plates. "What are you supposed to do about it?"

"Heck, I don't know," he says. "I think she's hoping I can give folks a heads-up, spread the word we might have a Peeping Tom running around. She didn't want to tell administration . . . so she told me. She seemed a little embarrassed about the whole thing."

"Maureen Stapleton hasn't been embarrassed a day in her life."

Miller shrugs noncommittally. "Maybe so. She sure was scared, though," he says, thinking it best, for the time being, to keep the other thing Maureen Stapleton had shared with him a secret for now, even from his beloved Rose: her show-and-tell of the Smith & Wesson snub nose .38 Special she keeps—fully loaded—in the bottom of her underwear drawer. *Old habit,* she'd told him. *But now I'm glad I have it.*

Rose scoffs. "I suppose I should feel lucky to be on the second floor. Keeps all the prying eyes away."

Miller laughs, picks off another piece of lemon bar from the nearest plate. "Anyway, I gave her my number, told her to call if it happened again."

"And what?" Rose says, hating the rising heat in her voice. "You're gonna hightail it to her bedroom in the middle of the night to catch a would-be burglar? Or some Peeping Tom?"

That Maureen is a hot-to-trotter, the dark voice in Rose's mind says with a raspy chuckle. *I bet he'll check on her, all right. Every damn inch.*

Rose mentally swats the dark voice away, sends it scuttering back to the shadows.

Miller sighs and shoves his hands into his pockets. "You're missing the bigger picture here, Rose. One might even say that you're missing the point."

Rose stares at him, coming back to the moment. She pushes

aside her petty, stupid jealousy, and replays what he'd said with a clear mind.

Then her eyes widen, and she gasps. "Angela."

Miller nods. "Angela."

Rose steps out of the warm kitchen, begins pacing the living room. "If Maureen really did see someone—"

"Says he was wearing a black ski mask," Miller adds.

"Then that could very easily have been who hurt Angela." Rose stops pacing, puts a hand to her forehead. "Who *killed* Angela."

"Regardless, I told Maureen to lock her windows, draw her curtains at night," Miller says, and plucks the two dessert plates off the counter, carries them to the coffee table. "I hate that she feels scared, but there's really nothing else I can do to help her. Still, it worries me. If someone is stalking around out there, and if they really did have something to do with Angela's death, we could have a very bad situation on our hands."

"That's not even all of it," Rose says, settling down into her usual spot on the couch whenever the two of them watch television, despite all thoughts of a crime show having been chased from her mind.

Miller sits down at the other end of the couch, then squints at her. "Oh? What am I missing?"

Rose looks at Miller, meets his eye. She wasn't sure before, but she is now.

"I was going to tell you . . . I met with the nurse, the one who found Angela's body this morning, as well as some new doctor. I was sitting with Tatum by the pond for a while, and she came out to meet me. I basically asked her if she thought Angela's death was an accident, or possibly something else."

Miller puts his hands on his knees, turns fully toward Rose, eyebrows raised. "What did she say?"

Rose purses her lips. "She said that, in her opinion, what happened to Angela was an accident."

Miller gives a short laugh of relief. "Okay, so what's got you worked up?"

"Miller, when I looked into Angela's apartment this morning, I noticed her living room window, the one facing the back lawn, was partially open. I could see the curtains fluttering."

"Huh," Miller says, rubbing a bristly cheek. "That's strange."

"And when I asked the nurse about it a few hours ago, she said she didn't recall if the windows were open or closed. Which I thought odd."

"Why's that odd? She was focused on the body, after all."

"Because," Rose says, "the first thing that woman did when she and Mr. Blackwell entered the room was walk over and shut the window."

Miller shrugs. "Maybe she forgot."

Rose nods, unconvinced. Some distant fact pecking at her brain, a loose thread in all of this that she can't quite put a finger on.

"Sure," she says. "Or maybe she's a liar."

9

Long after Rose and Miller finish their crime show—and Miller returns to his apartment and Rose to her large, empty bed—the three sisters enter the old asylum.

"Barb, light a candle."

The floor is dusty concrete, the air inside the squat building cold and stale. Other than the few stray beams able to find a wayward crack to shine through, offering a silver seam to penetrate the gloom, the boarded-over windows shut out the moonlight almost completely.

The front doors through which they'd entered—thick, wood-paneled double doors so filthy and warped they hardly opened—were padlocked, but the chain looped through the handles was so badly rusted that the sisters were able to pay Billy Evenson, one of the orderlies, fifty dollars to snap one of the chain links with a pair of bolt cutters.

"Just leave the chain looped through the lock and no one will know the difference," Bridget had told him when Billy arrived at their apartment for a maintenance call, presumedly to fix a leaking pipe, which, it turned out, wasn't leaking after all.

"Whatever, ladies. As long as you don't hurt yourselves or throw some mad rave, I'll hook you up, no problem," Billy said, pocketing the cash.

True to his word, Billy had snapped the chain later that very evening, much to the sisters' delight.

"It's a perfect spot," Betsie says, watching as Barb pulls one of several heavy black candles from her tote bag, sets it on the floor, and ignites the wick with a long-stemmed lighter.

"Come on, let's get started." Bridget clears some debris with a corn broom as Barbara begins lighting more candles, creating a circle roughly ten feet in diameter.

Betsie pulls a heavy piece of white chalk from a plastic baggie she'd tucked into the pocket of her sweater, carefully lowers herself to hands and knees, and begins to draw a circle onto the concrete, just inside the perimeter of the black candles.

"My knees aren't going to thank me in the morning," she murmurs, shuffling slowly forward to smoothly continue the circle.

"I'll do the interior," Bridget says, clapping lightly. "I know this is going to work. I just know it!"

"Shh, keep it down, Bridge," Barbara chides, her back aching from placing the candles. "There will be a lot of questions if we're caught out here."

Bridget nods and, for the next half-hour, the Baxter sisters complete the setup for the ritual they'd been planning since early that morning. The old asylum is a godsend, of course, since there would have been no way to pull off such a complex ceremony inside their apartment.

Not to mention that privacy, in this particular case, is paramount.

No, it wouldn't do for others to know what they were up to, so they decided to conduct the ritual at the asylum, and not to begin until long after the sun had set and most folks were tucked away into their beds.

It's best that way.

Not to mention that it seems rather fitting.

Summoning a demon, after all, is work best done in the dark.

THREE.

LITTLE GREEN MEN

1

The rest of the week at Autumn Springs passed without incident.

Angela's body was taken away, buried in a Buffalo cemetery with only a few family members in attendance. There was a light flurry of snow, and the pastor hired by her son made quick work of the scripture.

No one from Autumn Springs made the trip.

On Friday night, Rose played in a poker competition at the Community Center in which each resident was given $500 of "house money" chips and proceeded to go broke after ten hands of Texas Hold'em. Later, Miller called to let her know Tatum Bird was the big winner, ending the night with over $10,000 in fake money.

"In a moment of rare lucidity, he made a joke about using the cash to buy the Yankees a decent second baseman," Miller told her, chuckling over the phone.

"Now, Beauregard, I find this hard to believe. My God, Tatum couldn't possibly keep track of numbers, sequences, and such things. The man hardly knows his name."

There was a beat of silence, during which Rose could almost visualize Miller's bashful expression. "Well," he said. "I may have helped him with a hand or three."

On Saturday, Rose wakes early.

Her daughter is taking her to lunch, driving all the way up from the city, and Rose wants to look her best. She wishes she'd had time to go into town for a salon visit earlier in the week, but events at their quiet little community had taken a nasty, unexpected turn. After Angela's death, a day at the salon seemed somewhat frivolous and, at least in her mind, more than a little bit disrespectful, given the tragedy.

Now, after a light breakfast, Rose sits at her kitchen table, anxiously sipping a cup of coffee and looking at her watch, the wall clock, and her cell phone every few minutes, wondering what to do with herself.

She stares out the sunlit window and wonders if her grandson will be coming along, or if Sybil is leaving him with that *man*. What's his name. Raul something. Or no . . . Craig. No, that isn't it.

Well, what does it matter? the dark voice says. *The two of them aren't even married. They aren't even living together! A broken house from the get-go, and passing your poor grandbaby around like a—*

The landline rings and Rose jumps out of her skin, startled by the air-shattering sound. Most of her friends call on her cell phone, and she isn't used to hearing the loud, shrill braying of the house line. She stands too quickly, smacks her knee on the table leg, and cusses her way over to the phone.

"Yes? Hello?"

"Ms. DuBois?" A woman's bored, monotone voice.

Who the hell else would it be? Rose thinks grumpily, rubbing at her sore knee.

"This is she," Rose says, straining to keep her tone pleasant. She glances at the clock, noting it's almost noon.

Sybil.

"This is Cindy at reception? I'm calling to let you know that your daughter is here." A pause, as if a question had been asked. Then: "Shall I send her through?"

"She's on my visitation card," Rose responds, a thread of venom in her tone. She's happy to let her anger show a bit now that Sybil had been stopped in the lobby, as if she were visiting her mother in prison. "So yes, let her through, and please make sure that card is updated."

"Oh, I see it now. Yes, well, I'll let her know. Good morning," the receptionist says, and abruptly disconnects the call.

Dismissing her annoyance at the receptionist, Rose instead frets as she looks around the small apartment, trying to see it with Sybil's eyes, wanting to make sure nothing appears fussy or overly worn. That nothing appears *old*.

She sniffs the air, which smells clean, but cracks a window anyway, just to let some fresh air inside. The incoming breeze is chilly, but the scent of the nearby forest makes up for it, so Rose leaves it open for now.

Satisfied that things are proper (or proper as they're going to get), she goes to the front door, opens it wide, and waits in the hallway for her daughter.

2

Sybil arrives alone.

"Hi, Mom."

Rose hugs her daughter fiercely, then pushes her to an arm's distance so she can look at her.

Sybil isn't the spitting image of Rose when she was in her forties, but she's close. If anything, Sybil is prettier, lither. Her curly hair, which normally hangs past her shoulders, is pulled back, enhancing her wide brown eyes, showing off the smooth skin of her face and graceful neck. Still, Rose notices the worry lines on her daughter's forehead, the creeping crow's feet at the corners of the eyes. Yes, she is still young and beautiful, but a mother knows when things have been tough. She knows when a woman is worn down.

"You look tired," Rose says.

Sybil rolls her eyes, laughs. "Perfect. A really spot-on 'Mom' comment."

Rose waves a hand. "I'm allowed, I'm allowed. You didn't bring Roy?"

Sybil sighs, drops her eyes. "I wanted to, Mom. You know Carlo comes up on weekends, and I figured they could hang out while you and I had lunch."

Son of a bitch bastard.

"He could have come with you."

Sybil gives Rose a knowing look, but smirks. "Next time. Besides, I needed some alone time with my mother. Thought you might be able to bestow some parental advice on my situation."

"Oh, I see," Rose says, raising an eyebrow. "Well, in that case, lunch for two sounds perfect." Rose takes Sybil's hand and squeezes. "I'm so glad to see you, hon. Come on inside and I'll get my coat."

A few minutes later, as the two women step back into the hallway, Rose is caught off guard to see Miller standing nearby, looking momentarily baffled at the sight of her daughter . . . then recognition comes, and he smiles brightly, snaps his fingers.

"Sybil!" he says too loudly, but his excitement is contagious and Sybil steps forward to give him a hug.

"Hey there, Miller," Sybil says happily as Rose looks on, her mind working. Should she invite Miller to come along with them? No, of course not. This is bonding time between mother and daughter. No, no, there's plenty of time to see Mr. Miller.

"Hey there, yourself," Miller says, a head taller than Sybil and squeezing her tight. "Always good to see Rose's little girl."

Rose watches this encounter—her two worlds colliding—and has to admit it warms her heart to see them so naturally, almost reflexively, loving one another.

Miller looks over Sybil's shoulder and gives Rose a wink, which she reciprocates with a small smile. Admittedly, she thinks her friend Beauregard looks moderately dashing this afternoon: dressed neatly in a knit black sweater, khaki pants, and clean sneakers. His bushy hair is even somewhat combed, and his blue eyes twinkle brightly. Even from a few feet away, Rose can smell the peppermint on his breath.

"Hey, Miller, why don't you come to lunch with us?" Sybil asks, her smirk blossoming to a full-blown grin.

Rose tuts. "Honey, I don't think—"

"I'd love to," Miller replies, smiling grandly. He looks at Rose, who glares back, lips set in a hard line.

Then Miller looks to the floor, absently rubs the toe of one shoe into the dark red carpet. "But I would be a third wheel, I'm afraid." He lifts his gaze, buries his hands in his pockets. "You two ladies go have fun and catch up. Rose? I'll see you later?"

"Sounds fine," Rose says, a smidge annoyed at her matchmaking daughter for inviting him in the first place.

Everything in my life is the way I want it, she thinks stubbornly. *And I won't be made a fool of.*

Miller tips the brim of an invisible hat and turns to walk back down the hallway.

Sybil looks at her mother, accusation in her eyes. "That was rude."

"I . . . honey, I see that man every day. I only see you once a month or so. And like you said, we need to have some time alone. And since I won't be seeing my grandbaby, I think that's more than fair."

"Awesome guilt trip, Mom," Sybil says, but slips an arm through Rose's and leads her down the hallway. She leans in, lowers her voice to a whisper. "And if I didn't know any better, I'd say you were having boy trouble."

Rose scoffs. "He's a good man," she says. "A nice man."

"But?"

"But nothing, honey. The world is chock-full of good men and bad men. You know what the difference between them is?"

Sybil shakes her head. "Enlighten me."

"Nothing," Rose says, pulling her daughter close. "Not a goddamn thing."

3

Stan Swanson is eighty-six years old and a certified, life-long conspiracy junkie.

Over the years, he would quickly latch on to any "aluminum hat" theory he could get his hands on. Illuminati? You bet. Kennedy assassination? One hundred percent. Moon landing? Fake as perfect pearls. Whatever it was, he was on-board and totally committed. Didn't matter if it was toxic chemtrails or New Coke, he bought in and would die on whatever the conspiratorial hill of the moment happened to be.

Of course, none of the conspiracy theories he'd so avidly supported (and would continue to do so until he breathed his last breath) was bigger than the granddaddy of them all, the one he'd spent his whole life studying, whether it be from the newest book or the most obscure documentary.

Stan Swanson believes in *aliens*.

Area 51? Of course!

Little green men? Everywhere!

UFOs? Not even a question. Look at the data!

Not only does Stan believe in alien life, but his diehard views on abduction and flying saucers had been a big chunk of what cost him his first marriage, his wife having had enough of his "crazy talk" for the near decade they'd managed to stay together. Neither of his two children have spoken to him in years, thinking him batshit nuts and, even worse, blaming him for their bizarre, messed-up childhoods. And the few friends he'd once had—all of whom believed as wholeheartedly in extraterrestrial beings as he did—are dead.

Sure, Stan still cruises the websites and chat rooms, but it isn't the same. The new generation thinks everything is a joke, or a fake, or something to do more out of boredom than belief. Kids these days have the attention span of a goldfish, skipping from one thing to the next in a matter of days or, if they really hold out, weeks. For Stan and his (deceased) friends, however, aliens and conspiracies aren't distractions, or amusements. They are theories worth committing your *life* to: to study, research, collect data about and hopefully—if you are a little smart and a lot lucky—*prove*.

Yes, that is the dream! To have your "crazy" ideas brought to light by hard evidence, confirmed by eyewitnesses, by *indisputable* facts!

Sadly, it seems to Stan that no one really takes it seriously anymore. No one *believes* anymore. It's all just a malarkey sandwich with extra mayonnaise, nothing but *Hong Kong Phooey*, as his buddy Frank Mooney used to say.

But now, admittedly, Stan is the shell of what he once was. Somewhere along the way the brash, able-bodied, inquisitive young man with boundless energy he'd once been had turned into a hunched, white-haired, weak-kneed, doddering old fool.

Where had his life gone? How had the years gone by so fast?

And now, here he is, living at a retirement home. A nice one, admittedly; one that gives him the around-the-clock care he needs, and also one that costs him a pretty penny. But when he first took the plunge, he figured what the hell? Since his kids won't return his calls or reply to his emails (he isn't even sure where his kids live anymore or, even more frankly, if they are still *alive*), Stan scraped together his life savings, sold his New Jersey condo, and purchased an apartment at Autumn Springs nearly a decade ago, a place where he could live out his final years on this earth in relative comfort and top-notch care. Of course, he would be living those years with so many questions—so many *theories*—left unanswered.

To make things worse, a few years back (after a particularly in-depth physical) Stan had been given "invalid" status, forcing him to move out of his homey apartment and into a much smaller, much more depressing room in the Medical Center. The upside being it's a place where nurses and orderlies are available 24/7 to assist him, if needed.

He didn't argue.

Admittedly, Stan is relieved for the change. Getting out of bed every morning has become a challenge, he can't cook or clean worth a shit, and, on more than one occasion, he's had to call a nurse or an orderly to help him get his bare ass off the damn toilet (an old-school wall phone supplied for such a purpose). No, the sad truth of it is that, quite simply, Stan can't be on his own anymore.

Sure, he'd grumbled and complained to some of the residents about making the switch to full-time care, wanting to make a show of having a backbone . . . but deep down, Stan is *afraid* to continue living alone. Afraid that he'll wake up one morning and forget what his name is. Afraid he'll take a spill and not be able to alert a soul to help him get back up. Afraid he'll go hungry, night after night, because he can't make his own food, or even have the strength to get himself to the dining hall.

So yes, Stan moved into the Medical Center, along with all his books and DVDs, a nice television with all the channels he could ever want, a meager wardrobe, and two boxes of personal items. Everything that remained of a lifetime.

Hong Kong Phooey, indeed.

Of course, there are moments when Stan is depressed about it. Acceptance isn't a virtue, after all, it's a handshake with fate that one often accepts begrudgingly. He gets the most down in the dumps when imagining what it would be like to have a family that loved him or friends that cared about him. A special someone he could call on the phone and speak to, or trade stories with.

Instead, he relies on the kindness of nurses and orderlies and doctors, and the friendly nature of his new neighbors, to help fill the foul emptiness inside his lonely old heart.

So, as one can imagine, it's a pleasant surprise when—after slowly making his way back from lunch at the dining hall—Stan returns to his coffin-sized room (as he semi-jokingly refers to it) to find something peculiar waiting for him.

Sitting on his bedside nightstand is an envelope. One that most certainly had not been there when he'd walked out the door about an hour ago.

Inside the envelope is a letter.

Wide-eyed, Stan reads it all the way through.

Then he reads it again.

And again.

More excited than he's been in years, Stan closes his door for privacy, digs out some old stationary and—in his shaky, unsteady hand—begins to write back.

4

"I want you to move in with us."

Rose sits back in her chair, staggered—quite literally shocked—at her daughter's statement.

Between them sits the remains of Rose's quinoa salad and Sybil's Impossible Burger which, as Rose understands it, is a hamburger made entirely from plants.

"If you're going to have a burger, why not have a *burger*?" she'd asked after her daughter explained the vegetarian option.

"It tastes like a burger, but it's not animal meat."

"Then what's the point?"

"Because I don't eat animals, Mom," Sybil said with a sigh, having gone through this many times before.

And now, at the tail end of their time together, Sybil has dropped a bomb.

"What are you saying, Sybil?" Rose says, eyes wide with incredulity. "I can't come live with you. In the city? In that tiny studio apartment you and Roy live in? Where would I sleep?"

"No, Mom, listen . . . I just bought a house in the Hudson Valley," Sybil says proudly. "It's small, but it's a *house*. And now, since they've essentially kicked the entire design team out of the office, I can work from home full-time without worrying about waking up Roy . . . or us, you know, stomping all over each other."

"Kicked you out?"

Sybil shrugs. "They're looking to downsize their footprint, but whatever—it's a win-win! Now I can take care of Roy, which saves money on a nanny, and we can live in a bigger place outside the city. We both have our own rooms, plus a guest room, and there's like, grass and trees *everywhere*, not just in the parks, you know?"

"When did this all happen?" Rose asks, trying to catch up to her daughter's enthusiastic bombardment of revelations. *How did so much of her life change without my noticing? Without my having any idea at all?*

"Mom, I told you a year ago that I was looking to move."

Rose nods, still reeling. "I . . . yes, I recall. But I assumed it was somewhere in the city. Or that you were moving in with . . . you know . . . what's-his-name."

Sybil laughs. "Carlo. Which you know very well. I think you only pretend not to remember. You're snarky like that."

"And is he moving with you?" Rose asks, ignoring the jab.

"Unfortunately, no," Sybil says, and her eyes drop, her bubbly tone dampened by disappointment. "His work in the city would be way too hard of a commute. We want to, but it's just bad timing."

"And what about marriage?"

Sybil rolls her eyes. "Here we go."

"Well, why not?"

"Mom, don't be so old-fashioned."

Rose raises her eyebrows. "Oh, so commitment is old-fashioned now?"

"We are committed," Sybil says, shifting in her seat. "And he's an awesome dad, okay? Carlo commits every weekend to spending time with Roy. And with me," she adds, with a mild blush that Rose chooses to ignore. "And the truth is, that's all he can realistically do right now. At least until things change. But he's been really supportive of me moving, which has made the whole thing so much easier. Seriously, he's been great about it. And, you know, if things work out the way we hope, he'll eventually move in with us. But right now it's just not realistic."

"I see," Rose says, in a tone that indicates she doesn't see at all. Not one bit.

"So? What do you think? Wanna be roomies?" Sybil says, grinning like the little girl Rose remembers so fondly, eyes wide and hopeful.

Rose folds her cloth napkin, unfolds it, then folds it again. When she looks up once more into her daughter's face, she realizes that little girl is waiting for an answer.

Right now.

"Well, Sybil, I'm flattered. I truly am. And the idea of seeing you and Roy all the time fills my heart to bursting." She reaches across the table and scoops her daughter's hand into hers. "It's just . . . baby, this is all so unexpected."

Sybil nods, her smile softening. "I know, and I didn't mean to pull the rug out from under you. And I'm not saying we should go back to your place and pack up your shit—"

"Language."

"Sorry, *stuff.* But I do want you to think about it, okay? Roy would love seeing his grandmother more often, and I'd love to see you more, too. And now we've got the space . . . so why not?"

"Because you'd kick me to the curb the second you had a new man in your life, for one," Rose says with a dramatic sniff.

Sybil laughs. "Hello? I *have* a man in my life. In fact, I have two. And I love them both."

Rose grunts an acknowledgment but says nothing.

Sybil sits back as a waiter comes to the table and quietly clears the dishes. "Besides, you know I'd never kick you out. I'd have a live-in babysitter!"

Rose chuckles. "Now we get to the truth—"

"You know I'm kidding. Come on, Mom, seriously. What do you think?"

Rose lets out a held breath. "Honey, it's very sweet. *You* are very sweet. But, Sybil, the hard truth is that I'm getting old. I'm healthy now, sure. I can take care of myself and can do pretty much whatever I want. But what happens in five years? What happens if I have a stroke? Or fall over and break a hip? Or, God forbid, begin to lose whatever's left of my mind?"

"Mom—"

Rose shakes her head, cutting off Sybil's rebuttal. "Baby, I'm near eighty years old, and the last thing I want is you having to take care of me when I can't take care of myself. Making me meals, dressing me in the morning, walking me to the bathroom. It's you who'll be babysitting *me*, Sybil. So no. No honey . . . I can't ask that of you. I won't."

Sybil's face falls. A tear runs from her eye and she swipes it away. "I don't mind, Mom. I love you."

Rose smiles. "I know. But I won't be your burden, Sybil. Your mother? Yes. Always. Until the day I die. But I won't be your burden."

Sybil nods, but her eyes drop as she presses her hands into her lap. "Well, just know the invitation is there. It's always there, and you can accept it anytime. Okay?"

"Fair enough," Rose says. "Now, let's split some dessert while you tell me more about Carlo and why he can't live with his . . . partner, or whatever."

"Girl talk, got it."

"And don't worry about me," Rose says, lifting the dessert menu off the table. "I'm quite happy where I am, and that's no lie."

Sybil smirks. "I bet you are. That place is a goddamn frat house, but with all the drugs and none of the sex."

"Language," Rose says, eyeing her daughter over the top of the menu. "And you'd be surprised."

5

Stan goes for a walk.

Following the instructions he was given in the letter, he makes his way to the old gazebo on the back lawn. A long walk for him, but nothing he can't handle. Hell, it's probably good for him to get a few steps in and breathe some fresh air.

Even if it is getting cold as a witch's you-know-what, he thinks, stepping up into the large, empty gazebo. He recalls the instructions and easily finds the loose bench seat. He looks around to make sure he's not being observed, lifts the seat, and sets the envelope neatly underneath before letting it settle back into place.

Please confirm that you are willing and able-bodied enough to meet us, the letter had read. *We can take you to the place where the evidence has been hidden for many years. The time has come to bring in others, and we believe in you, Stan.*

After the anonymous letter detailed how and where Stan was to respond, it finished with a simple, if cryptic, sign-off.

Trust no one.

Stan is no fool, and he knows quite well that whoever wrote the letter could be one of the residents playing a cruel joke on him. But he can't help thinking there is a ring of *truth* to the contents. Heck, they said things in there he'd often believed himself—specifically, that aliens had been visiting upstate New York for decades, and had left traces of those visits behind.

In a chat room he frequented, many folks had stated there was *undeniable proof* of UFOs in the Hudson Valley area, stretching as far as New Jersey, Pennsylvania, even all the way up to Maine. Stan agrees wholeheartedly, and is also confident there are remnants of *ships* (and maybe even skeletal remains of aliens themselves) that had crashed in the area. The evidence is out there, buried deep in the surrounding forest, protected by the government so no one will ever build on the land and thereby discover what so many people already know, or at least strongly suspect.

That aliens exist. And they're *here*.

Normal folks simply have no clue about all the crazy stuff the government is up to. Hell, there's an atomic laboratory sitting less than a day's drive from Autumn Springs! There are even (so-called) abandoned—yet secretly active—military bases all over the state. Federal parks. Forest reserves. The DoD has their fingerprints all over the damn place! And Stan is quite certain, if not Grade-A positive, that the government is conducting tests on alien life-forms in hidden bases other than the well-known Area 51. Secret places where they experiment on the creatures so they can learn how to *communicate* with them and, ultimately, weaponize their technology.

And now, after so many frustrating years, there is a possibility that Stan—whose wife and kids had deserted him because of his beliefs—will finally get to see a *real* alien. The letter had been vague, but he could read between the lines easy enough.

There is only one form of evidence that would make them reach out to someone like him with such conviction:

They had *bodies*.

Or, maybe . . . just maybe . . .

A spaceship.

Stan knows it will be torture for him while he waits to find out more, to wait for another letter. For the next set of instructions. But he'll wait.

He's waited his whole life, after all. What's a few more days?

After double-checking to make sure the bench is settled correctly, and his letter safe beneath, Stan makes his way back to the Med Center and his room. He's worn out from all the activity and is confident that a nap will be just the thing to help him recharge for the evening. He's heard the dining room special tonight is shrimp scampi, and he doesn't want to miss it.

When he finally shuffles back into his room, knees and back aching from the exercise, Stan goes to his kitchen and opens today's compartment from his once-a-day pill organizer. Bleary-eyed from exhaustion, he knocks the assortment of pills into his palm, then takes them all with a glass of tap water. He smacks his lips and hums happily as he makes his way toward his bed for a nice, late-afternoon siesta.

Due to his tiredness—and the ritualistic nature of taking a group of pills each and every day for the last twenty years, give or take—Stan didn't notice the tiny purple capsule that had been added to his daily regimen.

He'd just swallowed them all without a second thought, eager to lay his head down for a nap, drift off to thoughts of the pulsing, colorful lights of UFOs, and the bulbous black eyes of little green men.

6

Rose is putting on a pot for tea when her cell phone rings. The saved image of a familiar face fills the screen, and she answers. "Hello, Miller."

"I just wanted to know how lunch went."

Rose puts a bag of chamomile in her favorite mug, leans back against the counter, and waits for the water to boil. She looks out the window toward the lighted path and the Community Center beyond. Dusk is fading fast into night.

"It was nice. I wish Roy had come."

"I bet," Miller says. "Sybil doing okay?"

Rose nods to the empty kitchen, takes a breath. She debates for a moment, then spills the question Sybil asked her at lunch—while also making it clear that she is wholly undecided in the matter.

After a long pause, Miller clears his throat. "I think it's lovely that she wants to take you in. She's a good daughter, with a good heart."

Rose nods absently, as if not sure whether it's lovely or not. "She's young, Miller. She isn't thinking about the big picture. About what happens in the future."

"Sybil's a grown woman, Rose. I'm sure she's well aware of what happens when people age. That us old folks need help here and there."

"She has no clue what it would be like—"

"C'mon, now. She's no ignorant child. What is she, forty-five?"

"Forty-six," Rose says, and pours boiling water over the teabag. "And yes, she is a child. I'm not sure she even has a 401(k)."

Miller laughs. "Sure, okay. Point conceded. So what are you up to now?"

"I'm making tea, then I'm going to read my book, and then I'm going to sleep."

"True crime or fiction?"

"Never true crime before bed. Too many nightmares. I'm working through a cozy mystery I like very much, although I think I know who did it."

"Yeah, that sounds about right."

"What about you?" she asks, and wonders for a moment whether she should invite him over for a late-night movie . . . then discards the idea.

"Oh, I was checking my Twitter earlier, but it's too damn depressing. No more social media for me tonight. A book sounds like just the ticket."

"A nice boring evening for both of us, then," Rose says, facing the window, watching the darkness take over.

"After the excitement of the past week, I'm looking forward to a few boring nights. Speaking of which, did you ever talk to Mr. Blackwell? You still sniffin' that trail?"

Rose sighs. "I don't know. What's the point?" She stirs a spoonful of honey into her mug, stares idly at the vortex of circling tea, tries to focus her thoughts. "Angela's gone, and nothing is going to change that. If the nurse says she fell, she probably fell. And besides, other than your little friend Maureen, no one's said anything about strange masked men looking into their windows."

"Gotta say, she sure was shook up, though."

"Hmm."

"Sounds like you've moved on," Miller says.

"Perhaps." Rose blows on her tea. "You disappointed?"

"Never," Miller replies. "Goodnight, Rose."

A few minutes later, Rose settles into her favorite reading chair with her book, but her mind wanders and she finds it hard to concentrate. She thinks about that open window in Angela's apartment, and what it would be like to live with Sybil. Why Angela had taken a bath so late at night, and how she would feel being so far away from her friends. To leave Autumn Springs. To leave Beauregard Mason Miller.

She recalls Miller asking if she'd moved on from Angela's death and surprised herself by telling him what she realizes is the truth: that maybe she had.

It all seemed so important a few days ago, but after Sybil's potential life-changing invitation, and the normal routine of life picking up where it had left off, it was almost silly now to think something nefarious is going on behind closed doors.

This is a retirement home, for goodness' sake, she thinks, the idea of some maniac stalking the grounds seeming more preposterous with each passing second. *No reason for anyone to bother us. And besides, they'd have to be out of their damn minds.*

What kind of crazy person would want to hurt a bunch of old folks?

Reassured, Rose takes a sip of tea and goes back to her book.

7

Owen dreams of a waterfall.

When he was a child, his mother took him to a campground with a twenty-foot wonderful waterfall that poured into a wide, deep river. The kids—and many adults—would sit among the smooth boulders at the top of the drop on a hot afternoon and let the ice-cold water rush past their limbs and over the edge, crash far below into a cloud of hazy moisture. Inevitably, you'd have no choice but to leap over the edge yourself, fly into that cloud of mist and plunge into the churning river, then surface, laughing and sputtering.

Being very young the first time they went—no more than seven or eight years old—Owen had been frightened of the seemingly long fall from the rocky top to the water below. But eventually, of course, he was peer-pressured into jumping by the other kids at the campground—some younger and smaller than he was, but most were bigger, older.

Those were the ones he'd wanted to impress.

Almost a decade later, his family returned to the campground. Owen, having grown into a teenager, had been excited to see the great waterfall again, prepared to leap—unafraid now—from its top. But on that second trip he'd been shocked at how pathetic the waterfall had become to him, how his perspective had shrunken the danger, the majesty, of what he held in his memory. Sure, it was still fun to jump off, but it certainly wasn't scary, and he was never able to recapture that sweet feeling of terror he'd had on their prior visit, nothing that could match the mad exhilaration of his first terrifying leap.

The teenager he'd become was disappointed. But, even more so, he'd felt *robbed*. As if a wonderful memory of his early childhood had been stolen, savagely ripped away, diminished. Forever tarnished.

He recalls how he'd sulked that entire weekend, unable to explain the existential crisis he was dealing with to his mother, how he'd just then—that very trip—realized growing up was not always a good thing—or a *cool* thing.

At the time, he'd thought to himself, quite philosophically, that getting older was nothing but a series of slow deaths of the people we once were, and how, with each death of our past selves, those held memories of past lives also died. Not forgotten, perhaps, but withered and lifeless. Colorless. Muted by time, made insignificant by the damning present and a relentless, bullying future.

As an old man, he would often recall that memory: his teenage realization that life was filled with tricks and trapdoors, and not all of them pleasant.

About a year ago, he'd told Angela about that waterfall, and about his teenager's philosophy of life's diminishing qualities. But she'd just laughed at him, called him a nihilist, and kissed him lightly on the cheek. "I'll be your waterfall, Owen," she'd whispered into his ear, and he'd hugged her then and cried softly into her shoulder.

Over these last couple years, Angela Forrest had become everything to him. He'd reached a point in his life when he no longer expected anything from fate, satisfied with what he'd been given over the last eighty years. But then, like a gift, this woman had arrived—a beautiful, spirited, funny, witty companion, a wondrous surprise waiting for him at the end of a long road. Someone who would take his hand and walk with him the rest of the way into the glorious unknown of his final years. Or perhaps even further, into that sweet hereafter, into the bright warm light of the beautiful thing that awaits us all.

His final waterfall.

But lying here, in the dark, Owen is forced to acknowledge, with a pang of despair, that Angela is gone.

To make things worse, his blessed abyss of sleep has been interrupted—not by a waterfall, or a memory of one—but by the sound of running water coming from the bathroom.

Groggily, he glances toward the partially open bathroom door, focuses on the light coming through the gap, the glow from a seashell nightlight he keeps plugged in there above the sink.

What the hell?

As he becomes more fully awake, Owen realizes something is very wrong.

For one, his hands are tied together.

For another, someone is in his bathroom. He hears them moving around, and being none too subtle about it, either.

"Hey!" he yells. "What is this?"

To his utter horror, the bathroom door swings open and a dark shape emerges, moves quick as a spider toward his bed. The figure is clad all in black and glides like a wraith, cutting like a shadow through the dull pink light coming from the bathroom. Before he can scream or even move—so frozen is he with shock and fear—the intruder is on the bed, straddling him, shoving a cloth into his mouth with such savage force that Owen feels it jam into the back of his throat and immediately begins to gag, his eyes wide and watering and terrified.

"Come with me, Romeo," a muffled voice says. Strong hands grip Owen's skinny biceps and yank him upward.

Before he can think to resist—to kick or struggle—he's thrown hard to the floor. Unable to break his fall with his hands, he lands face-first. A flash of white fills his vision as his nose crunches against the thin carpet and something in his back tweaks viciously from the brute force of being tossed from the bed. He groans into the rag.

Owen is even more stunned when the intruder grips his pajama bottoms at the elastic hip and yanks downward—removing his underwear in the process—and shucks the clothes aside with a chuckle.

"Don't get hard on me, Romeo," the voice says.

I know that voice, he thinks fuzzily, his mind a dark haze of pain and shock.

Spurred by terror, Owen begins to kick, tries to push the fabric out with his tongue—to *fight back*—when a knuckled hand taps him hard on the side of the head, then rolls him over onto his aching back.

"Look at me."

Reflexively, Owen glances up at the intruder, who now sits almost casually atop his bony legs, and sees a large knife held aloft, just a few inches from his eyes. The steel blade is serrated along one edge and razor-sharp on the other, the polished metal glinting with the murky pink light of the bathroom, where the bathwater—part of his brain registers idly—is still running.

"Don't move, or I might slip and send this thing right through your chest."

Owen snuffles out a gagged reply, and then gloved hands are gripping his flimsy white T-shirt. The knife stabs into the collar (poking his neck painfully) and cuts downward.

"Shit, look what you made me do," the intruder says, tapping the fiery wound in his neck, but there's a mad joy in their tone, a mocking disappointment.

Then the remains of his shirt are torn away, leaving him completely naked on the floor of his once docile apartment, a place he thought of as a sanctuary, a bastion of safety where he would peacefully spend whatever years were left to him.

And now he is going to die here. Oh yes, of that he is certain. And, almost assuredly, by the same monster's hand that took Angela.

Before he can think on it further—have time to lament or worry or drown in fear—the intruder abruptly stands, stomps around behind him, and grips him beneath the armpits. Owen whimpers and kicks as he's dragged backward toward the bathroom.

One last time, he looks at his room, his tousled bed, his life—praying for help, for answers—and then it's gone.

Cold ceramic tile slides beneath him as he's pulled into the bathroom and dumped to the floor. His legs are kicked aside by heavy boots and the door is closed, the water turned off. He hears light splashing.

A muffled, high-pitched voice. "Nice and warm."

Owen curls into a fetal position and weeps into the damp cloth in his mouth, wishing this would stop, wishing he could wake up and call Angela, take her to lunch and talk about all the things they were going to do together—the trips they would take while holding hands and sightseeing, or having fresh coffee on sunlit mornings, sharing their thoughts on movies, books, art . . .

The dream of a life never lived dissolves before his eyes, and his heart breaks.

He's lifted into the tub, his body immersed into the searing hot water. The spectre of death looks down on him, darker than the dark.

"This won't take long."

The knife strikes like a snake into his forearm, digs deep into the flesh, then begins to cut downward, ripping through tendons, shredding veins. Before he can gasp or beg or scream, a gloved hand grips his head and pushes him down below the surface.

Wake up, Owen, he thinks. *Please, please wake up.*

8

It's late, and Gopi knows that the best thing to do—the *smart* thing to do—would be to call it a night.

He checks his watch. Nearly 1 AM.

He takes the notepad from his lap and sets it on the coffee table, picks up his tumbler of scotch and takes a long sip, debating.

The apartment is in almost complete darkness, illuminated by nothing but the scrolling credits of *Black Sunday,* the 1960 black-and-white Mario Bava masterpiece (starring one of the original scream queens in Barbara Steele, who went on to work with such directors as Federico Fellini, David Cronenberg, and Jonathan Demme), as they crawl up the screen of his sixty-inch television.

Gopi is planning a double feature for the next movie night and, seeing as how it will fall during the week of Halloween, he figures some horror classics will be the perfect bill for a full house of novices. The only question now is what to do for the second film. *Black Sunday,* a wonderful story of witchcraft and the Devil, would show first, followed by a short intermission (bladders would be tied into hard knots by this point) and a brief Q&A before launching into the second movie.

He likes the idea of making it a Barbara Steele double-bill, which would give him plenty of options to choose from—everything from Corman's *The Pit and the Pendulum* (the current frontrunner) to Fellini's *8 ½. Shivers,* unfortunately, is not an option, although it is one of his very favorite Cronenberg films. No, he'd have a walkout on his hands after twenty minutes if he dared show that one. Best to play it safe with this group.

Struck by an idea, Gopi sits up and snaps his fingers. "Of course!" he says to the dark, empty room. "*Castle of Blood* is perfect." It's been decades since Gopi has seen the film and he's thrilled at the idea of diving into a classic—especially one that features a good dose of horror, a genre he favors above all others (even if he'd never admit such a thing, lest folks think his tastes lowbrow).

Now wide-awake with renewed enthusiasm, Gopi picks up the remote control and prays that the obscure film is available on demand. He squints as the dim scroll of credits flickers over to the television's main menu screen, bright as a new day's sun to his tired, dark-adjusted eyes. After a few moments of searching the different apps, he laughs in delight when he finds the movie available. And for less than a dollar!

I'll have to order the Blu-ray for the viewing, but there's plenty of time, he thinks as he purchases the movie, pausing the opening screen while he gets up to use the restroom and refill his scotch. There's no chance of going to bed now, of course. No chance at all.

After using the bathroom, and eager for the (very) late-night movie, Gopi is making his way back to the couch when he happens to glance out of a darkened first-floor window, the one facing Autumn Spring's back lawn, which is always pitch black after the path lights turn off at 10 PM sharp.

He stops, then takes a few cautious steps toward the window, squinting into the darkness, trying to understand what he's seeing . . . and then realizes what has caught his attention.

There are lights on inside the old asylum.

Well, not the actual building lights (any electricity that may have once run to the decrepit structure having been terminated decades ago), but *light.* By the orange, flickering nature of it, he'd say a candle.

A bunch of them.

"What the hell?" he says, and sets his empty tumbler back onto the table, Barbara Steele and *Castle of Blood* momentarily forgotten.

In his mind, he can't help replaying images from *Black Sunday*: A witch burned at the stake. A warlock in a ghastly mask, digging his way through an earth-torn grave, freshly released from hell.

"Nonsense," he mumbles, but continues to stare at the soft orange light—flickering in the distance like a warning—through the cracks of the asylum's boarded-up windows.

The night air is cold, but Gopi is prepared. He wears a black down jacket, a knit hat, leather gloves, and his warmest boots. The one thing he did forget, rather stupidly as it turns out, is a flashlight. He can't remember the last time he was out of his apartment this late and isn't accustomed to relying on nothing but moonlight to make his way somewhere on foot. To make things worse, the crescent moon is partially obscured by heavy black clouds, so seeing much of anything past a few yards is all but impossible. Instead, he uses landmarks. The gazebo, for one, stands sentinel about twenty yards ahead on his right. Beyond that, far to the left—toward the train tracks—pushed back against a towering wall of shadow-swollen trees, is the old asylum. An easy target for him to head toward, even in the dark, given that the candlelight coming from inside has created a beacon for his eyes to latch on to.

As Gopi stomps quickly past the gazebo, he begins to wonder if doing this is a good idea or a very bad one (he's leaning heavily toward *bad* on that count). From this distance, he can plainly see that someone is definitely inside the decayed building. The front door, although not fully open, appears to be slightly ajar, spilling a vertical seam of light. The boarded windows, badly aged and in desperate need of repair, are a fractured maze of jagged, flickering orange cracks.

Looks like a goddamn haunted house, he thinks, glad that the grass is swallowing any sounds of his approach.

As he gets closer, he hears something on the air . . . an indefinable ebb and flow of voices. Not singing, exactly, but rhythmic, and repetitive.

Is that . . . chanting?

Unbidden, Gopi's mind flings open the file cabinet of every old horror movie he's ever watched, flooding his imagination with images of devils, witches, and ghosts; of the demon-possessed and machete-hunting killers; of zombies, vampires, and were-wolves.

"You're being stupid," he whispers into the cold night air, his breath a drifting cloud of mist. "There's nothing out there but some kids or—"

As if cut with a knife, the chanting stops.

Gopi freezes in place, breath caught in his chest. With wide eyes, he watches the asylum, waiting for the voices to continue . . .

When the lights go out.

It's only now that Gopi realizes his mistake. By coming straight toward the building, he's put himself in direct view of anyone coming out the front door. With the dim exterior lights of the Green-view Apartments directly behind him, he'll stand out easily for anyone looking his direction.

Knowing he has little time, Gopi jogs to the right of the asylum, toward the trees and the trailhead, hoping he can get out of sight before he's spotted. As he nears the forest, however, a new sound permeates the chilled air.

The sound of something moving in the trees.

A squirrel, perhaps? No, this sounds . . . bigger.

Gopi stops his light jog only a few yards from the tree line and well to the side of the asylum. If he continues forward just a few more steps, he'll be in among the trees and closer to whatever it is that's rustling around in the dense woods. If he goes back toward home, he'll be visible—even in the dark—by whoever comes out the front door of the dilapidated building.

He's trapped.

Sweating, his heart beating from the unfamiliar, fear-induced adrenaline, Gopi hears more movement in the trees and strains his eyes to get a closer look.

Bright orange eyes stare back.

"Shit," he says, backing away from the trees, arms raised in a defensive posture.

He hears a creaking sound from his left as the front door of the asylum opens. He dares a glance in that direction, and gasps.

Someone is standing there, watching him.

"Fuck this," Gopi breathes, then turns his back on the asylum—on the dark trees and whatever creature stalks within them—and runs.

It's not until he's chugging his way past the gazebo, his heart racing as trickles of cold sweat slip from beneath his knit cap to run into his eyes and down his back, that he realizes he's being chased.

They're coming after me. Whoever it was in there, they're coming after me!

Gopi likes to think of himself as being in relatively decent shape, at least for a seventy-two-year-old man, but running, dear friends, is not something he has done in many years, and his body (especially the knees—the ones he'd thought of getting replaced time and time again) rejects the strained, awkward, painful exertion of each lumbering step. Regardless of his body's protestation, however, he continues to run because there is definitely someone—or *something*—following close behind. He can plainly hear the stranger's footsteps pounding the ground, the heavy breathing of something getting closer . . . closer . . .

But then, a stroke of luck. One of the upstairs tenants has come awake, either unable to sleep or needing a late-night glass of water—Gopi doesn't know and doesn't care—and the bright light of a second-story apartment douses the back lawn, followed by the shadowed figure of someone moving to look out the window.

Immediately, the footsteps from behind him disappear—vanishing as if they'd never been there at all. Inspired by the reprieve, Gopi doubles his efforts.

Moments later, panting heavily, his heart pounding painfully in his chest, he reaches the maintenance door at the back of the building—the one he'd smartly left wedged open, using an old broken brick kept by the door for just such purposes—and pushes his way inside. He kicks the brick away and throws his body against the door, locking it shut.

Thanking the gods that his apartment is on the first floor (a flight of stairs at this point most likely being the actual death of him), Gopi stumbles past the staircase and through a second door that connects to the well-lit, and almost oppressively warm, lobby. He glances toward the glass double doors of the building's main entrance, satisfies himself that no one is making their way inside to finish him off, turns to the right, and walks quickly down the hallway to unit 3—*his* unit—and safety.

After a few breathless seconds of getting his key to work, Gopi enters the apartment and twists the lock on the handle, wishing like hell he could bolt the door closed (a big no-no in a place where emergency access is regularly required). He peels off his hat, gloves, and jacket, lets it all drop to the floor as he makes his way across the dim room toward the kitchen, where he will pour himself a double and do his best to forget about the old asylum, the thing in the trees, and whoever it was that had been following (chasing!) him home.

Was it the thing from the woods? The shadowed figure in the asylum's doorway?

Or something else?

Shaking his head at his stupidity, he dumps the remains of the bottle of Dewars 12-Year into his glass and takes a long, burning swallow. Across the room, the frozen title screen of *Castle of Blood* glows dully, giving the room a gray, overcast light that does little to assuage Gopi's nerves.

Taking another sip of his drink, feeling a little better now that his heart is slowing, his skin cooling after the panicked run home, he debates whether to take a shower or just kick off his boots and flop down onto the bed.

As he weighs his options, he walks over to the couch, finds the remote control, and flicks off the screen, knowing there will be no double feature tonight. The last thing he wants to see is some demon reaching for the throat of a—

There's a knock at the door.

Gopi's blood chills at the sound. Standing still as a statue in the middle of his living room, a scotch in one hand and a remote control in the other, he stares at the closed door, the bar of hallway lit beneath it, and the shadows of two feet moving impatiently on the other side.

The knock comes again—soft, but persistent—and Gopi waits. Not moving, hardly breathing. Completely silent.

Finally, the shadows beneath the door move away, and he lets out a large, held breath. He drops the remote control on the couch and raises a shaky hand to finish off the scotch. There will be no shower tonight, he realizes, as he's suddenly swamped by tiredness, his mind and body desperate to strip off his clothes, climb beneath his blankets, and put this mad adventure behind him.

"Tomorrow," he mumbles. "I'll think about it tomorrow."

Satisfied, Gopi shuffles to the kitchen and sets his glass in the sink. Leaving the lights off, he crosses the living room, his mind cloudy with scotch and exhaustion, eager for a long, dreamless sleep.

Had he spared a look to his right while making his way toward the bedroom, perhaps to close the hand-stitched red curtains his dear, dead mother had once made with her own two hands, he might have screamed at the sight of the shadow-filled face staring back at him, as if patiently waiting to be let inside.

FOUR

VIOLENT DELIGHTS

1

Egor Abramov has a bad heart.

Whenever he leaves his room, he must always bring his bottle of prescription nitrates with him in case of an episode. His days of strenuous physical activity—of any sort—are long behind him. But he still has a lust for life and refuses to spend his days sitting in front of the television watching old reruns or, even worse, depressing news channels. He doesn't own a computer or a smart phone, so doesn't need to worry about doomscrolling (as the kids say) on social media. He enjoys long walks around the grounds and meeting with friends for meals. He plays chess anytime he can convince someone to join him for a game and even started a fledgling chess club (Community Center, Room 300, Monday afternoons at 3 PM) that has swelled to eight members, and counting, in just a few short months. He enjoys reading the classics, prefers Dostoevsky over Tolstoy, and is often found browsing the shelves of the Autumn Springs library for something he hasn't yet discovered. He has an innate curiosity, a drive to keep learning, to keep talking to new and interesting people, to spend time with friends and play whatever games his doctors will allow him to play (consisting primarily of chess, cards, and the occasional bocce tournament on the back lawn).

He doesn't even mind living in the Medical Center. At least he isn't down the hall with those poor souls in the hospice wing—the last stop on the Autumn Springs express. Sure, his heart is a constant worry, a troublesome ticking clock bumping and thumping in his chest—and after five surgeries there likely will never be a sixth—but he is determined to enjoy the years he has left, however many that might be.

He can still enjoy the good things in life: a decent meal, a good book, a long walk. A nice cup of tea.

Egor has never been a coffee drinker. Too much caffeine, and he doesn't like the taste. But he loves a good cup of tea: Earl Grey in the morning with lots of cream and honey, a chamomile or Egyptian licorice in the evening, unsweetened.

And so he is pleasantly surprised this morning when, after returning from breakfast at the dining hall, he finds a friend waiting in his room, a steaming pot of tea on the stove, and the chessboard set up on the kitchen table.

"To what do I owe the pleasure?" Egor says, already eyeing the chess pieces, considering different opening strategies.

"You up for a game?" his friend says.

Always, he thinks happily.

But first, a nice cup of tea.

2

Rose is pouring herself the first coffee of the day (she allows herself three cups, but nothing with caffeine after two o'clock, lest it affect her sleep) when there's a knock at the door. She sets her cup down, walks to within a few feet of the locked door, and stops.

"Who is it?" she says, hating the dark strands of fear slithering like poisonous snakes through her mind, through her heart. Despite warm leggings, slippers, and her favorite cable-knit sweater—the dark gray Patagonia that Sybil bought her for Christmas a few years back—she shivers.

I'm shaking, she realizes with a sense of unease. *Good Lord, when did I become so afraid?*

"It's the police, ma'am. If you don't mind, we have a few questions."

The voice is young, and male. Rose goes closer to the door, presses her eye against the peephole, and sees a policeman looking back at her, a grim patience etched on his face.

Rose pulls open the door. The man is alone, but Rose hears the unfamiliar sound of formal conversation from down the hall. She sticks her head out and peeks toward the lobby, where another officer is speaking to one of her neighbors. She turns her eyes back to the young man standing in front of her, and feels a renewed surge of fear.

"What's happened?"

The officer—who looks to Rose like he should be taking classes in college instead of wearing a holstered sidearm—only sighs heavily, as if tired of hearing the same question. "I'm not at liberty to offer any details, ma'am, but if I could ask you a few questions, we'd certainly appreciate your time."

"Who's we?" Rose asks.

The officer, who Rose notes has a name tag above his badge that reads FREEMAN, looks at her with confusion. "Ma'am?"

"You keep saying 'we', and I'd like to know who 'we' is."

Officer Freeman arches an eyebrow. "The police, ma'am. 'We' means the police."

"Did someone die?"

"Ma'am, if I can just ask you a few questions, I can let you get on with your day."

Get on with your *day, you mean,* Rose thinks, her agitation at the officer's attitude ruffling her feathers more and more with each passing second. But she only nods, crossing her arms over her thick sweater, wondering what new horror has occurred at Autumn Springs.

"Go on," Rose says, thinking that if this young man rolls his eyes at her she just might slap him across the face. "My coffee's getting cold."

Officer Freeman's expression tightens, like a man who goes to pet a dog only to be met with a deep snarl and a flash of wet, sharp teeth.

Rose spends the next few minutes telling the policeman her full name, how long she's been a resident, and informing him that: No, she hadn't heard or seen anything unusual last night.

When the officer closes his notebook, he offers a smile that chills her heart. "I appreciate your assistance, Ms. DuBois."

"Are you going to tell me what happened, or are we old folks supposed to sit in our fear all morning until we find out?"

Officer Freeman doesn't answer, but instead begins walking toward the next apartment.

As he turns to go, however, she grips him firmly by the arm. "I'd like you to tell me what's going on, young man, and I'd ask you wipe that smirk off your face while you do it."

The officer's smile disappears, replaced by a face of impatience and impending violence, a distorted mask she'd seen her own husband wear more than once. "Let go of my arm, Ms. DuBois."

Rose releases her hand, but her gaze on his remains steady.

For a moment, Rose doesn't think he'll answer, but then he

softens, as if suddenly realizing he's supposed to be one of the good guys.

"One of your neighbors died last night, okay?" he says, looking down the hall, as if to make sure the other officer can't hear him. "But look, he wasn't even in this building. So there's nothing for you to worry about."

"Who?" she asks, faces and names swirling through her mind like the balls in a bingo cage. She can almost picture the faces of her friends on each one, a dark hand reaching inside to pull another soul free. "Who was it, and how did he, or she, die?"

"I'm not allowed to say . . . *ma'am*," Officer Freeman says quietly, dark eyes locked on Rose, his face now creased with an annoyed frown. He takes a small step closer and lowers his voice. "But if I'm being honest? This is all a big waste of time, don't you think, Ms. DuBois? I mean, people probably die here every other day, am I right?"

As rain, the dark voice in her mind hisses, but Rose pushes it away.

Officer Freeman takes a step back. "Have a nice day, ma'am," he says, a little more loudly now, standing in front of Rose wearing that serpent's smile, like a doorman waiting for a tip.

Rose does not return the smile. Instead, she takes two steps backward into her apartment and slams the door in the man's face.

3

Detective Ernie Hastings stares at the corpse in the bathtub with mixed feelings.

On the one hand, he's grimly impressed with the vigor and thoroughness with which the man has torn up his arms. These are not hesitation wounds.

These are primal and angry. Determined.

On the other hand, he's annoyed that the old guy didn't find a more airtight way of offing himself. Not to mention, hygienic. Something that would require less paperwork and less cleanup. An overdose, perhaps. There has to be a way in this place to get a bunch of pills that will put you under for good. I mean, the joint is packed with sick and elderly folks, nearly all of them sporting a pharmacy on their kitchen counter.

No . . . he doesn't like this. It's *messy*. Messy as in cleanup on aisle four, but also messy as in: did he *really* do this to himself?

Hastings is forty-three years old and has been a homicide detective for seven of those years, but (ironically) has never been called to a retirement home before.

This is a first.

An average man in an average suit, Hastings has had a stellar, if not overly impressive, career. His cases almost always get closed, but his record has no legendary, headline-grabbing collar: no years-long manhunt of some nemesis that kept him up at night. He is no superstar on the force, and would never have a book or a television show based on his splashy cases.

But he's thorough. He has a bulldog mentality and is intelligent in the way of most good detectives. He isn't the kind of cop that sees killers around every corner, but he's open-minded and has never—*never*—ignored a lead.

Now, seeing this mess in the bathtub, he does his best to align his suspicions with his reputation and his standards. It isn't his job to find Murder where it doesn't exist, but it *is* his job to not let it sneak away, like a thief through the kitchen window.

If Murder's here, he's going to catch it.

So he stands by, patiently, *thoroughly*, studying the bathroom as the photographer snaps off shot after shot after shot, the *POP* of the flash every few seconds freeze-framing the scene in Hastings's mind. It's a sound he always associates with death.

The knife is in the tub with the victim, so no mystery there. He debates getting analysis done to match the cut with the knife, but it's not like a bullet, where forensics could narrow it down to a single, unique weapon. The wounds would tell a story, sure, but a bathtub full of blood tells a story, too. So what's the point? Nothing but more paperwork. More taxpayer money down the sinkhole.

Still, he thinks, *probably a good idea to run the analysis, even if it is pointless.*

Hastings had already heard back from the officers conducting interviews all morning. Turns out the vic's girlfriend had died— quite tragically—a week ago, and the man, Owen Duffield, had since become quite depressed. Locked himself in his room. Sat in the darkness for days. Probably stopped taking his meds (something an autopsy would verify). All signs point to suicide.

But.

Two violent deaths in one week?

Both vics relatively young, relatively healthy?

Nah, he doesn't like it. It smells funny.

Even in a place like this, where Death lives down the hall and throws a Tupperware party every Sunday afternoon, the idea of two violent incidents—broken bones, sliced wrists—in such a short span of time raises a red flag or three, regardless of how obvious both deaths happen to be.

Maybe too obvious? Too neat?

Perhaps.

Behind Hastings, waiting semi-patiently in the living room, is a crowd. The coroner folks are standing by, ready with a body bag and a gurney. With them is the administrator—a man Hastings can't quite get a read on, at least not yet—wringing his hands and looking pale as a sheet, probably worried about spooking the other residents and annoyed at the hullaballoo of the whole thing.

Hastings steps aside as the photographer slips out of the small bathroom.

"All done here, Ernie."

"Thanks, Jim," Hastings says. "Do me a favor and shoot the bedroom before the parade comes through. The bed, specifically."

"Sure," the photographer says, and continues snapping.

Hastings studies the bed again: the neatly tucked sheets and blankets, the meticulously folded clothes set on top. He scratches an unshaven cheek, and that phrase shows up in his mind again, like a flickering neon sign alongside a dark road.

TOO NEAT?

He sighs, turns back to the bathroom, hands shoved deep into his pockets, and ticks off all the reasons to write this one up as a suicide so he can focus on the next case.

No sign of a struggle.

No forced entry.

Second-story apartment, so no one came through a window (at least not without a ladder, but the latched window rules out even this possibility).

Neighbors reported nothing unusual during the night.

Victim was depressed, potentially suicidal.

No bruises or obvious marks on the body other than the cut wrists. At least from what Hastings can see. The water is dark red and nearly opaque, the head and shoulders of the corpse rising above the smooth crimson surface pale as vanilla ice cream, the eyes closed and sunken, the mouth stretched open in a rictus of pain and horror.

Doubt the marketing team will want this in the brochure, Hastings thinks, which reminds him of the administrator—who, it turns out, is the only one with access to the apartment other than the victim himself. Hastings will need to question him again before it's all said and done, but the guy has an alibi and besides, he's not the type.

It's never the guy you think it is, he reminds himself. *Like the neighbors always say: He was quiet. He was friendly.* Little did they know about the bodies buried in the backyard or the chained-up kid in the basement.

He'll keep an eye on the administrator.

Regardless, Hastings wants to know who else might have had access to that skeleton key of his—the one that gives full access to every apartment at Autumn Springs, to be used in case of emergencies—just to dot the *I's* and cross the *T's* on this, admittedly soft, investigation.

"All right, boys, come on in," Hastings says to the group waiting anxiously in the other room, noting the photographer has finished his work and exited stage right.

The coroner's men wheel in the gurney, and Hastings steps back and out of the way. Once the body is removed, forensics will come in to drain the tub and bag the knife, and anything else they think significant.

Hastings heads for the living room to have a chat with the administrator but stops to study the bed one last time. Folded neatly atop the clean, navy blue comforter are pajama bottoms, socks, and boxers.

No shirt, Hastings notes, then lets it go as another piece of useless data that his detective brain collects randomly and without filter. Like the fact that the curtains were all drawn shut when he arrived, or the state of the place being a total wreck, like a bachelor pad after a bender.

Except for the bed, of course. And let's not forget those creepily folded clothes.

Or the fact there's no note.

No explanation. No goodbye.

Died of a broken heart, Hastings thinks, then scoffs at his romantic rumination.

There's a loud, fleshy *splat* from the bathroom and one of the coroner men cusses. Hastings glances over in time to see a bare, badly gouged arm lying like a dead fish on the pink bathroom tile. Then he shakes his head and turns away, eager to speak once more with the administrator, wrap this whole thing up, get back to the station, and move on to the next case.

"So long, Romeo," he mutters in the direction of the bloodless arm, now being scooped into the black body bag, then leaves the bedroom.

4

Rose and Miller sit in silence, each of them lost in their own dreadful thoughts.

A bowl of cooling Penne Arrabbiata sits in front of Miller, a plate of salmon and rice—hardly touched—in front of Rose.

Word had rippled through Autumn Springs like stink on a breeze. Owen Duffield had been found dead by suicide that morning, less than a week after Angela Forrest's tragic accident.

With the dissemination of information, of course, comes insinuation.

For some, suspicion.

Rose has read her share of true crime books, and seen and read her share of murder mysteries. She knows that two violent deaths in such a short span of time is anything but common.

First, there is the brutal nature of the injuries to Angela. Second, based on what she's heard through the grapevine, are the savage details of what Owen had done to himself. She didn't know the man well, and sure, maybe there'd been an idea in her head that he might have had something to do with Angela's death . . . but to imagine him cutting himself up like that? For Rose, at least, it was hard to believe.

When she mentions her suspicions to Miller, he simply shrugs. "Maybe you were right about him being mixed up with what happened to Angela, and maybe what he did was out of guilt. No one really knows anyone, Rose," he says. "We all wear masks to some extent, and sometimes what's hidden beneath can be—"

"Monstrous?" Rose offers.

"Evil," Miller says, and stares blankly into his coffee cup.

Rose wonders if Owen Duffield had a monster hiding beneath *his* mask . . . or if what happened to him and Angela was something else entirely.

"You two look glum," a booming voice says, breaking Rose from her internal musings. She looks up to see Mickey Lake towering above them, a wide, welcome grin on his broad face. "Mind if I play third wheel?"

"Don't be silly, sit down," Rose says, happy for the distraction.

Mickey is always too loud, too happy, and too charming. A much-needed combination of attributes in a community filled with older, mostly docile types. Rose adores him in doses, but right now she's more than happy to have someone filling the void of sorrow in her heart.

Miller, she notices, is smiling as well, patting the broad shoulder of their friend as he settles into a chair that looks as if it can hardly hold his massive frame. "So glad you're joining us," Miller says. "It's been too long since we've had a good chat."

"Mickey, how do you stay so fit?" Rose asks, noting the muscled forearms of their friend, his gray cotton T-shirt all but painted onto his torso.

"Mostly body weight stuff," he says shyly. "Push-ups, yoga, some dumbbell work. Sometimes I use the shitty gym here, which serves its purpose. Look, at my age you got to be careful about free weights, so the machines they got here work okay."

As far as Rose knows, Mickey is about the same age as Miller—right around eighty—but looks quite a bit younger thanks to his shaved scalp, clean-shaven face, and bright blue eyes. And his physique, of course. She wonders what he must have looked like when he was playing football in his twenties and thirties—and has no trouble picturing him forty pounds heavier and even stronger than he is now, strong enough to push around men of equal or greater size.

Wouldn't want to see him angry, the dark voice in her mind says with a snicker, and Rose frowns, disturbed at the thought.

Like many of them, Mickey had chosen retirement home living because of what was to *come* versus the way things are now. That's the thing with most retirement homes: once you're too feeble, or sick, to live independently without professional care—to take care of yourself, in other words—they won't accept you. So in order to make sure you'll have the help you need late in life—when your body or mind is shutting down to the point where you can't manage on your own—you have to buy in early, while you are still (*relatively*) young and able-bodied. Like herself and Miller. And, of course, Mickey, who looks like he could wrestle an alligator, let alone make himself a meal or walk himself to the bathroom.

But it's also a nice community, Rose knows. And it's good to be around folks who are like you—who are of the same generation and move at the same speed, who have similar interests. A place where you can all watch out for each other. Where you can feel at ease.

Where you can feel *safe*.

At least, until now.

Mickey folds his thick arms on the table and hunkers low. "Look, given everything that's gone on this past week, I think it's time we three put our heads together about what's been happening around here," he says quietly. Conspiratorially.

Rose leans in. "What do *you* think's been happening, Mickey?"

He frowns, rubs absently at his scalp. "Hell, Rose, it's hard not to worry about it. Look, it's not just Angela and Owen that's got people on edge. I don't want to name names, confidentiality and all that, but there's been rumors of someone, you know, a stranger, walking around at night. Looking into folks' windows, freaking people out."

Rose and Miller share a look that doesn't get past Mickey.

"What?"

Miller clears his throat. "I know a resident who said she saw someone . . . someone wearing a black mask, staring into her window."

Mickey nods. "Exactly. But it's not just one resident, and it's not paranoia. There's more, lots more. Oh, shit, hold on. There he is." Mickey half-stands from his chair and cups a hand to his mouth. "Gopi!"

Gopi had entered the dining room looking slightly dazed, but turns sharply when he hears his name. Seeing Mickey and the others, he makes his way through the maze of dining tables until he reaches them.

He looks bedraggled, Rose thinks, noting the unkempt hair, the typically pristine moustache untrimmed, unwaxed. She studies his expression as he comes closer, tries to pinpoint what's off about him.

It's his eyes, she realizes. *They look . . . haunted.*

Suddenly, Rose wonders just how many residents have been concerned by the goings-on of the last week and feels a pang of remorse—of guilt—for thinking she might have been the only one.

"Hello, dear," Rose says. "Please, sit."

Gopi nods, pulls up a chair. "Thank you. How are you guys?"

Miller nods, shoves his plate of pasta to the side. "Worried, I guess."

Mickey puts a meaty hand on Gopi's shoulder, lowers his voice so only they can hear. "Tell them what you told me, Gopi. Tell them about the old asylum."

Surprised, Rose looks closely at the retired filmmaker, curious what new wrinkle this is all about. Gopi swallows hard, lowers his eyes. "As you guys know, my apartment faces the back lawn," he begins. "A couple nights ago, I was watching a movie, a wonderful film called *Black Sunday,* perhaps you've . . ." He glances at each of them, as if hoping they might want to change the subject to something more palatable, more *normal.* When he finds no takers, he sighs wearily. "Anyway, it was late, and I got up to use the bathroom—"

"And refill your scotch, no doubt," Mickey says with a grin.

"And that," Gopi agrees. "Like I said, it was late, around one in the morning, and I happened to glance out my window, toward the back lawn. And here's the thing. From my living room window, you can clearly see the old asylum back there."

"That place should be torn down," Rose interjects. "Such an eyesore."

Gopi nods. "Agreed, but at night I hardly ever notice it. I mean, the windows are boarded up, and the doors are padlocked, so it's just another shadow once the sun goes down. But last night I saw something. I saw lights."

"The trailhead's right around there," Miller says, also lowering his voice, although there's no one sitting with ten feet of the small group. "Maybe someone was just, I don't know, walking out to the old well."

"No one uses that trail," Mickey mumbles. "And certainly not at one a.m."

Miller nods. "Point taken."

"Besides, it wasn't that. I saw lights *inside* the asylum," Gopi says. "Like . . . I don't know, candles or something. There was flickering through the cracks of the doors and windows. Anyway, I decided to go out there and have a look. Probably not the smartest idea." He shrugs, smiles sheepishly. "Something a character in a bad horror movie would do."

"And what happened?" Rose asks.

"It was horrible," he says. "I went all the way out there, in the cold, in the dark, and I watched for a few minutes, you know? But then, the candles or whatever . . . they went out. And then . . ."

Gopi pauses, his eyes vacant, as if recalling a bad memory.

"Then what?" Miller asks, leaning closer.

"I don't know for sure . . . I mean, there was someone standing outside that building, and they were watching me. But in the woods . . ." Gopi shakes his head. "You'll think I'm insane."

Rose reaches out, puts a hand on Gopi's forearm. "It's okay. No one here is going to doubt you, and I think what you're telling us might be important."

"Okay," he says, swallowing hard. "I think there was something in the woods, and . . . hell, I sort of freaked out, you know? I started to run, and I swear someone was chasing me." Gopi looks up at them, eyes wide. "They followed me to my home, you guys. They knocked on my fucking door."

"What did you do?" Rose asks, her thoughts racing at this new information.

"Nothing, at least not that night," Gopi says. "But yesterday morning I called Mickey, and we both went out there again. Figured I'd bring some protection this time."

"That was nice of you, Mickey," Rose says.

Mickey shrugs, cheeks reddening. "Was nothing."

"So what did you find?" Miller asks.

"Nothing out of the ordinary," Gopi replies. "It was just like always. The doors were locked, the windows boarded. The doors were padlocked . . . we walked around, even peeked through a crack between a couple of boards, but there was nothing to see, just shadows and a dirty floor. And today I hear about Owen, and Mickey tells me that a few folks have seen someone walking around at night, looking into windows. It's all very strange."

"It's strange, all right," Rose says. "I wonder if what you experienced has any connection to what happened to Angela? Or Owen? Do we think some kind of night prowler is hiding out back there?"

"How would they even get in?" Miller asks.

Gopi shrugs. "I don't know, but someone was in there."

"Maybe someone from the staff?"

"With candles?" Gopi replies.

"They'd need a key to the lock," Mickey says, and a moment of introspective thought silences the table.

Gopi sits back, folds his arms over his chest. "It's definitely suspicious."

"We all need to be vigilant from here on out," Mickey says. "Eyes and ears open."

"What about the police?" Miller asks. "They were here this morning, dealing with Owen. Maybe they suspect something."

"No offense, Miller, but the police aren't going to do shit about folks like us," Mickey says. "I think we're on our own."

"Just to be clear," Rose says, eyes shifting from face to face. "We are all in agreement that there's something strange going on. That maybe the things that happened to Angela and Owen . . . aren't what they seem."

"I think it's a possibility," Gopi says, his naturally brown complexion turning pale, his mouth working, as if he'd swallowed something sour. "But assuming for a moment that Rose is right, I'm not even sure what we're talking about. I mean . . . are we saying there's someone responsible for all this? Because based on what I saw, what I experienced the other night . . . I'm not even sure what we're dealing with is human."

Miller chuckles. "Now we've really gone off the deep end."

"You weren't there," Gopi mumbles, but says no more.

"Regardless," Rose continues, "I think we can all agree there's something strange going on, and I for one think it needs looking into. And if the police aren't going to do it, then maybe we should."

"Now, Rose—" Miller starts, then clamps his mouth shut when Rose shoots him a glare. "Never mind," he says, hands raised in mock defense.

"But look, there's one more thing," Mickey says. "It could be nothing, and normally I'd be worried you guys would think I'm crazy, but after what Gopi just told us . . ."

"Easy . . ." Gopi says dramatically.

Mickey grins at his friend. "You know what I mean. And hell, I don't know, it might be relevant to all this stuff we're talking about."

"Go on," Rose says, exhilarated despite the horrible circumstances, and privately thrilled she isn't alone in her suspicions, at the idea that something at Autumn Springs isn't quite right.

Mickey grimaces, as if unsure, then blows out a breath. "Okay . . . well, it so happens that I got a buddy living at the Med Center. He was a neighbor of mine before he had to go into full-time care. Kind of an odd duck, but a sweet guy. I was visiting him this morning, and . . . aw hell, you guys. I can't. It's too weird. I think he better tell you himself."

"Tell us what? More ghosts and goblins, I hope," Miller says, and winks at Gopi, who scowls in return.

Mickey stands, puts his giant hands on the back of his chair, and looks at each of them in turn. "This could be a deep, dark rabbit hole, my friends. You guys sure you want to go down it?"

Rose looks up at Mickey for a moment, then she also stands, hands clutched tightly in front of her. "I'm in," she says, and turns to look at Miller, one eyebrow arched.

"Oh." Miller's eyes widen and he also stands, shoves his hands into the pockets of his baggy corduroy pants. "Yes, yes, I'm in."

Gopi raises his hand like a schoolboy. "I'll go, too. Consider my curiosity piqued. Besides, I'm a big fan of odd ducks."

Miller chuckles, then looks at Mickey. "Any hints on what's waiting for us down this rabbit hole of yours?"

"Conspiracies, Beauregard," Mickey says with a grin. "Conspiracies."

5

The four friends walk into the Med Center, smile and wave to a bemused Nurse Jarvis at the front desk, who smiles and gives a small wave in response.

"There a birthday party I don't know about?"

Rose steps over to the reception desk. "Hello, Mindy. We're here to see Mr. Swanson, if that's okay."

"Sure, of course. We love when our residents have visitors," she says cheerfully, her pixie haircut slightly disheveled, making her look even more like a child to Rose's eyes. "Our full-care and hospice babies don't get many people coming to see them."

Rose feels a pang of sadness at this, and makes a mental note to try and volunteer at the Med Center more often. "Wonderful. We'll just go on, then."

"Is it a special occasion, or . . ."

Rose turns back to Mindy, who's still smiling, but now there's a frank curiosity behind her expression. Unsure how to respond, Rose looks to her friends for help, and Miller steps forward.

"Nothing special," he says. "Mickey just wanted to introduce us, is all."

Mindy's eyes shift to Mickey. "That's so nice. One can never have too many friends, don't you think?"

"All the time," Rose says. She gives Mindy's perplexed look a goodbye wink, then follows the others toward the doors leading to the full-time care rooms.

As they cross the clean linoleum floor, past the clinic-white walls and bland beige doors, Rose tries not to think about the future. About getting to a point in her life—likely sometime in the next five-to-ten years—when she might also be forced to leave her comfortable apartment, with the plush carpeting and full kitchen, warm-colored walls and soft bed, her art and books, and her independence, behind. As they pass through the doors and into the sterile hall of full-time care, with the sharp smell of bleach reaching her nose, she tries not to think that one day this could be *her* home, that she'll need help to do basic things like use a bathroom or make herself a meal.

Lots of folks never need such care, Rose thinks as they continue on. *Lots of folks die happily at home after cooking a steak dinner and reading Faulkner. Some of us humans stay healthy and spry into our nineties, and there's nothing to say or do about it other than eat well, exercise as best you can, and know that some of us are lucky and some of us are not. And that's the truth of it.*

As for me, I'm gonna be lucky, she thinks. *No matter what.*

"Here's his room," Mickey says. "Hold on . . ."

He knocks lightly on the closed door, and a moment later a voice responds, albeit warily, from somewhere inside. "Yeah?"

"Hey, Stan. It's Mickey. I'm here with some friends."

"Mickey! Well heck, don't stand in the damn hallway, come on in," the voice says, the earlier caution turned cheerful. Mickey offers the others a bashful smile.

"Not sure if you guys have ever met Stan, but he's a trip. So be prepared."

Rose and Miller share a glance, but Gopi nods. "Okay, sure."

Mickey opens the door and they all step inside.

The sound from a TV perched against one wall fills the room, and all heads turn instinctively toward the screen, where a man is enthusiastically relaying images of ancient Egyptians and somehow tying them into a story about alien spaceships.

"You still watching this stuff, huh?" Mickey says, settling his big frame into a La-Z-Boy chair.

Rose takes a moment to study the room more closely, curiosity taking over briefly for politeness. She'd seen the full-time care rooms before, but they're all a little bit different. Like the apartment housing, some have bigger floor plans, some smaller. Unlike the apartments, the Med Center rooms are studio layouts, meaning you sleep where you eat, where you read and watch television. Not quite a hospital room, but not too far off, either. The few rooms she'd seen had small kitchenettes, full bathrooms, and a few pieces of furniture along with a medical-quality bed. Tatum's, for example, has an antique credenza, a couch, and an oak coffee table. But there are other things you couldn't help notice, even in the nicest, most well-decorated rooms.

For one, there is always a clear path from the hallway to the bed, wide enough for a wheelchair or a gurney. Second, the floors are smooth, and obviously faux, hardwood. No ridges, no seams. Not wood at all, but a tough linoleum made to look like hardwood planks to give the illusion of warmth. There is always at least one window with a nice view, and of course each room has a good-sized, wall-mounted television—the ultimate way to pass the time as one waits for each precious day to slide on by and disappear into the ether of the past.

Stan's room appears more lived-in than the others she's seen. There is a bookcase crammed with paperbacks, a stack of DVDs on a weathered-looking dresser below the television, and assorted bric-a-brac strewn on almost every surface. In addition to the (currently occupied) La-Z-Boy, he also has a small couch and coffee table. A tiny dining room table juts from one wall, two uncomfortable-looking metal chairs set on either side.

Stan himself is short and skinny with a mat of white stubble atop his bulb-shaped head, a thick tangle of white fuzz on his cheeks and chin. He has large, ever-searching brown eyes that are undercut by dark shadows and prominent cheekbones. He sits straight-backed in his bed, legs folded beneath him, eyes glued to the too-loud television. To Rose's untrained eye, she thinks that Stan doesn't look to be "all there."

If she were pressed to put a word to it, she might suggest that Stan looks . . . *high*.

"Hey, hey guys," Stan says distractedly, eyes bouncing from the TV screen to the faces of his visitors, to the window, and back to the screen, all in a matter of seconds while moving in a nonsynchronous, repeating pattern.

"Gopi, close the door, would ya?" Mickey asks.

Gopi, still standing halfway-in, halfway-out of the room, nods nervously, steps inside and closes the door behind him. He crosses his arms neatly and comes no farther.

Miller settles his lanky frame into one of the metal chairs at the dining room table. He glances over at Rose, who thinks he looks uncharacteristically uncertain, his eyes asking unspoken questions: *You gonna sit? Or should we run like hell?*

Rose gathers her wits, strides determinedly over to Stan's bed, and thrusts out a hand. "Hello, Stan. I'm Rose DuBois."

Stan looks at her hand, then up to her face, and smiles warmly. He shakes her hand gently, his skin soft and dry. "Sorry, I'm a little out of sorts today."

"It's quite all right; thank you for having us." Rose points to Miller. "That's Miller, if you don't already know."

Miller sits up, pinches the brim of his ever-constant invisible hat. "Nice to see you, Stan. We were in a book club together a few years back. We read . . . what was it?"

Stan's smile grows wider, and Rose sees a warmth there, an intelligence, and realizes she likes this man, even if he does seem— how did he put it?

Out of sorts.

"Sure, sure!" he says happily. "I remember. We read *Don Quixote*. Man, that thing was a million pages, but funny as hell."

Miller chuckles. "Right, right. That was a good one."

Rose points toward Gopi, still standing by the closed door. "And that's Gopi Sharma, another friend. He used to make movies."

To his credit, Gopi takes a couple more steps into the room, waves a hand. "A pleasure," he says, giving a near-imperceptible bow.

"Do you guys want coffee? Or a soda? There's a fridge there," Stan says, pointing to the small kitchenette.

"We're good, Stan," Mickey says, sitting up as best as he can within the cushioned sinkhole of the La-Z-Boy. "Would you mind pausing your show? I'd like you to tell these guys about what happened the other night."

Stan's smile disappears; his face drains of blood.

"I mean, if that's okay with you, of course," Rose says quickly, alarmed at the sudden change.

"No . . . I mean, yeah, it's fine." Stan presses a button on the remote control and the sound from the TV cuts off, which seems to leave the room itself paused, and deadly quiet, as if none of them are quite sure how to proceed.

Miller clears his throat, and Rose sits down on the edge of Stan's neatly made bed. "Do you mind?"

"Of course not," Stan says, but appears to be growing more nervous by the second.

"Let's start at the beginning, okay?" Mickey says. "Stan, why don't you tell us all about what happened. You know, with the letter and the, uh . . . visit."

Stan laughs uncomfortably. "You guys will think I'm crazy as a loon. Hell, who knows, maybe I am."

"You don't seem crazy to me, Stan," Rose says soothingly, fixating on Stan's eyes, the pupils of which appear fully dilated.

They must keep the folks here on some serious meds.

"Thanks for saying so," Stan says. "But it *is* a crazy story."

"Whatever you tell us," Miller says in his authoritative lecture hall voice, his *trust me* voice, as Rose likes to call it, "will stay in this room. No one here will breathe a word of it. That's a promise."

Stan nods, then drops his head a moment, as if considering. When he looks up, Rose notices some color has returned to his cheeks. "Okay, then." He points to the small end table next to the La-Z-Boy. "Mickey, the letter I told you about is stuck into that top book. Can you grab it and pass it around?"

Mickey pulls a tri-folded piece of paper from a hardcover book, opens it, then pries his body out of the cushioned chair and walks it over to Miller, who begins to read, brow furrowed.

"What's in the letter, Stan?" Rose asks.

"Proof," Stan says, then shrugs. "Proof that what I'm going to tell you isn't a lie and that I'm not batshit crazy."

"We wouldn't think that," Rose says. "Who's it from?"

Stan watches Miller as he reads, then turns his eyes back to Rose.

"The United States government," Stan says with a lowered voice, the quirk of a smile playing at the corner of his lips. "They want to enlist me."

"For what?"

"To meet the aliens," he says evenly, as if he'd suggested joining a Kiwanis club. "But that's not the cool part."

Rose watches as Gopi, sucked in by curiosity, walks over to Miller and begins to read over his shoulder. "What's the cool part?" she asks.

"That I've already met one," Stan says proudly. "It was standing right there, Rose, right next to where you're sitting now."

Rose glances to the empty space next to her; fights the instinct to shift her body farther away. "You mean . . . an alien from space? Like UFOs?"

"There's a ship out there in the woods, Rose, and I've been invited to see it," he says excitedly, grinning proudly at his visitors, as if expecting pats on the back or words of congratulations. When he sees everyone simply staring blankly at him, he turns taciturn, withdrawing back into himself. "I'm just waiting to find out when."

"Find out from who, Stan? The government?" Rose asks, eager to discover what's happening here, who could be torturing this poor man with silly letters, preying on his bizarre hopes. "The ones who wrote you the letter?"

"What? No, Rose, you aren't listening," he says, suddenly agitated. "I'm already past all that. I've accepted their offer, you see? And now I'm just waiting for one of the aliens to come back and get me."

Miller walks over to the bed, hands the letter to Rose. "So, there was an alien," he says. "From outer space, standing right where I'm standing now."

Stan scowls a little, as if worried he's being patronized, but nods, unable to contain his excitement. "Yeah, right there. I was sleeping, and it woke me up. I almost screamed, you know? But then I realized what it was, and I just waited and listened."

"It talked to you?" Rose asks.

"Of course. It spoke pretty good English. I mean, they've been studying us for decades, so . . ."

"What did the, uh, alien look like?" Miller asks.

Stan thinks a moment. "It was wearing a black cloak, like a robe. And it wasn't as tall as you, but more average height. Taller than the ones you've seen on television, anyway, or in documentaries. It had a big, gray, bald head and black, buggy eyes . . . to be honest, I thought it would be green, but more and more grays have been sighted in recent years, so I suppose it makes sense."

"Totally," Gopi mumbles, and Rose gives him a *hush* look.

"What's weird," Stan continues, apparently not having heard Gopi's quip, lost in his own retelling, "is that while it was here, my mind got, I don't know . . . sort of fuzzy, and I was seeing all these strange colors. I guess there's a telepathic aspect to how they communicate with us. Or maybe they just give off weird energy . . . like an aura."

Stan reaches out and grips Rose's hand, looks her in the eye like a child telling his mother a wonderful secret. Rose allows her hand to be held, and does her best to maintain contact with Stan's own wide, wild eyes.

His pupils, she notes again, are blown wide open.

"All my life I've studied this stuff," he says, a tear spilling down his cheek. "And I always hoped I'd have the chance to actually meet one of them, you know? To see a real alien creature. It's been my dream, Rose . . . my one and only dream. And now it's happening."

"And this creature . . . it invited you to see its ship?" Gopi asks quietly.

"Not yet," Stan says, pulling his hand back to wipe the tear away. "But I know it's going to. It said so in the letter."

Rose now looks at the letter, notes the printed government logo at the top. But there's no name. No address. Nothing more than an invitation to be part of a "select group" and to respond by . . . the gazebo?

What a bag of bologna, she thinks, but forces her expression to stay neutral as she has two disparate thoughts:

Someone is playing a very cruel joke on this man.

We're wasting our time here.

Rose turns to look at Mickey, who meets her eye and holds up a finger.

Just wait, that finger says, as if he knows exactly what she's thinking.

"Stan," Mickey says, "tell these guys what the alien said to you. You know, at the end, before it went out the window."

"It went out the window?" Gopi mutters brusquely, and Rose can tell he's doing his best not to scoff at the whole thing, to turn and walk out of the room in disgust. Not that he doesn't have his own tall tales.

"Tell them," Mickey prompts.

"Yeah, that part wasn't so good." Stan drops his gaze to the bed.

"What? What about it wasn't good?" Rose asks.

Stan looks up at them, eyes full of guilt. "I asked it, you know, if I could tell anyone about the ship . . . about *it*. But the creature said no. It said I was the only one who could see the ship. That I'd been *chosen*."

"Tell them the rest," Mickey says.

For reasons she can't explain, Rose feels a chill tickling the back of her neck, as if an ice-cold spider were crawling up her spine, toward her hairline.

Stan blows out a breath. "It said all the others, including you guys, I guess . . . are nothing but rotting sheep who deserve to die. That it would, uh, feed on the entrails of anyone who crossed its path, and, well . . . then it said it was going to kill everyone in this fucking place, one-by-one, for its own amusement."

Stan turns to look out the bedside window and shrugs.

"I mean, that was the basic gist."

6

As the group of friends exit the Med Center, Rose spots Tatum on his bench and excuses herself. She wants some time to think, and she always finds the best way to think on a problem is to think about something else entirely—an axiom she often relayed to her young students back in the day.

She waves goodbye to Miller and the others, then settles herself on the bench next to Tatum, who has a bag of fish food with him today and is tossing it into the pond, a few pellets at a time. Rose watches alongside him as the fat, bright, orange and yellow koi break the water's surface in bunches, tussling for the food.

"How are you today, Tatum?" she asks.

Tatum nods absently, stares at the fish. Suddenly, he bursts into laughter, then, just as abruptly, turns quiet once more. "I don't know, I don't know . . ." he mumbles, then tosses a few more pellets into the water.

"Well, I have to say, things are getting very strange around here."

Tatum looks at Rose, clears his throat. "Do you have my shovel?"

"Tatum Bird, what in the world do you need a shovel for?"

Tatum shrugs, points at the pond. "Need to dig this out. I had a shovel here—"

"I have not seen your shovel," Rose chides lightly, patting his shoulder to keep him soothed. "And you shouldn't be digging anything. Let the gardeners do that."

Tatum shrugs once more and chuckles, mumbles incoherently.

"Anyway, I want you to be careful," Rose says, hoping some part of what she's saying is getting through that thundercloud blowing around inside his mind. "I feel like things are going to get worse before they get better, if you know what I mean, and I think there's a danger here, Tatum. I think, perhaps, we are all in danger." She pauses, watches the bobbing, feeding fish for a moment. "I just need to figure out the who and the why, before someone else gets hurt."

"I need . . ." Tatum starts, then trails off. "Maybe we should go find Jack," he finishes, looking into the distance, toward the back lawn and the heavy dark line of trees beyond. "Maybe we go find Jack and then we can feed the fish."

Rose presses on, lost in thought. "First Gopi says something strange is going on in the old asylum out back, being chased by a pair of glowing eyes . . ." she tuts, shakes her head. "Now folks are getting visits from aliens. Meanwhile, people we love are dying. I just don't know—"

"I'd like to go home," Tatum says, a common refrain from his scattered, plagued consciousness, the plate tectonics of his mind ever shifting. This time, however, the thought strikes Rose in a different, more meaningful way.

"Maybe I do, too, hon," she says with a heavy sigh. "Maybe we should both go home."

Tatum reaches out and grips Rose's hand, forces her to turn her attention toward his blue eyes that, in this moment, look eerily lucid. Without a word, he flips her hand and places a small pile of pellets into her palm. Then he smiles and points at the pond.

"I see," she says. "Less talking, more feeding."

Tatum nods as Rose tosses a few pellets into the water, watches as the unsettling O-shaped mouths and lifeless black eyes of the koi attack with renewed fervor.

"There you go, Rose," Tatum says happily. "There you go."

Rose sighs, then chuckles. "I bet you were quite the ladies' man, Tatum Bird. You give good date."

Tatum also laughs and pats Rose's hand. "We'll wait for Jack," he says. "Okay, Rose? We'll wait right here."

Rose sighs heavily—mind buzzing with stress and worry, heart aching for the kind man sitting next to her—as she watches the fish, waits patiently for Jack to return, and wonders what new horror will befall them next.

7

Egor has no idea where the magazine came from.

He'd gone to dinner at the dining hall, having enjoyed a lovely minestrone soup with crispy sourdough bread, a glass of cold chardonnay, and chocolate cake for dessert. As he'd walked back to his room, however, he'd begun to feel a little light-headed but wasn't alarmed. If anything, he was likely overtired, but since he had nothing more to do with his evening except have a big cup of tea followed by a good night's sleep, he was confident he'd feel better in the morning.

When he returned to his room, he poured himself some tea left over from the afternoon pot, which he heated in the microwave before adding a few drops of cream and honey. He was just taking a long sip, thinking about his chess club tomorrow, when he noticed the magazine lying flat on the top of his bed. A magazine he'd never seen before . . . but still knows—knows almost instantly—what it is.

Porn.

He sets his mug on the kitchen counter, walks over to the bed, and looks down to see a lascivious-looking woman wearing nothing but see-through panties on the cover. Frowning, he picks up the magazine and opens it. Inside, there are many photos, and many kinds of women. All nude, of course. Some of the photos are tasteful, some less tasteful. In some there is a woman and a man, in others, two women. In a few of the livelier photos, there are *three* women.

In the middle of the magazine is a centerfold, opening to the image of a voluptuous raven-haired beauty lying on a white shag rug, her eyes deep and dark, her breasts magnificent, her hips tilted toward the camera in such a way that her privates are fully exposed. . . .

Egor's almost immediate reaction is to find the whole thing humorous. Most likely one of the cleaning people left it behind by accident, perhaps stealing a few minutes on his bed to choke the proverbial chicken. The idea bothers him, of course, but only mildly. He's too old to care about such trivial things.

As he thumbs through the magazine, however, studying each of the images, a different feeling rises deep inside him—one that, at first, he has trouble identifying. A feeling that he quickly, instinctually, recognizes, the result of hundreds of years of primal, lizard-brained evolution.

To his genuine surprise, and mild amusement, Egor realizes he is *aroused*.

"Silly man," he says aloud, stealing a glance toward his door to make sure it's closed, and feeling even more ridiculous for doing so.

Caught with a girlie magazine at the age of eighty-seven, he thinks. *Like a horny teenager hiding in the basement, hoping his mother doesn't come downstairs.*

To his even greater surprise (and somewhat less amusing), he notices that his body is responding—quite aggressively—to this new-found state of arousal. Looking down at the front of his pants, he can plainly see the distinct bulge of an erection pressing outward, begging for freedom from its cloth cage.

"Okay, Egor, that's quite enough," he says nervously, and sets the magazine down—face down—on the bed. He rubs sweaty palms on the sides of his pants, but can't help looking down with a sort of strange, nervous fascination at the swollen bump, waiting for it to subside. For a split second, he considers masturbating (*If I can remember how to do it*, he thinks only half-jokingly), just to get rid of the nuisance, then gets hit with another blast of light-headedness, followed by a discomforting flutter in his chest.

His heart is beating too fast.

"Silly, stupid boy!" Egor says out loud, trying to keep the itchy sound of fear out of his voice. "I have no time for such things," he mutters, disgusted by the sheen of sweat breaking out upon his brow. He wipes it away with a sleeve, tries to ignore the tightening in his chest, the feeling of his oxygen flow being constricted as his breathing shallows.

"A sip of tea, then I'll lie down," he mumbles, wondering why he's talking aloud to no one, wishing he'd never seen the goddamn magazine and furious at whoever left it in his room. He's also angry with himself, confused at why his body is reacting the way it is—why his ancient, comfortably flaccid cock is suddenly hard as a steel-plated rocket trying to blast off through the lap of his khaki pants.

It's not that Egor doesn't get occasionally aroused; he is still very much a *man* after all, and in relatively good health (other than his heart, of course). But this . . . this is something else.

This is madness.

Walking toward the kitchenette, Egor stumbles. Reaching for balance, his hand falls onto the table where he keeps the chessboard. In a flash that lasts only seconds, he glances down, clocks the pieces of the half-played game from that afternoon—part of his mind instinctively reaching for his next move—when his hand wipes across the wooden board, sending the pieces scattering to the floor.

"Damn!" he yells, wondering if the nurses might have heard, and part of him wants to hit the emergency call button—there are three placed strategically in different parts of the room—but he thinks of the magazine on the bed and his face reddens with the heat of embarrassment.

In fact, his *whole body* is hot.

And now his erection isn't funny at all.

In fact, it *hurts*.

Muttering curses, Egor continues toward the kitchen, stumbling on chess pieces in his socked feet, cursing as a sharp pain stabs into his foot (*likely the king*, he thinks). His leg buckles and he drops to the floor, wincing at the crashing pain in his knees as they hit the hard linoleum. Fighting panic, he grips the back of a nearby chair and climbs unsteadily to his feet.

He's panting now. His heart will not slow down and his body

feels as if it's on fire. Sweat pours off him and he no longer wants tea and he is no longer worried about being embarrassed. He wants *help*. He needs his heart pills, his nitrates, but he doesn't see them on the counter where he always—*always*—keeps them.

In your coat pocket, Egor. There's more in your coat pocket.

He spins, looking for his coat (doing his best to ignore the way the whole world is tilting), and recalls hanging it up in the closet after he took off his shoes by the door. But his vision is double now and there is sweat in his eyes and he's having *serious* trouble breathing. He takes a step and a pain unlike anything he's ever felt rips through his chest. His left side tingles, then goes numb. He tries to raise his left arm but it won't respond, and now there is a massive weight pressing onto his chest, as if an elephant were stepping on his rib cage, slowly shifting more and more of its bulk onto his frail body, crushing him to death.

There's some . . . by my bed . . .

Lurching madly, blindly, back toward his bed, Egor steps on a rook and his foot goes out from beneath him, twisting his ankle savagely enough to tear his Achilles. He screams out in pain and falls down sideways. As he tumbles to the ground, the side of his head slams into the hard metal bed frame at the foot of his bed, cutting a nasty gash into his temple.

Egor lands in a heap on the cold floor, heart thumping like a parade drum in his ears. He can almost feel the veins of his heart bursting, the flow of blood leaking into parts of his body that it should not be flowing or leaking into, and then his heart *squeezes* even more tightly, the organ demanding blood that is no longer coming.

And so the starving heart begins shutting down parts of Egor's body. It starts with the non-essentials, like arms and legs, followed, finally, by the brain and vital organs that—slowly, slowly—have their functionality dimmed, like a light being turned lower and lower. . . .

Egor stares with wide, watery eyes toward the entrance to his room where, from his low perspective, he can see the bottom half of the door—a stretch of white light running beneath it along the floor. He has just enough time left in this world to see the door open, to see a white spill of light enter from the hallway.

A pair of shadowed legs steps inside, then stands there, motionless.

Why aren't you going for help? Why aren't you yelling for nurses? Damn you, HELP ME!

As his vision continues dimming, dimming, Egor watches helplessly as the feet turn around and walk out. The door closes softly, and he has only time enough to think of the chess pieces (now scattered across his room) and what his next move might have been, and how badly he wishes he could have finished the game.

FIVE

FRIENDS AND LOVED ONES

1

It's late afternoon when Rose's cell phone rings with the distinct sound of an incoming FaceTime call, which means it's Sybil, because she's the only person who Rose would ever consider doing a video call with. Sybil and, of course, her little Roy.

When she answers the FaceTime request this time, she strikes gold.

"Roy!" she exclaims, likely too loud, but unable to contain her excitement at seeing that sweet little face filling her screen.

"Grandma!" Roy cheers just as loudly, bringing tears of joy to Rose's eyes.

Rose hears Sybil in the background, prompting Roy to say hello, to talk about himself, his time at school.

"What grade are you in now, Roy?" Rose asks, knowing the answer but wanting to get the boy chatting.

"First!" he yells, the way all small boys do when they're excited at knowing the correct answer to a question.

"And when are you going to come see me? I miss you so much," Rose says, trying to keep the quiver from her voice.

Roy looks to his mother off-screen, who says something inaudible, then he turns back to the camera, a huge grin lighting up his face. "Soon!"

"Well, I hope—"

There's a knock at Rose's front door.

Rose, who isn't used to unexpected visitors, is startled by the sound. "I . . ." she says, glancing from the door to the phone, flummoxed.

Damn whoever that is, and leave me be, she thinks, ignoring the stranger and turning her full attention back to her beloved grandson.

"Tell me about your friends, Roy? What sports are you playing?" she asks, likely overwhelming the child but wanting as much of him as she can get, knowing he'll grow distracted after a few min-utes and Sybil will take the phone back. "Tell me—"

The knock comes again. Louder, more insistent.

Then a voice.

"You awake, Rose?"

"Damn it," she mutters.

"What's wrong, Grandma?" Roy asks, sensing her irritation, just before the camera lurches away from her baby grandson toward Sybil, who looks concerned.

"Mom?"

"I'm fine, honey. There's someone breaking in my door," she says, then quickly adds: "A figure of speech."

Sybil smiles. "Well, it's a cell phone, Mom. You can walk with it."

"I don't want to walk with it," Rose grumbles, but gets up anyway and heads for the door. "Hold on!" she snaps. "Not you, Sybil . . . let me get rid of this pest. I want to talk to Roy."

"Who are you talking to?" a man's voice enters the fray from the other end of the call, coming through the video.

Carlo? Rose thinks. *Damn that man.*

On the screen, Sybil turns away and begins speaking to her boy-friend while the camera pivots to point at the kitchen floor.

Rose is beginning to lose her temper.

Arriving at her front door, she swings it open, ready to give who-ever it is a firm talking-to about the general politeness of calling ahead before knocking on someone's door . . . when she sees Miller standing in the hallway, looking as if he's seen a ghost.

"Rose, I . . ." He sees her holding the phone, looks even more stricken. "Oh no, I'm interrupting."

"Just come in and be quiet," she whispers, not unkindly (and not liking the expression on his face). "I'm talking to Roy."

Miller nods and steps inside, closes the door quietly and sits at the kitchen table to wait. Despite the interruption, Rose is actually happy to see him and knows he'll be good and quiet while she fin-ishes her call.

"Mom?"

"Yes, dear, I'm here. It's just Miller."

Sybil's smile widens. "Hey, Miller!" she says loudly, a singsong voice Rose knows too well.

Everyone's a damn matchmaker.

"Where's Roy?" Rose asks.

"Carlo just got here, Mom. So Roy's gotta run."

"Carlo can wait; let me speak to Roy another minute."

The camera lurches away again, and Rose hears muffled voices in the background—*arguing voices.*

Suddenly, Roy's face fills the screen. "Hi, Grandma, I gotta go. I love you."

Rose sighs, knowing she's beaten and hating that man even more than she did already. *Can't let me have two minutes.*

"Sorry, Rose, I have to get to work," Carlo says from the background.

Rose ignores him and focuses on Roy. "You go with your daddy, Roy. Grandma loves you very much and I'll see you soon."

"Love you, Grandma," Roy says, his attention already wavering amidst all the confusion. "Bye."

"Bye, honey," Rose says, and feels an emptiness open inside her chest that nearly breaks her heart. "I love you . . ." she adds, but Roy's gone.

She hears the sound of a front door closing, and then her daughter is back. "Sorry about that, Mom. I didn't think he'd be here for another hour."

"It's okay," Rose says, not meaning it but not wanting her daughter to feel badly. "I'm glad I got to say hello. But next time tell that boyfriend of yours two more minutes isn't going to hurt anyone."

Sybil frowns. "Yeah, Carlo's been acting off lately. It worries me, to be honest."

"Off how?" Rose doesn't like the direction of this conversation, but keeps her voice placid, unemotional.

That man better not do anything to hurt my babies.

"Sybil, if you're in trouble, you can tell me."

On her phone screen, Sybil rolls her eyes. "No, Mom . . . Jesus, nothing like that. You need to stop thinking that everyone is Dad."

Rose's eyes tick up to see if Miller caught the comment, but he sits quietly, tapping at his own phone screen like an imbecile.

"I'm only asking," Rose says quietly, turning her back on Miller. "I don't want you to live through what I did."

"I know, I know. But trust me, okay? It's not like that. He's just . . . off," Sybil says. "Distracted or something. He went away on a business trip for a few days but wouldn't talk about it. And every time I call him I get voicemail." She shrugs. "Anyway, not your problem. He needs to find a new job; this part-time sales thing is not working out."

"Sales? I thought he was working at some warehouse."

Sybil nods. "It's new. Just a part-time thing he fell into. He travels more now because of it, which is why moving to the house is going to be such a blessing for me. Working from home full-time will take pressure off all of us."

Rose glances at Miller, who is beginning to look impatient— which makes Rose even more apprehensive, since it's unusual for him to be anxious.

"Look, I got to go, hon. But I want you two to come visit me soon, okay? And tell that man to go sell his shoes, or whatever, and leave that baby with his momma."

Sybil laughs. "He doesn't sell shoes, Mom. He sells drugs."

Rose's eyes go wide, and in her peripheral vision she sees a similar reaction from Miller, who's overhearing everything. "Drugs? Sybil DuBois, you better not have my baby boy near any drug dealer—"

Sybil laughs again. "Mom, no, of course not like that. He sells pills, you know? Pharmaceuticals."

"Oh," Rose says, trying to settle her stirring emotions. "Well, hopefully it pays decent. I don't know much about it."

"Half the stuff he lugs around you probably have in your medicine cabinet," Sybil says. "Honestly, I should have him come up there with me next time I visit, introduce him to folks. He'd make a killing."

2

"I'm sorry to have interrupted," Miller says after Rose disconnects the call. He looks so shamefaced that Rose can't be angry at him if she wants to—which she doesn't. It's *good* to see her friend, and besides . . . he looks like he's heard some bad news.

Please, not again, she thinks, and sits down at the table across from him.

"What's happened? You look sick to your stomach."

Miller shakes his head. "Could be nothing. Could be . . ." He shrugs. "I don't know anymore, Rose. I don't know what to think."

Rose reaches out, takes one of his large hands in both of hers. "Tell me."

Miller looks up at her, and she thinks she's never seen him look older. "You know Egor?" he says. "The one who does the chess clubs on Monday?"

Rose nods. "I don't know him, but I know who he is."

"Well, he lives over in the Med Center, you know, full-time care, just a few doors down from where we were yesterday, listening to Stan Swanson's alien story."

"What happened, Miller?"

"He's dead, Rose," Miller says, shaking his head. "Poor man died of a heart attack."

Rose takes this in, thinks a moment before she speaks. "I'm sorry to hear that. He was long in years, if I remember."

Miller nods. "That he was. Eighty-seven, I think. And he had a history of heart problems . . . but it's not just that, Rose." He grips her hand tightly, looks her in the eyes. "Maybe I'm just being paranoid, or maybe I've been swept up in all the strange stuff happening here recently . . ."

He trails off, as if unsure how to phrase what he means, or is simply afraid of saying it out loud. Rose pulls back her hands gently, sits straight, eyebrows raised in a question. "Tell me what's in that shaggy head of yours, Beauregard."

"I'd say you're gonna think I'm crazy, but I think we've moved past such caveats," Miller says, his expression turning from one of sorrow to one of mild awkwardness. He lets out a heavy sigh and taps one fingertip steadily upon the tabletop, something Rose knows he does when he's thinking about a knot that needs to be untied. "You ever heard of priapism?"

"Doesn't ring a bell," she says.

"Hell, of course it doesn't. See, it's, uh . . ." He pauses, looks around the room, as if seeking answers, or help.

"Miller, come on, now. Out with it."

"Sorry." He takes a deep breath. "Priapism is a fancy word for what is more plainly called a death erection." His eyes lower in obvious embarrassment. "I googled it a few hours ago."

Rose folds her arms across her chest and frowns. "I'm curious to know how this information is relevant to our discussion."

Miller actually smiles a little, amused at her reaction despite himself. "Don't worry, I'm not getting saucy."

"Beauregard Mason Miller, what are you talking about?"

Miller pats the air with a hand and, despite her confusion, Rose is relieved to hear him chuckle again. The years wash away when he smiles.

"What I'm telling you, Miss Marple, is that it's been rumored Egor died with one of these . . . death erections. Which is very unusual for a man his age and very unusual for someone who has died of a heart attack. The blood would, well . . . it would stop flowing, you see, and that would . . ." Miller clears his throat. "That would be the end of that."

"I see," Rose says, clearly not seeing at all and desperately trying to piece together the facts he's abashedly telling her into some sort of cohesive picture.

"Look," he continues. "Let's say a man is hanged, okay? He'll have this happen, this rigor erectus or whatever."

"Is that a technical term, Beauregard?"

Miller looks at her, wide-eyed, then laughs. "I'm sorry, I'm sorry. None of this is funny."

Rose scoffs. "You're a damn schoolboy," she says, which makes Miller laugh all the harder. When he recovers somewhat, he sighs, wipes a tear from one eye. "Another term for it is angel lust," he says and, no longer able to contain himself, begins laughing so hard that more tears flow down his face.

Rose purses her lips with feigned annoyance but can't completely hide the smile brought on from his infectious amusement. "Are you quite finished?"

"Yes, yes . . ." he says, wiping his face. Then his laughter fades, along with his smile. "I'm sorry, I suppose I'm going a little mad with it all."

Rose leans forward. "Miller, I'm serious now. What does all of this have to do with what's been going on? Focus, please."

He nods. "Yes, ma'am. See, the thing is, Rose, there's another reason men sometimes die with this . . . affliction."

"Okay."

"It often happens when they have certain drugs in their system. Hormone drugs or antidepressants. But Egor wasn't on any of those. He had nitrate pills for his heart, some blood pressure medication, but that's all. Nothing, according to my research, that would have caused . . . that."

"Miller, how did you even get this information?"

"You know Billy, the big orderly? The one who will do anything for a buck?"

Rose sits back, arches an eyebrow. "You *paid* him?"

Miller nods. "I did. Anyway, he's the one who found Egor. I'd gone over to see a friend in hospice, a fella named Jim Percy, and saw the commotion. Billy and a nurse were banging on Stan's door. Apparently, he'd locked himself in, wouldn't let anybody come near him."

"Oh my Lord."

"Yup. He's either real shook up or he's gone completely off the deep end. Anyway, after I spent some time with my friend, I found

Billy hanging out by the nurse's break room and I asked him what the hubbub was about. He clammed up at first, but twenty bucks got him talking."

"And he told you about—"

"Uh-huh. Said Egor was 'pitching a tent.' His words," Miller adds, deciding to leave out the detail of the girlie magazine found on Egor's bed. "He also said the room was a shambles," he continues. "Which makes me wonder if there was some sort of struggle . . . hell, I don't know."

"What are you thinking, Miller?"

Miller shrugs, pulls a peppermint from his pocket, meditatively removes the plastic wrapping, and pops the candy into his mouth. "Not sure, Rose. But it's peculiar, don't you think?"

Rose nods, then stands.

Miller looks at her, eyebrows raised. "You going somewhere?"

"Not me. *We.* And please don't leave your candy wrappers on my table."

3

Miller and Rose walk through the lobby of the Medical Center without so much as a glance at the reception area. Rose notices it's Nurse Cooper manning the desk this afternoon, and she seems far too engaged with a phone call to worry about a couple residents heading toward the full-care wing.

They arrive at Egor's door and pause, surprised to find it wide open.

"The body is gone by now, right?" she asks.

Miller nods. "Down in the Morgue, waiting for transport. At least, it was a couple hours ago when I was slipping Billy Evenson my last twenty bucks."

"Okay, then," Rose says, and steps into the sunlit room.

"They must have cleaned up a bit; place looks orderly," Miller says, looking around.

"Like flipping a four-top during the lunch rush," Rose murmurs, noting the stripped bed, the industrial garbage bags sitting by the closet and dresser, presumably filled with Egor's clothes and whatever other worldly goods the man had at the end. A chessboard, however, is still set up on the small dining table, the pieces lined up neatly, as if waiting for a new game.

"They haven't dumped his meds yet," Miller says, having wandered to the kitchenette, where a few prescription bottles stand sentinel next to a daily pill organizer. Miller picks up the organizer, pops a few of the days open.

"What are you doing?" Rose asks, coming closer.

Miller shrugs. "Seeing if there's anything strange in his pills. But these all look okay. Blood pressure, of course . . ."

"You think someone slipped him something he shouldn't have had?"

Miller closes one of the small lids, sets the organizer on the counter. "I don't know, Rose. It crossed my mind."

"It's like that movie we watched a few months ago," she says. "The assassin who snuck into the hospital and swapped the old man's pills with poison."

Miller chuckles. "Yeah, I remember. Sure, could be something like that. Instead of poison, maybe something else."

"Something powerful," Rose says, thinking. "Something that stopped his sick heart like a train crash—"

"Hey, what are you doing in here?"

Miller and Rose spin to see one of the orderlies standing at the door. He's wearing blue scrubs and latex gloves. Rose steps forward, gives the man a warm smile. "Egor was a friend of ours. We just wanted to pay respects."

The man doesn't speak for a moment, then he nods. "I get it. Sorry for being jumpy." The orderly takes a few steps into the room, points at the counter. "Not to sound like a jerk, but you guys didn't take any of the meds, right?"

Rose and Miller exchange a confused glance. "Take the meds?" Miller asks. "For what purpose?"

The orderly shrugs. "Who knows? But it's our job to catalog all the meds before they get dumped. County is super strict about that stuff, and your friend is missing a few bottles we can't find." He looks around the room, blows out a breath. "At least not yet."

Rose steps forward. "What's your name, young man? I don't recognize you."

"Oh, sorry; I'm Jason. Got here a few weeks ago."

"Well, Jason, I'm Rose, and this is Miller."

Jason, unsure of himself, nods. "Okay."

"I'm curious, what bottles were missing?"

Jason grimaces. "I can't tell you that. Look, I'm sorry, but I've got to get this room cleared out."

Rose looks to Miller. "You sure it was your last twenty dollars?"

Miller frowns, then reaches into his back pocket and pulls out his wallet.

Walking back toward the apartments, Rose's mind is buzzing with the new information. "If someone took his nitrate pills," she says, replaying the information they'd paid for from the orderly, "then the possibility of someone being responsible for what happened to Egor suddenly has a lot more merit."

They stop near the koi pond, and Rose instinctively searches for signs of Tatum, but he's nowhere to be found this afternoon.

Miller looks down at her, a deep sadness in his brown eyes, and nods weakly. "I agree. I think you were right from the jump, Rose. Something funny is going on around here. And I'll tell you something else: I think folks know it. It's not just you and me who are getting the willies."

"What do you mean?"

Miller shrugs. "Whispers. I hear whispers. I hear some folks don't want to leave their rooms. I know that Liz Fisher up and left this morning . . . just called her kids in Pennsylvania and took a cab to the train station."

"Oh, Lord," Rose sighs. "Miller, what are we going to do?"

He reaches into his coat pocket, pulls out one of his peppermint candies, unwraps it, and pops it into his mouth. He plays with the crackly wrapper for a few seconds before Rose snatches it away, then looks directly into his eyes the way she would often look at a daydreaming student.

"Miller."

He looks back at her, working the candy in his mouth, and she knows he's debating what to say next. Perhaps unsure because he doesn't know. Perhaps unsure because what he says next might just lead them down a road they can't turn back from.

"I don't know, Rose. I admit, I'm a bit lost on all this . . . I don't even know what all this even is. What do *you* think?"

"I think we need to call a meeting with some like-minded folks," she says firmly. "And I think we need to start questioning some people who need questioning."

"But Rose, what would be the point? We're not the police."

Rose scoffs. "Like Mickey said, police don't care about a bunch of old folks. Look what's happened. Slip and fall. Suicide. Heart attack. All the victims in their eighties. You think police are gonna care about any of that?" Rose can't help thinking about the officer who came to her door. The cold look he'd given her, that serpent-like smile. *This is all a big waste of time, don't you think, Ms. DuBois? I mean, people probably die here every other day, am I right?*

Rose shudders at the memory, at the idea they might very well be on their own.

"Okay," he says. "Who do we talk to first?"

She takes Miller by the arm and steers him away from the pond, heading for home once more. "I think we need to regroup with Gopi and Mickey, and maybe a couple others. But Gopi first."

"Why him?"

"Because I want to know more about the lights he saw in the old asylum, the glowing eyes that chased him home," she says. "I want to know what's been going on in the dead of night."

"Only one reason anyone would be in that building," Miller says.

Rose looks up at him, waiting.

"To do something they shouldn't be doing," he says. "Or to hide themselves. Like vermin in the walls."

"Then that's where we start," Rose says, slipping her arm through his. "We smoke out the rats."

4

"I went to chess club today and heard people crying," Gopi says, shaking his head. "That's how I found out about Egor. Damn shame."

Mickey, Rose, and Miller sit quietly, listening to Gopi's update, the four of them sitting around a table in the dining hall, each having ordered nothing more than coffee. None of them having an appetite.

"And after hearing what you guys said about Egor," he continues, "it sounds more and more like something just isn't right about it. Strange way to die, that's for sure."

Rose spins her coffee cup slowly, Mickey and Miller also lost in thought.

"I'm referring to the erection," Gopi adds.

"Yes, we know," Rose says quickly, ready to move on. "But Gopi, you said you'd found out something else. What is it?"

Gopi nods. "Okay, so, ever since that night I went out to the asylum, I've been setting an alarm for two a.m., waking up just long enough to take a look out there for a few minutes. Most nights I've come up empty, but a few nights ago I saw someone walking out of that abandoned building," he says quietly, eyes darting left and right above the waxed tips of his moustache, as if afraid of being overheard by the wrong person. "They were wearing all black, and I don't know . . . they seemed . . ."

"What?" Mickey prods.

"Let me put it this way: the first thing I thought of when I saw that figure, clad in shadow, was 'I'm looking at Death right now.'"

Mickey's eyes go wide. "Like in that movie!"

"In a way, yeah," Gopi says. "So I kept watching, and then, just as I was thinking I should try to take a picture of it, I swear whatever the thing was turned its head and looked up toward my window, as if it *knew* I was watching."

Rose clutches the neck of her sweater and Miller wrings his hands atop the table, all of them more than spooked. "What did you do?" Mickey asks.

Gopi shrugs, bushy eyebrows rising. "What do you think? I backed the hell up, got out of the thing's line of sight. I waited a minute to let my heart slow down, and when I looked out the window again . . . it was *gone*, just like whatever chased me the other night, remember? It was like the shadows just carried them away, like a spirit. Or a ghost."

"No need for theatrics, Gopi," Miller says kindly.

"I'm not trying to be theatrical or paranoid," he says. "I just don't know how else to explain it. Anyway, last night it happened again."

"The strange figure in black?" Rose asks.

Gopi shakes his head. "No, sorry, I meant the *lights*. They were back. And this time I stayed up and watched for a while. It was almost a half hour before they finally went out, and that's when I saw them."

"Who?" Miller asks quietly, leaning in.

Gopi leans in so close his chin almost touches the tabletop, his voice so low Rose can barely make out the words. "The Baxter sisters," he hisses. "There's no doubt in my mind. There were three of them, and even though it was dark, I'm telling you, it was them. I'd recognize those hunched old witches anywhere."

"Be kind . . ." Rose says distractedly.

"Sorry," Gopi mumbles, then his eyes light up. "But seriously, what the hell were they doing out there? And who—or *what*—did I see coming out of that building three nights ago? Because it was definitely not some old lady, much less three."

Mickey unfolds his massive arms and lays his palms, gently, flat onto the table. "Only one way to find out," he says, looking from face to face.

Rose nods. "Right. We ask them."

Miller squirms in his seat. "You sure that's a good idea, Rose?

Those three are vengeful. Remember what happened to Will Soodik when he called Barbara a bitch for beating him at Friday Night Bingo? He woke up the next day deaf as a doornail. Doctors said it was neurological, but Will swears those women put a curse on him."

"That's a bunch of bull," Rose says, tugging her cardigan tightly over her chest. "Don't be silly, Beauregard."

Miller shrugs, but says nothing more.

"Alright, who wants to do it?" Gopi asks. "I mean, I would, but I have to prep for the next screening. . . ."

"We *all* go," Rose says. "All four of us. That way if they need to make voodoo dolls, they'll run out of stuffing after doing Mickey's and the rest of us will be safe."

Mickey looks at Rose in surprise, mouth open, and then begins to laugh.

After a moment, they're all laughing—laughing at their fear, their possible paranoia, and their unspoken relief at not having to go through it alone.

5

The quartet of friends find the sisters walking between the Community Center and the Seaview building. All three women are sweaty, frumpy, and grumpy, wearing stretch pants and loose sweatshirts, carrying towels and looking, all in all, worse for the wear.

"Hello, ladies," Rose chirps as they approach. "Wondering if you have a moment?"

The sisters stop on the wide path, looking warily at Rose and the others, and none too happy for having been waylaid.

"What is it?" Bridget snaps. "We're in a hurry."

Miller steps forward, spreads his hands. "We just have a couple quick questions. You see, we're trying to solve a little mystery."

The sisters glance at each other, then Bridget sighs, puts on a petulant expression of strained patience, and widens her eyes in a *well, go on* gesture.

"As you know," Rose begins, treading carefully, "there have been some strange things happening around here lately."

Barbara sniffs. "Hadn't noticed."

"What's this all about?" Betsie says, looking especially haggard. "We just did an hour of Vinyasa Yoga, and we're hot and tired . . ." She rubs the base of her spine. "And sore. I need Advil and a nap before our shows."

"My sister has a crush on Wolf Blitzer," Bridget adds, dabbing her forehead with a towel as Betsie blushes.

"Of course," Rose says, glancing toward Gopi and Mickey, who stand by silently and more than a bit awkwardly. *Jump in anytime, fellas,* she thinks, and is thankful when Miller speaks up again.

"Ladies, we don't want to hold you up," he says, feeling enough pleasantries have been bantered about and not wanting to lose their momentum. "But would you mind telling us what you've been doing in the old asylum out back? We're curious, is all."

The sisters exchange heated looks once again. Barbara opens her mouth, then closes it with a look from Bridget.

"How is that your business?" Betsie asks, seemingly anxious.

Miller lowers his voice. "Look ladies, folks around here are worried. Hell, they're *scared*. Three deaths in just over a week, and more than a few people have seen someone wandering the grounds at night, looking into windows."

Gopi takes a step closer, face stricken. "I was chased."

Miller shoots him a glance, then turns back to the sisters. "We're just trying to get to the bottom of what's going on. If anything."

Bridget looks momentarily defiant, then softens. "We heard about Egor. That's too bad. He was a nice man."

Miller nods. "So . . . will you tell us what you've been up to?"

Barbara sighs once more, even more dramatically than the first. "Fine. But not here. It's freezing, and my sweaty leotard feels like snakeskin. Come on up for a minute and we'll talk."

Rose smiles. "Thank you."

As the sisters begin walking toward home, the others following a few steps behind, Bridget turns her head pointedly toward Gopi and Mickey, who stop, wilting under her glare. "Not you two," she says sternly. "We're not having a damn dinner party."

"It's okay," Miller tells them. "We'll catch you up later."

Mickey and Gopi nod, appearing to be more relieved than upset, and trail off as the others continue toward the apartments.

As they enter the building, Rose spares a glance at Miller, who has turned back, wearing a hangdog expression, to watch their friends walk off.

Most likely wishing he was walking away with them, she thinks, and wonders, with a sense of dread, what they are getting themselves into.

6

Rose has never been in the Baxter sisters' apartment and always wondered how all three of them fit into one of the Autumn Springs footprints, given there are no two bedroom units and even the one-bedroom places are less than a thousand square feet.

She didn't have to wait long for an answer.

"Are those bunk beds?" Rose asks, knowing it's horribly rude but unable to resist glancing through the open door of the bedroom and observing the stacked beds. "I'm sorry," she adds quickly. "It's none of my business."

"Unfortunately," Barbara huffs, then shrugs. "But it works out fine. It's the only way we could stay together."

"We looked at apartments and even some small houses," Bridget adds, tossing her towel onto a couch and settling down next to it. "But we're not in the best of health, and we have no other family."

"So if one of us were to have a medical issue," Betsie interjects, moving to the tidy kitchen to put on a pot of water, "or God forbid *two* of us, we'd be in big trouble."

"Better to be where there's help if needed," Barbara adds seamlessly, as if the three of them were a hive mind, each speaking the same thought in turn.

Likely not too far from the truth of it, Rose thinks, eyes bouncing from one sister to the next as they chime in.

"Tea? Or coffee, perhaps?" Betsie asks, and both Rose and Miller shake their heads.

"No, thank you, Betsie," Miller says.

Rose is surprised (and mildly abashed for *finding* herself surprised) at how clean and orderly the apartment is. A part of her, truth be told, was expecting dream catchers in the windows, shelves of jars filled with dark fluids and undefinable blobs of human organs, wooden bowls overflowing with flies' wings and bat teeth. Instead, she notes matching tins of everyday herbs on a cute antique spice rack, a jar of instant coffee, a small blender for smoothies. The furnishings are not black and dreary, and there are no cobwebs hanging in the corners dotted with fat black spiders. Instead, the couch and chair are a matching set of plush crimson, the room completed by a teak coffee table and a gorgeous, midcentury credenza with a flat-screen television on top.

These aren't witches, Rose realizes, feeling sillier with each moment that passes. *They're just three old ladies who rely on each other, trying to make a nice home for themselves and taking it day-by-day, like the rest of us.*

"So, I suppose you want to know about the demon we've been trying to summon," Bridget says evenly, accepting a cup of coffee from her sister.

Rose's thoughts burst like a bubble, and she looks at Miller with wide eyes. To his credit he only nods, makes his way to the plush red chair adjacent the couch, and settles into it.

"I suppose we do," he says. "If that's what you three have been up to back there."

"Well, we certainly can't draw chalk spell circles in here," Barbara says with a huff, as if stating the obvious. "It would stain the carpet."

Betsie walks over from the kitchen, hands Barbara a mug of something Rose certainly hopes is tea, and settles down next to Bridget on the couch. "Not to mention lighting all those candles would set off the smoke detectors."

"They're quite sensitive here," Barbara murmurs.

"But most of all," Bridget continues, "we had to have complete privacy. Summoning a demon like Haures is no small thing."

"We need room to operate," Barbara adds.

Rose looks from sister to sister to sister, unsure what to do with herself as all the seats seem to have been taken and she feels awkward, and a little bit lightheaded, standing next to the kitchen while taking this all in.

Barbara seems to notice and smiles at Rose. "Here, honey, come sit with me at the table. You look a bit peaked."

Rose smiles back as best she's able and steps to the dining table, which she notices overlooks the front lawn and the rear entrance of the Community Center.

"Uh, if we could back up a bit . . . who is Horace?" Miller asks, sitting forward in the chair and setting his elbows on his knees.

"How-rez," Betsie enunciates. "And he's a very important demon."

"To us he would look like a leopard or a big cat," Barbara adds. "But stronger and, well, immortal."

"He's an animal?" Rose asks numbly.

"He's a deity, dear, but that's the shape our feeble human minds would see him as, yes," Betsie says, eyes alight with admiration. "His true form would likely drive us insane. So, if he comes across your path, you'd assume him to be a panther or a cougar, I suppose. Opinions vary."

"We almost had him once," Barbara says with a bright smile, as if she were talking about meeting one of the Beatles instead of a four-legged demon. "But we couldn't hold the spell, so he got, you know . . . sent back."

"We're looking to make a deal with him," Bridget continues. "We need protection from the evil in our midst and, in exchange, we'll offer him one of our souls."

Rose starts to speak, finds her tongue inoperable, and so simply stares, gape-mouthed, at Bridget, who blows lightly on her tea before taking a slurpy sip from the mug.

"Your souls?" Miller asks, eyebrows raised.

"Well, just one," Betsie replies absently, pulling a stray hair from the thigh of her tights.

Barbara taps Rose's forearm and she nearly jumps out of her skin, but manages—just barely—to stay seated. "We're gonna draw straws," she says quietly, wearing a mischievous grin.

"Or we'll just let him choose," Bridget adds, shrugging. "The point is that we need protection, and I think you two know it. As do those two chuckleheads we left outside. It's no secret there's a killer on the loose at Autumn Springs."

Despite herself (and the outright bizarre nature of the conversation) Rose sits up, excited to feel that someone else, someone outside their circle, at least, is having the same thoughts she is: that something is very wrong with how Angela and Owen—and possibly Egor—died.

Or, if one were to put it another way: how they were murdered.

"We certainly have our suspicions," Rose says, finding her voice. "But if I may leave the, um, demon part of it aside for now, what makes you so sure there's a killer?"

The three sisters share a glance, one that does not go unnoticed by either Rose or Miller, then Bridget gives a little shake of her head. "We promised not to tell."

"Whatever you tell us will not leave this room," Miller says. "I swear it." He looks to Rose, meeting her eye, and she nods along.

"Of course," she says, meaning it. "I promise, as well. We won't betray your confidence. But if we're right about this, then lives could be at stake, possibly our own. So please, ladies . . . what do you know?"

"Well . . . for starters, Angela didn't slip and fall down," Betsie says solemnly. "She was attacked."

Bridget sets down her coffee. "There's a man who lives next to Angela, a chicken-legged, bobble-headed creature by the name of Henry Barber. He's been here for a decade. Old coot must be almost ninety by now."

"Yes, I met him," Rose says excitedly. "What about him?"

"He came to us the day after they found poor Angela's body," Barbara says, forcing Rose to swivel her head toward her and making her feel like she's watching a tennis match. "He was frightened and wanted us to give him something for protection."

"Another demon?" Miller asks, eyebrows raised.

The sisters all chuckle, and Bridget replies through a sly grin. "No, dear. That's for us. In the end, we sent him away with instructions on how to draw a very basic hexafoil on his door."

"And a small amulet to keep around his neck," Barbara adds.

"Easy fifty bucks," Betsie says, and the sisters all break into giggles. "Just like the old days."

"But we did make him tell us what he was so worried about," Bridget says. "In order to increase the power of the marking and the talisman charm. Or, at least, that's what we told him."

"The coward spilled everything," Betsie says with a scowl. "He heard the whole thing and didn't lift a finger."

"And he lied to the police," Barbara adds. "He was afraid that, if he squealed, whoever killed Angela might come for him next."

"What did he hear?" Rose asks, reeling from this new, and damning, information.

"Well, he described it as a loud struggle," Betsie says. "Oh, and he heard Angela call out at one point, real faint like."

"Then he barricaded his door while that monster poured a bath," Barbara adds sadly. "Trying to make the whole thing look like an accident."

Miller shakes his head. "So why don't you tell someone? Tell Mr. Blackwell or that detective. Maybe he could get the truth from Henry."

"We promised him, Miller," Bridget says. "Just like you've promised us."

"Besides, he'd just deny it, and without his confirmation I doubt the police would believe us," Betsie says.

"They'd think we were just paranoid, crazy old ladies."

"It's not like the police care about a bunch of elderly folks, anyway," Barbara adds, and her eyes lock on Rose, as if reading her mind. "I think you agree."

Rose clears her throat, not liking that dark, penetrating look.

"I suppose I do," Rose says, secretly wondering if she means it, and is saddened to realize that she does. At least for now.

"And because of what Henry Barber told you, you're trying to find your own protection," Miller asks, "by raising this demon?"

All three sisters nod in unison, then Bridget stands from the couch with a groan. "We'll get old Haures up here, don't you worry.

Couple more tries and we'll bag him. And then he'll make sure nothing happens to me, or my sisters, and he'll kill the son of a bitch doing this," she says, her face hard with determination. With belief. "Now, if you'll excuse me, I need to take a shower and put on some clothes that don't smell like trash day in the Bronx."

Betsie also gets up, and Rose realizes the collusion has come to an end. As she stands, Barbara's cool hand grips her own, and something slides from the woman's palm into hers. When Rose looks at her, a question on her face, Barbara just gives her a timid smile and a quick wink.

"Well, thank you for the information and the time," Miller says, his knees popping like cracked walnuts as he gets up from the chair. "And good luck with your demon," he adds, doing his best not to sound pandering.

"Don't you worry about us," Bridget says. "You two just take care of yourselves."

"And watch your backs," Betsie adds.

When Rose and Miller are in the hallway, she opens her clenched hand to study the small item Barbara had slipped her: a silver charm, molded into the shape of a hand, a wide-open eye etched across the palm.

"What's that?" Miller asks.

"A gift from Barbara," Rose says. "I assume for protection."

"Protection against what? Ghosts, demons, or madmen?"

"All the above, I guess," Rose says with a shrug.

"A ward against evil."

Rose nods, then tightens her hand on the charm, the silver metal cool against her palm, hoping that whatever magic it contains will be enough.

7

Hastings reads the email again, the tip of his ballpoint pen ticking against his teeth in irritation.

This is good news, Ernie. This is good *news.*

Forensics could not find any discrepancies between the wounds on Owen Duffield's wrist and the knife found in the bathtub—the weapon he'd supposedly used to cut open his arms, allowing his blood to pump into the warm water like a broken inkwell.

The autopsy did note a small nick on the victim's collarbone, which could have easily been done by accident when the old guy was climbing into the tub, or sometime before. A footnote Hastings catalogued without much enthusiasm.

Despite the chief's mild irritation, Hastings had ordered the analysis, along with sending a small team into the room to vacuum hairs, wipe for fingerprints, and keep an eye out for blood that might have missed the tub or DNA that might be someone's other than the victim.

Nothing. Nada. Nathan.

So yeah, this is good news. He can sleep at night knowing he'd gone the distance with the old man's suicide, crossed his *T*'s and all that shit, and now he can move on to the next case.

And yet.

This morning he'd gotten a call from the precinct letting him know, as a courtesy, that another resident had just died at Autumn Springs. Heart attack. Death certificate stamped and approved. But, you know . . .

Another one.

In what? A week?

He wants to go back out there. Snoop around. Ask more questions. Interview the staff. Chat with friends of the deceased. Maybe take another crack at the neighbors.

See if something doesn't line up.

He'd brought the idea to his boss, even asked for a couple uniforms to tag along, but Chief Christie all but laughed him out of the building.

"People dying at a retirement home is not exactly a front-page headline, Detective," he'd said, filling his coffee cup from the brewer he kept in his office for personal use, the coffee being the far more expensive *low acidity* type. Hastings didn't mind. He figured the chief needed it. They all did.

"I know, Chief, but this feels off to me. I want to give it another go-around."

"Nah," Christie said, shaking his fat-jowled head. "You got other shit to do. I've seen your caseload. Your focus needs to be elsewhere."

"Chief—"

"Old people die, Detective," Christie said, the joviality in his voice replaced with cool steel. "Nothing shocking there. Plus, there's no evidence of foul play, no alarming loose ends, no suspicious evidence. You got a slip 'n' fall, a heartbroken lover offing himself, and a heart attack that killed a guy who—wait for it—had serious heart problems. No . . . this is not something you need to spend time on."

So Hastings had gone back to his desk, pulled out another case file and went to work. The chief was right about one thing: he has a massive caseload and there isn't nearly enough time in the day, even with his constantly working well into overtime. Unpaid, of course.

Still . . . something nagged at him about that place. Those deaths.

Something funny is going on at Autumn Springs.

He can almost *feel* it.

If nothing else, he'd like to have one more chat with the administrator. What's his name? Blackwell. Jerry Blackwell. He'd already looked at the guy's file in the database but found nothing noteworthy. When he'd questioned him, however, the guy seemed antsy. Maybe not guilty, per se, but definitely anxious.

Probably because one of his residents ripped his arms up with a kitchen knife and bled himself out in the bathtub.

Yeah, maybe.

Or maybe it's something else.

Regardless, he wants to get in a room with the man for ten minutes. Poke and pry under the hood a bit, find out what his story is. What makes him tick.

Why would a young, sharp guy like that be in charge of a retirement home?

Odd, for sure. Not suspicious . . . but odd.

Noteworthy.

Just like it's noteworthy that Blackwell has access to every room at Autumn Springs, knows the schedules for the entire staff— including the cleaning crew, the nurses, and everyone else who deals with the residents. He can be anywhere, do pretty much anything, and no one will be the wiser.

Hastings shakes his head. *You're leaping, Ernie. There's no motive, no reason a guy like that would want to hurt—much less kill—any of the nice old folks who live there.*

"Fine, fine . . ." Hastings mumbles to himself, letting it go, letting his mind absorb the new case file in front of him.

For a couple minutes, it actually works.

"Goddamn it." He pushes aside the folder, spins around in his shitty, squeaky chair, and stares out the window at the gray sky beyond, the chewed tip of his pen tapping once more against his teeth.

Someone else croaks up there anytime soon and I'm gonna go verify the cause of death myself, he thinks, absently watching a broil of storm clouds approach from the east. *I don't care if it's a goddamn stroke in their sleep; I'm going up there to sniff around.*

Hastings watches the incoming storm, his brain itching in the way it does when he's missing something, when the red flags are being pushed around by a wind of doubt and those highly trained detective-grade bullshit detectors are flickering to life.

There's something about that administrator I don't like, he thinks, slightly thrilled at the idea of creating a suspect list. *That guy dresses too nice. His hair is too perfect.*

Much like these recent deaths . . . he's too damn neat.

In Hastings's experience, when something appears too perfect on the outside, it often means there's a seething chaos just below the surface, as if that visage of perfection is a shield—or a projection—so others can't see the darkness beneath.

Like a mask.

It's possible, even probable, that one could rip off that tidy, smiling face to find a monster staring back at you—all yellow eyes and sharp, snarling teeth.

Look at Ted Bundy. Handsome, charismatic. *Nice.*

But underneath? An unspeakable horror.

Is Jerry Blackwell a monster behind that efficient veneer?

Perhaps.

Hastings just prays that no one accidentally gives that mask a tug, tries to have a peek at what's beneath.

Because that hideous, ghastly face will be the last thing they ever see.

8

Rose is exhausted.

After the strange meeting with the Baxter sisters, she met up with Libby Sue Thompson, Jill and Jerry Pickford, and Bob and Ellie Nash (who had recently celebrated sixty years of marriage) for a sushi dinner.

The food was wonderful (it always was at Tsunami, where the chef, Ryo—who they all knew on a first-name basis—was the only one who prepared the fish), but she'd drunk too much hot sake and now feels the beginnings of a headache at the center of her forehead. Too much alcohol, combined with Jerry Pickford's somewhat loud personality and Libby Sue's gossip, had been a recipe for disaster.

Still, the sushi was excellent, and Rose had badly needed to get away, if only for a few hours, just to clear her head and get some much-needed perspective.

But now she is glad to be home, away from her brash, gossipy friends, the hustle and bustle of the town, and that dreadful shuttle van, which—since the driver is a chain-smoker when not behind the wheel—always smells like an ashtray.

She locks her front door (wishing, for the first time since moving to Autumn Springs, that she could deadbolt it as well) and flicks the wall switch, turning on the overhead light. She's eager for some hot tea and possibly a bath. Before she can ruminate further on either option, however, she steps on something—something that must have been slipped under the door.

Rose looks down to see a square, linen-colored envelope beneath the toe of her boot. She bends over (wincing only slightly at the tightness in her tired lower back, the dull ache in her knees from so much walking) and picks up the strange delivery. Across the face of the sealed envelope, written in bold, flowery cursive, is her name:

Rose

Carrying the envelope with her, Rose continues into her apartment, clicks on the standing lamp next to her couch, then flicks another switch by the kitchen to illuminate the shaded bulb that hangs over her dining room table. She sets the envelope on the table and makes herself a cup of chamomile tea.

Not used to getting mail shoved beneath her door (all the residents had locked postal boxes just off the Community Center's main lobby), she sits at the table, a hot mug in hand, to study the envelope more closely. Outside of her name there's nothing else written: no address and no sender information.

"Very strange," she mumbles, then opens the envelope.

Inside is a thick, oversized card covered with fine handwriting, neatly scrawled in bold red ink:

Greetings Ms. DuBois,
You are invited to a salon.
Attendance is mandatory.
Your host is Sandra Freeman.

-

WHERE: Greenview Apartments, Unit 28
WHEN: Friday, October 12th, at 7 p.m. sharp

-

Please do not bring anything but your sparkling personality.
Drinks and food will be served.

Rose scans the card a moment longer, shrugs, then casually turns it over, enjoying the feel of the heavy linen cardstock. Centered on the back of the card is a single, handwritten line, and Rose wonders if it's on all the invitations . . . or just hers.

There is much to discuss.

Despite her tiredness, Rose smiles. Surprises are few and far between as one gets along in years, and most of them unpleasant. It was the pleasant ones you held on to. The ones that gave life a little jolt of fun, a little kick in the pants to the day-to-day churn of watching time pass by, standing still as friends and loved ones die.

She sets the card neatly against the dining table's centerpiece—a blue, baked-clay vase Sybil had made for her in junior high school—and sips her tea.

Nice to have something to look forward to, she thinks, then stands and takes her mug to the bedroom, ready now for that hot bath and a good night's sleep.

Maybe, when I wake up, all this nonsense will be just that: nonsense. And, after a few days, we can forget all about this toil and trouble and get back to our lives. Get back to enjoying ourselves and living in peace.

As things turned out, it would be the last optimistic thought—and the last good night's sleep—Rose DuBois would have for quite some time.

9

Stan can't sleep, and yet he feels like he's dreaming *all the time.*

Curled up in his bed, the sodden sheets coiled around him, he sweats profusely. His tongue is dry as sandpaper, his eyes wide and watery. He doesn't even notice the tears running down his cheeks, dripping off his chin onto his pillow. The television is on but plays nothing but the same show, over and over and over: *Aliens Exist!*

It used to be one of his favorites, but something must have gone wrong with the app and now he's become so sick of the damn show he could vomit. At one point he turned the television off but hated the dark silence even more, so he quickly clicked it back on—turning the volume up loud enough to fill the room with noise—and crawled back into bed.

Now he's worried about the sounds coming from the hallway. Whoever—*whatever*—is out there, he fears, wants to get inside and hurt him. Possibly *eat* him. He thinks maybe—just maybe—there are giant insects out there, their long, wet mandibles clicking hungrily, scratching at his door with one multi-jointed black leg. He was forced to yell at one of them earlier. Told them he wanted to be *LEFT ALONE*, that he was *JUST FINE* and didn't want anyone to come inside his room. His room . . .

Is full of colors.

The walls are rainbows, and there's strange music flowing through the air like currents of wind—long, sinewy tendrils of yellow, purple, and green. The music emanates from the bathroom, the kitchen, the air-conditioning vents. Melodies layered with other melodies sing to him, tell him things no one could possibly know. *Private things.* Buried secrets he's kept for years. For decades.

But now the music has burrowed deep inside his head, and the walls have become a shifting, pulsing smear of impossible colors. When he shuffles around the room, his feet feel like they're sinking into the floor. His body feels brittle as burnt clay and he's waiting for it to shatter, to break apart into multiple versions of itself, so that if he were to look into a mirror he would see his face and the back of his head at the same time, below which would be several extra limbs, flowing like seaweed, each one terminating in an uncountable multitude of fingers.

Soon, he knows, whatever is scurrying around in the hallway will find its way in. Whoever—whatever—is out there will *break* in if they have to. Heck, they'd already told him as much! One more night, and that will likely be the end of it—then they'll come inside, riding the streams of multicolored music, through the vents and beneath the door and from the shadows they'll come, they'll come!

His imagination racing with images of man-sized insects prancing into his room to gobble him up, to drink his blood and *crunch, crunch, crunch* on his bones, Stan is so badly frightened that he trembles and whimpers and pulls the sheets even more tightly to his chin, wishing he could simply close his eyes and make it all go away, that he could fly from this place—travel far, far away from the creatures that want to hurt him.

A distant, more logical part of Stan's mind knows that he desperately needs to sleep, but another, much louder part, feels that he must stay vigilant—must continue to monitor his surroundings and make sure nothing gets in, that the walls don't melt and expose another world, a hideous nightmare world where there are black seas and pale skies and unspeakable creatures—

TAP, TAP, TAP.

Stan's head jerks toward the window. The curtains are drawn tight.

"Go away!" he yells, knowing it's one of those things from the hallway, the ones that make the shadows under the door. "I'm sleeping," he mutters, wishing the colors would fade, that the walls and floor would become solid once more.

TAP.

TAP.

TAP.

Stan shifts his body toward the window, ready to shout at whoever might be out there—when he recalls what the gray-skinned alien had told him:

You've been chosen.

We want to show you the mothership.

We'll come back for you.

"Hey!" Stan yells, hoping it's not too late.

His fears and worries dissipate in a jolt of drugged adrenaline as he throws himself out of bed, shuffles quickly to the window, grips the (*slippery—why are they slippery*) curtains with both hands and yanks them apart.

"Ah!" he cries, startled by a monstrous, alien face only inches from his own, their two heads separated by nothing but the thin glass of the window. Stan gawps as large, black eyes stare blankly at him; the gray, bulbous, bald head cocked to one side in curiosity. The creature is wearing the black robe again and, as Stan watches in wondrous horror, it raises a long, gnarled finger, tipped with a sharp black nail, and points to the latch on the window.

Open up.

Stan nods, hating the way the alien's face blurs when he does so, then flicks the latch with shaking fingers. He raises the window. Freezing cold October air blasts inside.

"It's time, Stan," the alien says, and backs away a few steps.

Stan looks down at his bare feet, his thin pajama bottoms. The chilled air rips effortlessly through the fabric of his baggy V-neck undershirt. He shivers.

"Wait, just let me get my coat and shoes."

The alien simply stares and says nothing. Stan, terrified to miss this opportunity, walks quickly to the closet, sticks his feet into a pair of worn-out moccasin slippers, pulls on a blue hoodie sweatshirt, and scurries back to the window in time to see that the alien is already walking across the dark clearing, melting into the night's long shadows, heading toward the wall of tall trees, beyond which the river flows.

Moving slowly, so as not to hurt himself, Stan gingerly puts one leg through the window, then sticks his head through and looks down. There's little drop to speak of—no more than a couple feet—but it's still awkward for him. He's not the nimble youngster he once was, the one who'd sneak out the window and climb effort-lessly down the trellis in the middle of the night to meet Suzanne Weathers for a smooch in the park.

No, Stan is *old* now, and it hurts like hell to squeeze himself over the sill, his balls taking the brunt of the damage as he shifts his weight through the opening.

"God*damn*," Stan groans, then brings his other leg through be-fore dropping awkwardly to the grass, ignoring the twinge in his bad knee as his feet hit the cold ground. "Hold on," he hisses at the back of the retreating creature, his breath clouding in the cold night air.

Up ahead, however, the alien continues to stride away—nothing more than a dancing shadow gliding across the silver, moon-kissed grass, moving quickly toward the trees.

Toward the spaceship.

Grinning like that schoolboy he once was—the one who'd snuck out at night to kiss a pretty girl in the park—Stan follows.

10

I can't see! Why can't I see? Oh, God, where am I?

Stan had run headlong into the dark trees, the moon and stars above quickly blocked out by a heavy canopy—the twisted black arms of branches and leaves. The ground is sodden and dense with the detritus of a long autumn, the season now near death, slowly strangled by the icy hands of the oncoming winter.

"Wait!" he yells, gasping for breath, blinded by the sudden darkness.

For a moment, he stops, flattens his hand against the rough bark of a tree. He turns around but can no longer see the way out, the way back. "Wait . . ." he mumbles, panting, sweating, searching for the right direction, praying he didn't lose the creature.

"Here!" the alien hisses from nearby. Stan spins to see the large gray head, those lidless, shining black eyes, just a few feet away. "This way."

Stan waves weakly, wondering why all the trees are dancing, shaking their rumps to an old tune, something from a cartoon he once saw as a child. "I'm coming," he says. "Don't leave me."

"You want to see the fucking ship or not? I'm freezing my ass off," the alien says, then turns and disappears into the trees, its voice trailing back through the dark.

Stan nods, not knowing what he's even nodding about, and follows.

After a few minutes of navigating ankle-breaking roots and forehead-smashing branches, Stan sees a shimmer of light ahead—as if the air were filled with fireflies or diamonds—and gasps.

He bursts from the trees—heart racing, his slippers long lost, his bare feet wet, scratched, and numb with cold—and stares at the magnificent thing ahead.

The creature stands in the clearing, facing him. One clawed

hand is held up and out theatrically, as if presenting the eighth wonder of the world. "Behold!"

Stan stares, open-mouthed, at the creature and the tall structure just behind it, his drugged, tired mind working to piece the images into something he can understand.

"But . . . where's the ship?" Stan says, eyeing the tall structure, a swirling light at the top acting as a beacon, one that shines with all the colors of his imagination.

"At the top, Stan," the creature says triumphantly. "The ship is docked at the top. And the sooner you get your ass up there, the sooner we can fly away from this place and into the great beyond!"

"Move it, champ," the creature says from behind Stan, having prodded him toward the stairs at the base of the tower.

Stan stares up at the swirling colors of the ship with a sense of awe. He doesn't question why there are stairs instead of a tractor beam or why the ship perched atop seems rather *small* compared to what he'd seen in so many UFO documentaries. He just wants to get up there and see it.

After all, he's been *chosen.*

And so he climbs, the metal stairs icy cold beneath his bare feet, seeming to go on forever.

High above his head, however, Stan can almost hear the pulsing of the ship's engine. As he climbs two flights, then three, then four, he finds himself looking outward—not at the trees, but *over* the trees. The stars once more in full bloom, the fat moon all but bursting from the night sky. Stan imagines he can almost reach out and pull that plump white moon from its orbit—as if pulling a plug from a tub—and the entire universe would drain through, flowing back to the beginning of time.

"A black hole," Stan mutters, jaw sagging, a slick line of drool stretching down from one corner of his mouth, catching the moonlight.

"Keep moving," the alien snaps.

But Stan is panting heavily now, his heart pounding. His bad knee throbs painfully, and he feels like maybe—just maybe—something here isn't right. The stars are swirling around him, as if the universe were moving in fast-forward—days blurring into nights, years shooting by in mere seconds, eons spinning past as the entirety of outer space swells and contracts like the lungs of God. Sickened by it all, Stan feels bile burn the back of his throat as he puts one foot in front of the other.

"I think I'm gonna puke," he says, then stumbles to a stop on the next landing, crying out when his knee cracks down on the hard metal.

He grips the ice-cold safety bar, leans over the side, and vomits into the night.

"Jesus Christ," the creature says, as if disappointed.

Stan stays on his knees, filth staining his chin, chest heaving as he stares at the dark purple sky, the scattered stars. A new clarity appears at the fringes of his mind, and suddenly—as he looks around at the dark night, far above the tops of the trees—he wonders where he is, and how in the world he got here.

"I want to go home," he whines, ashamed of his childlike helplessness.

Behind him, the alien pulls a long hunting knife from the folds of its cloak, the metal blade glimmering in the dim silver moonlight, one edge smooth and sharp, the other jagged as witch's teeth.

"Get the fuck up," the alien says. "Or I'll stick this so far up your ass it'll pierce your tongue."

Anal probe, Stan thinks wildly, swallowing bile, recalling a thousand images from the countless documentaries he'd seen, the ones showing dramatic and vivid re-creations of humans getting experimented on by savage, heartless aliens. Terrified, he gets shakily to his feet, turns toward the next rise of steps, and keeps climbing.

Minutes later, when they finally reach the top, Stan is out of breath and out of energy. His knee is screaming bloody murder, his brain is heavy with exhaustion and doubt and confusion, his body wracked from lack of sleep and food and (despite his not knowing it) the hallucinogenic drugs coursing through his blood.

He looks around at the interior of the ship. At the bright, colorful lights, at the . . . wooden floor? He notes a weathered worktable, upon which rests an ancient CB radio, unpowered and lifeless.

"Welcome to the mothership," the alien says, and jabs Stan in the shoulder with the tip of the long knife—just enough to break the skin. To get the man's full attention.

"Ow!" Stan howls, and the alien laughs.

"Time to fly, Stan!" the thing shrieks.

Stan spins around, confused. His heart is strained to a breaking point, his shoulder burning from the fresh wound.

"Don't hurt me," he whimpers. "I'm ready to go! I'm ready—"

The alien lunges like a musketeer and jabs the blade's tip into Stan's stomach.

"Ow," Stan cries out, doubling over. "Stop," he says, holding up one hand. "Please, just hold on a second—"

"Time to go, Stan," the alien says somberly, its gray head wobbly on its black-cloaked shoulders, its large, monstrous hands palms-up at its sides, long rubbery fingers still wrapped awkwardly around the knife's hilt. "You've reached the ship, just like I promised. And now it's time to fly."

Stan drops to his knees and begins to cry.

"Please . . . I just want to go home."

The colors behind Stan's eyelids fade to shades of gray and, when he opens them, the world comes into renewed focus. His feet are frigid with cold, his nose caked with snot, his teeth chattering. He looks up at the alien, one of his hands clenched to his bleeding gut. "How did I get here?"

"Through trust and determination," the alien says, then pulls off its hands and lets them fall to the floor. The knife disappears into the folds of the cloak.

Stan watches, with a new kind of terror, as the creature lifts its head from its shoulders. What hides beneath is not a face, but a head made of slithering, writhing snakes with scales of silver oil, their mouths hissing, teeth snapping at the tails of the others as they slick together as one.

"Time to go," a growling voice says from deep inside that mound of serpents. Then the creature takes two quick steps toward Stan and thrusts out its hands (*human, they're human!*) to grip the front of his hoodie, lifting him easily to his feet.

Stan groans, wide-eyed, as the squirming, hissing head comes closer. He screams, hot urine running down one leg, as a pair of dark yellow eyes widen from within the nest of slick coils, the black abyss of a mouth emerging from the mask of horror. Of evil.

"It's been fun," the voice says.

With a gentle but firm grip, the creature takes Stan by the arms and turns him around so he's facing the swirling, colorful lights of the night sky. It eases Stan forward, step by step, until his bony hips are touching the waist-high railing of the cabin's outer walkway.

"Do you see the stars, Stan?"

"Yes," he says, the sky once more a blurred, abstract image of reality. "Yes . . . they're beautiful."

The alien rests a hand on Stan's shoulder, whispers into his ear.

"Keep looking at the stars."

Stan does.

"We've left planet Earth, Stan. We've breached the atmosphere to enter the void," the voice says. "Right now, we're hurtling through outer space at light speed. Entire galaxies are flying past us, each of them bursting with all the colors of creation. We're racing toward a distant planet . . . an alien planet far, far away. A planet filled with impossible wonders. Just like you've always dreamed."

Tears flow down Stan's cheeks. He nods.

"Thank you," he says. "Thank you."

The hissing of snakes grows momentarily louder, and then . . .

A perfect silence.

The world has stopped. The stars once again stationary. The swirling colors have diminished to reveal the perfect beauty of a plum-colored sky, a crater-strewn moon, a mist of silver-lit clouds. A window to the infinite.

"You're welcome," the creature whispers.

Then it shoves Stan up and over the railing, watches him fall eighty feet to the hard, cold earth far below, where his body lands with a muffled *thump*.

The entire way down, Stan doesn't scream.

Instead, he thinks—with a sense of awe and wonder—about the vast, astounding miracle of the universe.

SIX

EYE OF THE STORM

1

Hastings stands in the early morning mist.

Early birds chirp from the surrounding trees, huddled around the scene like grim witnesses, veiled in haze.

Twenty feet ahead of the detective lies the crumpled, broken body of Stanley Swanson, who committed suicide in the middle of the night by climbing a retired fire tower, then jumping from the top.

Apparently, Stan had been having "episodes" over the last twenty-four hours or so, and the nurses had been doing their best to coax him out of his room, albeit without success. This morning they'd finally forced entry, a doctor in tow, and found Stan gone, his window open wide. After twenty minutes of searching by a makeshift party made up of cleaning crew, nurses, orderlies, and one very annoyed doctor (who wanted to know why he hadn't been called earlier about Stan's state of mind), they'd found the body.

Another suicide.

Supposedly.

Hastings instructs the officers to tape off the area, tells forensics to do a sweep of the room at the top—a room that contained, somewhat oddly, a battery-powered disco ball (the kind you'd buy at a party supply store for twenty bucks, likely left by some kids), a broken ham radio, some empty beer cans, and little else. He doubts they'll find anything of value and has a pang of guilt about making the poor bastards climb the fire tower, but hey, sometimes the job sucks.

Leaving them to it, Hastings makes his way back to the retirement complex. He walks to the window where Stan made his exit. The grass is wet with morning dew, and there are no telltale footprints. No half-smoked cigarette. No index card that says *A MURDERER WAS HERE.* Just . . . grass.

Wouldn't make a lick of sense, anyway, he thinks. It's not as if someone could have forced the guy to climb out a window. If threatened, he could have walked into the hallway and yelled his head off, or pushed a button to have a nurse come running. No, he went out the window because he *wanted* to.

Because he wanted to kill himself. Because his brain had turned to jelly, his body was a constant source of pain and discomfort, and he was possibly—maybe even probably—inspired by the bathtub job done by Owen Duffield. So he shimmies out the window, walks to the fire tower, climbs . . . and jumps. Goodnight, Irene.

Regardless, Hastings will have the window dusted for fingerprints, just to cover the bases, but also because he doesn't like it. Too many deaths in too short a time. Two suicides only days apart? Nah, he doesn't like it one bit.

Back inside the Med Center, near the room where Stan lived, Hastings speaks with the nurse who was on the overnight shift. The one who was supposed to be taking care of Stan Swanson, the old man who'd just checked himself out of full-time care to become a sack of meat, half-frozen to the ground in the middle of the woods.

"Paranoid, erratic, mild hallucinations—"

A nurse named Annie Cooper rattles off symptoms like they're the names of friends coming to a dinner party.

"Sounds pretty serious," Hastings says.

But the nurse just shakes her head, tapping her foot in a way Hastings identifies with someone jonesing for a cigarette. "This is the Medical Center, Detective. A way station between retirement and death. The people we treat here suffer from dementia, Alzheimer's . . . half of them have had strokes or heart attacks in the past year. They're *old*, Detective. Shit, just this morning one guy kept telling me I was his granddaughter. And he's one of the *healthy* ones. So, no, it's not out of the question that a patient would rant and rave about seeing things, or question reality, or be paranoid that someone is trying to hurt them. My own grandfather, who raised me—and who I took care of for almost a year while he was slipping away into that horrible black cloud of dementia—would sometimes call relatives and tell them I'd chained him up in the basement. That I was stealing all his gold."

Hastings raises an eyebrow. "Did you?"

Nurse Cooper laughs in a jagged, almost cruel way, and now he can tell she's *really* begging for a smoke break. "Are you kidding? He was in so much debt it was a race to see if he would die before the bank took his house. That man didn't have gold in his fillings."

Hastings nods. "Regardless, I'll need a list of Mr. Swanson's medications."

As Nurse Cooper prints out the smorgasbord of pills Swanson was consuming, Hastings thinks through his game plan for the morning.

Of course, his immediate thought is to sit down with the administrator, Jerry Blackwell, and gather his take on the incident.

And find out where he was last night.

After that, he'd play it by ear. The chief didn't like him coming in the first place, but even he knows that an obvious suicide needs a signoff from homicide, so he has some leeway, and some time, to poke around a bit.

Hastings leaves the Med Center with a printout from the acerbic Nurse Cooper in his pocket, then walks until he hits the paved pathway that will lead him to the other buildings in the complex (complete with color-coded strips designating the correct path to each). As he walks, studying the multi-colored lines beneath his feet, he debates who to question first. Does he go find Blackwell at the Community Center? Or should he talk to the rest of the night staff, the ones who were supposed to be making sure people like Stan Swanson didn't do anything stupid? Like leap to their death from the top of an abandoned fire tower, or crawl out a window so they could die in the middle of the woods like a goddamn animal.

"Excuse me? Detective?"

Hastings, realizing he'd been lost in thought, turns toward the voice. He sees an elderly woman—a resident, he assumes—waving at him from a nearby bench. Sitting next to her is an older, more frail-looking resident who, unlike the woman, doesn't seem interested in much other than feeding the fish in a small, nearby pond.

Hastings gives a little wave back and decides there are worse ways to spend his time than interviewing a few locals. Before he can approach, however, the woman stands, says something to the man sitting next to her (while reassuringly patting him on the shoulder), and makes her way toward him.

I recognize her, he thinks as she comes closer, the clearing mist defining her features. *Yeah, she was hanging around the hallway outside the room where the guy opened his wrists.*

They meet on the path, and the woman extends her hand. She wears a pretty blue dress, a thick wool sweater, and a tidy black hat. She has a kind, open face, but hard eyes that have seen a few things, he thinks. Hastings pegs her as a retired nurse or perhaps a former schoolteacher, one who the kids loved dearly and feared like hell.

"Hello, I'm Rose DuBois," she says. "And you're the detective."

"Guilty," Hastings says, taking her hand. "How are you today, Ms. DuBois?"

"Well, I'm not so good, Detective."

"Please, just Ernie is fine."

Rose smiles, and it lights up her face.

This woman was a knockout back in the day, he thinks. *Hell, she still is.*

"That's kind, and just Rose, then, since we're friendly."

"You got it, Rose. What seems to be the problem?"

Rose studies him a moment, those hard eyes searching his face as if looking for defects, and Hastings makes a mental note not to take this woman lightly. Sure, her neighbors' minds might be flying the coop, but Rose still has everything wired correctly up there. You could see it in her expression, the one that said: *I'm watching you, so tread carefully.*

Hastings thinks this is pretty good advice and makes sure to keep his patronizing detective voice—the one he uses on the delusional, high, and paranoid—in his pocket.

"The problem," Rose says, her smile disappearing like a magic trick, "is that an acquaintance of mine jumped to his death last night."

Hastings nods. "Of course, I'm sorry. I wasn't sure everyone knew, or knew him."

Rose's smile returns, if only partly. "The grapevine at Autumn Springs is efficient and well powered, believe me. And a murder, well . . . that news travels at the speed of light."

Hastings is about to reply, but the words snag in his throat. He coughs into his hand, looks around furtively to see if anyone is in earshot. "You said murder?"

Rose nods. "I did."

"And why, Rose, do you think your acquaintance was murdered? Seems like a clear-cut suicide to me. To most people, I'd think."

"Just like Owen Duffield was a suicide? Like Angela Forrest was an accident? And Egor Abramov?" she says, listing the dead like accusations. "And you are not most people, sir. You're a police detective."

Rose's smile widens, but her eyes are sharp, determined. Hastings knows she's weighing the substance of him, judging his value, and the thought makes him incredibly uncomfortable.

"That's true," he says carefully. "But I gotta say, and I mean no offense, Rose, but things like this do happen in . . . well . . ."

"In places filled with old people, is that right?"

Hastings shrugs. "To be frank, yes, that's right. In fact, people in places such as this one, well, it's just not that uncommon, Rose." He watches her face closely, gauging her response, wondering if this woman is the provider of light—of insight—he needs right now. "And I think you know that."

"I suppose," Rose says with a sigh. "But us elderly folks aren't all as close to the ground as you'd imagine."

Certainly not as close as Stan Swanson is, he thinks darkly, and lowers his eyes.

"Look, I meant no offense."

Rose lifts a hand. "None taken. My point is that we aren't all ready to drop like flies. Hell, most of us are fit as fiddles. This place isn't a cemetery, Detective, it's an active community. And *your* job," she says, wagging a finger at his chin in a way that makes him feel like a scolded schoolboy, "is to protect our community."

Hastings nods. "That's true, Rose. And that's why I'm here. I'm not ignoring these incidents. But, to be honest, there's really nothing overtly suspicious here. My red flags are at half-mast, and my Spidey-sense isn't tingling, you know what I mean?"

A small lie, he thinks, *but no reason to bring the water to the fish.*

"Unless maybe you know something I don't?" he adds, raising an eyebrow.

Rose purses her lips, studies him even more closely than before.

He waits, meeting her eye.

"Can I trust you, Ernie?" she says finally. "Can I trust you to take me seriously and not think I'm some old crazy lady, full of conspiracy theories and paranoia?"

Hastings laughs. "Rose, I know we've just met, but if there's anything I'm certain of in this world, it's your stone-cold sanity. I mean that."

Rose laughs along with him, turns and slides her arm through his. "I'm glad to hear it," she says, leading him toward a building he hasn't been to yet. Through the windows he sees tables and chairs, folks having breakfast. "Because I have some things to tell you and some people I'd like you to meet."

Hastings thinks again about interviewing the administrator, the Medical Center staff . . . he thinks about the other cases he needs to follow up on this morning . . .

Then he pushes all of those follow-up items out of his mind, knowing they'll be waiting for him when he's ready, and also knowing he wants to hear what Rose DuBois has to say.

So he walks with Rose toward the dining hall, happily so, to meet her friends.

2

In Greenview 11, Bill Rutherford has lost his teeth.

He'd woken at the usual time that morning, then gone into the bathroom to gargle mouthwash and pull his dentures from their glass of overnight cleaning solution—just like he did every morning, like he'd done every morning for the last four years, ever since he had those last remaining soldiers yanked out by the town dentist and was fitted for full upper and lower dentures. Yessir, Bill's life had changed immediately—for the better—and he'd felt a lot less guilty about the cigar habit he'd had since his forties. With the new dentures, there wasn't a whole lot more damage his precious cigars could do (to his teeth, at least).

But now he has a problem, because his teeth are not where he'd left them the night before. Either that (and this would be an entirely separate, and much more terrifying, concern), or he'd simply done something with them and completely forgotten what that "something" might have been.

"Losing my damn mind . . ." he mumbles as he searches the bathroom counter, the wastebasket, the toilet, and the shower. Bill spends the entire morning searching every inch of his bedroom, living room, and kitchen.

He even checks the fridge.

Nothing.

No teeth.

"I'll be double-damned," he says, debating what he should do next.

Like most residents, Bill is nervous about mental health. Nervous that if the doctors and nurses get wind that ol' Bill Rutherford might have spilled some brain cells onto his pillow overnight and is now, as they say, "losing his marbles," those doctors and nurses might just decide it's time for Bill to move out of his cozy apartment in the Greenview building and into one of the generic, sterilized, full-time care rooms of the Medical Center.

No thank you, Bill thinks, working his gums. *Not interested.*

And so, Bill continues to search . . . until there is nothing left *to* search.

Not wanting to explain himself to the other residents, nor to the caretakers who roam the grounds, or the staff of the Community Center and dining hall (and definitely not the doctors or nurses, oh Lord no), Bill instead makes himself a can of soup, sits down at his kitchen table, and hopes to God that the memory of what he'd done with his teeth will come back to him.

After a few minutes, he gets up to check the fridge again. This time, he figures he'd better check the freezer, too.

3

Nurse Mindy Jarvis is tired, but now is not a good time to call out of work.

Besides, she has a lot to do.

All of her normal chores and usual patient rounds, of course, but now she also has to deal with the fallout of two recent—and rather sudden—vacancies.

She considers getting Tatum from his bench to bring him home, but figures he'll be okay a few minutes longer. So, instead, she grabs a couple file boxes from the storage room and heads down to Stan Swanson's old unit to start gathering his stuff for transport. Clothes, books, personal items . . . all of it will need to be boxed, labeled, and sent with the body to the funeral home. If none of the family want to claim any of it while it's still at Autumn Springs, they can do it while making burial arrangements. If nobody shows up to claim the stuff (or claim Stan himself) at the funeral home, it will all be unceremoniously chucked in the trash, and the state will step in to dispose of the body—the corpse will be burned, the ashes boxed and buried in a landfill somewhere.

And just like that: no more Stan Swanson.

Of course, when most residents without family move into Autumn Springs, they sign every horrible form you can think of:

Power of Attorney.

Do Not Resuscitate.

Last Will and Testament.

Upon a resident's death, any bank or stock accounts will be closed and all funds allocated to the Autumn Springs Retirement Home, LLC, per the unit purchase agreements. That is unless another name—bestowed friend or family member—is listed as the beneficiary.

Sometimes Mindy wonders just how much money this place is

raking in off the corpses of the unloved, the deaths of the un-wanted. Following on the heels of this thought, she thinks how Mr. Blackwell has it pretty darn good, and wonders if the slick administrator lines his own pockets while reaping those financial windfalls. Perhaps he gives himself a vague "fee" for each transac-tion, or each closed account.

He sure does dress nice, she thinks. *And has a pretty sweet car, to boot.*

Mindy sighs. It's none of her business and, truth be told, she doesn't really give a shit. She isn't long for this place—no sir, no ma'am. She has big plans for herself, for her future, and Autumn Springs is nothing more than a pit stop on her winding journey. Great things lie ahead, she knows. Great things.

For now though, she has to push her dreams aside and pack up crazy old Stan's bullshit into boxes, then get the cleaning crew in there to do a serious once-over (perhaps even a twice-over) before they can move in the next resident.

With the two flat file boxes tucked awkwardly under one arm, Mindy reaches Stan's room, pushes through the door . . . then stops cold.

"Oh," she says, and is embarrassed when one of the folded boxes she carries slides gracelessly to the floor. She looks down at it, kicks it off of one white sneaker, then addresses the man standing by Stan Swanson's bed. "I'm sorry . . . should I come back?"

"Not at all," Blackwell says.

He calmly folds the two letters he'd been reading, then slides them deftly into his coat pocket. "I'm all done here."

4

Hastings can't believe what he's hearing.

Sitting with him at the dining hall table is a behemoth of a man named Mickey Lake, an effeminate Indian man named Gopi (who has a bushy, handlebar moustache waxed at the tips in an impressive imitation of Hercule Poirot), a tall, lanky, retired professor in a tweed jacket named Miller, and Rose DuBois.

The professor picks at his unusual breakfast: a generous slice of apple pie nested beside a giant scoop of vanilla ice cream, and Hastings wonders momentarily if the man is hypoglycemic with the way he's putting it all down. Miller notices Hastings's stare and gives him a wink.

"Sweet tooth," he says.

Hastings nods, instinctively liking the guy. Liking *all* of them and, if he's being honest with himself, surprised at the mental acuity of the group. To his bemusement (and mild embarrassment), he can't help but wonder why these folks are stuck in a retirement home when they could obviously be living anywhere they wanted.

But then he takes a beat and rethinks it.

Community. Friendship. Activities. Care as needed.

Not such a bad deal.

Hell, in thirty or so years I might be this place's newest resident.

Hastings shakes off the stray thoughts and focuses on what these locals are trying to tell him, every one of them seemingly convinced that the incidents at Autumn Springs are anything but natural, accidental, or suicidal.

According to these nice folks, it's *murder*.

And Hastings is starting to believe them.

"So wait, wait, wait, wait . . ." he says, stalling for time so he can think for a moment, the barrage of new information too much, too fast. "You guys are telling me that somebody dressed up in an alien mask, then climbed into Mr. Swanson's room through a window and told him he'd been chosen by the U.S. government . . . to go see a *spaceship?*"

"Believe me, we know how crazy it sounds," the big guy, Mickey, says with a shrug. "But that's what Stan told us. And now, one night later . . ."

"He's dead," Hastings says, the words bitter in his mouth.

Mickey nods grimly. "And look, Detective, you don't have to take our word for it, or even Stan's word for it, I guess, because there's proof. There's the letters. We all saw them, all of us together, and there's no way Stan did all that."

Hastings thinks about it for a moment, tries to understand—tries to *reason*—why someone would do that to an old man. And, to be frank, why the old man in question would buy into it. Why would he climb eighty feet of steep metal stairs in the middle of the night and jump to his death?

Nothing made sense.

But it did make him curious.

"And Stan even wrote a reply," Rose says. "He told them he was on board with whatever silliness he'd been convinced of. Then he told us, told *all* of us, that he'd had a visit from this alien."

"And you think the alien came back," Hastings says in a lowered voice, wondering what the chief would think of him for saying something so ridiculous out loud. Hell, even *he* thinks he sounds nuts.

But Rose just nods, hands folded primly atop the table. "My hunch is that whoever visited him that first time returned last night, and that's who drew him out of his room."

"If everything you're saying is accurate," Hastings says, turning over the possibilities in his mind, "and assuming Stan was telling you the truth, it means that whoever did all this knew the victim personally. The killer must have known about his obsession with aliens and conspiracies, which means it had to be someone . . ."

He lets the thought trail off, catching himself.

Easy, Detective, he thinks. *You're talking to civilians here, so let's keep those theories to yourself.*

But it's too late. He'd run his mouth off—overly excited by the idea of his suspicions being founded in something real—and now all four of his new friends are staring at him with wide, borderline frightened, eyes.

"Someone who lives here," Rose says, finishing the thought for him.

"Or works here," Gopi adds.

Miller, having finished his dessert and pushed the plate aside, offers a shrug. "It could very well be someone we know. Someone we see every day."

"But hold on," Hastings asks, wanting to turn the conversation. "Let's say you guys are right, that he was tricked into climbing out his window and walking halfway to Maine through dark forest in the freezing cold. Why climb a fire tower? Why jump?"

"Maybe he was threatened?" Mickey suggests.

Hastings nods. He'd had the same thought, of course, but something about it feels off. All that effort by the killer, just to stick a gun to the back of the guy's head?

That would be no fun at all, a voice inside Hastings's mind whispers.

It's a voice he sometimes gives murderers when working a case, when he's trying to get inside the head of the enemy in the hope of understanding them, figuring out what they're going to do next. It's also a voice that makes him feel dirty and a little sick, a voice he sometimes drowns out with one too many shots of whiskey, just so he can have a good night's sleep.

"I don't have an answer for you, Detective, but I'll add this to the pile of loose facts," Gopi says, glancing at the others, hoping for backup. "He seemed really off when we saw him. As if he'd been . . . I don't know, drugged or something."

"He looked high as a kite," Mickey adds, and the others nod.

Miller leans in, taps the tabletop lightly with his knuckles. "Which would play into what happened with Egor."

Rose looks abashed, which gets Hastings's attention, but he turns to Miller. "Sorry, you've lost me. You're suggesting there's a connection?"

"Didn't you hear how Egor died?" Miller says. "Weren't you notified?"

Hastings nods, perhaps just a tad defensively. "Yeah, of course. The officer who took the call knew I'd just been up here for the, you know . . . other thing. He told me it was a heart attack."

Miller leans in, lowers his voice. "He died with an erection, Detective. A big old boner. *Postmortem.*"

Hastings laughs, assuming he's being put on, but the sour expressions on the others' faces gives him pause. "Come on," he says, finding black humor in the realization that talking to four elderly people about murder cases involving aliens and a dead man's erection was absolutely *not* on his bingo card for today. "There's a million reasons something like that could happen."

Miller shakes his head, and Hastings makes a mental note—much like with Rose—not to pander to this man, who had taught for decades as a college professor and likely had more master's degrees than the entire precinct combined.

"Not a million," Miller says. "And you know it. I agree with Gopi. I think he was drugged. Something that would make his bad heart give out. Something sly and sinister. Something that would appear natural to the naked eye."

"It's simple: check his blood and find out," Mickey says. "Isn't that part of a normal, you know, autopsy or whatever?"

"I—" Hastings starts, then shakes his head, now slightly embarrassed, and worse, feeling like he's letting these nice people down. "We didn't do blood work on him. There was no autopsy. And, per his wishes, he was cremated yesterday."

The others sit back in their chairs, absorbing the setback.

"I just keep thinking . . ." Mickey says, then shakes away the thought.

"What?" Miller asks. "Go on, man. This is a safe space." He looks toward Hastings, his eyes asking a question to which there's only one correct answer. "Right, Detective?"

Hastings clears his throat, nods. "Of course."

Mickey glances around the table, then lets out a held breath.

"Mickey?" Rose says, a worried look on her face.

The big man smiles but, studying him more closely, Hastings has the realization that the guy isn't looking so hot. He's perspiring badly, and his face is splotchy and pale.

"I was just thinking," Mickey repeats, gathering his thoughts as he pats his forehead with a dinner napkin, "that, you know, what if this is just the beginning? What if things are gonna get worse before they get better?"

"Eye of the storm," Gopi mumbles.

Miller puts a comforting hand on Gopi's shoulder, and the entire mood of the table fizzles, from the eager sharing of knowledge to a dull depression, a prescient sorrow for things that have happened and things that are yet to come.

"Just so I'm perfectly clear," Hastings says, leaning forward onto his elbows and lowering his voice, making sure he's not overheard by any nearby tables, "you four are telling me that someone is murdering the residents here." He pauses, looks into each face, and sees nothing but steadfast determination. "That there's some sort of serial killer at Autumn Springs."

Rose pats the top of Hastings's hand and gives him a small, sad smile.

"Look who's catching on."

5

After the longer than expected detour (one that included a Western omelet, since they wouldn't hear of him leaving the table without breakfast), Hastings says goodbye to Rose and her friends.

"Listen, I'm taking everything very seriously, and I appreciate what you guys have told me," he says, meaning every word. "At the same time, I'd ask you keep a lot of these theories to yourself. We don't want to scare people, and we don't want a panic. There's still a very good chance this could all be coincidental. You may look back on all this and just think of it as nothing more than a very bad week."

He gives each of them his card, which has his cell phone number and an email address. "Anything else comes up, give me a holler. If you ever feel you're in any immediate danger, call 9–1–1."

Once outside the dining hall, Hastings decides he's going to speak with some of the Medical Center employees before finding Blackwell. He doesn't want to miss the morning shift staff and knows Blackwell will likely be around for most of the day.

As he approaches the building, he notices a small group of residents standing on an adjacent crest, all of them watching something down below and speaking animatedly with one another.

Hastings detours off the path and walks up the gentle slope toward the group. A couple of them notice him coming and prod the others, who turn and watch him approach. A few appear slightly ashamed, while a couple others seem downright angry.

"Good morning," Hastings says, offering his best smile . . . which immediately slides away when he sees what it is they're looking at.

To one side of the Medical Center is a small loading dock, beside which is a paved employee parking lot that can hold maybe six cars—likely for visiting doctors and a few of the more high-priority staff. Parked there now is a white cargo van with the word CORONER splayed across its side—along with the seal of New York State—in bold black letters. Just beyond the parking lot, toward the thick trees and bubbling river, three medical examiner staff members are fighting a gurney over the tall grass. The corpse of Stan Swanson (covered in thick white sheets and strapped down securely) lies atop.

"All right, folks," Hastings says in his well-practiced tone of both friendliness and command. "I think it's best you all move along now. Go have a nice breakfast or just head on home."

A thimble-sized old lady with a frizzy aura of fine white hair and oversized glasses turns toward him, a scowl on her face, and jabs a pointed finger into his chest. "This is America!" she says. "You don't tell us what to do."

"Take it easy, Marie," one man says. He's wearing a dark sport coat, New Balance sneakers, and a frayed baseball cap. "He's with the police."

"I don't care!" Marie answers, and then, much to Hastings's shock, begins sobbing into her hands. "It's so horrible," she moans.

"Jesus," Hastings says, pulling a clean handkerchief from his lapel pocket. "Here, miss. I'm sorry this is upsetting you."

She reaches out and takes it, crying into the fabric.

"He's right," the man in the sport coat says to the others. "We should go. This is morbid."

"Poor Stan," another man says, his face pinging a memory in Hastings's mind.

"Excuse me," Hastings says, and is mildly embarrassed when everyone in the small group turns to look at him, but he keeps his eyes on the man who spoke. "Did you know Mr. Swanson?"

The man shrugs. "We all know each other, more or less."

Hastings nods, his mind working . . . and then he remembers.

"You're Henry, right? You live next door to Angela Forrest."

Henry grins widely, obviously pleased to be remembered. "Sure, that's me." He points a bent finger at Hastings, a crooked smile on his face. "You're a detective, all right," he says. "Got a mind like a steel trap."

Realizing they're not needed, or wanted, a few of the others wander off, most likely taking Hastings's suggestion to have breakfast (which appears to be a rather drawn-out, leisurely affair here at Autumn Springs) or head back home. Henry turns toward two others that have lingered.

"This is Bob and Ellie Nash; they live in Seaview."

"Nice to meet you," Hastings says.

"Awful business," Bob says, his wife nodding along. "Just awful."

"Yeah, quite the rash of misfortune," Henry agrees, all of them looking back toward the parking lot once more, just in time to see Stan Swanson's body being loaded into the rear of the van. "It's like we're cursed or something."

"Did Stan have many friends?" Hastings tries to keep his voice conversational, not wanting to spook the trio.

Henry shrugs, shakes his head. "Before he moved into full-time care, we were friendly enough," he says. "But you know, not a lot of us like hanging around the Med Center."

"Too depressing," Ellie Nash mutters, leaning into her husband for warmth against the cold.

"So, folks in full-time care, they don't get a lot of visitors?"

"I suppose you could say that, but it's not like they're a leper colony," Henry says, showing off a row of strong teeth with a wry smile. "Unless you're in hospice care you're free to do whatever you want, for the most part, so we see them at different activities. And there's volunteers who visit everyone there, so they never feel too isolated. Heck, there's even a schedule in the Community Center where folks can sign up. I've done it myself a few times. But I'd say they're closest with the nurses and the staff that work there. You know, the people they see every day."

The coroner van doors slam closed; the staff climb back inside. Moments later, it pulls out of the parking lot and onto a service road. All four of them watch it go.

"Anyway, nice seeing you again, Detective. Well, not *nice*," Henry says, giving him a nervous look, "under the circumstances. But you know what I mean."

"Sure," Hastings says, and watches as they all turn to leave now that the show's over. "Hey, Henry? One more question?"

Henry turns back, a *there-then-gone* look of irritation on his face.

Likely wants to get out of this miserable weather and have a hot cup of coffee. And I don't blame him.

"Shoot."

"The volunteers you mentioned, is there anyone who sticks out as being especially generous with their time? You know, someone who's always on that schedule you mentioned?"

"You mean like a regular?"

Hastings nods. "Yeah, exactly."

Henry thinks for a moment. "Well, there's a few who would fit the bill . . . but I can think of one guy who's over there nearly every day." Henry shrugs. "Got a good heart, I guess."

"And who would that be?"

"His name is Beauregard," Henry says, absently scratching at the white growth of stubble on his cheek. "But everyone calls him Miller."

6

After their sit-down with Detective Hastings, who Rose thinks is a genuinely good-hearted man (and who probably believes about one-tenth of the things they'd told him), she tries her best to socialize versus isolate.

As she is wont to do in the afternoons, she sits with Tatum by the pond, and he even lets her take him for a walk around the grounds. She knows he enjoys sitting inside the gazebo on the back lawn, and so they rest there for a few minutes before making their way back.

Later, she stops by the Community Center for Trivia Tuesday, which takes place in the large game room, a space filled with several tables and shelves crammed with every board game and card game known to mankind (although many of them are missing a few pieces). Trivia Tuesday isn't a whole lot more than a game of *Trivial Pursuit* on steroids, played with groups instead of individual players.

Her group loses.

In the evening, she and Miller watch three hours of a new crime show they'd become hooked on. She makes a simple pasta dinner for the two of them (topped with her secret homemade tomato sauce) and he brings a bottle of red wine.

Wednesday is Bingo Night, and Rose finds it noteworthy that attendance is much lower than usual. Miller mentioned that a lot of folks were staying inside, afraid to go wandering about on their own, many not even wanting to risk group events. She's deeply saddened by this and hopes that if enough time passes—without any further incidents—folks will go back to their normal routines without worry, or fear.

On Thursday, Rose attends a 10 AM exercise class, which is essentially dancing in place to music from the eighties while a young woman from town—one who grins hard enough to break glass—

barks nonsense she apparently thinks motivational, followed by some light stretching. Rose makes a note to avoid that instructor in the future.

Later that night the facility arranges for a pianist to perform in the main lobby, along with Happy Hour cocktails served from a makeshift bar and passed hors d'oeuvres, which consist primarily of cheese and crackers, deviled eggs, and bruschetta. The pianist is good—not great—but keeps things lively enough and plays all the classics (Rose is partial to Gershwin and can't stop smiling while he performs "Jasbo Brown's Blues" *and* "The Man I Love"). Still, it's a nice gesture by the administrator and likely done in the hopes of cheering the place up a bit. Or, at the least, distracting those who have fallen prey to the creeping paranoia permeating throughout the community like dark, brittle weeds.

Friday, of course, is the day of Sandra's party.

The morning and afternoon are uneventful, and Rose finds herself losing a bit of the tension that had gripped her so strongly earlier in the week.

There have been no more accidents, no more suicides, no more drama. No strange activity in the asylum, and no masked strangers seen creeping around in the dark. The concert, she thinks, went a long way toward calming things down, perhaps giving them all a little perspective on what the real world offers (along with a reminder that the very idea of *murder* should remain firmly outside that reality, left to fiction novels, television shows, and big cities, where it belongs).

She'd texted Miller earlier in the day, and they agreed to go up to Sandra's place together. That way neither one of them will be stuck having to make uncomfortable conversation with whoever else has been invited. Besides, the invitation was very clear about the timing:

7 PM *sharp*.

Rose checks her watch. It's just past 6:30, and she still isn't sure what she wants to wear. She'd be embarrassed to show up in something too formal or too casual.

In the end, she plays it safe and wears a simple black dress, adorned with a necklace strung with pretty golden leaves that her mother left her when she passed. After some brief internal debate, she decides on pumps over sneakers and her favorite black cardigan, blissfully cashmere.

At 6:45, just as Rose is touching up her makeup, there's a light knock at the front door. Her pulse quickens and she feels a flush rise to her cheeks.

It's not a date, Rose DuBois. It's a group get-together, and the man is simply walking with you down the hallway.

Satisfied with the way she looks, Rose checks her face in the mirror one last time, pats her hair, picks a piece of white lint off her sweater, and goes to greet Miller.

7

The Baxter sisters decide that tonight is the night.

Outside, the tired October sun is already setting, the cold gray sky turning a bruise-purple, the horizon a smear of blood.

Despite their desire for privacy, they don't feel the need to wait until early morning (Barbara is still suffering the effects of a cold from the last time, when they marched out to the asylum at 2 AM, the temperature damn near freezing).

And so, in the late evening, the sisters gather their things and wait for darkness.

"I'm quite confident this is the time we'll get the bastard," Bridget says.

"Agreed," adds Barbara.

"Not to be a downer, but if it doesn't work, I think we might want to consider alternatives," Betsie says, staring out the window toward the back lawn, watching the trees slowly blacken, absorbed by dusk's heavy shadow. "Besides, nothing more has happened, has it? Maybe we're all being a bit paranoid about the whole thing."

"Tell that to Henry Barber," Bridget says. "Remember what he told us? Remember how scared he was?"

"True," Barbara adds, then sneezes into the sleeve of her puffy black jacket. "He's fairly confident that someone killed Angela Forrest, and I believe him. Especially after the others."

"Stan Swanson, most of all," Bridget says, nodding. "Brainwashed, most likely."

"Maybe he was hypnotized," Betsie says.

"Or someone used black magic, infiltrated his thoughts."

"That's why we need to get this done. Tonight," Bridget says firmly. "We need to raise Haures from the depths of Hell, have him root out and destroy whatever this evil is, and be done with it."

"A soul for a soul," Betsie says wistfully.

"Amen," Barbara adds, then sneezes twice in quick succession. "Jesus Christ, I say it's dark enough, ladies. Let's get this over with before I sneeze to death."

The other sisters nod in agreement.

It's time.

8

Maureen Stapleton studies herself in the full-length mirror. Her cherry-red sleeveless gown is likely too much for a bunch of old fogeys, but to hell with it. She's gonna flaunt it while she's got it, and at the ripe old age of seventy-eight years, she definitely still has it. That's what proper dieting, daily exercise, and a committed amount of money spent on masks, creams, and—yeah, okay—hair dye can do for a woman.

As she straps on her high heels, Maureen is grateful she doesn't have to walk to the Seaview building for Sandra's soirée. Not at night, anyway. For one thing, she doesn't have to worry about putting on a heavy, cumbersome coat. For another, she doesn't have to worry about being accosted by whoever is out there murdering people.

Theoretically.

But now it's almost time to go, and she's happy with her outfit, the way it holds her curves. Her empty stomach gurgles, then settles. On the off-chance she needs to shit later, she'll claim she forgot something and come back to her own place for a minute—no harm, no foul. She tries on a smile, lowers the wattage a smidge, then nods.

Turning her body to inspect her backside, Maureen glances down at the nearby nightstand and sees the .38 Special handgun resting there, fully loaded. She hasn't opened her curtains after sundown since she saw that creep staring in at her, and the gun hasn't left her bedside for a minute.

She briefly debates stuffing it into her two-thousand-dollar Dolce & Gabbana calfskin handbag (a material extravagance she's never regretted), then decides it's both unnecessary and a bad idea. She'd shown it to Miller, who she hopes to get into her bed at some point in the next century (if he would only stop fawning over the angelic Rose DuBois, who apparently walks on perfumed air as far as Beauregard Mason Miller is concerned). Still, she isn't worried. It's just a matter of time.

Maureen closes her eyes, takes in a deep breath, then lets it out. Looking back at the mirror, she gives her reflection a final once-over, tucks a stray bit of black lace from her bra behind the silky red cloth of her dress, adjusts her tits for good luck, then plucks the .38 Special off the nightstand and shoves it into her handbag.

Better safe than sorry.

SEVEN.

THE PARTY

1

At promptly 7 PM, Rose knocks on the door of Greenview 28.

"Hello, you two!" Sandra squeals, opening the door wide. "Please come in! Welcome, welcome . . ."

Sandra is wearing a sequined silver dress Rose thinks (somewhat cattily, she admits) would be more appropriate for a twenty-one-year-old at a New Year's Eve party than an eighty-two-year-old woman having a dinner party. But who is she to judge?

Rose DuBois, you're becoming an old fuddy-duddy, and if you don't want to become a miserable, lonely old bitty, you best nip that nonsense in the bud.

"Thank you, dear," Rose says. "And thank you for inviting me."

"Of course," Sandra says, then leans closer and lowers her voice. "I think it's past time we all get together and chat."

Rose nods, even as her smile falters. *At a cocktail party?*

Sandra turns from Rose to the man beside her.

"Good to see you, Mickey," she says, then goes up on tiptoes to give him a quick kiss on the lips, and a fleeting thought goes through Rose's mind that there might be something between the two of them. By the way he grimaces at her kiss, however (looking as if he's going to be sick), Rose gets the idea he's not all that interested.

Breaking away from Sandra, Mickey gives a quick wave to the group and heads to the table for a drink.

Rose couldn't help but be surprised when she had pulled open her front door, just about five minutes ago, to see the hulking Mickey Lake standing there instead of Miller.

"Mickey?" she'd asked, eyes wide with surprise. She'd even glanced to either side of him, as if Miller were hiding behind the big man.

Mickey had shrugged, a sheepish expression on his face. "Miller asked me if I'd escort you to the party. He probably wouldn't want me telling you, but he's got some IBS issues. He doesn't sound great, to be honest."

Rose had only stared at him for a moment, unsure what to say.

"You know, Irritable Bowel Syndrome? Probably constipated—"

"Yes, I know what IBS is, Mickey, thank you."

"I told him to drink some fiber, heat up a hot water bottle, get some sleep."

"Sorry . . ." Rose had said, trying to regroup. "Strange he didn't text or call." She'd tried to smile, not wanting to offend her friend. "It's just not like him, is all."

Mickey shrugged again, wiped perspiration off his forehead with a large handkerchief. "He only called me a bit ago. If he's sick, he might not be thinking that clearly. Or, you know, if he's stuck in the bathroom—"

Rose had held up a hand, not needing the image. "It's okay, let me get my things and we'll go."

And now Rose stands alone at the threshold of the small gathering, feeling out of sorts, worried, and—in a petty way she doesn't like one bit—annoyed with Miller. She considers texting him, but he's probably in bed with a hot water bottle on his stomach, and she doesn't need to make a fuss.

Still, she wishes he were here or that she were with him, helping.

He's not your husband, Rose. You can stand on your own two feet, and he's a grown man who can care for himself.

Rose frowns and tells her dark inner voice to crawl back into a hole somewhere . . . but realizes the voice is right. She'll check on Miller tomorrow, and tonight she'll socialize and have a nice time. She knows he'd want her to, and the thought comforts her. So, focusing on the party, Rose takes stock of who else is in the room.

A handful of people are already standing around the apartment (obviously the ones who took the arrival time to heart), holding glasses of wine or, in the case of Bob Nash, a bourbon. Jazz music plays softly from a hidden source, the furniture organized in such a way that no one will be isolated, and the lights are warm and forgiving. Rose notes, with a pang of envy, that the living room is considerably larger than her own, Sandra having sprung for the larger floor plan usually reserved for couples. But it's not as if Autumn Springs would ever turn down a sale.

Other than Bob and Ellie Nash, Rose nods hello to Maureen Stapleton (looking stunning in a tight-fitting red dress), Libby Sue Thompson, and Jim Percy, who Rose thinks looks far too young to be in a retirement community (although word has it the man is pushing seventy years, even if he looks a decade younger).

"Wine?" Sandra asks.

"Maybe a pinot grigio," Rose says, noting the small array of options on the dining table. "Thank you."

There's another knock at the door and everyone—including Rose—is amused to see Gopi enter with Mary Reynolds at his side. Sandra hustles over to say hello, handing Rose her glass of wine as she passes by.

Once the last two guests are ushered inside and given drinks, their host addresses the room. "Welcome, everyone!" Sandra says, tapping the side of her wine glass with a small dessert spoon. "I'm so glad you're all here. I have yummy appetizers in the oven, so if it gets too stuffy let me know, and I'll crack a window. There's lots of wine, and booze, and even a few beers in the fridge. As you've seen, there's more food on the table here, so don't be shy. Make sure you eat and drink while you can; you'll need to keep up your strength for the games I have planned for later." Without waiting for a response, she plucks up her smartphone from the kitchen counter and taps a few buttons. Immediately, the music goes up a notch.

Impressive, Rose thinks, hoping that whatever Sandra has planned won't be anything too ridiculous. *Stop worrying and have some fun for once.*

For once agreeing with her inner voice, Rose wades deeper into the room to mingle, intent on enjoying the night, whatever it may bring.

2

Mickey had initially decided to bail on the party.

He hadn't been feeling so hot lately.

At first, he thought maybe he had a bug. Virus, or something. But he didn't have a temperature. There was no cough or scratchy throat. He just felt . . . *off.*

He'd been eating okay. Plenty of appetite. But the last few days his head felt fuzzy and his heart would do an occasional rumba deep in his chest, or he'd wake in the middle of the night sweating profusely and thinking there was someone standing beside his bed, watching him.

It never turned out to be anything but shadows, of course, but the last couple nights he'd slept with the lights on, just to avoid that middle-of-the-night terror from happening again. It isn't that he can't take care of himself, and he highly doubts any killer would want to go toe-to-toe with him . . . but he also gets the sense that— assuming there actually *is* someone behind all this—they're going about it a different way.

Subtle.

Like with Egor and Stan.

Making it all look like misfortune instead of murder.

And maybe, just maybe, that's exactly what it is.

Misfortune.

Buckets of it.

Making things worse, he'd spent the last couple days feeling anxious, feverish. Constantly sweating. If he were being honest with himself, it felt eerily similar to how it had been taking steroids for a couple years near the end of his football career: overly amped, barbed-wire tense, and dangerously quick to anger. Prone to violence. Yesterday afternoon, he'd shocked himself by throwing a remote control at the television hard enough to crack the screen when his Yankees lost in extras to the Tigers.

After the game ended, he spent most of the night in the bathroom, suffering from a constant, dehydrating, painful flow of diarrhea that had him popping Imodium tablets like they were breath mints. The last few days his stomach had felt churlish, acidic. He figured it was something he ate but, for the most part, he'd made his own meals this past week and nothing stuck out as being an obvious culprit. Because of the stomach issues, the only things he'd eaten in the last forty-eight hours were toast and water, crackers and Sprite, and a couple plain, thoroughly cooked chicken breasts for dinner, seasoned with nothing but his tabletop salt and pepper shakers.

This morning, however, he'd woken up feeling better. His head was still a little funny, and there was a twitch in his eye he didn't like, and he *did* punch a hole in the wall when he stubbed his toe on the goddamn bedpost while getting up to take a leak at 6 AM, and sure, he'd hardly slept last night, and when he *did* sleep he woke up in a pool of cold sweat, his sheets and blankets kicked to hell and his heart knocking against his rib cage like there was a coked-up woodpecker in his fucking chest, but . . .

But.

All in all, he felt slightly better than the day before.

And so, he decided to come to the party after all.

Before he took a shower and got dressed, he cooked himself a steak—lots of salt and pepper to prep the meat, a fat slice of butter in the pan—and wolfed it down, wanting to fill his belly so he wouldn't get lightheaded after a couple glasses of wine. Knowing Sandra, he'd have trouble keeping his glass empty, so he was planning ahead.

After the steak, he got dressed (hating the sweat already beading his bald head and neck), popped a pre-party Imodium—just in case—and had a nice evening stroll while walking from Seaview to Greenview, the night crisp but windless, the cool October air a balm on his overheated skin.

He was just entering the building when he got the call from Miller, asking him to swing by Rose's place and escort her to the party, that he'd taken—quite suddenly—ill.

"No problem. You just take care," Mickey had said, before instructing him to drink a glass of fiber substitute and hug a hot water bottle.

Rather than wait for the rickety elevator, he took the stairs to the second floor. When he came out of the stairwell, he saw Gopi kissing Mary Reynolds in the hallway. He purposely pretended to not notice, and turned the opposite direction to collect Rose.

By the time they arrived at Sandra's door, Mickey wasn't feeling so good, wondering if maybe whatever Miller had was contagious.

He waved to the rest of the group and went for a drink, praying he could hold it together a couple hours, a small part of him beginning to worry there might be something going on with him he didn't fully understand.

After a few minutes, Sandra strolled up next to him. "Hey," she'd said quietly, whispering the suggestion of spending the night in her bed.

"Not tonight," he replied bluntly, perhaps cruelly. He was beginning to feel stifled in the black sport coat, and the idea of sex made his already churning stomach flip nastily. Feeling bad about letting her down, he pecked her once on the cheek, then mumbled in her ear, "Sorry, I just need a drink."

As he filled a glass with red wine, he thought again about that cracked television screen, about the fist-sized hole he'd left in the wall, and hoped he wouldn't do anything tonight to embarrass himself.

Or worse, hurt anyone.

3

Sandra's unit at 28 Greenview is on the south side of the building, facing the well-lit walkway and courtyard, directly across from the hulking Community Center. Sandra's pleased about her location (as well as the extra square footage of her unit's larger footprint) because her views are so much nicer than those that look north toward the back lawn, the weathered gazebo, the wall of trees, and that horrid abandoned asylum, which she thinks looks more like an animal pen than a place where they once cared for the sick or dying (albeit decades ago).

If she stands at her bedroom window and looks east, she can see the little park with the koi pond, and she's still far enough from the train that she hardly ever hears it passing, even if some residents complain about the noise (seemingly *all* the time).

A night like tonight—with all the lights blazing and people having fun, the window cracked to let the chill night air seep in and the chatter of a party leak out—makes her feel *alive*, like she'd felt as a young girl, living in a studio apartment in the city, taking classes at NYU. Admittedly, she gets off a little on the idea of other residents walking by on the path below, looking up at the bright windows and hearing the bright voices and wondering who is throwing a *party* at Autumn Springs and why the heck weren't they invited? Not that Sandra is sadistic, or cruel, or that she desires attention (although she sort of does); it's because it reminds her that, even at seventy-eight years old, she is still a *person*. Someone who likes to have fun, to flirt, to sleep around . . . to host a party.

After all, it's not her fault she and her friends aren't just sitting around doing crossword puzzles, watching the news, and waiting to die.

And if she enjoys broadcasting that feeling to the rest of the community, that's her right. Besides, perhaps the joy will be contagious, inspire others to host their own parties, or do something that makes them feel just a tiny bit younger. Perhaps it will remind them that age doesn't define you, that life is still a vibrant beast, full of light and music and laughter and friends and love and sex and sure, yes, okay . . . *danger.*

Because that's the shit that makes life worth living.

So now, as she glances out the window to see a group of dark-coated residents coming out of the Community Center and glancing up toward her apartment, she gives a little wave, and a smile, and then turns back toward the vibrancy of her guests, her full-of-life world, relishing the warmth it gives her heart to see them all here.

She spares a look for Mickey, the hulking bear that he is, and recalls—with a pleasant shudder between her legs—their last night together, how wonderfully large he felt in her arms and inside her. After that night a few weeks ago, she'd hoped it might develop into something more, something deeper.

But then the "incidents" happened. Or, if one were to believe the rumors, the *murders.* She knows that Rose DuBois and her constant companion, Miller (he of the somewhat suspicious, last-minute stomach bug), have been sniffing around, and later on she's going to insist they spill the beans on what they've discovered. Her, and the others gathered tonight, deserve to know the truth. It's a topic relevant to every person here, some of whom, she knows for a fact, agree with Rose: that there's a killer on the loose at Autumn Springs.

But first she's going to have them all play a game. One she hopes will get everyone in the mood, so to speak, to have a frank conversation about it all.

It's a quirky little game called *Murder in the Dark.*

And it's about to start.

4

Rose was never very good at mingling, which is why she prefers the company of close friends, where she doesn't have to watch every word she says or worry about coming off as cold or unfriendly (something she's been accused of in the past). As she sips her wine and approaches Gopi, one of the only partygoers she knows well, she feels the bitter sting of not having Miller by her side and doesn't know how to feel about that . . . void. She's not one to feel dependent on anyone, so her initial response to missing him is annoyance at herself and an unfair anger with him. Another part of her, however, wonders if it means something more, something deeper that she hasn't fully examined yet.

If only she could trust that deeper feeling.

If only she could trust *him*.

"Hello, Rose," Gopi says, one arm possessively wrapped around Mary's waist. "Heard Miller is sick."

"I heard the same," Rose says. "How are you, Mary?"

"I'm fine," Mary says with a light giggle that Rose forces herself to grin at, the other option being to lightly slap the silly woman on the cheek. "Say, did you hear about Gopi's little adventure the other night?"

Rose nods. "I sure did. Hard to know what it all means, though."

"Well, there's not much mystery to it anymore, right?" Gopi says, sipping a second scotch and already slurring his words, albeit mildly. "I mean, it was the sisters the whole time."

Rose's eyes flick to Mary, then she turns to see if anyone else is listening in. Given the size of the room, Rose figures most of them are, even if they're pretending not to. "Seems that way," she replies, not wanting to break their word to the Baxter sisters about keeping quiet on the matter. "But that's talk for another time."

"Ooh, are you guys talking about the Baxter sisters?"

Rose turns to see Libby Sue Thompson at her elbow.

The gossip queen of Autumn Springs.

"Not really—" Rose starts, trying, and failing, to cut Libby Sue off at the pass.

"I heard they've been up to some strange things," Libby Sue says breathlessly, her snowball-pale cheeks flushed red with wine. Her blue eyes bulge beneath thick eyeglasses, and her floppy mound of dull yellow hair shakes with urgency as she speaks, as if the woman were wearing a wig that wasn't secured correctly atop her head. The wine in her glass splashes dangerously as she gesticulates with excitement. "Some people are saying it's their fault that folks are dying so strangely." She leans in closer, lowers her voice to a half-hearted whisper that Rose is certain the whole room can hear without effort. "They say the Three B's have put a curse on Autumn Springs," she hisses, eyes big as saucers and blazing. "I've even heard they conjured up something to take out their enemies. Something not natural, something not even *human.*"

Gopi laughs, but Rose can sense the tension lying beneath it. The fear.

"Or maybe they're nothing but serial killers. Madwomen!" Mary says, showing the whites of her eyes in a way that makes Rose think *she* might be the one with too many nuts in her fruitcake.

I wish Miller were here. He'd know how to squash this madness, how to put Libby Sue in her place without her even knowing he'd done it. For the second time that night, Rose wonders if she should go check on him.

He's just a few doors down. I could be there and back before—

"Okay, everyone!" Sandra announces, once again pinging the side of her half-empty wine glass with the small silver spoon, quieting the room. "It's time to play a game," she says, then grins madly. "I hope you're not afraid of the dark."

5

"Everyone find a chair, if you please," Sandra says, bustling about the room to adjust furniture. "If my math is right, there should be enough seating for everyone."

All the guests eventually do find a place to sit, many of them mumbling with excited curiosity. Sandra opens her music app, turns down the jazz a touch, then picks up a top hat she'd brought in from the bedroom—a relic she'd purchased at a downtown thrift store years ago—and holds it aloft toward her audience.

"In this hat are playing cards. One for each of you," she says. "I hope you all brought your reading glasses . . . anyway, one of them is an ace. Whoever draws that card is the Killer."

"Oh, really, Sandra—" Rose starts, but Sandra hushes her.

"I'm aware it's topical, Rose," Sandra says. "But c'mon, a little levity couldn't hurt?"

Rose grimaces, but holds back any additional comments.

"The rest of them are face cards—kings, queens, and jacks." Sandra looks quickly to each of her guests, wearing a sly grin. "The potential victims! Now, once you all have your card—and don't show anyone else, of course—we'll turn out the lights."

Mary, sitting next to Gopi on the couch, sits forward, an anxious look on her face. "Oh, I don't know—"

"When all the lights are out," Sandra interrupts, raising her voice to override further protestations, "the person who has the ace will silently move about the room and, well . . . *kill* people."

"This seems awfully childish," Libby Sue says nervously, and a few others mutter in agreement.

"No, no . . . I've played this before," Jim says. "It's fun. Just don't trip over anything."

"Everyone needs to spread out, and no holding hands!" Sandra says, shooting an over-the-top glare at Gopi and Mary. "I'll set a timer on my phone and, after five minutes, we'll turn the lights back on and see who's dead and who's alive."

"How does he . . . or she . . . kill people?" Maureen asks, clutching uneasily at her handbag.

"It's simple, you guys. Whoever is the Killer, you just go up to people and tap them on the shoulder. Or, if you want, you can whisper, 'You're dead.' But you can only kill *four* of us, so that's where your murder spree ends. We need a few people to survive or the game won't work. As for the victims, once you've been tapped, you must not say *anything*, then you need to lie down and play dead—"

"Lie down, hell," Bob Nash says jovially, and several others nod in agreement. "If I lie down on this floor, I ain't getting back up."

"I think I'll just sit on the couch," Libby Sue adds. "The floor is much too hard."

Sandra scowls at Libby Sue, then her eyes jump to Mickey, who looks pale and sweaty. He's slumped in his chair, staring at his hands.

Is he mumbling to himself? Sandra thinks, then pushes him from her mind for the moment. She's clinging desperately to her smile and her patience—a feat becoming more and more difficult as her guests push back on her (brilliant) game idea—and turns her attention back to Libby Sue, who is being a goddamn grouch about the whole thing.

"Fine, then just . . . stand still and don't talk or move."

"Then what?" Rose asks.

"When the lights come back up," Sandra continues, "whoever has survived will guess who the killer is. Whoever guesses right wins the game. Now, let's push all the seats and stuff against the walls. The bedroom is not off-limits—don't worry, I've put all my lingerie away—or you can hide in closets, the bathroom, wherever."

Rose takes a deep breath as the others stand and begin pushing chairs and end tables toward the walls. She looks at Gopi. "I don't like this."

But Gopi just looks back at her and winks. "Don't worry," he says. "If I kill you, I'll be quick about it."

6

The Baxter sisters are inside the old asylum for the last time.

The candles are lit. The magic circles are just as they left them, their chalk-drawn symbol of incantation unharmed.

Barbara produces the *athame*, the black-handled blade that will cut open the door between their worlds—like birthing a baby via C-section—and let Haures through into the earthly realm.

During their last two attempts, they had managed to draw some power from the netherworld, creating just enough energy to establish the door. But it had taken all of their meager power—and their constant flow of incantations—to hold it, even for a few minutes, which was not nearly enough time (and not enough energy drawn from the five points of power: air, fire, earth, water, spirit) to complete the ritual and let them to open the portal fully, allowing the demon to pass through and remain.

So tonight they start earlier, and even with Barbara's cold they all feel much more energized and determined than they had during the previous two attempts, motivated by the fact that, since their last try, another incident had occurred.

Another resident dead.

They're running out of time.

Bridget can't help think back to how scared Henry Barber was the day after Angela's murder, the poor man having heard, through the thin walls, the sounds of the killer's brutal attack. How he'd told them, scared out of his mind, that he was convinced someone had killed Angela Forrest.

"I mean, who's next?" he had babbled, sitting in their living room, sipping from a mug of strong coffee while they offered him what meager magic they could, which boiled down to a crude hexafoil and a store-bought amulet, one they'd painstakingly spoken a spell over.

Bridget sincerely hopes they had kept the man safe. Sure, they made a little money, and perhaps they jested a bit too much about him when they were alone (mostly due to their own nerves), but she didn't like seeing anyone so frightened.

She didn't like feeling so frightened.

But now, tonight, they will summon the demon—the sixty-fourth spirit from the key of Solomon, Great Duke of Hell, the fiery-eyed cat, Haures—who will strike down the killer and accept the bargain: once their corporeal forms cease to function, their spirits departing this plane of existence, Hell will have one of their souls for eternity.

Bridget prays it will be hers.

For the next thirty minutes, the three sisters fill the empty, ruined building with their chants, candles flaring, the circle glowing dimly, humming with power.

They are close . . . so close.

It's Betsie, in the end, who breaks the spell.

"Do you smell something?" she asks.

Barbara and Bridget, already growing tired—and annoyed at being jarred from their meditative incantations—look at her sharply.

"What's wrong with you?" Barbara asks, sweat dripping down her back from exertion. "We can't stop now."

Bridget is about to snap at her sister as well . . . then sniffs the air. "Wait . . . I smell it, too."

Barbara snorts and snuffles, then shrugs. "With this cold I can't smell a thing. What is it?" Then her eyes widen with excitement. "Wait! Is it sulfur? The scent of Hell? Should we cut open the portal?"

Betsie and Bridget exchange a look across the chalk circle but don't reply. After a moment, Betsie stands, sniffing at the air more urgently. She moves toward a dark corner of the destitute, dusty lobby. "No, sister. Not sulfur. I think . . . it smells like . . ."

Bridget also stands, eyes widening. She glares at the candles, at the doors.

"What is it? What's wrong?" Barbara asks, small tendrils of fear slithering up her spine, her alarm growing as she notes the look on her sisters' faces.

Fear.

Bridget meets her gaze. "It smells like gasoline."

7

The curtains have been pulled shut.

The cards handed out.

The lights turned off.

The apartment is absolutely, entirely, dark.

Rose hears breathing; some of the others shuffle around nearby.

There's a giggle from the bedroom.

Likely Gopi getting fresh with his date, she thinks, refusing to be unnerved by the complete darkness, by the presence of some folks who are friends, and others, if she's being honest, who may as well be strangers.

They'd all spread out in the dark. Some tiptoed into the kitchen. Some crept into the bedroom. Rose thought it would be a good idea to stand behind the gray club chair she'd been sitting in, the one that faced the living room from the corner. She noted the small gap when Sandra was passing around the hat and tucked herself behind it once the lights were turned out. She had to give it a little nudge to make room, but she takes comfort at having a barrier between herself and whoever is wandering around in the dark, tapping shoulders, whispering into ears that they're "dead."

She's not sure where Mickey went off to. For all she knows he's the Killer, so probably best not to stay close to anyone. Admittedly, Rose is slowly becoming amused with the game, at hearing the nervous laughter and occasional whispers from the guests. It reminds her of playing hide-and-seek as a little girl, when she'd—

Somebody a few feet away knocks into a table and curses. *Sounds like that Jim fellow. And if he's moving around, he might be the Killer.*

But then someone else bumps into the chair she's hiding behind. There's an annoyed grunt, followed by the sound of heavy breathing coming from right in front of her. The body moves to the side of the chair. Hands pat against the wall only inches from her shoulder, as if searching for a light switch.

"Too dark, too dark," the person says quietly, and she immediately recognizes it as Mickey. "Goddamn . . ." he mutters under his breath. "I need to get out of here."

Rose almost says something to him. Is he sick? Perhaps he's too embarrassed to say so in front of his friends? Maybe she should—

"Hey!" a woman yells, and the sound cuts through the dark like lightning. "Watch what you're touching."

Maureen?

I guess someone missed a shoulder, Rose thinks, and smiles at the silliness of it all—as if they were children instead of grown adults, copping feels like teenagers.

"Someone's lying on the floor," another voice says. Libby Sue, perhaps. "What if they're really hurt?"

"No one's really hurt; now be quiet," Sandra orders. Rose thinks she's somewhere near the kitchen.

More random shuffling and bumping noises come from the spacious apartment, and Rose figures the five minutes must be almost up by now. Which is fine with her; she's tired of standing behind this chair, she—

A hand paws her head, her shoulder.

Tap.

Rose almost screams, but then takes a breath, lets it out. Her heart pounds in her chest, beating much too fast for her liking. But that's the game.

I guess I'm dead.

Whoever touched her moves away, and she wonders how they missed running into Mickey, who she doesn't hear anymore.

"Okay, five minutes are up; everyone stop!" Sandra announces happily. "That means you, too, Killer."

There are some lighthearted, if anxious, chuckles. Mumbled voices.

Seconds pass.

"Sandra?" someone says. "The lights?"

"I know, they're . . ."

Rose hears the muted click-click of a switch flipping up and down.

Up and down.

"They're not coming on."

"Not coming on?"

That's Mickey.

The voices in the room begin to grow agitated.

When Maureen speaks, Rose thinks she sounds a little . . . hysterical.

"Turn on the lights, Sandra," Maureen says, her voice high-pitched, as if panicked. "Someone's over here with me!"

"I'm trying!" Sandra snaps, sounding a little nervous herself. Rose hears other switches being tried, perhaps a floor lamp.

"Careful!" Gopi says.

"Open the curtains," Rose says to whoever can hear her, trying to keep her (*dead, I'm dead*) voice steady. "That will let in some light."

"I got it," Bob Nash says from across the room, and one set of curtains is thrown open . . .

Showing nothing but more dark.

"Where are the pathway lights?" Libby Sue.

"Okay, enough of this shit. I want out of here." Maureen.

Possibly . . . *crying?*

"Relax, folks. I'll get the front door. The hallway light will help," Jim says, but Rose can't place his location. He sounds far away.

Not near the front door at all.

"I'll get it," Sandra says.

A few seconds later, Rose hears the sound of the handle turning, the creak of the door opening.

But no light.

"The hallways are dark . . ." Sandra says stoically, as if stunned.

"Don't fucking touch me, I said!" Maureen wails. She's closer now. Trying to get to the front door. Trying to get out.

"I have a gun, damn you!" she announces, near sobbing.

"Jesus!"

"Maureen, relax!"

"Did she say a gun?"

"Stop it. Stop this—"

Then Rose hears Mickey.

"He's here!" Mickey screams, followed immediately by the sound of heavy footsteps tromping around the room. Something crashes. "He's here! The killer's here!"

"Oh my God!"

Someone falls, cries out in pain.

"Everyone just relax!" Sandra yells.

The room erupts with a gunshot. A photographic flash fills the apartment, freeze-framing its panicked occupants—eyes wide, mouths agape. There's a heap of clothes (someone's body?) lying on the carpet.

A woman screams.

Rose covers her ears, shuts her eyes tight. She cries out: "Stop it!"

And then the fire alarm goes off.

8

"I think we need to leave," Betsie says.

"Agreed. Something's wrong. Blow out the candles," Bridget says. "We'll come back later . . . or tomorrow."

"This might be a waste of time," Barbara sighs.

"You may be right—" Betsie begins, then gasps when there's a loud pounding on the front double doors.

Barbara shrieks, and all three sisters put their hands over trembling hearts.

"Who is that?" Betsie whispers.

"Probably just a staff member wondering why they see lights in the building," Bridget says. She puts on a weak smile. "Looks like we've been caught, ladies."

Betsie tries to smile back but feels watery inside, her flesh crawling with fear. "I'll just put out the candles."

"Fine, and I'll have a talk with our friend," Barbara replies, and walks quickly to the abandoned asylum's front doors.

As the last candle is extinguished, the room turns pitch black. Other than the dull lines of moonlight leaking through the boarded windows and doors, the sisters are swallowed by the dark.

Barbara reaches the doors, agitated that their session has been interrupted (and privately frustrated that their summoning doesn't seem to be working). She's afraid for herself and her sisters, and that fear grows claws as she goes to meet whoever has frightened them, eager to give an earful to the asshole who thinks it's funny to scare three old ladies.

With this in mind, she tugs hard at the doors.

They rattle loudly, but don't budge an inch.

She pulls again, knowing damn well that the clipped security chain was left completely off when they entered, so there's no reason the doors shouldn't open.

And yet.

"Bridget?" Barbara says, tugging again and again.

She can plainly hear the chain rattling against the metal handles, but it won't release. It's as if someone had come by, knowing they were inside, and locked it.

"What's wrong?" Bridget asks, sidling up next to her.

"It won't open," Barbara replies, trying to keep her voice level, not wanting to show her panic. "Do you suppose it's stuck?"

Bridget grips the handle and yanks hard. When the door hardly moves, she shakes it like one might throttle a naughty child. "Oh, come now . . ." she says, voice cracking with fear.

"Sisters!"

Barbara and Bridget turn back toward the dark room. They can barely make out Betsie, who stands in the middle of the open space, atop the incantation circle. One of her ghostly arms is raised, pointing toward a far wall.

The sisters look, and now they see—see much better, in fact, than they could only a moment ago. Because now there are flames flickering at the edges of one of the boarded-up windows.

As they watch in stunned horror, the flames crawl up the old wood, orange fingers reaching high enough—in mere seconds—to tickle the spiderweb-clogged beams of the ceiling.

Before they can react there's another sound at the doors, just a few feet from where they stand.

Someone is laughing.

"I'd move back if I were you," a high-pitched voice says.

Then there's a *splashing* sound, and the sharp stink of gasoline fills their nostrils. Both women step quickly away.

"Bridget—" Barbara breathes, and clutches her sister's arm.

Within moments the front doors are creeping with flame. Smoke begins filling the long, cold room. Behind them, more planked windows are catching fire, one by one, as if the person outside is walking gleefully around the building, igniting each gasoline-soaked window as they go.

All three sisters move toward the center of the room, clinging to each other in a tangled mass of limbs and black lace.

Betsie is crying. "Oh no . . ."

"It's okay," Barbara says through tears. "Someone will see the flames. Someone will come."

"Help!" Betsie cries, but they all know yelling is futile. There's no one close enough—other than the one lighting the building on fire, of course—to hear them.

"Sisters, be strong," Bridget says. She kisses them each on the cheek. "Come, we're so close. If . . . if the worst happens, we'll know we've tried our best."

"I'm so scared," Betsie mutters, eyes wide and wild. "But yes, let's finish if we can. I love you both very much."

"I suppose we don't need to relight the candles," Barbara adds, giving them both a brave, sad smile.

"We have all the fire we need. Now, let's continue," Bridget says confidently. "Help will come." She holds out her hands and they are quickly gripped by her sisters, the three of them standing atop the intricately drawn circle.

They resume the ritual.

As the Baxter sisters hold hands and chant, an incandescent light comes from the floor—from the incantation circle. Flames curl inward and slither across the ceiling. Smoke fills the brightening interior like rushing storm clouds, and the heat begins to eat the cold, warming their cheeks and hands.

Through their recitations, Bridget silently prays to the spirits of the earth that she is right. That someone will save them. *And if not, then I will return from Hell as a vengeful spirit, and I will find this evil creature . . .*

As flames pluck eagerly at the edges of her dress and lick at the ends of her hair, she gently takes the black-handled athame from her sister's shaking hand, grips it tightly in her own.

. . . and I will cut out their black, beating heart.

9

Red flashing emergency lights from the hallway pulse through the apartment's open door. The *WEE-OO WEE-OO WEE-OO* of the fire alarm blasts through the building, effectively deafening its (mostly) hearing-impaired residents.

Rose stumbles out from behind the chair, trips, and falls to a knee. Grimacing, she gets up and makes her way to the front door. Shadows pass by in the hallway—other residents fumbling their way toward the foyer. As Rose nears the apartment door to join them, a giant body storms past her, knocks her back to the ground; this time she lands on all fours, a knife of pain shooting into one knee. She catches a glimpse of Mickey's large frame bursting past just as she hits the carpet. Almost immediately, however, firm hands are gripping her by the arm. Miller kneels down.

"Rose!"

Miller!

"I'm fine. Help me up."

Miller helps her to her feet and together they stumble blindly down the hallway, where ghost-like shadows, eerily lit by the emergency lighting, move like wraiths escaping purgatory.

"If the power's out, the elevator's out," Miller says in her ear, putting one protective arm between her and the shuffle of other residents.

"The stairs," Rose says, and they make their way toward the foyer and the stairway leading to the first floor.

"I can't use the stairs!" someone yells, but Rose can't make out the identity of one of the older residents, standing with their walker as others push roughly by. "I'm going home," they say stubbornly, apparently deciding they'd rather burn than deal with any more of this bullshit. Rose hardly blames them.

Miller follows another couple through the stairwell door, and they all slowly make their way down. After a few steps, someone trips and tumbles, then screams out in pain. Rose is certain she hears the *crack* of a snapping bone.

"Jesus Christ," Miller mumbles.

Rose nods but says nothing, concentrating on each step so she doesn't meet the same fate.

They reach the landing, where several residents are trying to help the fallen woman, who doesn't appear to be responding, then all of them are inching down the stairs to the first floor and the emergency exit. The fire alarm wails and wails, and Rose fights a sharp rise of claustrophobia while climbing down the dark, crowded stairwell, bodies pressing behind her, nearly causing her to misstep.

When they reach the bottom, she does her best to let those pressing around her get through the door first, before she and Miller follow, making their way into the blissfully cool night air, onto the vast swath of the back lawn.

She sees the fire immediately.

The old asylum is an inferno.

10

Outside, a crowd has gathered.

The fire alarm has been silenced.

At some point, power to the Greenview Apartments building had been restored.

The blaze at the base of the tree line is arched high into the night sky, reaching twice the size of the asylum itself, which must have been fine kindling for whatever spark caused it to catch fire.

Some of the trees have also begun to burn, and sirens are closing in from a distance as the local fire department makes its way toward Autumn Springs.

Rose and Miller walk as far as the gazebo, where they watch in silence as the building burns. Miller turns to look at her, studies the red glow reflecting off Rose's wet cheeks, giving her an ethereal beauty. A luminescence.

He reaches out and takes her hand.

She doesn't pull away.

Instead, she leans into him, and he puts an arm around her shoulders. Many residents are crying, some are yelling for others to *get back*. A few are laughing, projecting thoughts of *good riddance* to the eyesore.

"Miller, did you hear what happened upstairs? A gun went off. . . ."

"I don't know, Rose. All the lights went out, I woke up, then I heard what I thought was a gunshot. I jumped out of bed to come get you the hell out of there." He squeezes her shoulders. "We'll find the others, find out if everyone's okay."

"Mickey ran out ahead of me," Rose says, not wanting to describe how he'd knocked her down, how he'd been talking to himself.

"Chaos," Miller says. "I don't know what's gotten into everybody."

"They're scared," Rose says. "I'm scared."

"Yeah," he says, nodding. "Me, too."

Rose wonders if there's someone lying dead or wounded in Sandra's apartment.

I just hope everyone's safe. . . .

Then she recalls what Gopi had told them about the Baxter sisters, and the old asylum. She looks up at Miller—half his face is in deep shadow, the other half flickering with orange light. "Do you think the sisters are in there?" She nods toward the fire. "Doing that silly ritual?"

Miller's eyes widen. "I don't know. I suppose it's possible. Didn't Gopi say they'd used candles the other night? Maybe they burned the place down somehow."

"Or summoned a demon," she says, only partially in jest.

"Sure, sure," Miller agrees. "And that right there is a doorway to Hell. Flames from the lake of fire."

"Don't say that," Rose says, and rests her head against his shoulder.

Ten minutes later, fire trucks and ambulances have made their way to the dirt service road between the railroad tracks and the Greenview building. Clusters of firemen run hoses toward the blaze.

As the residents look on, the asylum's roof caves in. Sparks fly up into the night. Gasps and groans come from the large gathering, watching from a distance.

Rose looks around. To her relief, she sees Gopi and Mary, his arm around her as she sobs. Rose meets his eye for a moment, and he nods.

I'm okay.

She nods back, and continues scanning the crowd. She sees Mr. Blackwell—wearing an expression of horror—talking animatedly with some of the firemen. For the first time since she's known him, he's not wearing a suit. Just jeans and a leather jacket. She wonders, absently, how he got here so fast.

She does *not* see Maureen Stapleton, or the Nashes, or Mickey, or Sandra, or Libby Sue, or Jim Percy, and she prays that no one was hurt tonight.

"I hope the sisters weren't in there," Rose says.

"If they were, it's all over now," Miller says quietly. "Hell, I don't even know if it matters anymore."

Rose grips his unshaven chin in her fingers, and gently turns him to face her. His eyes are ablaze. A tear glistens on one cheek.

"Miller, what are you talking about?"

"I don't know, Rose. I guess it just feels like this whole place is burning. Not just the old asylum, but all of Autumn Springs. It's like we're all on fire." He turns away to watch as a sea of sparks float into the night sky, adding to the stars. "And we just don't know it yet."

EIGHT

BODY COUNT

1

Hello.

I don't think we've met.

No . . . definitely not. I never forget a face.

Although, that can't be right, can it?

I mean, at some point or other . . . I've met everyone.

Anyway, I'm goddamn freezing. It's cold down here in the Morgue.

Oh, I apologize. I mean *Storage.*

Yes, ma'am, it's chilly. Cold as a witch's tit, am I right?

Although, I can think of three witches that aren't so cold anymore.

Crispy, yes. Blackened, like chicken left too long on a grill.

Nothing but ashes now, scattered to the wind.

Just like that . . .

No more sisters. No more witches.

Of course, you were just an innocent bystander. Took a tumble down the stairs during the mass exodus, did we? Yeah, that neck looks good and broken. Good lord, the way your bone is pushing against the skin . . . like it's pitching a tent. Surprised that sucker didn't punch right through, but you got some pretty flexible flesh there, so . . .

Small blessings, I suppose.

But again, and I can't make this clear enough: not my fault. Seriously, don't blame me from the afterlife, because you were a clear-cut accident.

Unlike the others.

Yes . . . those were planned. *Extensively* planned and, if you'll pardon the double entendre, executed.

Hmm? What's that? You died because the power went out?

I could see that argument, sure. But do you blame God if you fall down at night and crack your damn skull? No, of course not.

Look, I'm not going to debate you on this. Besides, you're just a shriveled, ice-cold, stiff little corpse now, so you shouldn't be talking anyway.

That said . . . did I use my stolen skeleton key (you know, the one that says *DO NOT DUPLICATE*—whoops) to enter the janitor's closet, wrench open the electric box, and throw the main breaker for the entire west side of the campus?

Yeah, okay. That was me. But I needed the confusion. I needed the *chaos*. And, in my defense, there *are* security lights in the halls and stairwells. Dim, hellishly red emergency lights, sure, but they did come on.

Anyway, water under the bridge, am I right? And besides, I have good news:

You're not going to be down here alone much longer.

The long play has been a gas; don't get me wrong. At first, I was just happy to get another one under my belt. It's been *years*, lady. Haven't had a kill since I was back in the big city, playing my games with the homeless folks at the shelter. I've been good for a while now. Honest! An old-fashioned, fabric-of-society contributor.

But I got *itchy*, you know?

And when I got here . . . gosh, it was almost too easy.

Like a box of chocolates.

But I took my time. I *planned*. Stan, for instance, was complex, but also a lot of fun. A perfect kill for the Halloween season, what with the mask and all, am I right?

And Egor . . . well, at least he died happy.

But time, I fear, is running short, and I must accelerate things.

And besides, the cupboards of my secret pharmacy are nearly empty. That haul of synthetics was tricky to acquire. It's amazing what one can find on the internet these days. The dark web has all kinds of goodies, and if you combine that with a few online pre-scriptions from an authorized medical facility? Ringo bingo: you've got a box of good times.

Purple capsules full of LSD—for mental health reasons, of course.

Liquid sildenafil. Also known as boner juice. And, as fate would have it, barely detectable when mixed into a cup of tea.

And, all the way from China, two packets of good old-fashioned plant food, aka *bath salts*. Less commonly known as synthetic cathinone, and more commonly known by such playfully wistful names as Vanilla Sky, Stardust, and White Lightning.

And, last but not least, a little bottle of HCN.

Sweet cyanide. Just in time.

By the way, the warnings on these packages—*NOT FOR HUMAN CONSUMPTION*—crack me up. As if.

I mean, come on. I think Stan kind of *enjoyed* his LSD phase, don't you?

Not sure the big guy is digging it, though. He's looking a little rough. Dumbass must think he has a seventy-two-hour flu.

To be honest, you never know how this stuff is going to work. You hope, of course. And you plan, like I said. But there are always *variables*. Things you can't foresee . . . which is why it's all a game.

A game I like to play.

A game I always win.

You hear me, you dead bitch? No one cares about you. No one but me.

To the world out there, you're all just sacks of rotten meat.

And I'm the fucking grinder.

Anyway . . . look. It's been great chatting. I just popped down because I'd heard there was an honest-to-God accident last night, and I couldn't resist seeing you with my own two eyes.

Now, you just sit tight. And don't let the bedbugs bite.

And don't worry.

Remember what I said.

You'll have company soon.

2

After it was determined that all three Baxter sisters had perished in the fire—their charred, but relatively whole, bodies intertwined in a death embrace amidst the rubble—Administrator Blackwell called an emergency town hall for all residents on Sunday morning, at 10 AM sharp, in the main Community Center Activity Room, which is the only room outside of the dining hall that can accommodate all the (remaining) residents.

Sunday Scrabble was cancelled.

3

Maureen Stapleton has locked herself in her room.

Miller and Gopi try to speak with her, to coax her out, pleading through her locked door, and doing their best to not bring up her firing a gun at the party.

Maureen informed the inquiring men that she would come out of her room "when hell freezes over." Given that no one was hurt by the gunshot (Sandra had found a neat, dime-sized hole in one wall, just a few inches above floor level), and not wanting to exacerbate an already tense situation, they told her to give them a call if she needed anything and left her to dwell alone in her fear.

As for Sandra, the following morning she reached out to all the partygoers and confirmed that no one had been grazed by the bullet that ended up in her wall, and that everyone was in good health.

Well, almost everyone.

She hasn't spoken to Mickey.

It seems no one can find him.

Since he'd been the first one to bolt out of the room (nearly knocking Rose ass over kettle in the process), however, assumptions are that he'd survived and is simply hiding out somewhere, much like Maureen. Either that or he'd left the premises altogether, along with two or three others who decided to take impromptu trips to the homes of relatives, or even local hotels.

Still, if he *had* left, it would be strange for him not to tell his friends first, which causes some worry.

The night of the fire, and for the first time in decades (she doesn't bother doing the math), Rose does not sleep alone.

Angry, sad, and deeply frightened, she asks Miller (who assures her that he is feeling much better) to stay the night. He obliges in the way of a gentleman: sleeping fully clothed (minus only his shoes) atop the bedding next to her.

In the morning, the two of them have a light, stay-at-home breakfast. They speak little of the fire, of the party, or of the sleepover.

4

In Greenview 11, Bill Rutherford has found his teeth.

To his surprise, he finds them sitting neatly on his bathroom counter, half-hidden by a box of tissues.

Now hold on, he thinks. *I would swear I looked there! Hell, I checked the entire countertop.*

The pang of doubt, however, lasts for only a few seconds before his joy—and relief—at finding the expensive dentures takes over. He debates soaking them in the solution for the day but is so excited to have his teeth back he simply plucks them up off the counter, gives them a quick once-over (*they look clean to me*), and pushes them giddily into his mouth. The pleasure of biting down onto something solid (versus soft gums) is glorious.

He lets out a sigh of contentment, then smiles grandly at himself in the mirror, exposing as much of the clean white teeth as he can.

"You handsome old bastard," he says to his reflection, then chuckles at himself, thinking he'll be a lot more handsome when he puts some pants on.

As he walks back into his bedroom, he feels a wave of light-headedness and figures he'd better make himself something to eat before heading to the town hall, relishing the idea of chomping on food again.

"Yes sir, yes sir," he mutters happily as he plops down on his bed and sticks one pale, bony leg into a pair of khaki pants. "Things are looking up!"

5

Including the hospice and full-time care, there are approximately eighty residents at Autumn Springs. Of those eighty, eight have died in the past two weeks, including Esther Pound, who snapped her neck tumbling down the stairs during the fire alarm.

Six more have left the retirement home of their own accord (whether temporarily or permanently, no one knows for sure).

Two have been transported to St. Vincent's hospital (on the night of the evacuation, Sylvia Fair broke her leg falling over a chair when the power went out, and Vic Roberts suffered a heart attack on the back lawn after running from the building and into the cold night).

Of the residents who remain, a handful refuses to leave their rooms.

And Mickey Lake has seemingly disappeared.

Rose doesn't do a head count, but looking around the large Activity Room—the fluorescent-lit space where they hold bridge tournaments, Bingo Night, and Sunday Scrabble—she estimates there are fewer than fifty residents in attendance. Most are folks who live in the two apartment buildings, but she spots a few wheelchairs and walkers around the perimeter, along with more nurses and orderlies than she's ever seen in one place since the day she moved in. She guesses around ten of the residents in the room are from the full-time care wing of the Medical Center.

The hospice folks, of course, will not be coming.

How many more rooms will be sitting empty in the morning? she wonders. *And should one of them be mine?*

The administrator stands on a raised stage at the front of the room—the very same stage that children would occupy when they came to sing for them on holidays or to put on a Christmas play. He taps a microphone to make sure it's turned on, then addresses the residents.

"Thank you all for coming," he says. "As you know, we suffered a horrible tragedy on Friday night, one for which we are still searching for answers. And look folks, I'm not going to beat around the bush, okay? I want to be honest with you. You deserve that." He clears his throat, takes a breath. "Esther Pound died from a fall while exiting the Greenview building. Bridget, Betsie, and Barbara Baxter were killed in the fire."

A wave of mumbles pervade the large room—but there is no shock, no panic. Not yet. This information had already spread like the fire itself through the mouths of residents and staff.

"We don't know what the sisters were doing in the building or how it caught fire. But the local fire department is looking into it. To that end, if you see anyone walking around that area over the next few days, rest assured they are here in an official capacity. Furthermore, I realize there are concerns about a few other incidents that have occurred these past couple weeks, most notably the suicides of Owen Duffield and Stanley Swanson."

"Suicides my puckered white ass!" someone shouts, and now the murmurs that fill the room are more urgent, edging toward panic. Anger.

Blackwell puts up his hands, presses the air. "Please, please . . . we don't need gossip and suspicions entering the fray. There's already enough tragedy on our doorstep, let's not bring panic into our home along with it."

There are some nods, some shaking of heads, but the pervasive grumbling of the group goes from a boil to a simmer.

Somebody coughs loudly—a wet, hacking sound—and Rose looks across the room to see Bill Rutherford sitting in a chair, head bent, hands on his knees. She's about to tap Miller on the arm about it when Blackwell says something unexpected.

"That said, I do think, until such time as things are fully investigated, we need to implement a curfew for all residents."

Voices rise—

Bill Rutherford continues to hack—

Blackwell speaks more loudly, cutting through the dissension.

"Starting tonight, all residents will be asked to be in their homes by nine p.m. There will be no shuttles into town past five p.m., and all public areas will be closed following dinner hours, at eight p.m. sharp."

More raised voices.

"We're not children!"

"This is nonsense!"

"Why do we need a curfew? What aren't you telling us?"

"Furthermore . . ." the administrator says, almost yelling now to make his voice heard over the hostile responses and ignoring those who have stood from their chairs, pointing at him in righteous anger. "I have temporarily hired a security company. They will have guards walking the grounds overnight, every night. These guards will stay outside the buildings but will monitor the surrounding areas. If they see anyone out after curfew, those persons will need to verify their identity, after which the guards will escort the individuals to their homes."

Lee Truby, a ninety-year-old spitfire of a woman (who leads a weekly crochet class that never has an empty chair), stands from her table and stabs a finger toward the stage. "Gestapo bullshit!" she screeches, and now more people are standing, yelling.

Orderlies and nurses, all wearing blue scrubs and sneakers, begin milling through the crowd, trying to calm people down. Someone shoves one of the orderlies—a young brute of a man Rose doesn't recognize—and she sees his face redden as he turns to snap at whoever pushed him. A few elderly folks cower. One of the nurses, who Rose *does* recognize as Nurse Cooper by her height and broad shoulders, has her hands on Lee Truby's elbow, desperately trying to calm her down.

Rose looks at Miller, concern in her eyes. He stares back with an equally worried expression and is about to say something . . . when his eyes flick to the stage, and widen.

"Oh no."

Rose turns in time to see the hulking form of Mickey Lake

pulling himself up onto the stage, just a few feet from the (now very nervous looking) administrator.

Blackwell stares, wide-eyed, at Mickey, who has the appearance of a madman in his flapping, button-down shirt and disheveled sport coat, the same outfit he was wearing at the party Friday night.

"Mr. Lake, please go sit with the others—" Blackwell starts, but then Mickey is on him. He takes a wild swing at the administrator, who throws his arms up to absorb the punch but is still knocked to the stage floor by the power of the blow. Mickey stands over him, huffing and puffing like a giant wolf, as three male orderlies rush to the front. The big man turns toward the crowd, eyes wild, and grabs the microphone.

"There's a killer among us!" he roars. "We're all going to die! All of us! We—"

Before he can say anything further, one of the orderlies—a man almost as big as Mickey himself—reaches him, but Mickey charges the orderly like a wild boar, dips his shoulder into the other man's chest as if tackling a running back, and knocks him clean off the stage. The orderly crashes down onto a nearby table, sending three of the seated residents to the floor, where they land in awkward heaps.

The other two orderlies—Rose recognizes Bobby and the man they met the other day, Jason something—have now reached Mickey and are wrestling him to the stage floor as he screams like a demon in frustration and horror.

Meanwhile, Mr. Blackwell has gotten back to his feet. His tidy suit is not so tidy anymore, but he manages to speak calmly into the microphone. "I need a nurse to bring a sedative up here, *stat*."

Rose notices two of the nurses run from the room, seemingly to get something strong enough to slow Mickey down, when a loud scream—a scream of undeniable terror and despair—cuts through the noise and chaos.

Everyone turns to see a man dancing in the middle of the large room. Anyone standing nearby begins to back hurriedly away.

No, he's not dancing, Rose thinks, watching Bill Rutherford stagger in circles, eyes bulging, hands clutching at his throat. *He's choking.*

"I can't breathe!" Rutherford yells, his voice horribly garbled. "My mouth," he says, stumbling to a knee. "Oh, God, help me!"

He coughs so roughly that Rose clutches at her own neck, can almost *feel* the tissue of his throat tearing to shreds. Even from a distance, she notices his blood-speckled chin as a squirt of dark red ejects from his mouth and onto the white linoleum floor.

Then Bill Rutherford jerks backward, back arched, hands clawed.

"AAACCCKKK!" he screams, his voice now a gurgle, blood spraying the air, then throws himself sideways into a nearby table, sending two chairs flying.

Two of the remaining nurses run to his side. Now that he's down, people push forward, wanting to see—*needing* to see—and Rose, God help her, is one of them, with Miller at her side.

Through arms and bodies, Rose watches Bill's twisted body writhe on the floor, shaking like a man possessed by a legion of devils, his legs kicking wildly.

"Good Christ, his mouth," Miller says into her ear, and Rose pushes forward until she can see the man's face, which has turned cherry red.

Thick white foam, tinged with dark crimson, pours from his mouth, covering the lower half of his face as his heels pound a staccato beat against the floor. A nurse tries desperately to push her fingers into the mess between his lips, hoping to keep his tongue from going down his throat and choking him to death.

"I can't separate his teeth!" she yells in a high-pitched, panicked voice to the nurse on her knees next to her, who Rose recognizes as little Mindy Jarvis, trying desperately to assist by putting her hands on Bill's jaw, as if to pry it open.

Through the tumult, Rose catches movement on the stage and glances up to see one of the other nurses running toward the collapsed form of Mickey—held down now by a group of four orderlies—with a large syringe clutched in one of her hands. Rose notices that the big orderly—the one who'd been knocked off the stage, rivulets of blood dripping down one gashed cheek—is shrieking at the nurse to *hurry the fuck UP*.

Rose watches as the nurse jabs the large syringe into Mickey's thigh.

Meanwhile, Bill Rutherford has gone still. A last drizzle of foam pushes out from between his lips like a party trick.

"He's dead!" someone screams.

Around the room, people are holding each other. Many are crying. A handful have left, possibly never to return.

Rose notices Mr. Blackwell standing—forlorn, adrift—on the stage. Next to him is the pile of bodies holding Mickey down as the shot does its work.

Staring dumbly at the dead man on the floor, Blackwell's face is chalk-white and limp with shock, his expression confused and horrified and helpless as that of a little boy who has just watched his mother get run down by a truck, right in front of his eyes.

6

In Seaview 26, Libby Sue Thompson is on the phone with her grand-daughter, Stephanie Reynolds, a twenty-three-year-old New York City resident married to an ambitious young man with a year left at Columbia Law School. Contrastingly, Libby Sue's only daughter—Stephanie's mother—lives in a Texas trailer park with an ex-convict.

The two women are her only surviving family.

"Hey Grandmama," Stephanie says, answering on the first ring.

After a few pleasantries, Libby Sue explains, as tacitly and care-fully as she can, that she'd like to come stay with Stephanie and Craig (the lawyer in waiting) for a little while. That she'd be happy to sleep on the couch and would be no trouble at all.

"Grandmama," Stephanie says slowly, "our apartment is the size of a tinderbox. You know that. You visited here a few years back, remember?"

"I remember . . ." Libby Sue says, not remembering at all and hating the surge of acidic panic rising in her throat. "But sweet-heart, I need a place to stay for a while—"

"What's wrong with the retirement home?" Stephanie asks. "Are they kicking you out?"

"No, no," Libby Sue says, thinking furiously. "There was a fire . . . the buildings are no good until they clean them up, hon. I just need a place—"

"I'm sorry, Grandmama," Stephanie says, sounding as if she means it. "There's just no way. Craig and I have four hundred square feet, hon. Our kitchen is so close to our bed I could fry eggs with my head on a pillow. I'm sorry."

In Greenview 10, Cristina Mancini is on the phone with her only son, who works in finance and has a beautiful home on Lake Michigan.

"Mom, it's not great timing," her son—the man she raised while working two jobs, who she put through college, who she gave *birth* to—says. "The kids are going on winter break in a month and we're planning a big trip to Switzerland. Eli's a big snowboarding nut now, did I tell you that?"

Cristina connects that Eli is her oldest grandson, but she hasn't spoken to the boy since he was six years old, so she has no shitting clue how much he may or may not like snowboarding. "Randy, I just need to come stay with you for a few weeks. Please. A spare bedroom is fine."

Clanging pots in the background. Children fighting. Her daughter-in-law—that bitch Margaret—threatening everyone with violence.

"Look, Mom, I'll send you some money, okay? I'm going to Zelle you a thousand dollars. Get yourself a suite at one of the local hotels. Seriously, treat yourself. You deserve it."

"Randy, what the hell is Zelle? Look, please—"

"I'm sorry, Mom."

To the best of Cristina's knowledge, the money never comes through.

In Greenview 5, George McKee begs his oldest daughter to let him come to Florida, to stay for a while with her and his grandkids.

"Daddy, we're going to Disney World next week, and then J.P. has friends coming in from Detroit. We're all going fishing, like chartering a boat. It's been planned for months."

"I like fishing."

"Dad . . ." His daughter lets out a sigh. "Honestly? It's just not a good time."

In Seaview 7, Carmela Rodriguez is on the phone with her ex-husband, a once-upon-a-time kind man, who remarried twenty-two years ago and now has three grown children. She pleads with him to help her.

She has no other family.

After several minutes of him refusing her in any—and every—way possible, her ex finally gets fed up when she begins to cry, when she tells him she's afraid for her life.

"People are dying, Richard," she says, embarrassed by both her tears and her uncontrollable fear.

"Of course they're dying, Carmela; it's a goddamn retirement home," he says, before disconnecting the call.

"That one was always a drama queen," he says to his wife, who'd been watching the call from the kitchen with narrowed eyes. He sets down the phone (after silencing it), gives her a reassuring smile, and asks her what's good to watch on Netflix tonight.

In Seaview 12, eighty-three-year-old Michelle Hall is telling her only living son (having lost one to cancer and another to a motorcycle accident), who lives in Los Angeles and works in movies, that she loves him very much and to take good care of himself.

"I love you too, Mom," he says. "But look, I gotta go. I'm on set and they could call me any second. Bills to pay, you know?"

"I understand," she says. "I just wanted to say hello. I love you, honey."

"Love you, too, Mom. Take care."

Michelle holds back tears until she disconnects the call.

I've lived a good long life, she thinks, and finds herself looking around her small apartment, as if seeing it for the first time. The pale sunlight slanting through the window feels like a warning. She's never felt so alone.

Waiting for the ache in her heart to subside, she lowers her face into the cushions of her sofa and weeps, thinking of her beautiful boy.

It's the last conversation they ever have.

7

"I couldn't possibly leave," Rose says. "Not right now."

It's Thursday afternoon. Rose had been debating if it was too late for a nap or whether to push tiredly through the evening and get to bed early, when Sybil called her cell phone, upset at seeing the news about the fire at her mother's retirement home. A fire in which *three* people burned to death.

"Why?" Sybil says, sounding a bit hysterical to Rose's ears. "Why can't you leave, Mom? We're all moved into the new house, and . . . okay, no, it's not all set up yet, there are boxes everywhere, but you'd have a bed, and you'd be *safe*."

"Honey, I'm safe here," Rose says, debating the truth of her words but trying her best not to let Sybil hear the hesitation. "And besides, the fire wasn't in any of the occupied buildings. It was an old eyesore way out back, a building that should have been torn down years ago."

"But people died, Mom. There was a piece about it on the news. They said three women burned to death in that fire."

"I'm aware, honey, and yes, it's horrible. A tragedy. But frankly, and I don't mean to sound heartless, they really shouldn't have been out there in the first place." Rose reaches into her pocket, pulls out the small silver charm Barbara had given her, looks down at the hand with the open eye etched into the palm, as if watching her.

"Okay, but when we had lunch, you mentioned that someone else had just died. A friend of yours."

"That's true," Rose says slowly, stalling. "But you know, the police said that was an accident—"

"The police?!"

"Sybil—"

"Holy shit. Look, I know you, Mom. There's something you're not telling me."

"Language," Rose says, putting a bit of steel in her voice, just enough to quell her daughter's rising agitation. "Sybil, please relax. I told you I'd think about your invitation, and I am thinking about it. But for now you need to focus on getting your house set up and taking care of that sweet grandchild of mine. You don't need to worry about me."

"Well, I am worried," Sybil says, deflated. "I'd feel a lot better if you would leave that place. You have options, even if most people don't."

"I know, and I'm grateful," Rose says. "But I don't know . . . it would be hard to leave my life here . . . my friends."

"You mean Miller," Sybil says, and Rose can hear the smirk in her voice.

"I mean no such thing."

Sybil chuckles. "What's up with you two, anyway? I can feel the sexual tension from here."

Rose frowns. "Don't be crude. And there's nothing going on, as you well know. We're good friends. And at my age, that's really the best you can hope for. Or need," she adds quickly.

"Well, I like him."

"I like him, too. I . . ." Rose pauses.

"What?"

"What happened with me and your father . . . it makes things difficult sometimes."

"Mom, come on. There are good men out there, and Miller seems like one of them."

Rose shakes her head. "There's so much I don't know about the man, even though we've been friends for years now. He's . . . I don't know. Secretive about things. About his past."

"He's not the only one," Sybil says quietly, reflecting.

"That's different," she says. "I don't even know if the man has family. Or an ex-wife, or three ex-wives."

"Yeah, sure. And maybe they all died in mysterious ways."

Rose is about to scold her daughter for being a troublemaker when her cell phone buzzes. She holds it away from her face, sees Miller has texted her an hourglass emoji.

Speak of the devil.

"Hon, I'm sorry, but I have to run. I'm supposed to be somewhere in ten minutes."

"Fine, fine . . . Where are you headed?"

"Just over to the Medical Center," Rose says, grabbing a warm sweater off the back of the couch. "I need to go see a friend."

8

Miller and Rose stop at the reception desk, where one of the nurses is typing notes into a computer. She's skinny and pale with long red hair that's messily thrown into a rushed ponytail. Rose recognizes her as the one who injected Mickey during the town hall.

"Hello," Rose says, using her most congenial tone. "I don't think we've met. My name is Rose DuBois, and this is my friend, Beauregard Mason Miller."

"Just Miller is fine," he says with a wink, and Rose is pleased to see him also pouring on the charm. "All my friends call me Miller, since Beauregard is a mouthful, and two last names confuse folks. You see, I took one from each of my moms." He leans in closer to the nurse and whispers, as if dispelling some great secret. "No hyphen."

The befuddled (and very unimpressed) nurse glances from one of them to the other, her fingers still hovering over the keyboard, as if frozen. She does not reciprocate their smiles, nor their friendly tone. "Okay," she says. "So what can I do for you?"

"We'd like to see our friend," Rose says. "Mickey Lake? He was brought in here yesterday."

The nurse scoffs, and Rose sees cruelty in her watery blue eyes. "Yeah, that's not going to happen. That guy is seriously dangerous."

Miller leans forward, as if to speak, but Rose holds up a hand, her eyes never leaving the nurse. "What's your name, dear?"

The nurse looks at Rose warily, as if confused by the power she has over the tall, bearded man in the tweed coat and furrowed brow. "Angie."

"Okay, Angie. Here's the thing. That man? The one you think is so dangerous? He's our friend. And I know he was agitated yesterday . . . we all were, right? I mean, that fire really shook folks up."

But Nurse Angie is already shaking her head. "He wasn't 'shook up', ma'am," she says, finger-quoting "shook up" to make a point.

"He was delusional and violent. He threw Big Jim off the stage, and that guy weighs like three hundred pounds. I was scared for my life."

"I'm sorry about that," Rose says. "And I'm sorry about . . . Big Jim. I hope he's okay."

Angie scoffs again. "He's fine. He can take a hit."

"Well, that's good to hear," Rose says, tapping the reception desk lightly with one fingertip. "And all I can tell you is that we've known Mickey Lake for many years, and he is the gentlest, kindest man I've ever met. Isn't that right, Miller?"

"One hundred percent," he adds, and Rose hears the crinkle of him opening a peppermint.

"Look, you guys seem nice, but I'm afraid it's not possible. Mr. Lake is restrained, heavily sedated, and is to have no visitors."

Rose's eyes widen with surprise, and her congenial tone vanishes behind one of incredulity. "Restrained? Who ordered such a thing?"

"Doctor Kincaid, ma'am," Angie responds, and Rose is convinced she sees a smugness in those thin lips.

This is an unkind woman, Rose thinks. *Not just unhelpful . . . but unkind.*

"Nurse Angie, please," she says. "Can't you just let us in for a minute? He's all alone in there, and I'm sure he's scared out of his mind. We're his *friends.*"

"Ma'am, I'm sorry. You can't visit—"

"Rose?"

The voice comes from the direction of the elevators, and Rose looks over to see young Doctor Kincaid standing there in his white coat, holding a clipboard, a bemused smile on his face. "Finally coming in for that checkup?" he asks, approaching the desk. "How's the reflux?"

Without waiting for an answer, the doctor turns toward Miller, extends a hand. "Hello, we haven't met. I'm Doctor Kincaid."

Miller shakes the doctor's hand, gives him a warm smile. "Beauregard Mason Miller. My friends call me Miller."

Rose distinctively hears Nurse Angie mumble *Jesus Christ* under her breath, and thinks Doctor Kincaid heard it as well, because he gives the young woman a decidedly unhappy glance.

"Doctor," Rose says, trying and failing to keep the desperation out of her voice. "We're trying to see our friend, Mickey Lake. The nurse tells us he's in restraints and isn't allowed visitors. But he's a good person, Doctor. And we think it will do him a lot of good to see some familiar faces, and perhaps—"

Kincaid holds up a hand, nodding. "It's okay, Rose. It's okay. It just so happens I agree with you. How about this? We all go down there together and I give you five minutes. But if he gets agitated again, I'll need you to leave, okay?"

Rose looks at Miller, who raises an eyebrow.

Your show, Rose.

"That sounds fine," Rose says, and Kincaid gives her a kind smile, a sharp contrast to the frown currently gracing Nurse Angie's pale, freckled face.

"Okay. This way," he says, and points his clipboard toward the hospice side of the building.

"He's in hospice?" Miller asks, and Rose can hear the quiver of anxiety in his voice. She doesn't blame him for being anxious.

She feels the same way.

Doctor Kincaid looks momentarily uncomfortable, then shrugs. "Sometimes our hospice patients get worked up . . . confused. To protect our staff, and the patients themselves, we sometimes need to secure them. We can't have patients yanking out their catheters and feeding tubes."

"So you tie them down," Miller says. A statement.

Kincaid sighs. "It's very humane, Mr. Miller. And oftentimes, the only option."

"And that's why you've got Mickey over here?"

Kincaid nods, and there's a sadness in his eyes. "He's heavily sedated and out of sorts, I'm afraid. I know he's your friend, but the truth is he's a big, strong man, and he scared the hell out of most of the staff. He'll stay restrained until he calms down and passes a psych evaluation. Sometimes, these things just happen."

Rose gently touches the crisp white sleeve of the doctor's coat. "I'm sorry. What just happens?"

Kincaid stops in front of a large wooden door, turns to face them.

"Mental collapse," he says. "Paranoia, delusion, rage—"

"Madness," Miller says quietly, as if to himself.

Kincaid nods. "Sure. Madness."

Then he pushes open the door.

9

Rose gasps at the sight of her friend.

Mickey lies on a narrow medical bed wearing nothing but a flimsy blue hospital gown, a stained white sheet tucked beneath him. There are metal guardrails mounted high on either side of the bed and heavy gray straps—secured to the sturdy guardrails—are attached to his wrists and ankles. He's wearing white medical restraint gloves that look like oven mitts on his giant hands, heavily taped to each wrist. An IV drip runs into his arm and a catheter tube slips out from beneath the hem of his gown. He's hollow-cheeked and pale, his shadowed eye sockets sunken, his body emaciated, which Rose knows is impossible since he's only been here forty-eight hours.

He's lost the weight of his soul, she thinks sadly, unsure where such a dark thought had come from but unable to deny its validity.

Mickey, eyes open, watches them as they walk in, then he raises those bloodshot eyes to the ceiling and groans. Even though he's restrained, he has somehow managed to knock the top sheet and blanket to the floor, leaving his body exposed to the cool air.

"Oh my God," Rose says quietly.

Even Doctor Kincaid looks abashed at the sight of his patient. "I'll get a nurse in here when we leave, we'll clean him up and get that bedding back in place," he says quietly, then moves to the foot of the bed and plucks up a chart, flips through a few of the clipboard's pages. "He's sedated right now, to keep him relaxed, but not enough to knock him out. We did some bloodwork but it looks like we're still waiting for results. We think he might have been on something, probably a strong narcotic, that brought about his current state of paranoia and violence. We'll know more soon, then we can treat him properly and hopefully get him out of here and back to his life."

"Does he have to have those restraints?" Miller asks, his expression filled with horror and disbelief.

"I'm afraid so," Kincaid says, sounding genuinely despondent. "This morning he attacked a nurse, nearly choked her to death before we could get his hand pulled away. He's big and strong and, I'm sorry to say, not in his right mind. But please know we don't do this to be cruel or solely as a treatment mechanism; it's also for his own safety. Mickey has pulled out both his IV and catheter once already, and we can't have that happening again."

"No, of course . . ." Rose says, taking a (cautious) step toward the bed. "Mickey? It's Rose and Miller, hon. We came to visit you."

The big man turns his head. His eyes are not empty, as she'd expected, but filled with the impotent rage of an angry, caged lion, a wild beast that would tear her limb from limb if it could.

One gloved hand jerks hard against the restraint, and Rose flinches.

"Get me the fuck out of here," Mickey rumbles, eyes darting between Rose, Miller, and the doctor. He pulls his arms against the restraints, face reddening, neck veins bulging.

Kincaid steps forward, rests a hand on Mickey's bare ankle. "Take it easy, Mr. Lake, we're going to get you—"

Mickey lets out a gasp, shakes his head violently from side to side, then bellows so loudly that Rose covers her ears, tears springing from her eyes.

"GET ME OUT OF HERE!"

"Mickey, please—" Rose begs.

He turns his head toward her, eyes burning with pure hate. "Get me out of here! Get me out of here! Get me the fuck out of HERE!"

Miller puts a cautious hand on Rose's elbow. "Rose—"

"Mickey, please—"

"Get me out of here you goddamn fucking *bitch*!"

"I'm sorry, but we'll need to sedate him again," Kincaid says, voice shaky. "It's not good for him to be this upset."

The doctor drops the chart onto the foot of the bed and walks quickly into the hallway to call for a nurse, leaving Rose and Miller alone with their friend.

Miller steps forward with confidence, knowing their time is short, and grips Mickey's restrained wrist. "We're here, Mickey. And we're going to help you, okay? We're going to get you out of here."

Mickey, as if seeing them for the first time, goes slack, eyes wide and scared—all the rage emptied away—then looks up at Miller. "Please help me," he says. Tears run from the corners of his pleading eyes into the thin, sterile pillow. "I'm not supposed to be here."

"I know," Miller says, moving his hand to pat the big man's shoulder. "Hang in there and we'll be back. We'll get you home."

Rose steps next to Miller and runs a hand over Mickey's forehead. "Be good for the nurses and doctors, Mickey. Be good for them and they'll let you go."

Mickey stares at her, desperate and strained, then lets his head fall back, the fight gone out of him. "I'll try," he says, and it's the first time since their arrival he seems like his old self, the gentle bear Rose has come to treasure as a dear friend.

When Kincaid returns, he's followed by Nurse Mindy, who's holding a syringe, and a large orderly Rose recognizes as the man who was pushed off the stage. Big Jim. She sees the violence brewing in his eyes and prays Mickey won't give them any more trouble.

Instead, Mickey glares daggers at them—and just like that their friend is gone, a madman taking his place. "Fuck you!" he screams. Miller pulls his hand free of Mickey's shoulder as if burned. "Fuck all of you! Let me out of here!"

"Is that the Ativan?" the doctor asks. Rose thinks he sounds the slightest bit rattled. "Just five milligrams."

Mindy nods. "Five milligrams, doctor."

More calmly than Rose would have thought possible, Mindy walks to the IV stand and plunges the needle into the port connecting the tubes. She gives Rose a quick glance of recognition as she depresses the plunger, then pulls the needle free.

Mickey sits up, then rams his head and torso back down onto the bed.

It's like he's possessed by devils, Rose thinks hollowly. *My God.*

Again, Mickey sits up, slams himself down.

"It's not working," Miller says, eyes wide.

Mindy shakes her head. "Any more than that could kill him."

"Do something!" Rose yells.

Kincaid looks at her, and for the first time she sees something other than warmth and congeniality in his eyes. This time, she sees something much closer to controlled anger. "You have to go now, I'm sorry," he says, using a tone that does not welcome discussion. He turns to the orderly. "Escort them out, Jim. We'll need to get the chest strap on him."

The big orderly takes a step toward them and, to Rose's moderate surprise, calmly extends a giant paw toward the door, speaking gently. "I'm sorry, but you have to leave right now," he says. Then adds, somewhat more quietly: "You don't want to see this."

"Come on, Rose," Miller says, touching her elbow.

As they get to the hallway, Rose now in tears, they look back to see the orderly and the nurse fighting Mickey down onto the bed. A massive Velcro strap is flung across his chest and secured, and the last thing they hear from their friend is a deep, throat-wrenching scream.

Rose thinks it is the howl of a man burning in the flames of Hell.

10

Badly shaken, Rose and Miller walk down the hospice corridor, away from the fading, heartbreaking screams of Mickey.

As they walk, each silent, lost in their own despairing thoughts, Rose can't help glancing through open doors, looking in on the poor souls too sick to care for themselves: the ones who will need no more healing, no more prayers. There is no more ambiguity as to what is happening to them and what the end result will soon be; all that's left are the chores of making them comfortable, and the question of how long they can hang on.

When she spots a familiar face, Rose hesitates.

"What is it?" Miller asks.

"You go on," she says. "I'm gonna say hello."

Miller peeks through the doorway and sees Tatum Bird sitting in a chair, gazing out the window at the late afternoon sun, which is already on its way down the sky's backside, heading west for the big sunset show—the same one it offered each and every day.

"I'll talk to you later," he says, giving her a wink and a tip of his invisible hat. He pops a peppermint in his mouth and walks away.

Rose watches him go for a moment, then enters.

"Hello, Tatum," she says, walking across the room to stand beside him.

Rose notes the tidy hospital bed, the orderly way his Yankees cap and sunglasses are set on the dresser. The television is on but silent, showing a baseball game he doesn't seem to be paying attention to.

Tatum doesn't turn to greet her, doesn't stand and smile and say, "Ah, my dear Rose," and reach out his arms to offer a hug.

Just once, she wishes he would, wishes he would look at her and really *see* her, remember who she is and what they might have talked about the day before. She wishes she could have known Tatum Bird before his second stroke, before his mind flew the cage and fluttered away into the gray stormy sky of dementia. Yes, she would like to have known that version of Tatum Bird. She would have liked it very much.

She pulls over a plastic visitor's chair and sits next to him, matches his gaze out the window at the pretty, if waning, day. "Not going to the pond today?"

"No food," he responds immediately, giving her a jolt of surprise.

"No fish food, you mean?" she asks, leaning forward, turning her head to look into his eyes, wondering if she'd see a spark there.

But he doesn't respond, simply squints and shakes his head a little. After a few moments of comfortable silence, he slaps his thighs and looks at her. "Time to go," he says, then smiles. It's a beautiful smile, and it blows away some of the darkness in Rose's heart. "Time to go to work."

Rose nods. "Of course, we'll get you to work. But let's just sit and look outside for a bit first, okay?"

"Okay, okay," he says, sounding disappointed, if understanding. "It's important that I get to work today." He begins to stand. "I gotta go; I have to go."

Rose places a firm hand on his forearm, lowers him gently back down. "Now hold on, Tatum Bird. You just sit with me for a minute. I want to spend some time with you."

He waves a hand in her direction but settles back down. It saddens her to see how skinny his arms have gotten, the blue T-shirt he's wearing draped on his shoulders as if hung on a hanger made of bones. "Okay, Rose," he says.

Rose turns around, making sure there isn't a nurse or a doctor standing behind them, then leans closer to her friend. "I'm scared, Tatum," she says. "I'm scared of what's been happening here . . . happening to our friends. I don't want to leave, but I don't want to get hurt, either."

"No, no . . ." he mumbles, eyes intent on the darkening sky.

"I could go live with my daughter," Rose says, pressing on. "She *wants* me to. Can you believe that?"

Something in Rose's tone makes Tatum smile, and he gives a little laugh. "No . . ." Then he shrugs. "I'm not sure; I don't know."

"But I can't leave my friends," she continues, sliding a hand over one of his, giving it a light squeeze. "I can't leave you, or Miller, or Gopi, or any of the others living here who I consider friends and neighbors. Who would I talk to every day? What would I do at my daughter's house except get in the way? I love my grandchild, but I don't want to be a live-in babysitter, or a cook, or a maid. I *like* my freedom. I like being independent. You know what I mean?" Rose shakes her head and continues, mumbling more to herself than to Tatum. "I don't know what to do. I've been on this earth nearly eighty years, and sometimes I still don't know what's right."

Tatum nods, then stands. He pats her shoulder. "I need to find something," he says. Rose is about to protest again but remains patient while he makes his way to the dresser, opens a top drawer, and pulls out a picture frame. He comes back and sits down, hands the picture to Rose.

"My buddy," he says.

Inside the worn frame is a photograph of a much younger Tatum Bird, his arm around a beautiful woman with raven-black hair, both of them smiling brightly. There's a young, sheepish-looking teenager standing beside the woman, hands buried in his pockets. At their feet is a chocolate Labrador, grinning at the camera like there's no tomorrow.

"The famous Jack," Rose says. "And who's this pretty lady? That your wife?"

Tatum smiles, nods. "That's Jack," he says.

"Right, but this is your wife, remember? What was her name, Tatum?"

Tatum looks into Rose's eyes, still smiling. "Have you seen Jack?"

Rose sighs, sets the picture in her lap. "I'm afraid not. But you have a beautiful family," she says, wondering what happened to them, what tragedy befell his son—or befell their relationship—that the young man isn't here right now, sitting with his father.

She wonders how long ago his wife was taken away, how long

before the memory of her existence was erased by the changes in Tatum's brain.

He takes the picture from her lap, looks at it a moment, then sets it gently on the floor next to his chair. "You should go," he says.

"You want to be alone?"

Tatum taps her knee gently with the side of one hand, gestures toward the window. "You should go," he repeats.

"You mean leave Autumn Springs?" she says, playing along. "Go home to my daughter? Is that what you're telling me, Mr. Bird? That's your life advice?"

Of course he's not saying that, Rose. For all he knows he's telling you to run to first base, thinking he's back coaching Little League baseball games.

But to her surprise, he nods.

"Yes, Rose," he says, clear as a bell. "You should go home."

11

Gopi takes his Beaulieu 4008 movie camera from the case and sets it on the table. He'd been into town that morning to pick up his order of Super 8 reversal film, his preferred film type for creating lovely, high-contrast black and white movies, and is excited to film something again.

He'd planned on asking for volunteers, thinking it would be a fun exercise for many of his neighbors to be part of making their own movie: An Autumn Springs Original Film. He'd spent the last few months writing a thirty-page script that could be filmed using the interiors of a couple units, exteriors utilizing parts of the grounds, with the finale filmed at the old asylum—where their hero, a gaunt detective (Gopi had Miller in mind for the lead role), tracked down a villain (to be played by Mickey, who had already agreed to the part and had given surprisingly nuanced feedback on the script), and shot him dead.

Now, of course, it seems that all his best laid plans of mice and men have gone awry. What with the horror of the last couple weeks—not to mention the destruction of the asylum—the once promising hope of making the film has been unceremoniously shoved into the abyss of lost dreams, a badge nearly every filmmaker in the world wears proudly, if despairingly.

Gopi smiles to himself as he opens the camera. *A typical Hollywood movie production,* he thinks. *Everything gone to hell at the eleventh hour.*

With the asylum gone, there can be no finale. Mickey, of course, is now in the Medical Center, most likely drugged to the tits and crazy as a rabid dog. No villain.

As for his dream of asking volunteers to help with the production? Also not going to happen.

Even worse, Gopi will have to cancel the next screening. And rightly so. Showing a horror film would be in incredibly bad taste, even if it is a classic piece of cinema from the late, great Mario Bava. Perhaps it could be postponed to a later date.

When people stop dying, he thinks.

With a heavy sigh, he pops open the yellow box of 8mm film and loads it deftly into the camera.

That done, he raises the Beaulieu (which, to a layman's eye, looks similar to a science-fiction gun from a fifties pulp magazine) and points the lens at the wall of his apartment, focusing on the painting by an artist named Mark Licari: a brown flowerpot with a vicious green plant sprouting from within, dripping with flies and slugs. He rolls a few seconds of film, just to be sure everything's loaded okay, and is about to check the focus settings on the camera . . .

When there's a knock at the door.

Must be Mary, he thinks, a warmth spreading in his chest. He checks his watch. *A little early, but that's okay.*

He sets the camera on the couch cushion beside him, stands, and goes to welcome his girlfriend. Before letting her in, he pauses to smooth his moustache, gingerly pinches the waxed tips, then opens the door.

"You're a bit early—"

A figure, clad in black from head to toe, cocks their head at him.

Gopi takes a step back, brow furrowed.

Then, he realizes.

He holds up a hand.

"Wait—"

The masked figure lunges forward and buries a ten-inch bowie knife hilt-deep into Gopi's belly—punching through shirt and skin.

Gopi's mouth opens wide to scream, but the intruder clamps a hand over it while pushing him backward, then kicks the door closed.

The pain in Gopi's stomach is fire, and the impossible feeling of the blade pushing through his gut floods his mind with blinding terror.

White flashes—like popping bulbs—fill his vision.

He's pushed back, back, deeper into the apartment. He stares, goggle-eyed, at that hideous black ski mask, a raised black hood pushing the face even deeper into shadow, the eyes and mouth covered in semi-opaque black fabric, so that even the color of the killer's eyes are hidden.

Gopi's heel catches the edge of a rug and he trips, falls backward. The killer rides down with him, knees landing on either side of his hips, one hand still on the hilt of the knife, the other covering his mouth and nose.

"Ever heard of *seppuku*?" a deranged voice asks, one that Gopi thinks he recognizes, but in his terror, his panic, he can't think—

"Like a zipper," the killer says, then chuckles as the knife saws sideways, opening Gopi's stomach.

Unlike the other murders, this will not look like an accident.

After a few moments, during which Gopi bucks and spasms and nearly passes out from shock and pain, the masked killer sits back against the couch, breathing heavy, watching Gopi desperately suck in short, broken breaths, his stomach a gory mess of intestines and blood, hands probing his innards with a gentle sort of wonder, as if trying to push it all back inside.

"And look, it's still a beautiful day," the killer says, turning to glance at the nearby window, a wall of warm sunshine reflected on its glass.

There's a light knock at the door, and the masked head jerks toward the sound.

Gopi, despite his pain—despite his sheer, mind-numbing terror—shifts his eyes toward the door, his mouth working silently.

The killer's face hovers into Gopi's view, now only inches away, close enough that he can feel hot breath through the cloth.

"That would be Mary," the killer whispers, that strange voice muffled by the fabric of the mask. "I'd suggest you stay quiet. Unless, that is, you'd like her to join our little party? It's up to you, man. I'm good either way."

Gopi stares at those blackened eyes, his breath coming in strained, shallow gulps, and manages to nod.

A gloved hand pats his cheek.

"Good boy."

After a few minutes of Mary calling out and knocking, she finally goes away, likely thinking Gopi is waiting for her at the dining hall, that perhaps she'd misunderstood where they'd be meeting.

Gopi, now pale as a sheet, pulse slowing to an irregular crawl, lies still.

"Well, this has been fun, but it's time for me to shove off," the killer says, standing. "I look forward to seeing your friends later. God, I have so much to do, so much to do . . ."

The killer walks toward the window.

Gopi's eyes move to the couch, where the protruding lens of his Beaulieu camera sticks out slightly, no more than a foot above his head. Using all of the life left in his body—all his remaining strength and willpower—he reaches one bloodied hand up . . . higher . . . higher . . . until his fingers grip the lens.

He pulls.

The movie camera slides off the edge of the couch and drops hard onto his chest, landing with a soft thump he doesn't even feel. With two blood-soaked hands, he turns the camera atop his body until the lens is pointed in the right direction.

Feeling around with numb, shaking fingers, he finally locates the grip, then depresses the button that brings the camera to life.

The last thing Gopi feels in this life is the gentle vibration of the camera on his chest; the last thing he hears the familiar, comforting shutter of film flowing through the machine, capturing his last moments through a hungry lens . . .

Aimed directly at the killer.

Rolling . . . he thinks.

Then thinks nothing more.

12

Detective Hastings is ready to go home.

He's had a hell of a day, and he's dead on his feet. Unlike those hard-boiled types one sees in television crime shows, he isn't heading to his favorite hole-in-the-wall bar to drown his hatred for the world in a bottle of bourbon. Instead, he's heading to the gym for an hour of light weights and some time on the treadmill before dinner at home, a glass of wine, and a good night's sleep.

As one of only three homicide detectives in their precinct, Hastings always carries an unusually robust caseload, and he likes to stay in relatively good shape, even if that means finding three hours a week to fit in his (very base level) workout. He prefers to be sharp, so he doesn't drink much—well, not *that* much. Sure, his job isn't all that taxing when compared to big city homicide detectives, but even so, it's the way he operates.

Sure, most of the deaths he's called out for are quick and painless, other than the paperwork, and most cases don't necessitate calling in forensics to scour a scene for days while the pathologist runs a million tests on a cadaver. In his experience, a suicide is a suicide. An overdose is an overdose. If a guy falls off a cliff, it only takes a few hours to find out if he slipped, jumped, or maybe—just maybe—was pushed. Was there a husband or girlfriend or stranger nearby? If so, what was their relationship like? How far from the edge did the victim land? Had he or she been depressed?

Sure, Hastings has a suspicious mind—it's a prerequisite for the job—but he isn't *overly* suspicious. He's a realist. He doesn't conjure up a crime where there's no crime, and he doesn't invent stories to fill a narrative. Nine times out of ten the victim purposely shot themselves, or took one hit of heroin too many, or slipped and fell off that proverbial cliff. Not everything is a conspiracy. Not everything is a murder.

So when the phone on his desk rings, and he scoops it up and listens to the forensic pathologist tell him that the old man who died foaming at the mouth at Autumn Springs Wednesday afternoon had been poisoned, he takes a beat before jumping to any wild conclusions.

"What kind of poison?"

"Still waiting on the tests," the doctor says. "Cyanide is the first thing that comes to mind given the state of the body, the organs . . . but it must have been slow since he was walking and talking before the reaction, right? So, this isn't popping a capsule. He'd have been dead in minutes."

"Slow how?"

"It'd have to enter his bloodstream over time. A few hours, give or take. Hell, I don't know, Detective. We're not even a hundred percent sure it's cyanide. Not yet, anyway. But if you're asking for my knee-jerk opinion, that's it. Regardless, we'll know for certain when the tests come back from the lab."

"And how soon is that?"

"Not sure," she says. "I was told this wasn't a rush."

"It wasn't," he says. "But based on what you're telling me, it is now."

"Okay, well, I'll see what I can do to expedite things, and I'll call you the second they come in. I'd say twenty-four hours."

"Jesus, Doc . . ." Hastings runs a hand through his hair. "Suddenly, I'm not sure I have twenty-four hours."

13

Night falls.

A full moon ripens in the black expanse amid a dusting of cold stars.

Autumn Springs is quiet as a graveyard.

Mickey stirs.

The room is cold and dark; a distortion of blue light filters through the window, moonlight mixed with ocher sky that softens the far wall, gives the entire room a hazy, dreamlike feel, even though he knows he's awake.

He strains against the confining straps on his arms, legs, across his broad chest. Testing them gently. He's been drugged, he knows that, but he somehow feels . . . *better*. Less agitated. As if his mind has been returned to his noggin, despite still being a bit foggy from whatever sedatives they're pumping into him. He turns his head to look at the IV drip, then turns the other way. Through the dim room, he can barely make out the door to the hallway, which appears to be closed.

Need to get a nurse, he thinks. *Explain that I'm feeling better. Get these straps taken off me. Or at least my chest . . . I feel like I can hardly breathe.*

Mickey raises his head as best he's able, looking for some sort of a call button, but sees nothing below the edge of the restraint strapped across his torso. He paws around with one gloved hand, then the other, feeling around for some kind of button or bell . . . anything he could use to call for help.

He finds nothing.

"Damn," he mumbles, and settles his head back against the pillow, focuses on steadying his breathing.

He thinks about Rose and Miller coming to see him . . . but the memory is jagged, distorted. He remembers yelling at Rose, at the doctor. Grabbing a nurse—

There are flashes of wandering the apartment building hallways, lost and angry. Looking for the killer? Yes, that's right. Then ending up in the Activity Room and attacking Mr. Blackwell—

What was I thinking?

"Oh, God, what a mess . . ." he says softly, sorrow and regret flooding through him.

What the hell was wrong with me?

He thinks back to the previous few days. He hadn't taken any strange pills. He hadn't been drinking heavily . . . and certainly hadn't done any recreational drugs. Hell, he hasn't touched that shit since his twenties.

Maybe I just . . . snapped. A sort of mental break? God, I want to get better. I want my mind back, my life back. I'll . . . I'll just lie here until someone comes. Nice and calm. Focus on my breathing. Then, I'll be polite, I'll be rational. This will all get worked out in no time. And then I'll apologize to . . . well, everyone. Rose and Mr. Blackwell. That nurse I almost hurt. And I'm sure a few other—

Mickey's inner dialogue abruptly halts.

The door to his room is opening.

He hears the soft creak, sees the top of the door swing inward, spilling white light across the ceiling and the far wall, wiping out the underwater dissolution of the moonlight, bringing things into sharper relief.

Mickey squints against the light, then settles back, takes a deep breath, lets it out. *Just need to explain that I'm better now. That I'm calm now.*

I need to get these restraints off.

The door closes softly and Mickey waits for a nurse to come into view. He's eager to speak with someone now that he's lucid, convince them he's not some raving lunatic.

Seconds tick by, but no one appears.

He *hears* them near the base of his bed. A rustling of fabric . . .

Probably checking my chart.

Then an idea, slick and cold as an ice pick, settles into the base of Mickey's spine. A frigid finger that slowly trails up his back until it reaches his thick neck, makes his mind tingle with fear.

No. No way. You're being paranoid.

It's a nurse; it's just a nurse.

"Hello? I'm . . ." He clears his parched throat. "I'm awake."

"Good," a voice says, soft in the darkness.

Is that a man or a woman?

The sound is high-pitched and distorted, as if someone's doing a funny voice for show. As if playing a character.

Oh no . . . please God . . . it can't be . . . not now.

Not like this.

The visitor steps into Mickey's view and, at first, he wonders if his mind is playing tricks on him again. It's dark, after all.

But no . . . the person is wearing all black, and their face is covered in some sort of material that turns them into a walking void, a head made of darkness and shadow.

Inhuman.

"You," Mickey says calmly.

Pushing away the rising fear—the panic—in his chest, he forces himself to *think*.

To find a way out of this.

He quickly debates his options:

I can beg . . . Or . . . I can yell. Yeah, I'll scream for help. If I can just get my hands free, I can grab this son of a bitch and throttle—

Before he can do any of the above, however, a gloved hand comes toward his face and begins pushing fabric into his mouth, stuffing more and more until Mickey's eyes bulge with terror.

I'M BEING CHOKED!

But then the pushing stops. A leather glove taps his cheek. *Good boy.*

A gag, then. Okay, fine. But I'm still alive, still alive!

Mickey rotates his wrists, his ankles, praying by some miracle a strap has come free, a mistake made in his favor.

But there's nothing. His wrists, his ankles, are strapped down tight. His hands secured in the medical mittens.

He's stuck. Trapped.

Helpless.

"Hey, big guy," the voice says, that high-pitched, scratchy hiss sounding more animal than human. "I sure hate to see you like this. You were doing so well."

Mickey can only stare blankly at that black mask, that hollow face.

"Too much salt in your diet, I think," the killer says, patting Mickey's stomach.

With one last, sudden charge of resistance, he convulses, bucking against the restraints.

In a nanosecond of pleasure—the last Mickey will ever experience—the shadow figure takes a jerky half-step backward, as if not completely sure the restraints can hold the big man down. Then there's a light chuckle from behind the mask.

"Jesus, you are strong," the killer says. "I mean, with all those drugs in your system, you were like a raging bull. Oh, yeah, I guess I can tell you now. I might have spiked your salt and pepper with a nasty stimulant—sort of like if you did cocaine, meth, and ecstasy all in one. You've been digesting that shit for almost a week, by the way. In small doses, of course. Still, it did quite a number on your brain, huh?"

One gloved finger taps Mickey's forehead—*tap, tap, tap*—before pulling away.

Mickey groans, tries not to gag on the (now quite damp) cloth tickling the back of his throat.

"Just so you know," the killer says quietly, bending over, now only inches from Mickey's face. "I'm going to smother you to death in a minute. But first, I want to let you know that I gutted your buddy Gopi earlier today." A chuckle. "I split him open like a pig at the slaughterhouse. His guts were *everywhere*. It was nasty but also, you know . . . awesome."

A fat tear spills down Mickey's temple. His eyes glisten with despair, with horror.

"And when I'm done with you," the killer continues in that same terrible whisper, "I'm gonna get your friends. I'm gonna get *all of them*. You guys have sort of become my, um . . . special project. My *coup de grâce*, as the French would say. A deathblow that will put this whole horrid fucking place out of its misery."

The killer grips the pillow beneath Mickey's head and jerks it away. Mickey's neck twists painfully and another panicked moan crawls up his throat. He tries to speak, to beg, to plead for his life—

"You know, I've seen this done in movies a hundred times, but I never actually tried it on anyone. I'm super curious to see if it works."

The killer holds up the pillow, as if presenting a grand prize.

"Shall we give it a try?"

Mickey shakes his head back and forth, pulls madly at the restraints, bucks his hips up and down. The wide strap across his chest slides upward, edging into the base of his throat.

Free—if I can just get my body free! Maybe I can flip the whole damn bed, the crash will bring someone running, I just have to . . . please! Give me one more . . .

The pillow slams down onto his face, the pressure of a hand, perhaps even two, pushing down onto his nose, his cloth-stuffed mouth. He turns his head, fills his nose with air. *It's not working! I can breathe!*

I'll play dead, I'll buck for a bit, then struggle, then play—

But now the pressure moves, the stuffing of the pillow tightens, once more finding his mouth and nose, and he tries to twist his head once more, to find air, but the hands are strong, and now he's beginning to find it hard to breathe. Panic building, he tries to push the cloth out of his mouth with his tongue, but the weight on his face is complete, is total.

No . . . no!

Mickey jerks his head violently to the side, but the pressure stays, and now things are getting tricky. The more he struggles and squirms, the more the chest restraint slides off his broad chest and toward his neck, pressing roughly, tightly, against his throat—as if being held there by an unseen hand, crushing his windpipe—and all the while his body is *commanding* him to breathe IN through his mouth, but all he sucks in is more damp cloth, which is now slipping down his throat, making him want to gag, to throw up. If he could only clear it . . . but his mouth is a no-go. Nothing in, nothing out.

Instead, he focuses on breathing through his nose, but the pillow is shoved down so tight, and there's no air there . . . a trickle at best . . .

"Come on, motherfucker . . ."

Mickey hears the killer's strained voice, but now it's distant, distorted. His thoughts are becoming muddled, confused. His face is hot, his body has slowed its thrashing, his limbs have gone numb. His heart is pounding, but it's getting slower, slower. . . . He'd give anything to lift a hand to his face and yank the obstruction away, pull the cloth from his mouth, escape this suffocating darkness, clear his vision so he can see the moonlight one last time.

After a few more seconds, his brain begins to slow, then shut down in a mad final surge of bursting neurons. Behind his eyes there's a blinding white flash—then another, and another.

His body, meanwhile, has become impossibly heavy, as if made of stone. A dead weight that quietly sinks into the murky depths of a great black sea.

Sinking . . .

Sinking . . .

And then, all feeling is gone.

The darkness consumes him, and his ethereal spirit tears apart from the flesh—forever free now of that heavy burden—and streaks away, away, toward an endless silver horizon and whatever lies beyond.

NINE

EXODUS

1

The air is brittle cold, the sky overcast, a hard, unforgiving gray. A light morning mist covers the ground, gives hazy skirts to the distant trees. Instead of the outdoors feeling open and expansive, there's a pressure in the air, as if the earth itself were being squeezed, the concrete sky trembling with the stress of not bursting apart and hurling the inhabitants crawling below into the void of outer space. It's the kind of morning that makes one feel as if they're trapped in this world, vacuum-sealed in God's Tupperware for later use.

Rose sits in the gazebo, a navy blue, ankle-length coat draped over her housedress; a brown knit hat she'd made herself covers her head and ears. She stares at the dense, distant trees, her back to the buildings, and silently weeps for Mickey Lake, her lost friend.

After a few minutes, she takes a few deep breaths of cool air—hoping to steady herself—then gives in and weeps some more.

Ostensibly, she'd come out to the gazebo to have a look at the bench where Stan Swanson had left his missive for the government, his written agreement to visit an alien spacecraft. Beneath the bench, however, she'd found nothing of interest. A roly-poly bug, a crouched daddy longlegs. But no clues.

Other than the fact the killer knows this entire place inside and out. Knows about a secret space beneath a bench and can move like a phantom through rooms and hallways, past nurses and orderlies and residents.

Whoever it is lives *here,* Rose thinks, and the thought sickens her, worries her mind like a devil's crossword puzzle.

Six letters that mean *Destroyer of Lives.*

KILLER.

Rose had tried calling Hastings using the number on his business card. She'd left a message, asking him to please come, to please *investigate* this newest horror.

He hasn't called back.

No, she doesn't think any police will come, or care. Not for a doped-up, crazy old man who died in the night, his mind so far gone that the doctors and nurses had put him in restraints—the equivalent of a modern-day straitjacket.

We're on our own, she thinks, hating the truth of it.

After inspecting the bench where Stan had put his letter (*the killer was here, right HERE*), Rose sat down, wanting some quiet, enjoying the peace, comforted that the chilled air matched her mood. The somber morning allowed her to open her heart and mourn the news she'd received upon waking—a phone call from Miller letting her know Mickey had died in the night. Some kind of freak accident.

"He struggled like a mad dog, and the chest strap slipped up to his throat. Poor bastard strangled himself," Miller had told her, his voice sounding tired and old. "At least, that's what the nurse told Jesse Garcia, a hospice resident who knows Bob Nash, who told his wife Ellie, who told Libby Sue—"

"Who told everyone," Rose said, her breath stuck in her throat as she sat up in bed, staring blankly at a window. She hardly noticed when the train rumbled by a few moments later, right on schedule.

"The gossip queen," Miller agreed, but did not laugh.

Rose had disconnected the call and put on her coat and boots, feeling the need to do *something*—needing to get out of her apartment, away from the residents, from all the horror and death and despair.

Now, sitting in the gazebo—the cold air working its way beneath the layers of her protection, settling on her exposed lower legs, hands, and face like the breath of Death himself—she ponders what's happening, and what she's going to do about it.

For a few minutes more, she allows herself to absorb the solitude. The quiet peace. Despite the brittle morning air and the pain of losing her friend, she finds herself able to relish the nearby singing of birds—a gentle, rhythmic trilling that kindles the tiniest spark of hope inside her hurting heart.

The birds go on singing, she thinks. *Despite all the horrors of this world.*

She takes a tissue from her coat pocket, blows her nose, sniffles away the last dregs of her open sorrow, and wipes the chill, wet tears from her cheeks.

Enough tears, Rose. You have to think now.

If someone here is doing this, then they must have access to the rooms and to the Medical Center. Someone who would not arouse suspicion if they were seen, day or night, walking the grounds or the hallways . . .

Rose sits up straight, an idea ringing in her mind.

She looks at her watch, sees it's just past 9 AM. It's a Saturday, but that won't matter. The man works every day but Sunday, and if he isn't in his office, he'll be around somewhere.

She'll find him. She'll speak with him about what's going on.

Administrator Blackwell, she decides, is her best place to start.

And, if she's being honest with herself, her number one suspect.

2

Rose lucks out.

She finds Blackwell at his desk, clicking away at a keyboard, his brow furrowed in concentration as he stares at a computer screen. She watches him from the doorway for a moment, waiting for him to notice her. When he continues to work, she gently clears her throat, startling him. He stares at her, gaping and wide-eyed, as if she'd caught him watching pornography. He rapidly clicks the mouse a few times, presumably closing whatever windows he'd had open, and she's about to apologize when his face lights up into a genial smile and he stands—dressed in a neat brown suit, even on a Saturday.

"Ms. DuBois," he says. "What a pleasant surprise. How can I help you?"

Rose returns a weak smile. For the first time since she's known him, she notices just how *tall* the man is. How *fit* he looks under that suit.

"May I sit down a moment?"

The administrator hurries around the desk, adjusts one of his visitor chairs a fraction of an inch. "Please, please. Of course."

Rose hasn't been in the administrator's office for a good while. A year or more, she guesses. She spent some time here when she first moved in, of course. A couple years back she came to see him about moving to a different apartment, one that was far away from the tracks of the CSX freight train.

Booked for years out, I'm afraid, he'd said in that nearly undetectable pitch of a British accent, the one barely hanging on from the years of his London childhood.

The office is plain and inoffensive, like a therapist's office might be. Calming artwork on the walls—seascapes and mountain ranges—simple but elegant wood furniture that's both antiquarian and utilitarian. The floor is covered with plush, dark gray carpeting, and the tan-painted walls are warmed by a hint of umber. It's all very soothing, Rose thinks, wondering why, then, it feels so sterile. So cold.

Rose sits in the chair, puts her hands in her lap, and waits for Blackwell to regain his own seat. "So," he says, putting on his usual congenial expression, the one he wears like a mask.

"So," Rose says. "I'd like to speak with you about Mickey Lake."

The administrator's set expression softens like heated wax; his smile dissolves. "How did you—"

"And Angela Forrest," Rose continues. "And Owen Duffield, and Egor Abramov—"

"Rose—"

"And while I'm here, let's have a chat about Stan Swanson, the Baxter sisters, and Bill Rutherford. Hell, might as well throw poor Esther Pound in there, to boot. Although I think that one was actually an accident." She leans forward, eyes locked on his. "Am I missing anyone?"

"Now, Rose—"

"To be more pointed," she continues, undeterred, "I'd like to talk about *you*, Mr. Blackwell. I think we should discuss the deaths of all these people who were in *your* care."

The administrator is momentarily stunned by the tenacity in Rose's voice—his face a cloud of guilt and shame—but then he grimaces, stands quickly from his chair.

For a split second, Rose readies herself to scream, as if the man were coming around the desk to put his hands against her throat and strangle her to death right then and there. She shrinks back when he comes near, then relaxes as he goes past her to the door, shuts it softly. She doesn't like him behind her—not one bit—but he quickly moves back to his side of the mahogany desk, sits back down, and folds his hands neatly atop a clean leather blotter. He takes a breath to steady himself then looks into her eyes, as if daring her to see deception in his heart.

"Rose, I'm not going to patronize you."

"A good start," Rose says, attempting, for the time being, to keep derision out of her tone.

"You're a smart woman, Rose. I know that," he says. "And you also know that I'm very aware of what goes on in our community, and believe me when I say I'm just as concerned as you about the recent deaths here at Autumn Springs. Now, I'm not saying that I believe it's foul play or that there's some . . . *person* . . . responsible for these things . . ." He sighs, turns his hands, palms up. His eyes are troubled, maybe even frightened. "But I'd also have to be pretty thickheaded to think it's nothing more than a streak of bad luck."

Rose is surprised at the admission but keeps her face serene, her voice neutral. "Sounds like you're of two minds."

"A good way to put it," he says. "Look, my job is to make sure every resident here is being given the best care, the best *life*, we can offer. I think of everyone here as family, Rose, and it's hurt me terribly that so many have . . . passed on . . . in such a short window of time. And yes, I admit, it's suspicious."

Rose sits forward to speak, but Mr. Blackwell holds up one hand, staying her a moment.

"That said, accidents do happen. Suicides *do* happen. The people in this community are dealing with a lot more than just old age, Rose. Many are sick. Many are confused. Many, I'm sorry to say, are depressed. As I said, it's my job to offer the residents here the greatest of care, and we all do our best—the whole staff—to give comfort, and help, and treatment when and if needed. But sometimes . . ." Blackwell sits back, shrugs one shoulder. "We fail. And that's a hard truth. A hard reality. One that I take very personally."

"Mr. Blackwell," Rose says, placing a hand on the edge of his smooth desk. "My mother used to say that if you're walking around with a stick up your ass, that pain you're feeling isn't hemorrhoids. It hurts because you got a stick up your ass."

The administrator's eyes crinkle in confusion. "Sorry?"

"You got a stick up your ass, Mr. Blackwell, and you're talking about hemorrhoids."

"I'm not sure I—"

Rose shifts forward in her seat, dark eyes blazing. "Someone is killing my friends, administrator," she says. "And I think you know it."

Blackwell shrinks in his seat, eyes hooded. "I know no such thing, Rose. And I might caution you against saying such things to residents or anyone else."

"And why is that? You don't want to start a panic? After what happened in the Activity Room the other day during your curfew announcement? Bill Rutherford was foaming at the mouth like Cujo—"

"A seizure," Blackwell says weakly.

"Point is, there's *already* a panic, Mr. Blackwell. The people here are frightened half to death. Many, as you damn well know, are leaving or at least trying to. Some are stuck to this place like it's flypaper." Rose shakes her head. "You're not running a retirement home, Mr. Blackwell. You're running an octogenarian orphanage. Autumn Springs is full of lost souls with nowhere to turn, nowhere to go, otherwise you'd have a full-blown exodus on your hands."

"Rose, please," Blackwell says, a ring of desperation in his voice. "We need to be rational. We need to keep this contained."

As soon as the words are out of his mouth, Rose can tell Blackwell knows he'd slipped up—his lips tighten, the hands folded on the leather blotter curl into tight fists.

"What I mean to say—"

Rose sits back in her chair, eyes wide. "Oh, I know what you mean, administrator. You mean if word gets out that the old folks at Autumn Springs are being slaughtered like pigs in a sty, that property sales might slow down a bit. Maybe stop altogether. Is that right?"

Blackwell sighs, shakes his head. "As I said, my number one responsibility is to provide the best care for the residents here."

"While also taking care of the corporation that owns this place, I presume. Make sure appearances are held up so when grandma is brought here by her desperate children, they all think it's a hunky-dory idea, that they can sleep at night knowing they're giving her a good life instead of pushing her into a cow chute. You need to keep selling units, Mr. Blackwell. And all this . . ." Rose waves her hand through the air, as if swatting slow fat flies. "All this death is making things awkward, isn't it?" She raps her knuckles on the desktop, looks into the man's eyes. "All this murder, I mean."

"Okay, Ms. DuBois," Blackwell says tiredly. "Your point is made. Unfortunately, I have a lot to do—"

The cell phone on Blackwell's desk vibrates. The screen lights up with a new message. He glances at it casually, then his brow furrows.

Rose looks from his face to the phone.

Something's happened, she thinks, praying she's wrong.

Blackwell lifts the phone, taps the screen, and reads a text message.

"What is it, Mr. Blackwell?" Rose says lightly, wanting to know. *Needing* to know what's happened. "Please, tell me."

Blackwell looks at Rose, his face pale, his brown eyes troubled. "Have you seen Gopi Sharma recently?"

Rose feels cold fingers crawl up her spine. Her hands tingle, and for a moment she doesn't breathe. "I saw him Wednesday, at the meeting you called," she says, her voice no more than a whisper through numb, trembling lips. "What is it? What's happened?"

"Nothing," he says quickly, then shakes his head. "Probably nothing."

"What? Please, is he okay?"

"I'm sure he's fine, Rose." He sighs heavily. "Mary Reynolds has requested an emergency wellness check."

"I think they're a couple," Rose says distantly. "Why is she asking?"

Blackwell stands, opens a drawer, and pulls out a fat ring of keys.

"Because he's not answering his door," he says.

"You mean this morning?"

Blackwell looks down at her with haunted eyes. "Since yesterday."

Rose stands as well. "I'm coming with you."

Blackwell moves to the door, pauses as he holds it open for her. "I was going to suggest otherwise, but what would be the point?"

3

Mary Reynolds stands in the hallway.

Rose notices right away how distraught the woman is. Her hairdo, normally combed neatly to her shoulders, is tufted in places, as if she's been gripping clumps of silver hair with clenched fists. She's dressed, but her outfit is all wrong—hiking pants and a formal blouse, the buttons mismatched, giving her a decidedly *uneven* look.

There are several staggered doors open along the length of the hallway, nervous residents standing at the thresholds—all wringing hands and wide, nervous eyes.

Gopi's apartment, Greenview 3, is near the end of the hall, facing the back lawn. George McKee, who lives next door in unit 5, is one of those standing anxiously nearby at his open doorway, face lined with concern.

"I haven't heard him come or go," George says as they approach. "It's been real quiet. I hope he's all right."

Blackwell puts a comforting hand on the man's shoulder. "I'm sure it's fine. Please don't worry."

George takes a shaky breath, lets it out, and tries on a smile that makes him somehow look more sad than happy. He turns to address Rose, who stands a few feet back. "My daughter says she's taking me fishing. Her and her whole family."

Rose returns the smile, knowing a lie when she hears one. To the best of her knowledge, in all her years as his upstairs neighbor, George hasn't had a single visitor.

"How nice," she says.

"At least, I hope so. She's thinking on it."

Blackwell moves on past George and—to Rose's surprise—gives Mary Reynolds a quick hug, whispers something in her ear. Mary nods, sniffles, and takes a step toward Rose. Without either of them speaking, Mary slips an arm beneath one of Rose's—each of them supporting the other—as they watch Blackwell fit his master key into the door.

He pauses, glances at Mary. "I better . . ." he says, then gives a good hard knock. "Mr. Sharma? It's Administrator Blackwell. Sir, are you there? Can you answer?"

"Should we get a nurse?" Mary asks.

"Yes, I . . . sorry, I rushed here and . . ." Blackwell says, edging toward flustered. "Let's just . . ."

Rose thinks the man is hesitant to go in, to see what might be inside.

He's frightened, she thinks, and moves a hand to cover Mary's, which is clutched tightly to her arm. *Lord, please let him be okay.*

Blackwell pushes open the door, takes a single step into the apartment, and lets out a cry of such utter horror, such deep-welled *despair,* that Mary bursts into tears.

"What is it?" she wails. "Oh, God. What is it?"

Blackwell steps back into the hallway and slams the door closed. When he glances back toward George, Rose, and Mary, his face is white as a sheet. "Please don't come closer," he says, pulling a cell phone from his pocket. Rose notices he's dialing 9–1–1.

"Mr. Blackwell?" Rose asks. She feels lightheaded, her tongue heavy. "Should I get a nurse?"

He looks at her and shakes his head. "No, it's . . . nobody opens this door," he replies, his voice quivering.

Someone answers his emergency call, and Blackwell turns his back on the two frightened women, the gawking neighbor. He puts a hand against the wall for support.

"Yes," he says. "I need to report a murder."

Mary's scream fills the hallway.

4

Detective Hastings arrives shortly after Blackwell shows two armed, burly policemen the dead, mangled body in Greenview 3.

Upon arrival, the officers had immediately ordered all the residents on the floor to stay inside their apartments, then proceeded to roll CRIME SCENE tape across the threshold. Shortly after, four more officers arrived.

Now, one policeman stands sentinel at Gopi's front door while another calls the coroner's office from the foyer. Two others head out to the back lawn, where they cordon off a large square of grass with thin wooden stakes and more of the bright yellow CRIME SCENE tape, making sure no one comes near the two windows of Gopi's apartment or the area that surrounds them.

Hastings enters the apartment with latex gloves on his hands, paper booties on his feet, and surveys the bloody scene with a grimace. With genuine remorse (and more than a bit of frustration) he thinks this death could have been prevented if he'd followed his instincts earlier, and if the captain had seen fit to take what was happening at Autumn Springs more seriously. Perhaps, if they'd had a police presence here this past week, this wouldn't have happened. If . . . if . . . if . . .

Poor bastard, he thinks, recalling the brief conversation he'd had with the victim less than a week prior. He'd been smart, Hastings recalled. Quick and astute. The best kind of witness. A man of depth he could have seen befriending in another life.

Now his guts are spilled onto the living room floor, his blood crusting the carpet, his body a ruin—torn open by a savage, ruthless hand.

Hastings studies the surroundings. The closed window was, most likely, the killer's point of entry and exit. He notes a strange device on the floor next to the body. *A camera?* The coffee table is knocked askew from what he assumes was a short, brutal struggle.

Staring at the scene, part of him still can't believe it.

A killer. A goddamned *killer.*

How many other deaths is this maniac responsible for?

Anger boils in Hastings's chest as he thinks back on the other victims. In his mind, he flips through the grim, gory photographs in his files.

The two suicides?

Possibly.

The man in the bathtub—yeah, okay. Strong candidate.

But the guy who jumped off the fire tower? How?

Or what about the fella who was poisoned?

Again . . . how?

Cyanide in his pudding?

Only moments ago, Hastings was briefed on the former football player who'd died in the night. How he'd gone seemingly mad, become totally unhinged.

How he'd suffocated to death.

A freak accident with a medical restraint.

Pretty far-fetched for an accident.

And the fire? The three sisters?

Jesus Christ.

Am I dealing with a serial killer . . . in a retirement home?

Hastings stares at the gutted corpse and does a quick body count in his head.

Ten dead in two weeks. *TEN.*

Slow down, Ernie, you're jumping to conclusions. No way all ten are murders.

Okay, smart guy. Then how many?

Half?

More than half?

Hastings makes a note to order complete autopsies and blood work on the other victims (outside of Egor Abramov, he of the death-by-hard-on, whose body is nothing more than a pile of ashes; ditto for the Baxter sisters, whose charred remains have gone to the big oven in the sky).

I could exhume the woman that started this horrible streak—the supposed slip and fall. And her boyfriend, the one who slashed his wrists. And Stanley Swanson.

Dig them up and have them all examined.

Okay, let's say you get the go-ahead. You're looking for . . . what exactly?

Hastings recalls the conversation he'd had with the four elderly residents the other day, over a cup of coffee in the dining hall. When all of this felt like wild speculation.

What had the one guy said? Beauregard. The one they call Miller.

He said the guy with the bad ticker had been drugged.

Quite a guess.

Quite a leap.

Hastings will speak with Mr. Miller again. And with Rose, who seems to have suspected quite a bit early on. At the time, Hastings had thought her smart but a smidge paranoid. Perhaps desperate for something to cling on to out of sheer boredom. He's ashamed to think that now, to realize he'd dismissed her warnings so easily.

He'll need to speak with Rose again.

He'll need to speak with *everyone.*

As he studies the room, the mutilated body, two thoughts come to mind.

One, if the killer was being subtle before, this signals a significant change in his modus operandi. The murder scene is a lot of things, but subtle isn't one of them.

Because he's escalating things, Hastings realizes. *Because he knows his time is growing short, that there's only so much he can get away with. Our killer is showing the world that he's no longer a myth. A ghost. A figment of the imagination.*

This bloodbath is the killer's way of saying "Howdy-ho, everyone!

"I'm real, and I'm HERE."

But the killer isn't just getting antsy.

He's getting angry.

It's a thought that gives Hastings a nasty churning in his gut. If the killer is making this personal—getting reckless, showing their hand—it means they're either very stupid or very smart.

Smart enough to know that the game is almost over.

That the clock is ticking.

Soon, Hastings knows, the killing will stop, and this madman will vanish back into the ether from which he came.

But not yet. Not until they kill more.

But how many?

Who else?

Once more recalling that get-together in the dining hall, Hastings pictures the folks he'd been sitting with. There were four of them, all suspecting foul play, all trying to convince him there was a murderer on the loose.

Mickey Lake. Gopi Sharma. Beauregard Mason Miller. Rose DuBois.

Two down, two to go.

Which leads to Hastings's second thought:

Mr. Miller and Ms. DuBois are, in all likelihood, next on the killer's list.

He hopes he's wrong about that. After all, he'd been wrong before.

He'd been wrong plenty.

5

Rose sits at her kitchen table, numb with shock and impossible grief. The detective sits across from her, a notepad open in front of him.

Most of his questions have to do with the previous deaths, wringing her memory dry about what she suspected *before*, back when they'd shared a coffee. Was there anything else? Anything he'd been unaware of or dismissed?

Rose answers his questions, but she is growing tired. So very, very tired.

Too much, she thinks. *It's too much. I feel as if my heart has been broken, the pieces mended with cheap tape, then broken all over again.*

I'm in pieces.

But Rose also realizes, with a mild jolt of surprise, that she is more than just sad—more than just devastated or frightened.

She's *angry.*

"You and your friends, you guys mentioned drugs. That the killer had been using drugs somehow."

"Speculation," Rose says, shrugging. "It's just . . . if you'd seen Stan Swanson before he died. He looked *high,* you know what I mean?"

Hastings nods. "I do. Blasted pupils. Erratic behavior."

"Paranoia," Rose adds. "I kicked a kid or two out of my classroom when I knew they'd been smoking dope, or something worse, but this was a whole other level."

"And the nurses, the doctors . . . they didn't notice?"

"You'd have to ask them but, if I'm being honest, I think it's because, after a while, the nurses don't really *look* at us anymore. Not really. The folks who live in the Medical Center, they're not ailing from things that can be cured. They just need help getting out of bed sometimes, or getting to the bathroom. They can't cook their own meals. And the orderlies and nurses, they just sort of go on autopilot.

I'm not saying they mistreat those under their care, or that they aren't good people . . . but I've seen them in action, Detective. I've watched them enter a person's room, turn the bed, collect the dishes, and not so much as glance at the person who lives there. I've seen them ask my friends if they need to use the bathroom while staring at their phones, then walk out like they had a hot date waiting for them back at the nurse's station."

Hastings nods. "And erratic behavior around here isn't necessarily a showstopper."

"I'm afraid not. But regarding the drugs, we know about that man with the heart attack and the stiff pecker, but what about Mickey? He was *restrained*, Detective. Let me tell you, Mickey Lake was one of the gentlest souls I've ever known. I've never seen him raise his voice or lose his temper. Not once. Then . . . what? He's attacking Mr. Blackwell on a stage, in front of God and everybody?"

"Okay," Hastings says, making a note before looking back at Rose. "And you thought there was something similar going on with Mr. Swanson?"

Rose's eyes go wide, and Hastings squirms under the impression that she's looking at him like he's the biggest idiot on planet Earth.

"Why else would he be out there in the middle of nowhere?" she says. "Climbing a damn tower in the dark? Why else would he think aliens were visiting his room? Or getting letters from the government?"

"I hear you, Rose," Hastings says with a sigh. "I'm just trying to understand how he was lured out there, and if he was drugged—if he was *high*, like you said—it might explain it. To some degree, at least. But I want to ask you about those letters, because despite our search we never did find them. Any ideas?"

Rose purses her lips. "No. My guess is they were thrown out with the rest of his things. But listen to me now . . ." Rose reaches across the table, puts her cool fingers over Hastings's wrist, and waits for him to look into her eyes. "I think your killer is preying on us, Detective. A lot of folks here are plenty old, I'll give you that. But there's *old*, and then there's old and sick. Old and mixed-up.

Old and weak. You get me? I think this man is playing with us like someone might fool a child into getting inside their van. Preying on our innocence, our naivete, our ignorance of things that could hurt us. This person is more than just a killer, Detective. He's sadistic."

Hastings nods. "I agree with you there. I mean, yeah, it's sick, Rose. Truly. And this person, and I'm sure you've had the same thought, is connected to Autumn Springs somehow. They'd have to be."

"Yes, I agree," she says, pulling her hand back. "I assume you're doing background checks on everyone?"

"Yes, ma'am. On the doctors, the staff, you bet."

"What about the residents?"

Hastings laughs, but it fades quickly when he sees her dour expression. "Come on, Rose. No offense, but you think there's an elderly Jack the Ripper in one of these apartments? Takes a lot of strength to kill someone, Ms. DuBois."

"No offense taken, and while I admit many of us are on the fragile side, or maybe we aren't still holding all the cards God originally dealt us, there are plenty of us who are stronger than you might realize. Who have every bit of our minds, too. We might be forgetful, or we might not hear so well, but character doesn't change, Detective. If this person killed before they moved here, why not now?"

"You really think it could be someone who lives here?" Hastings asks, but does so thoughtfully, as if turning the idea—the possibility—over in his mind.

"There's precedent," Rose says, straightening in her chair. "I googled it."

Hastings frowns at her. "Rose, you shouldn't be doing that."

"There was an older couple who murdered drifters who came by their farm . . . in Missouri, I think it was," Rose says, ignoring his admonishment. "Murdered a dozen people. They were both in their seventies."

"Okay—"

"A man named Little killed over sixty women. *Sixty*. Kept killing on through his early seventies."

"I know that one, actually," he says, tapping his pencil on the table. "Samuel Little. Studied him along with Bundy and the rest."

"And you mentioned Jack the Ripper," Rose says, leaning forward as if sharing a secret. "There was a Granny Ripper, too. Killed a dozen people, right up through her sixties. Now, being in your sixties isn't that old, granted. But you see my point."

"You really need to stop reading this stuff," Hastings says teasingly, but Rose can tell she's got him thinking.

"I'll do as I please," she says with a sniff, and gives a look out her window, the uncaring day on the other side yawning its way toward dusk.

"Fair enough," Hastings says with a chuckle. "There's a couple other things I'd like to talk to you about, though."

Rose looks back at him with interest. "Okay."

"First, I want you to take a look at something. It might be difficult, and I probably shouldn't be showing you, but you seem to know a lot about what goes on here, and . . . hell, I don't know, maybe it will mean something more to you than it does to us."

Hastings picks up his phone, taps the screen, and turns it around so Rose can see it clearly.

"Oh, God . . . is that . . ."

"Yes, I'm sorry if it's—"

"It's fine." Rose takes a deep breath, then gently plucks the phone from Hastings's hand, stares more closely at the image. "What am I looking at exactly?"

"That's Mr. Sharma's forearm. He wrote it in blood before he died."

"Oh, sweet Jesus."

"Rose—"

"I said I'm fine; now let me look," she says, knowing she sounds snippy but doing her best to push through this horror, to be of some use to the young man.

The image is a close-up of the inside of Gopi's forearm. Written on the flesh, in finger-painted blood, are three symbols:

BMM

Rose thinks a moment. Hastings watches her carefully.

"It looks like . . ." she starts, frowning.

"Rose?"

"It just . . . oh, wait, I know." She snaps her fingers. "Did you find a camera in his room? A movie camera?"

He nods. "We did."

Rose hands the phone back to the detective. "Gopi used to brag, all day and all night, about his strange old camera, one that used film he had to order special. Eight-millimeter film, he called it. I saw the box once. Eight-M-M. Just like in that photo." Rose sighs, looking wistful. "He was going to make a movie next week . . . and poor Mickey, of all people, was going to act in it. I actually read the script," she says, swiping away a tear. "It wasn't very good."

"Okay, then. The obvious message here is eight-millimeter, as in the type of film in the camera we found, the one you're describing."

Rose hesitates for only a second. "I'd say so, but I'm no detective."

Hastings narrows his eyes at her. "Something else on your mind, Rose?" He smiles coyly, as if trying to read her mind, as if he were holding her deepest, darkest secret on his tongue, wondering if he should say it out loud.

I don't care for that look, Rose thinks. *That's the look of suspicion, probably the one he gives murderers in a small, cramped investigation room.*

No sir, I don't care for it one bit.

It's Rose who looks away first.

"Do these three symbols mean something to you?" he asks, leaning in. Pressing. "Something other than the camera film?"

Rose figures that's why he showed her. He knew about the camera all along, and the film. *He's fishing. Well sir, there ain't no fish here to catch. Not today.*

Rose folds her hands atop the table. "No, Detective. I guess I'm just wondering why you're showing this to me. You already know what it means."

Hastings's face relaxes, his eyes soften, and his smile becomes more genuine. He shrugs. "True, but another perspective never hurts. But you're right, we've already bagged it and our techs are going to develop the film that was inside, just in case there's something on there, something that can give us a lead on who did this."

"Okay, then. I'm sorry I wasn't more help."

Hastings pockets his phone. "No, Rose. I was wrong to ask. I guess I'm a bit desperate. I don't think time is on our side here. Which brings me to something else, something I'm hesitant to bring up."

"Well, get it out, and I'll let you know if it stings."

"Okay, here it is," he says, and folds his arms atop the table. "I don't want to frighten you, or overly worry you, but I think . . . well, and this is just a hunch—"

"You think I'm next," Rose says, and her eyes slide toward the window once more, frowning at the day.

Hastings hesitates, then sighs heavily. "It's a possibility. Given who this lunatic seems to be targeting, I think he might have it in for you and your friends. For whatever reason."

"Because we're meddling," she says, turning her gaze back to him.

He shrugs. "Could be that, could be something else. Could be nothing."

"So what should I do? I can't put a bolt on the door; it's against policy. I can lock my windows, but lucky for me I'm on the second floor. If they want to come in here and get me, there's not a lot I can do about it. Maybe I should get a gun."

"I wouldn't advise it," he says, not picking up on her sarcasm. "And yes, I think you're right. I think he can probably come in here any time he wants. So I wouldn't answer the door unless you know who's on the other side."

"Wonderful," Rose says, the heat of anger on her cheeks. "So, I'm to stay locked up in fear? That's your answer? And what do I do if he comes in the night? While I'm asleep? What then? I'm helpless, Detective. We're all helpless here."

"I know that, Rose," he says quietly.

His eyes fall to the table, and she would swear the man is blushing. As if . . . *embarrassed*. Like a child caught stealing from a cookie jar.

"What?" she says.

He doesn't look up. He doesn't meet her eye. "Let's just say, hypothetically, that you *were* next on this psycho's list." Now he does look at her, and there's a sadness in his eyes. "We'd be a step ahead, Rose."

For a moment, he just watches her . . . waiting.

And then, she knows.

A fear so deep and heavy fills her heart that, for a moment, she forgets to breathe. In a series of flashes, she sees her friends—killed and cut up. She sees Miller, popping a peppermint into his mouth and taking her hand in the dark. She sees her daughter, her grandson, and she sees a glimpse of herself, somewhere in the future, sitting alone in a small room, watching the sun disappear behind the trees, wondering what it was all for.

She recalls a quote from a book she once read—a brick of a novel about good and evil at the end of the world: "*Love always comes due in blood.*"

After a few quiet moments, she nods.

"Okay," Rose says quietly, and then turns toward the window once more—toward a life that was once safe—to gaze at the shattered remains of a sanctuary she thought impenetrable from anything but the cold, ethereal hand of death itself.

But now there's a snake in the garden, and it must be cast out.

"Okay."

6

It's a bright, brittle Sunday morning. The sun is pale, the sky an icy blue shell, fragile as fine China.

Rose and Miller sit at their usual table in the dining hall. They've picked their way through a light brunch, and Miller is just finishing his dessert ("The sugar helps me think," he'd said when ordering, slightly embarrassed). Rose sips decaf.

It's been twenty-four hours since the discovery of their murdered friend.

When the CRIME SCENE tape went up, there was no keeping what happened a secret, and the residents—with good reason—recoiled in fear and horror at the news of a violent murder in their community. Those who were able to find alternate places to stay, did so. Many refused to leave. Many could not.

Rose looks around, noticing the emptiness of the dining hall. "How many have left, do you think?"

Miller glances around, shrugs. "Not so many. Maybe ten . . . maybe a dozen." He takes a sip of coffee after finishing off his bowl of ice cream. "Wish we could at least bolt our damn doors," he says, wiping his mouth with a napkin. "I don't like knowing anyone with the right key can come on in whenever they please."

"And what happens if you have a stroke or a heart attack?" Rose shakes her head. "The staff needs to have access."

"I suppose," he grumbles, absently spinning the porcelain mug on the table.

Rose takes a nibble of cold toast and—trying for nonchalant—says, "I spoke with the detective this morning."

"Oh? What did he want?"

"He thinks you and I are in danger," she says. "That we have targets on our back from whoever did that to poor Gopi."

Miller nods. "Are you worried?"

"I suppose I'd be stupid not to be."

"Then why don't you leave?" Miller leans forward to rest on his elbows. "Go stay with Sybil and Roy. Get out of harm's way."

"There are police here now. I saw a car parked out front."

"Yeah, but they can't be everywhere. They can't protect everyone. I think you should go, Rose, even if it's for a few days or a few weeks. Maybe they'll catch this lunatic by then and you can come back."

"What about you?"

Miller smiles sadly. "I've nowhere to go." He pauses, as if debating something . . . then lowers his eyes. "I had a daughter once, but she died years ago. Cancer."

Rose sets down her mug, eyes wide and hurt. "I had no idea. I'm so sorry."

He waves a hand, but she can tell it pains him to think of it. To remember.

"It was a long time ago."

"What was her name? If you don't mind my asking, that is. I know you don't like to talk about your past, and I don't want to be intrusive, I—"

"Caroline," he says. "Anyway, she was the end of the line, so to speak."

"So . . . she didn't have children? There's no grandkids running around?" Rose asks hesitantly, feeling as though she's walking on eggshells. Or through a field of land mines. "I'm sorry to be curious."

Miller shrugs. "I don't mind, Rose." He looks up to meet her eye and smiles sadly. "There's not much to tell, and I don't like dwelling too much on what was. Besides, family or no, I wouldn't leave even if I could. This is my home, for better or worse."

"I agree with you there," she says, resisting the desire to push further, to ask about Caroline's mom, about the rest of his family.

But he's right: the past is the past. At our age photo albums aren't filled with memories, they're filled with lessons. In some cases, with warnings.

"Well, I'm glad you're staying."

"Likewise."

"And since that's decided, and if I'm being honest, there are one or two things I'd like to follow up on."

Miller gives her a stony look, one that makes her slightly uncomfortable. "Rose, this sleuthing thing might have been entertaining at one point, when we weren't sure if these things were accidents or something else. But now we *know*, Rose." He taps a finger against the tabletop. "There's someone lurking around here who is deranged, who is sick. Who is *killing* folks. Killing our friends."

Rose straightens in her chair. "Yes, Beauregard, I'm well aware."

"And you just said that you could be a target. So why are you fooling around with this?" Miller shakes his head. "We're nothing but a couple retired teachers, Rose. I'm just an old man with too much tweed in his closet, and you should be playing cards and reading cozy mysteries, not hunting serial killers. You should be packing a bag, not . . . hell, I don't know, sticking your nose where it doesn't belong."

Rose bristles. "What I do is my business, Miller. If you don't want to help, that's fine. But I am not a child to be reproached."

"Then stop acting like one!" he snaps.

Anger bursts from Rose like a bomb, one whose timer has finally ticked to zero. She slaps a hand onto the table, shaking the ceramic cups and plates, her normally serene voice harsh as a whip. "Jesus Christ, Miller, do you think I *want* to die?"

Miller's eyes go comically wide as he sits back, one hand raised in a vague gesture of self-defense. Heads have turned throughout the quiet dining hall, forks paused in midair, as if Rose has somehow stopped time.

"Yes, I'm old," she says. "And yes, you're old, Beauregard. We're all so goddamned *old*!"

"Rose, please—"

"But that doesn't mean I'm dead," she says, tears filling her eyes. "I have so *much* I want to live for. I want to see my grandson grow into a man. I want to have a thousand more days with my beautiful daughter. I want to see sunsets and watch the seasons change. I want to have fun and enjoy my life. I want to read, and travel . . . and I want to *live*. But part of living means not living in fear, Miller. Part of living means doing what's difficult, what's frightening, what's *right*, even if it puts you in the path of danger. Do you understand? I want to live, damn it, not be shoved onto some dusty shelf or locked inside a closet for my own safety."

"We are living, Rose," Miller says, his own face now stormy and defiant, his voice raised to her for the first time in their brief history. "This is life! This, right here! Me! Yes, that's right. I'm here, too, you know. And I care about you, and I want you to be safe, that's all I'm saying. My God, woman," he says, his voice choked with emotion. "Why do you hate me so much?"

Rose's expression goes cold, her eyes stern. She stands, drops her clutched napkin onto the table. "I don't hate you, Miller, as you well know. But I'll not be told what I should or should not be doing. Not by a man. Not by anyone. Not by you."

"Rose—"

"Enjoy your fucking coffee," she mutters, then walks away, promising herself she'll hold back the tears burning her eyes until she's outside or, better yet, back home.

She so badly wanted to tell him what she's planning. Part of her hoping she *could* tell him, that it would bring her comfort to know he was thinking of her.

To know she isn't alone.

But she is. And that's okay. That's her choice.

She is alone, and vulnerable . . . and in grave danger.

Now, however, she means to use that danger to her advantage.

If the killer wants to come for her, let him come.

She'll be ready.

7

Rose sits beside the koi pond feeling sick to her stomach—partly due to her argument with Miller, partly from nerves for what's to come. Tatum is not out here today, so she sits alone and watches the fish buoy to the surface, their shiny bright faces reaching for the sun, mouths agape in the hopes of a floating bug or a tossed pellet.

She calls her daughter, praying she's got the timing right, catching them at home between school and dinner. In the distance, the setting sun burns ocher above the trees, lengthening shadows, cooling the air as day prepares for night.

"Mom?"

"Hello, baby," Rose says.

For the next ten minutes, Rose talks to her daughter. The indifferent sun lowers itself into the western horizon. At one point, Roy hops on the call, and Rose tells him that she loves him. That she'll see him soon.

When she hangs up, dusk has crept in like a clandestine lover, wrapping itself around her in a cold embrace—one she shirks off with a shiver.

Despite the cooling air, Rose stays by the pond and watches the sunset to its conclusion, savoring the day's glorious curtsy, as if it were just for her.

As if it might be her last.

8

Rose opens her eyes to the pitch-black darkness of her bedroom.

The clock on her nightstand informs her it's just past 2 AM and—after a moment to pull herself out of whatever dream she was having—she's completely, terrifyingly, awake.

But she doesn't move.

She lies very still, and very quiet, in her bed.

Listening.

After a moment, she hears it. The sound of someone moving around in her apartment—through the living room, coming closer.

Rose shifts her weight—quietly, slowly—so she's lying on her back, head propped up on a pillow, eyes fixed on the solid black rectangle of her bedroom door.

Even though she's prepared for this (as prepared as anyone can be), and even though she was *positive* it was going to happen just the way it's happening, she is still petrified with fear.

Quietly, she waits . . . and waits, her breathing steady and deep. She lowers her eyelids as much as she can while still being able to see.

Sleeping, she reminds herself. *You're sleeping, Rose.*

And then, after what feels an eternity, a shadow slips, like black liquid, through her bedroom door.

Is this what Angela saw on the night she died?

And Owen?

The killer steps to the foot of her bed, stops, and stares down at her.

Rose opens her eyes.

She takes in the killer's black clothes, the shadowed, masked face. Something glints in the killer's hand, but it's not a gun, or a knife.

It's a needle.

Rose doesn't move, doesn't breathe.

Slowly, the foot of the duvet is lifted by a gloved hand, pulled back and away, exposing Rose's bare feet.

The killer hesitates, as if watching her in the dark, then reaches out and touches her right foot and grips it, holding it firmly in place.

Lowers the needle.

"No!" Rose screams. She kicks at the hand, yanks her feet away and sits up straight in the bed, her back pressed against the headboard. "No more!"

The lights come on.

Rose winces against the bright overhead light, pain searing her eyes. The killer, now fully exposed, the darkness pulled away like a magician's handkerchief, takes a step backward, head turning left and right—confused, upset.

Scared.

"The fuck?" a roughened, high-pitched voice says, and then a plain-clothed police officer steps out of the bathroom, gun drawn, pointed right at the killer's chest.

"Don't fucking move!" the officer yells.

The killer spins, as if to run back into the living room, when the apartment door bursts open and two more men storm into Rose's small apartment—a uniformed policeman and Detective Hastings. Rose can't see them, but she can *hear* them—hear them yelling for the intruder to *PUT YOUR HANDS IN THE AIR* and *DROP THE NEEDLE* and *GET ON YOUR FUCKING KNEES!*

But the killer does none of these things. Instead, the intruder kicks the bedroom door shut, twists the lock on the knob and, tucking the syringe into a coat pocket, grabs a long, thin can clipped to their side. Before the cop standing in Rose's bedroom can fire his gun, the intruder drops to a knee and spins, arm extended. The air is filled with a *hissing* sound and then—from one second to the next—the whole room turns toxic.

Rose's eyes immediately begin to burn. Her throat clenches painfully and she begins to gag. The officer—one arm thrown defensively over his face—stumbles back toward the bathroom door.

For a split second, the killer stands at the foot of Rose's bed, fully exposed, staring at the old woman cowering and coughing into her blanket. Through burning eyes, Rose takes in the image.

Tall. Lithe.

Black ski mask.

Black hooded sweatshirt.

The bedroom doorknob rattles. A body slams into it.

The killer looks directly at Rose for one more moment, then turns toward the window, throws it open, and climbs out. There's another concussion as someone slams once more into the bedroom door, followed by curses. Rose glances back to the window but now sees nothing but a pair of gloved hands gripping the sill.

The killer hangs on for a moment . . . then drops.

The bedroom door bursts inward.

Rose screams.

Hastings runs to the open window, looks down, then yells into a radio mic clipped to his shoulder that the "perp is heading west, toward the tracks." The uniformed policeman, meanwhile, has turned and bolted from the room. Rose hears muted yells from the hallway, most likely her neighbors filing out to see what the hell is going on.

Hastings dips his head out the window, looks straight down toward the ground. "Dropped into a goddamn hedge," he mumbles, then turns to look at Rose. "You okay?"

"Yes," she says, even though her body is trembling with adrenaline and fear. "Just shaken up."

He nods, looks at the other officer, now leaning against the doorframe of the bathroom, fresh water from the sink dripping down his face. "What about you?"

"I'll live," the man says. "Fucking mace. Probably bear mace by the way it's eating through my eyeballs." Then the policeman walks to the bed and hands Rose a damp washcloth. "You should cover your mouth and nose until this shit's aired out."

Rose takes the cloth as Hastings paces, chewing his lip in frustration. He looks at Rose once more, face filled with regret, then turns his back on her to stare into the night. "You should've just shot the fucker."

The other man grunts and goes back to the bathroom sink.

But he didn't shoot him, Rose thinks, knowing she won't be sleeping any more this night. *And now, most likely, I've made this maniac angry.*

Perhaps even vengeful.

Rose opens her hand and stares at the small charm there. The silver, all-seeing eye stares right back. She wonders, somewhat numbly, what was in the needle. Would the contents of that syringe have killed her?

She thinks not. She thinks that would be too neat. Too clean. Too merciful.

No, Rose has an idea the killer wanted her incapacitated.

That he wanted to take his time with her.

To kill her slowly.

She shudders at the possibilities of what might have been, and now that everything has gone wrong, she thinks that maybe Miller was right. She should not be hunting killers. She should pack a bag and leave, like so many others have already done.

A weight settles on her mattress, and she looks up from the silver charm to see Hastings sitting at the edge of her bed, watching her with sorrowful eyes. "I'm sorry, Rose. I'm sorry to have put you through this."

"My choice," she says quickly, without conviction. She wipes her eyes and face with the cloth, sets it neatly atop her blanket. The plain-clothed officer exits the bathroom, heads for the hallway. Most likely to join the hunt.

"So . . . what happens now?"

"Now?" Hastings says, eyes roaming the room in search of answers. "Now we put a man at your door, and we find another way."

Rose nods. "You want to hear something strange?"

Hastings holds up a finger as his mic squawks. Rose catches enough to know that they're still searching. That the killer has slipped away.

Hastings mumbles a response, then glances toward the window with a look of frustration, as if wondering how such a vanishing trick had been performed. Then he returns his full attention to Rose. "Shoot."

"It's about the Baxter sisters," she says. "When they were burned up inside that old asylum, they were trying to summon some sort of vengeful demon. They believed they could conjure the thing, that it would destroy this horrible person. That's why they were in there; they were doing this crazy ritual when the building caught fire. Can you believe that?"

"If I didn't know any better," he says, "I'd say they summoned you, Rose. You've got this guy on the run."

"Perhaps. But I think he's done playing games with us, Detective," she says, feeling tired, weak, and very old. "You know what else I think?"

"No, tell me."

Rose smiles at him sadly, a tear spilling from the corner of one red, irritated eye.

"I think the worst is yet to come."

TEN

CHECKMATE

1

It's an ice-cold morning.

Hell, they're *all* cold now, what with October creeping its way toward Halloween and, in the months to follow, another crappy New York winter.

But that's all right.

This won't take long.

I sidle up to the bench, all casual-like. Just going for a stroll, everybody. Nothing to see here. Pay me no mind.

I take a moment to look around for anyone who might be watching . . . but there's no one. God almighty, this place has turned into a fucking ghost town. My box of chocolates has been severely depleted.

For my purposes, however, it works out just fine.

Now I can relax a bit, take my time with these last few.

Sure, having the cops loitering around isn't the greatest, but those guys are worthless. One sits in a squad car in the parking lot, another hangs his fat ass at reception, flirting with the doe-eyed dimwit who works the desk. There haven't been any new residents, so no one's working undercover. Probably hard to find eighty-year-old cops.

Still, I'm none too happy with last night's festivities. I mean, damn. That crazy woman almost had me! And to think how I'd planned everything out in such detail—the rope was standing by, the propofol syringe ready to knock her out cold.

It *infuriates* me that I probably won't get another chance at that nasty, meddling bitch. I'd love nothing more than to push her down a flight of stairs one day. Maybe I'd get lucky and she'd break her damn neck like poor Esther Pound, or crack her head open and bleed out.

Is it poetic? No, not really. Which is a shame.

Because she deserves poetry.

Still, I might have a shot at her yet.

In the meantime . . . a little payback.

You fuck with me?

I fuck with you.

"Hey there, Tatum," I say, flashing my warmest smile.

He looks up at me, a Yankees cap askew on his head, his blue eyes sparkling and distant as galaxies. "Have you seen Jack?" he asks.

Because of course he does.

"You know what?" I say, sitting next to him, ignoring the gawping, creepy fish just a few feet way. "I have."

His smile makes my whole damn day. It really does.

2

Where am I?

What is this place?

I need to find Jack. My boy. My good boy.

Someone holding my hand. Not Rose.

Rose . . .

Who is Rose?

I had a shovel.

"I think he's just over here."

Okay, okay. Let's go. Let's go to work. I need my hat.

Wait . . . I need to go back for my hat.

"Hey, big guy, this way."

"My hat," I say.

"Uh-huh, it's on your head, dummy."

I need to get my hat, and I need to get to work. I don't want to be here.
I've never been here before. This isn't my house—

"Okay, let's go," I say, and turn to go home. *I want to go home.*

"Whoa, hey, we're looking for Jack, remember? Your dog, Jack?
He's right down here, near the creek."

Jack. Yes, yes . . . my dog. My good boy. He'll be home soon. We'll talk
to Rose and watch the fish. I like the fish.

Okay, let's go. Okay, then.

"Just through these trees."

I need to get to work. I'll take Jack and my wife, my baby boy. What's
his name? I don't know, I don't know.

Oh! I don't like this. It's cold! I don't like this—

"Like going for a swim. We're gonna find Jack, okay? But first a
little swim."

Swim? I went swimming once with Jimmy Lowell. In the old lake
by the farm. He caught toads. I hope Jimmy got back okay. His father is
a bad man. Gets mad at Jimmy and beats him. I hope he gets back home

okay. I should go check on him. I don't want to be here; my legs are cold and wet.

I don't want to be here.

"Like being baptized. You ready?"

Where are the fish?

"One, two . . ."

Hands grip me hard—it hurts!

NO! Stop!

Time to go, time to go, time to go!

OH! Wait . . .

It's . . . no . . . I can't breathe.

Can't see.

Can't breathe!

Please . . .

I . . . I . . .

. . .

It's quiet . . . and dark.

And suddenly, it's bright.

Oh God, so bright! So warm!

So *incredible.*

A brilliant meadow, the most beautiful I've ever seen. Colors I've never seen!

I run, run, run toward the light. I'm so strong! So fast!

I hear something behind me and turn. . . .

My boy!

Jack races up to me, grinning and panting and young, his chocolate coat shining as if he were formed from sunlight, from stars. I kneel and he barrels into me and I fall over onto my back, laughing as he whimpers with pure joy—licks at my face, my arms, my hands.

"Jack! Good boy!" I say, laughing. I hug him and kiss his head.

Finally, he lets me stand, and together we continue walking through the meadow, toward the light. He runs ahead, runs back. Barks and spins.

My Jack.

Just ahead, I see them both waiting for me. Waiting for us.

What a life!

What a life. . . .

3

Hastings is sent a link to a video file.

The total runtime of the video is just over eighteen seconds.

The video is the only footage captured by Gopi Sharma's Beaulieu 8mm movie camera on the day he was murdered. Hastings prays this might be the key to solving this thing. He desperately needs a win with this case—even a small one.

He'd gone through the background checks on all the employees of Autumn Springs: the affiliated doctors, the cleaning staff, the nurses, and the orderlies. Even Blackwell.

Especially Blackwell.

Nothing. Everything tidy. Everybody legit.

He'd reluctantly agreed with Rose on the residents, but that was trickier. He needed a court order to get social security numbers and full names from Blackwell, who wasn't handing it over otherwise. Honestly, Hastings understood. Guy could lose his job.

Still, the way things are going, the administrator's job is tenuous at best.

"Fucking ethics . . ." Hastings mumbles.

Regardless, he'd requested the warrant and hoped it would be coming soon. If not today, then tomorrow. After that, it would take another two to three days to run over eighty background checks. Of course, the hospice patients aren't exactly suspects, and a good dozen or more of the residents have moved out. Presumably.

Didn't matter; they would all have to be looked at.

In the meantime, Hastings is curious what Gopi Sharma had managed to capture with his archaic movie camera.

He takes a slug of sour coffee and clicks the link to the file's secure location on the local police server. The window opens, filling his computer screen with a still frame of what appears to be carpeting, captured in grainy grayscale.

He hits Play.

The first few seconds of the fuzzy, black-and-white video are jagged and wild, as if the camera had been caught in a storm. For a flash, it's pointed at the victim's face, his glazed, haunted eyes staring back into the lens, and then the camera is tilted upward, capturing the out of focus shadow of someone with their back to the camera, walking away toward the blown-out contrast of a sunlit window.

"Come on . . . turn around, you fuck. Say cheese."

The window is opened and the dark blob of the killer slips through it, into the blinding daylight. For a couple seconds, nothing happens. Then, from outside, the killer steps *back into frame.*

"No mask," Hastings mumbles, leaning in.

After exiting, the killer had removed the ski mask and had, inexplicably (and quite stupidly), gone back to close the window without wearing it.

But the face is so out of focus—the contrast of the shadows and light so blown out and dramatic—that Hastings can hardly tell what he's looking at.

Regardless, his detective mind takes notes:

Caucasian, definitely. Dark hair . . . yeah, okay. Maybe.

Eye color? Height? Distinguishing marks? Impossible.

Male? Female?

Unknown.

Young? Old?

Unknown.

"Shit," he says. "Shit, shit, shit."

In the video, dark arms reach up, obscuring the already distorted face even further, and pull the window shut. Then the killer disappears, and the camera POV jags hard left to show a blood-spattered couch.

At least I think that's blood, he thinks. *Hard to tell when the film is black and white.*

And then the short clip ends, along with any strength—any life—the victim must have had left in his ravaged, bleeding body.

Hastings watches all eighteen seconds, then plays it again.

And again.

And again.

He freezes the frame of the killer's face multiple times. He leans so close to the screen his nose is nearly touching it.

He'll order video analysis, of course, but he knows it's a dead end.

"You almost got him, Mr. Sharma," Hastings says.

He thinks about the dying man's strength running out, the camera falling to the carpet before he takes a shaking, bloody finger and writes a message of hope on his own flesh. The conviction he must have had to think that clearly—to even *try*—knowing he was moments away from death, from tipping into the eternal abyss . . .

"Hell of an effort."

Hastings is moving the computer's mouse to close the video when his desk phone rings. He scoops it up while staring at the full-screen image of the blood-spattered couch, thinking about the victim's failed heroics.

"Hastings."

He listens, then leans back in his old, squeaky office chair, and covers his tired eyes with one hand.

"Christ . . . I'll get over there right now," he says. "Don't touch anything."

He punches a button to open another line, dials the four-digit number for forensics, and tells them to prioritize the lab analysis they received a day ago from the exhumed bodies of Stanley Swanson and Mickey Lake.

"I need to know if there are any narcotics in their system, any prescription drugs, any stimulants," he says when he gets a tech on the line. "Anything that wasn't taken for high blood pressure—scratch that; just give me everything. Today, please . . . Yeah, push everything else, understand? Okay then, by end of day. Thanks."

Hastings checks his watch. Just past noon.

He's going to need to meet with the administrator right away.

It's time to shut down Autumn Springs.

4

Rose sits at her dining room table, eyes open, staring at the wall.

Her cell phone rings and rings. She hears the *ping* of messages arriving.

She ignores it all.

Buried deep in her psyche, she knows that part of her is in shock, and now is the worst possible time to be making decisions. Regardless, a half-hour after finding out about Tatum Bird, she pulled herself together enough to call her daughter and tell her she'd like to come stay with her for a while.

Or, if it was okay . . . indefinitely.

Rose blames herself for what happened to that poor, dear man. Her friend.

Another friend.

She blames her ego, her lack of foresight, her mistake at not realizing just how badly the killer would want revenge.

And that's what this is—oh yes, she knows it for a fact.

Revenge.

She knows it in her heart. Not because she is arrogant or self-important—nothing so subjective as that. She knows because when she'd returned to her apartment, after a light breakfast at the dining hall, there had been a Yankees cap resting on her bed.

His Yankees cap.

When Rose had seen it, sitting there on her neat bedspread—*staring* at her, *mocking* her—she'd felt so many emotions it was impossible to keep them straight.

Violation, first and foremost.

That the killer had come into her room, into her *home*, after what had happened only a night previous, and touched her things, defiled her sense of safety, of independence.

Then white-hot terror flooded her veins. She knew who the

hat belonged to, of course. Knew what it meant. And yet she prayed—oh, she *prayed*, dropped to her knees and prayed to God— and then she dialed the number for the Medical Center, asking where Tatum Bird was and was he okay?

The nurse who'd answered seemed annoyed at first. Then, per- haps hearing the tone—the utter despair—of Rose's voice, told her to hold. Two minutes later, the nurse picked up the line again and said she'd have to call her back. Before she hung up, however, she said that Mr. Bird was being searched for and asked if Rose knew anything that could help locate him.

Rose told her she did not, and ended the call.

But she *did* know something. She knew that Tatum Bird was lying dead somewhere. That he had, in the broad light of a new day, been taken away and murdered. Somehow, impossibly, murdered.

By someone who knows him. Someone who would not attract suspi- cion.

After the call, Rose had let out a sob, then slapped herself hard in the face. "Not now, Rose DuBois," she'd said. "Not yet."

Finding the card for the detective, she called his cell phone and told him about Tatum being missing. Then she told him about the hat.

"I'll get over there right now," he said. "Don't touch anything."

He means the hat. It's evidence now.

Evidence of a murder.

My whole world is a crime scene.

Rose had felt a surge of disgust, of anger, but held it in check as best she could. "I won't, Detective."

But he'd already hung up.

Good. Get your ass down here and end this nightmare.

A couple hours later, Hastings himself knocked on her door. With him was a young woman in plain clothes, who he introduced as Detective Williams.

"May we—"

"Of course. Please."

Hastings sat Rose down on her couch, then told her they'd found Tatum's body in the creek. Early indications were that he'd drowned. *Been* drowned.

"Honestly, I would have normally considered it to have been an accident, but now—"

"Everybody's slipping on banana peels and dying around here," Rose said.

"But now," Hastings continued. "This makes things more clear." He turned to the younger detective. "Let's bag the hat, give the place a once-over. Try and pull prints from the door handle, although the perp is always gloved."

"Can't hurt," Williams said.

For the next few hours, Rose sat at her dining room table, drinking tea and ignoring her phone. No one came by the apartment while the police dusted for fingerprints, inspected the floor, photographed her bed, and asked her questions.

"Anything else unusual?"

"Anything missing?"

"What time did you leave for breakfast? What time did you return?"

Rose didn't mention that she'd thrown up her breakfast of ham and eggs. All it took was the thought that, while she was sipping coffee and picking at her plate of food, her friend was only a couple hundred yards away, hidden by thick foliage, being pushed beneath the water of the creek. The same creek where visiting grandkids sometimes played. While she ate, he suffered. While she was safe, he was confused and scared.

And then he died.

And now, Rose feels empty—scraped clean of emotions such as rage, or love, or guilt, or fear. Devoid of that magic-dust feeling of companionship. She is a shell. An empty vessel. If she could, she would disappear and never return.

In a way, she thinks, *that's exactly what I'm doing. Yes, yes, dear friends. It's time for Rose to disappear.*

There is another emergency meeting being called, of course. This time by the police department. Rose will go, and then she will pack.

And when her daughter arrives at six o'clock (the earliest she could manage), Rose will leave this place behind.

And that . . . will be that.

5

Hastings looks on in disgust as the uniformed officers roll out a CRIME SCENE barrier like it's caution tape on a parade route.

Might as well keep rolling it out—this whole goddamn place is a crime scene.

A parade of death.

The body lies face down on the grass next to the stream—hatless, of course—as a photographer attacks it with his camera, moving from one angle to another as if shooting a half-dressed supermodel for the cover of *Vogue* magazine. Two women from the coroner's office stand by with a body bag and a gurney, waiting for Annie Leibovitz to wrap it up.

Behind him, a couple nurses look on, crying their eyes out and holding each other, but Hastings doesn't even bother noting either their identity or their existence. It doesn't matter. He's going to drain this pool, dry this killer out, catch him or, at the very least, force him to move on to another hunting ground.

His stomach churning with guilt and rage, he turns away from the scene and notes that Blackwell has finally arrived and is now standing atop the rise, looking down in horror. *Time for a meeting, administrator,* Hastings thinks, heading up the hill.

It's time to clear the killing grounds.

6

Rose enters the Activity Room, knowing she's a few minutes late, but had wanted to make sure she'd put on her face. Not for vanity, but for strength. Wouldn't do for folks to see how cried-out she was, how haggard and tired. Maybe she could help others feel empowered, even as she readied herself for retreat.

Rose DuBois, you are nothing if not a walking contradiction, the dark voice says with a chuckle, hiding like a spider in the corner of her mind.

Yes, she knows it's true. She's not proud of it, but her emotions and actions can often seem paradoxical, even to her.

Help people, but run away. Be kind, but not loving. Be friendly, but not trusting. Be strong, but only to hide your weakness, your constant fear.

Rose knows she is damaged goods. Has known it for near forty years. She once thought—after Barry's death—that she would become the woman she'd always wanted to be, that she would no longer let herself be manipulated, or allow herself to be yelled at, or put down. *Abused*. But she'd been naïve. She hadn't realized how deep the scars in her psyche ran—how they'd cut across the roots of who she once was. How they'd disfigured her heart.

For decades she'd hidden the pain, the torment. Hidden it from her students, her friends and peers, her daughter. She moved to Autumn Springs hoping for a fresh start, desperately needing to be out of that place in Brooklyn, where so many horrific memories huddled in shadows like vengeful spirits, waiting to creep into her bed while she tossed and turned to flood her mind with nightmares, sit on her chest and steal her breath.

And, for a while, she'd done okay. She'd done *better*. She made new friends and let them into her heart. For a time, she even considered *love* being a part of her new life, then dismissed it. Rebuked it.

It was too much. A bridge too far.

And she was too weak.

Damaged goods.

As she enters the large room, part of her looks for her friends, then realizes—with a sharp stab of sorrow—that many of them are now gone. Sweet, loveable Mickey, and talented, whip-smart Gopi. Her dear, dear Tatum, who she prays has found release from his caged mind in the afterlife, that he's playing with Jack in Heaven.

In fact, many of the folks she knows even moderately well seem to be absent. The room is no more than half full, perhaps forty or so residents remaining. The ones with nowhere else to go, she imagines. The ones who are alone.

She spots Maureen Stapleton, Libby Sue, and Carmela Rodriguez . . . and the man who lived next to Angela Forrest, Henry something or other. There's Ginny Gavin and old, cranky Lee Truby. Bob and Ellie Nash, surprisingly, are still here, holding hands at a far table as they wait for the meeting to begin.

Mary Reynolds, she notes, is not present. Nor is Sandra Freeman.

And near the front, sitting alone at a table, wearing his rumpled tweed coat, is Miller. She debates ignoring him, finding a seat near the back, but he's already found her with his eyes, given a small wave. She waves back and walks toward his table.

You have to tell him, she thinks, knowing how badly it will hurt. *He deserves to know you're leaving. That you might never return.*

She sits down beside him and he studies her, arching an eyebrow. "Forgive me?"

"Nothing to forgive," she says. "Miller—"

Before she can go on, however, Detective Hastings and Administrator Blackwell walk onto the stage. Nervously, Rose wonders if there are any more surprises in store—a drugged-up resident attacking the detective, perhaps, like some sort of mad play, the retirement home version of a penny dreadful.

As the detective introduces himself to the gathering, Rose finds herself glancing at Miller. Despite every effort, she can't help thinking about their fight, his rising anger, and the strange reveal that he had a daughter. Why would he keep that from her?

And the photo, of course, the dark voice in her mind whispers gleefully. *Remember what you saw in the photo?*

Sure. She remembers. It was written in blood on her dead friend's arm.

8MM.

Or was it BMM?

That's what you thought at first, wasn't it, Rose? You saw that photo, and you thought they weren't about a camera at all, that they were INI-TIALS.

His *initials.*

Beauregard Mason Miller. BMM.

Because you can't trust him. You can't trust any man, especially those who profess their love—who project that impossible, deceptive kindness. Because those are the ones that TURN on you. Those are the ones that GET you.

The ones that HURT you.

Of course, the rational part of Rose's mind knows Miller couldn't possibly have anything to do with the murders. He'd found her when the power went out, while the Baxter sisters burned.

But where was he when that old building was set on fire?

In bed with a stomach bug. How convenient.

Rose scoffs at the voice.

Well, he couldn't have been the one in my room the other night, she retorts. *Dropping from a window twenty feet to the ground?*

Ridiculous.

Of course . . . there were *other* murders.

Maybe he isn't a killer, but maybe he helped?

Maybe he only killed *some* of her friends.

Like Gopi, the sly voice whispers, and Rose can almost picture the voice's wide, fang-toothed grin as it fills her thoughts with doubt.

What about Tatum? Somebody—someone he trusted—led him to that creek. And somebody drugged Stan Swanson and Mickey. Someone who could move around here freely. Someone who wouldn't draw attention.

And what of this daughter? that voice continues. *C'mon, Rose. You don't have to be Agatha Christie to wonder if that daughter had kids— kids who would be adults now. Like that nice doctor who you think might have a dark side. Or one of the orderlies. Heck, maybe he's in cahoots with a crazy grandson you don't know about.*

I mean, really, at the end of the day, what do you really know *about him?*

He could be anybody.

He could be ANYTHING.

". . . and so we're asking that, until further notice, you all seek alternative accommodations for the time being. A couple weeks, at least."

Hastings's voice cuts through Rose's thoughts, and with a shake of her head she does her best to focus on what the man is saying.

"Maybe there's a family member who can take you in, or a friend? Or hell, maybe take that trip you've always wanted," he says with a watery smile, as discordant murmurs rise from the group.

A voice rings out from the back. "And what if there's nowhere for us to go, Detective? I tried, damn it. My kids, they're all busy! Too busy for me."

Another voice: "You want me to travel? Are the police paying expenses, because I certainly don't have any money, and I'm not allowed to drive anymore."

A general rumble of agreement from the others.

They're all trapped here, Rose thinks. *Trapped in a cage with a killer.*

I don't know if this place is purgatory or Hell itself, she thinks. *How can you run from the only place you're wanted? The only place that will have you?*

"I want my lease broken, Blackwell!" Bob Nash yells, standing and stabbing a finger at the stage. "To say that things here are un-safe would be the understatement of the year."

Now more people stand, yelling at the administrator, who looks to Rose as if he's plum out of answers, while Hastings calls for calm.

Maureen Stapleton also stands, but instead of addressing the stage, she looks toward the gathered group, aggression in her dark eyes. "Well, I'm not leaving, but I'm going to tell all of you right now, or at least *one* of you, that I'm armed. So if any of you bastards takes a single step into my room . . ." she glares from face to face, her own expression stretched into a snarl, "I'll blow your fucking head off."

More raised voices join the fray, and Hastings grabs the microphone. "Okay, ma'am, let's not escalate things, please. Officer Volk, will you please . . . Yeah, let's ask her to step outside so we can check permits? Ma'am . . . folks . . ." He holds up two hands, desperately trying to quiet down the suddenly vocal residents.

"We should've taken that thing away from her after what happened at the party," Miller grumbles, more to himself than to Rose.

Rose nods, but strongly doubts Maureen would have given her gun up to anyone, especially after the events of the past week.

"Look, folks, obviously I can't force anyone to leave," Hastings says, his voice having become terse, frustrated. "And I understand if there are money concerns or if you don't have a place to go, but it's my job to tell you that the situation here is dire, and that the police can only do so much from a preventative standpoint, okay? We can't watch everyone all the time. So if you decide to stay, I'm telling you now, you'll be doing so at your own risk."

Now *everyone* is standing, pointing and yelling at the stage. A red-faced Lee Truby lifts up her walker, shaking the tennis ball feet toward Hastings in a fiery rage.

Bad move, Detective, Rose thinks. *These people are already scared and helpless; now you're telling them their home is a lions' den, and you've just let loose the lions.*

Blackwell steps up to the mic, putting a calming hand on the detective's shoulder, who is visibly upset with how things are going. "Okay, everyone. Calm down, please. Look, I'm here, and I'm not going anywhere. The staff is here, and we will continue with the uninterrupted care you've come to expect. In addition, we are going to have security guards walking the grounds twenty-four seven, as well as some of the officers you see standing around the hall here. They'll be monitoring the comings and goings of all individuals and keeping an eye out for anything even remotely suspicious." He looks around the room, makes eye contact with a few residents.

Folks have stopped shouting, and the louder rumblings have quieted. Blackwell nods, as if satisfied, then continues. "To that end, and for your own well-being, we're implementing a six p.m. curfew. We want everyone home and safe before dark."

More grumbling, but Blackwell rides over it, undaunted. "And please bring a buddy with you to lunch or dinner or if you just want to walk the grounds, okay? But look, folks, things are going to be fine. I promise."

Rose notes that Hastings is scowling at Blackwell, likely not appreciating him making promises he can't possibly keep, but the administrator's little speech has the right effect on the gathering. Folks have sat back down. Many are nodding. Even Lee Truby has dropped her walker back to the floor, though her hands remain tightly clenched around the handles.

Before Blackwell can continue, however, a shriek fills the room. All heads turn to see Maureen Stapleton—her gun clenched in both hands and pointed toward a police officer, who is slowly backing away, hands raised.

"Don't you fucking touch me!" she screams.

Of the four uniformed officers in attendance, two have drawn their guns.

"Wait!" Hastings yells. He climbs awkwardly off the front of the stage and walks quickly toward Maureen and the officer closest to her, whose eyes are darting nervously around the room, as if debating how to proceed. Hastings points at the other two uniformed policemen, both creeping closer, guns pointed. "Officers, lower your weapons!"

"Drop that gun, ma'am!" a bull-necked cop yells, ignoring Hastings's command as he takes another step closer to Maureen.

"Stay back!" Maureen shrieks, beyond hysterical, pivoting the extended gun from person to person, whether they be cop or citizen. "All of you, stay back!"

Hastings approaches slowly, one palm held out in a pacifying gesture. "Your name is Maureen, is that right? Look, Maureen, I know you're scared, and things are tense, but we are police officers. We are here to *protect* you, not to harm you in any way. Whoever is doing this to your neighbors, your friends, they're not wearing a police uniform, all right? But you need to put the gun down; you need to put it down *right now*."

Rose watches in horror as Maureen looks at Hastings—then glances at the bull-necked officer pointing his gun at her—with an expression of surprise, as if she'd just woken up, or snapped out of some strange hypnotic state. She stares at the gun in her hand with disbelief, as if she has no idea how it arrived there.

"Okay," she says quietly. "I . . . yes, okay . . ."

As Maureen begins to lower her gun, Bobby the orderly, who stands a few paces behind her, biding his time—and most likely wanting to impress the police he so much admires—leaps forward to grab her from behind. One meaty arm wraps around her waist like a python, physically lifting her from the floor, while the other swipes madly at the hand holding the gun.

"No!" Hastings barks.

When the gun goes off, the shot is so loud it sounds like a thunderclap in the large room—so loud that Rose's hands leap to cover her ears.

Michelle Hall, who'd been watching the bizarre scene play out from a couple tables over, jerks backward off her chair, a cloud of red mist filling the air where her head had been only seconds prior.

Terrified screams fill the room as folks leap up from their chairs in a mad panic. Some hobble toward the exits; some drop to the floor. A few crawl beneath their tables.

Rose feels Miller grab her hand and *tug*. She looks over at him in disbelief, sees him kneeling next to her, his eyes wide and begging.

For one insane moment in time, she thinks: *My God, is this man proposing?*

And then she's dropping from her chair to the floor as more screams flood the room. Maureen Stapleton shrieks like a woman gone mad, and Rose realizes, with a cold dread, that she likely has.

And maybe, just maybe, we've all gone mad. And not just a little bit, either—oh no—but FULL BORE, ladies and gentlemen. Yessir, we've entered "stark raving" territory, and there may be no going back now. There may be no escape.

Certainly not for Michelle Hall, who Rose can now see from her new vantage point below the table.

The dead woman lies motionless on the linoleum floor, her gaze aimed blankly at Rose from across the room with her one remaining eye, twirls of silver hair soaking in a growing puddle of blood, lumpy with bits of skull and brain.

Or perhaps death is the escape, Rose thinks numbly, letting the shock carry over her in menthol-cool waves of obliviousness and relief as she stares into Michelle Hall's wide, empty eye.

Perhaps it's the living who are entombed.

And it's the dead who are the lucky ones.

7

Honestly? I couldn't have done it better myself.

8

Rose waits in the lobby of the Community Center, sitting in a comfortable club chair, a suitcase at her feet. The piano sits empty today, and the large room is silent but for the sporadic typing of the night receptionist, the occasional trill of the phone. Looking around the large room, Rose realizes that she likes the lobby and wonders why she hasn't frequented it more often during the weekly Happy Hour, when they wheel in a temporary bar and pipe music through the speakers set into the ceiling. Aside from the receptionist desk, you could almost mistake it for a country club—the furniture is dark, the lights warm, and the walls a deep rose color that makes her think, in some way, that it's *her* color. Maybe, one day, she'd paint one of her apartment walls a similar color, liven the place up a bit.

If she ever comes back, that is.

"Rose?"

Rose turns toward the voice, embarrassed that she'd been caught daydreaming.

Of course he'd known. Of course he had.

"Hello, Miller."

Miller settles into the matching club chair beside her own, a Tiffany-style floor lamp between them, a red oriental rug beneath their feet. He glances at her suitcase, then into her eyes. "I don't want to put my nose where it doesn't belong," he says uncertainly.

"No, it's fine. I was going to tell you, honestly. But with all the chaos, I just figured it would be best to just . . . go." She shrugs, embarrassed at the idea—of him thinking—that she'd been sneaking away.

You're sneaking away, all right, the dark voice whispers. *Without a word. Like a field mouse scurrying for shelter, hoping to avoid the hawk's shadow.*

"Is it permanent?"

"No. At least, I don't think so," she says, wondering if it's the truth. "But you know . . . it's like the detective said: It's not safe here right now."

"Of course, of course. And I agree, by the way. You know I do. You should be somewhere safe. Guess this makes me the last man standing," he says with a chuckle, trying to bring some levity to his heartbreak.

Always trying to make me smile.

"It appears that way," she says, feeling a well of guilt and shame open inside her, at the bottom of which lies a deep, wounded love for this man. "But listen, Miller, while we have a moment, I think there's something else you should know."

Miller raises his eyebrows, then listens, without interruption, as Rose tells him about Hastings asking her to play possum in hopes to snare the killer. How it had almost, miraculously, worked.

Almost.

When she's done, he shakes his head, and she can tell he's upset, that he's biting his tongue. "I see," is all he says, unable to meet her eye, his face half-shadowed by the shaded lamplight.

Rose reaches out and takes his hand. "Miller, there's so much more you should know. I haven't been forthcoming, and that's not fair to you. But we'll talk soon, I promise. I'll call you and . . . I'll tell you everything. About who I am inside. About my past. About the husband who made my life hell for fifteen horrible years. It may . . ." She takes a deep breath, then lets it out in a sad, weary sigh. "It may explain some things about me. About us. It may explain why a woman who is nearly eighty years old is terrified to go on a date, afraid to let someone inside, or get too close."

Miller studies her as she talks, and she hates seeing the pain in his eyes, the worry that he may have somehow, inadvertently, opened old wounds.

"But you know I'd never—" he starts, leaning forward and clenching her hand tightly. "Whoever hurt you, Rose, I'm not that man. Not all men are evil."

Rose looks at him with pity—enough pity for both of them.

His naivete. Her misfortune.

"But some are, Miller," she says. "And some's enough."

Miller shifts in his chair, and she can see him looking for a loophole, for a thread they can follow together.

Finally, he simply sighs, as if beaten. "I'd never hurt you."

That's what they all say! the dark voice shrieks, with a hint of glee. *C'mon, that's classic behavior. Besides, look at him. He's probably involved in this—*

OH, SHUT UP!

"Rose? What's wrong?"

Rose pulls back her hand, looks away in shame. In regret. "Miller, just know that I'm still working on myself. I'm still, all this time later, trying to figure things out. I'm trying to learn how to trust . . . but it's hard for me." She sniffles, pulls a tissue from her pocket, wipes her nose. "There's so much you don't know."

"Okay," he says soothingly. "Okay. But know this. I'm here for you. There are no strings when it comes to my feelings for you. I'm your *friend*, Rose."

Rose looks toward the glass double doors of the parking lot, gazes at the darkness falling in the world outside, the world she'd left behind and is now returning to.

Where is trust?

Is it out there, in the dark?

Or is it sitting next to me, asking to hold my hand?

"Miller, I have to ask you something," she says. Knowing time is short, Rose turns back to him, locks in on his big, sad eyes. "You didn't have anything to do with it, did you? With any of it?"

He stares at her for a second, uncomprehending. Then it dawns on him what she's asking, and his eyes widen; a rush of blood reddens his cheeks. "Excuse me?" His voice is thick, choked with emotion and disbelief. "Rose, what are you—"

"I saw a photograph of Gopi's arm," she says softly. "You know, after."

Knowing that the only way through the fog of her mistrust is to simply power forward—to get all of it into the open—Rose releases the floodgates of her doubts, her fears, and speaks in a rush, not wanting to chicken out, not wanting him to stop her before she can say everything.

"At first, I thought it was your initials, you see? B-M-M. Beauregard Mason Miller. Of course, I know that's silly. Impossible, even. And then, from one second to the next, I realized Gopi had been thinking of that fool camera, the one he was wanting to make a movie with, remember? But then you said you had a daughter, and how did I not know that, Miller? Why would you not tell me that? And I thought, what other secrets? What other things is this man keeping from me? And I'm sorry. I'm a little unsure of myself, if I'm being honest. Of what to believe. Of what I can trust . . ."

Rose trails off, shakes her head, her heart aching more and more with each word, until it hurts too much to continue.

Miller stares at her for what seems an eternity, as if trying to understand who this woman is sitting across from him.

For a moment, Rose thinks his eyes look much like Tatum Bird's—lost and fragmented—the mind behind them nothing but a thundercloud ignited by random flashes of lightning bolt thoughts, scattered and momentary, then gone.

"Please say something," Rose says.

Miller looks away, as if in a daze. "Is this why you're leaving?" he asks. "Are you running away from *me*?"

"I—"

Rose's cell phone rings, shattering the tension of their conversation, filling the quiet of the large lobby. She pulls it from the pocket of her coat, taps the screen.

"Hello, honey. Yes, I'm just inside . . . no, no reason to park. I'll come out. Give me a minute and I'll come out."

She hangs up and is surprised to see Miller is no longer sitting beside her. He's standing a few feet away, hands shoved deep into the pockets of his pants, his eyes studying the floor.

Rose stands, takes a step toward him. He takes a half step back, one hand leaving its pocket, raised between them.

Stop.

"Miller?"

But he doesn't look up. Doesn't meet her eye. Doesn't hug her and tell her that it's fine, that he cares about her and will wait anxiously for her return.

For a moment, he doesn't move at all.

And then he turns his back to her, head still bowed. His tweed sport coat hangs loosely, the coat too long, too baggy. The coat of an old professor who'd lost the mass of youth.

Rose knows she's hurt him, hurt him terribly.

"I just wanted to explain," she says.

Without a word, Miller walks through the warmly lit lobby, toward the rear doors that lead back to the apartments—toward life, toward home.

Toward a love that might have been.

Toward moments, past and future, that are now lost, never to be regained.

9

I watch the bitch leave.

I gotta say, for all my planning, all my *work*, all my intuitiveness about people, I didn't see this one coming. Even after the other night.

No, I thought Rose was made of sterner stuff.

I thought Rose had *agency*.

In the back of my mind, I kind of hoped she was going to be my final girl, you know? I could almost picture us standing in the rain, the moon above a dim bulb darkened by midnight clouds, toe-to-toe.

No more mask. No more deceit.

Just me and her, ready to have it out one last time.

Not exactly a fair fight, admittedly. But one can dream.

But now the dream is gone. It just folded its tents and left town, leaving me with nothing but table scraps.

I should have known killing the dumdum would drive Rose to ruin. In fairness, I did try—tried very hard—to kill her first.

But you know what? Sometimes things don't work out.

The truth is, you don't always know what someone will do or how they'll react. You can hope for a certain outcome, sure. Of course. You set things up like a chessboard and watch it play out, move by move, waiting to fuck that queen.

Hmm, but this? This I don't like.

I don't like it one bit.

That said, momma didn't raise no quitter. So . . . maybe there's a way to finish what I started. Maybe, if I do it *just right*, I can bring things to a proper close.

Final girl and all.

I've got lots to think about. Lots to plan.

But it feels good. It feels right.

One more game.

But for now, I'm gonna handle a small piece of business. And look at that, he's right there, strolling just ahead of me under the halo lamplights of the path.

I check my watch. Just past six o'clock.

Tut tut, my friend. You're out after curfew, and that's a no-no.

Don't you know it's dangerous around here at night?

Don't you know it's a great way to get yourself killed?

ELEVEN

FINAL GIRL

1

A few quiet days go by, and Rose is happy.

She loves her daughter's new home. It's not big, but the shared rooms are spacious and get plenty of good light. She loves the original hardwood floors and warm color palette Sybil has selected for the paint and furnishings. Rose's own bedroom is cozy but has a nice-sized closet for her things, a private bathroom, and a pleasant view of the tidy backyard (which is fenced off so Roy can't wander), which features a small patio deck that is just the right amount of weathered. Beyond the fence, the ground slopes downward toward a large copse of the Hudson Valley's ever-present trees.

Though Rose's room is quite small (smaller than her bedroom at Autumn Springs, which is saying something), it's just big enough for her bed and a dresser, which is all she really needs. The house's living room is busy, being the central location for Roy's playthings, the television, a couch, and a comfortable reading chair.

But Rose doesn't worry about needing her own space, and Sybil doesn't seem to either, using her bedroom as an office during the day. It's Roy, of course, who rules the house, as six-year-olds do, the women gleeful, hopeful spectators on his great journey, carried along by his boundless energy and enthusiasm for life.

As for the events at Autumn Springs, Rose has heard not a peep.

She doesn't know the fate of Maureen Stapleton, who was handcuffed and driven away in the back of a police car directly after the shooting of Michelle Hall.

She doesn't know if the remaining residents are still there, or if they've left. Or if there have been any further incidents. In other words, she has no clue whether anyone else has been murdered, or shot, or stabbed, or drugged, or has jumped off a tower.

She hasn't heard from Detective Hastings or Administrator Blackwell.

She hasn't heard from Miller and wonders if their relationship is forever broken by her paranoia, by her irrational fears. By her past.

No calls, no emails, no text messages.

On Friday night, two days after she'd left, Carlo comes over for his usual weekend stay, and the tidy house suddenly feels like a *small* house.

Sybil makes spaghetti and meatballs (Roy's favorite). Rose bakes a pie.

When Carlo arrives, Rose watches him carefully.

Like a hawk, one might say.

She watches how he interacts with her grandchild and contemplates whether the child seems reluctant in any way to interact back. But they both seem natural, and happy, and comfortable. And that settles Rose's nerves a smidge.

Even more closely, however, she studies the way he is with Sybil—scrutinizing their interactions, looking for signs of hesitation or discomfort. Is he overdoing it to impress the mother-in-law? Is Sybil stiffening at his touch?

But again, Rose notices nothing that sets off alarm bells.

Nothing that raises any red flags.

Still. She doesn't trust him, and she knows that might make her unreasonable, but she doesn't care. She only has one daughter. One grandchild. And she will never let this man—or anyone—hurt either one of them.

She's done what needed doing before, and she will do it again if necessary.

But even Rose has to admit that dinner with the young family is pleasant. Peaceful. Carlo talks of his new job selling prescription drugs, and he listens attentively when Sybil speaks of her job, or about some of the things Roy's teachers have discussed with her, or the relatively bland details of how the new house is becoming a home. At no point does he interrupt her, badger her, or mock her.

And that's a start.

"I had planned a little trip to the automotive museum with me and Roy tomorrow afternoon, but I was thinking maybe we should hang around the house," he says, spearing another meatball from the large bowl in the center of the table. "I know you've been having a hard time, Rose, and I thought you might like to have more time with him."

Rose nods and worries to find herself liking the young man.

Well, at least not hating him. Yet.

"That's very thoughtful of you, and of course I can't get enough of my baby boy. But you two should go. I'll have plenty of time with him when you're back."

Besides, Rose thinks, *a quiet afternoon with my daughter sounds like a nice change of pace.*

She turns to Roy, who sits in a booster seat, sucking in noodles, one-by-one, giggling as each reaches its slurping end. "We're talking about you, little boy, about how much your grandma loves you," she says, and Roy's smile washes over her—warms her.

Heals her.

"Now, who wants dessert?" Rose asks.

"Me!" Roy shouts, raising his hand, one cherubic cheek smeared with pasta sauce.

"Me as well," Carlo adds, reaching out to clean spilled spaghetti that had leaped from Roy's plate to the tablecloth. "That pie smells incredible."

"I'll get it; you all sit and relax," Sybil says, then stands to clear dishes. Sitting at the table, being waited on by her daughter, spending time with her grandson, Rose feels her first pang of regret since arriving at her new (*temporary?*) home. A churning guilt settles in her stomach at how comfortable—how *safe*—things are for her here.

She thinks about Miller up there in Autumn Springs. Alone, possibly afraid. And what is she doing? Having dessert with her family. Surrounded by loved ones while he's surrounded by death.

Of course, she hasn't exactly reached out to him, either. She still wakes up in the night, thinking about the blood scrawled on Gopi's arm, how she immediately leaped to the idea it was initials. Miller's initials.

Ridiculous, she'd think in the dark night, lying in a bedroom she doesn't recognize. On a couple of those nights she'd look to the bedroom door, wondering if it would creak open, if an ink-black shadow would slip inside her room, come stand by the foot of her bed.

Sometimes, in her frightened imagination, that shadow would simply stand by her feet, staring down at her. Then those gloved hands would reach up and slowly . . . ever so slowly . . . lift up that horrible black mask to reveal a chin, then a grin of white teeth, then a pair of eyes she'd recognize.

No, she hasn't texted once to check on her friend. But she will.

Tomorrow, she thinks, feeling cowardly. *I'll call him tomorrow and we'll catch up. Assuming he'll even answer the phone.*

Assuming he'll even want to speak to me.

Rose wonders about that. About the things she'd said to him. How badly she must have hurt him . . . and knows there will need to be a lot of mending done if they want to continue as friends. Once this killer is arrested, and it's safe for her to return, she and he will have a good long talk.

Of course, you haven't told him everything, *have you, Rose?* her hateful inner voice says, filling her mind with images of her past. *No, not everything . . . if you did, you'd be cutting that cord for good because you know he'd never want to be near you again. Not if he knew the whole truth.*

No one would.

Be quiet, Rose thinks, ignoring the voice and its taunts.

I'll call him tomorrow, and that's that.

Satisfied to have won her internal argument, Rose dips the corner of her napkin into a glass of water, then dutifully wipes tomato sauce off her grandson's chubby cheek.

2

The next day, the four of them spend the morning at a nearby park, just half a mile from Sybil's new home. They walk back in time for lunch, after which Rose and Roy take quick naps while Sybil catches up on emails and Carlo rakes leaves from the backyard.

At 2 PM, Carlo and Roy leave for the automotive museum. "We'll be back by six at the latest," he says, getting Roy's shoes properly tied.

"Can you make it five?" Sybil asks. "I want to give him a bath tonight before bed, so it would be good if we had dinner before six."

Rose notes a shadow of annoyance cross over Carlo's face—there and gone in an instant, but most certainly *there*. She watches him closely as he pats Roy on the knee and offers Sybil his most patient smile.

"Sure," he says genially. "It's just that it's a long drive to Saratoga Springs, but we'll make it back by five, no problem."

"Thank you, love," Sybil croons, likely knowing she's overmanaging, so gives him a quick kiss on the lips to make up for it.

Rose looks away.

Now it's just after four, and the day is shuffling its way toward dusk. Rose sits on the living room sofa with a book, feet up on a stool, a hot mug of herbal tea at her side. Sunlight slants in through the curve of bay windows behind her, offering what's left of late afternoon warmth and perfectly lighting the book's pages.

Sybil is in her bedroom office, likely working on a design for a client, and Rose is just considering the merits of a snack . . . when her cell phone rings.

Not recalling what she'd done with it, she pats her pockets, then the sofa, before seeing the phone on a credenza across the room, where she'd plugged it in to charge.

Damn.

She sets down her book, pushes herself off the couch a bit too quickly (not liking the twinge in her left knee as she does so), and works her way over to the phone. She unplugs it and checks the caller ID, which is saved in her contacts as MEDICAL CENTER. Thinking she might have forgotten an appointment with that young doctor (and briefly wondering why they'd be calling on a Saturday afternoon, even if that was the case), she answers.

The voice on the other end is a woman's.

"Ms. DuBois?"

"This is she."

"I'm so sorry to bother you," the woman says. "I'm calling on behalf of Doctor Kincaid? Luckily he was in the office today . . . it's regarding Beauregard Mason Miller?"

Rose feels a cold pit open wide inside her stomach—the gaping mouth of a forming abyss—and swallows hard.

"Okay," she says, and turns around so she can look out the bay windows.

If it's bad news, she wants to be looking at sunlight when she hears it.

"Well, I'm not sure if you're aware?" the nurse continues. "But you're listed as his emergency contact."

"No, I didn't know. Please, what's happened to him?"

He's been murdered.

He drowned in his bathtub—isn't that strange?

There was a fire in his apartment, and he didn't escape.

He was shot.

He fell down a flight of stairs and broke his neck—what are the odds?

He was torn open, cock to chin, with a hunting knife.

"He's fine," the nurse says.

Then, as an afterthought: "Well, I mean . . . he's fine *now.*"

Is this young lady going to tell me what's happened, or are we going to chat about the weather? Rose shuts her eyes, takes a shaky breath to calm herself, lets it out.

She shoves away her annoyance at how the woman speaks. It's the same way some of her students used to talk, with a bizarre up-tick at the end of each sentence, as if everything they said was a question instead of a statement.

But there's something else tickling her brain.

I know this voice, she thinks. *I know it but can't quite place it.*

"Nurse, please just tell me what's happened. I don't mean to be rude, but you're scaring me."

Overhearing the conversation, Sybil steps out from her bedroom, worry etched on her face. "Is that Carlo? Is Roy okay?"

She looks to her own phone, as if wondering if she missed a call.

Rose shakes her head, holds the phone away from her mouth. "Autumn Springs," she says in a rushed whisper.

Sybil is momentarily relieved, then looks as if she's about to ask for more information. Rose pats the air with a palm. *Hold on, honey, I'm working on it.*

If this crazy bitch will stop beating around the bush and give me details, you'll be the first to know.

"Okay, well, I don't mean to frighten you," the nurse continues. "But Mr. Miller was brought into the Medical Center with chest pains. We sent for an ambulance, but like I said, Doctor Kincaid was here? The EMTs checked him over and wanted to take him to St. John's, but he refused. And since he appeared stable, the EMTs left him with us. He's resting in the full-time care wing. Mr. Miller, I mean, not the doctor." The nurse snorts a little laugh, as if any of this is the least bit amusing.

"Nurse," Rose says slowly, forcing herself to be calm. "Can you please just answer one question: Is Miller okay, or not?"

There's a pause.

An *annoyed* pause, Rose thinks.

"He's resting," the nurse says.

Rose considers all this for a moment.

That voice . . . almost . . . phony? A put on?

It definitely *sounds* like a woman, and she claims to be a nurse.

Or someone pretending to be one.

"I see," Rose says, her mind moving in a thousand different directions. "Do you think I need to come up there?"

"Oh, are you not in residence?"

"Not currently. I'm . . . I'm away."

"Oh," the nurse says tersely, as if Rose had flicked her nose with a finger. "Well, I mean, it's up to you? But before he went under he asked for you—"

"Asked for me?"

"That's right. Frankly, I assumed you were his wife? But like I said, he's stable now. So if you're traveling, we can just let him know you weren't able to come in. When he wakes up, that is—"

"It's okay," Rose says, interrupting. "I'll come tonight. I just wanted to make sure he's all right."

"I'm sure he'll be glad to see you," the nurse says. "We'll see you soon, then . . ."

Think . . . Think . . .

"Oh, nurse? One other thing," Rose says quickly. "Can you please make sure the doctor knows that Mr. Miller is diabetic? He's on a fairly strict diet, and it's important he's not given certain foods. Can't have sugar, of course."

Another pause.

"Of course," the nurse says, but the bubbly, whimsical, valley girl tone is gone now, as if they were suddenly discussing things of a more serious nature than chest pains and EMTs. "I see it here on his chart. Don't worry, we'll keep the sweets away from him."

Rose shuts her eyes, and her hand clenches the cell phone more tightly, as if she's afraid she might drop it to the floor. "Very good," she says quietly.

"See you soon, Ms. DuBois."

"Wait, nurse, can I get your—"

But the call is ended, and Rose is already thinking of what she needs to do next.

"Mom?"

Rose looks at her daughter, wondering if her baby girl can see the fear in her eyes. She hopes not and does her best not to alarm her, even going so far as to offer a small smile. "It's about Miller."

Sybil steps closer, puts a hand on her mother's arm. "What about him?"

But Rose barely hears her. She's looking at the clock on the wall, doing the math, wondering if there's any way she can get back to Autumn Springs before nightfall.

She doubts it.

"Gimme a second." Rose goes back to her phone screen, taps her contacts, and calls Miller's cell phone.

It goes straight to voicemail.

Sybil squeezes her arm lightly. "Mom, what about Miller?"

Rose sighs, knowing what she needs to do.

She's never felt more afraid.

"He's in trouble."

3

After the call from the nurse, Rose and Sybil decide that Carlo will drive her back to Autumn Springs—about forty-five minutes if traffic isn't too bad—that very night, and Sybil will keep her bathtub and bedtime schedule with Roy.

"Mom, something doesn't feel right about this. You seem really worried. It's like you're . . . I don't know . . . scared."

"I'm fine. I'm just worried about Miller. Now, I should pack some things."

Going into the small bedroom, Rose shuts the door, sits on her bed, and tries Miller's cell phone one more time. *Please answer,* she thinks, hoping to hear his groggy voice letting her know that he's okay—just a little indigestion, perhaps, but nothing serious. Nothing to worry about.

Again, the call goes straight to voicemail.

Rose has never been good at texting (hates it, actually), but she sends Miller a quick follow-up text anyway, telling him to call her the moment he gets the message.

That done, Rose searches her phone history for another number and is relieved when she recognizes it from her call records.

Detective Hastings also does not pick up, but Rose has no more time to wait.

She leaves him a long message, filling him in on things and letting him know her plan. Then she disconnects and—doing her best not to panic, nor rush to any conclusions—packs up her things and waits impatiently for Carlo to return.

As promised, Carlo arrives back at the house by five o'clock.

Rose is waiting by the door.

"Carlo, I need a favor. And I'm afraid I can't take 'no' for an answer," she says, within seconds of the young man and the small boy entering the house.

Carlo looks at Rose, a haze of tiredness in his expression, but sees the determination on her face, the suitcase at her feet. He glances toward Sybil, who looks back with a stony glare, every equal to her mother's.

Realizing he has no choice, he simply shrugs. "Sure, Rose. What do you need?"

When they are ready to go, Rose gives hugs and kisses to her daughter and grandson, then climbs into Carlo's pickup truck. She notes, without realizing she's even doing it, that the truck is well maintained, the interior clean. A glance to the back seat assures her that he has a proper booster seat for Roy. He sees her looking but says nothing as she buckles herself in, hands gripped tightly in her lap.

"We're in a hurry," she says.

"You got it, Rose," Carlo replies, and pulls on to the two-lane, tree-lined road that will lead them back to Autumn Springs.

They drive northeast along one of the many snakelike, narrow upstate roads, winding through ancient forest as if they were racing toward a far-off castle in a stagecoach, one pulled by eight white horses instead of a V-8 engine.

Outside the truck's cab, the sky has darkened to a cobalt blue. The traffic is scant, so they make good time along the twisting road, despite being buffeted by gusty winds that bend the branches of the dense trees walling them off on either side and cause the leaves to wave wildly, like things gone mad.

After a few minutes pass, Rose decides it's time to have her chat with Carlo. It isn't one she's looking forward to, but things are in motion now, and she feels it's best to settle those things that can be settled.

"Thank you for doing this, Carlo," Rose says, breaking the silence that has permeated the cab since they left the house.

"Of course. It's Saturday, so I'm free. As you know, I spend my weekends with Sybil and Roy, so I rarely plan anything that doesn't involve them. And Sybil says your friend is sick?"

"Yes, seems so."

"That's too bad."

"It is," she says, knowing she's procrastinating but unsure how to begin.

When in doubt, speak the truth.

"Carlo, I can see you're good with Roy. And I know you and Sybil have a good relationship—"

Carlo starts to respond, but Rose holds up a hand. "It's best if you let me get through this," she says. "It won't be easy for me."

"Oh, shit," he breathes, but nods. "Yeah, okay."

She doesn't scold him for the language. They're past all that now. Well past.

"Carlo, you may not know this, but I was once married to a man named Barry Wise for fifteen years. Sybil's father, obviously. I'm sure you've heard stories."

Carlo nods, but says nothing.

Good boy. We may get through this yet.

"But there are things you don't know. There are things nobody knows. Not even Sybil." Rose shifts in her seat so she can look at him—give him her full, undivided attention from the world outside the windows. "And I fear I may not get another chance to talk to you, to tell you what it is I want to tell you."

"Okay . . ." Carlo says, eyes glued to the road ahead, as if afraid to look toward the old lady in his passenger seat, the one giving him all kinds of willies at the moment.

"Barry was not a good man, Carlo. But there was a time when he *was*. At the time I married him, he was. I'd swear it on a stack of bibles. Once we'd been married for a few years, though, things changed. He lost his job, for one. Began drinking, as men who lose their jobs are wont to do, as if the answers to life's problems sit at the bottom of a bottle."

Rose shakes her head a little, takes a breath, then continues.

"At first, he just got ornery. Snappy. Hard to live with. One minute he'd be sulking around, the next minute he'd be throwing a glass against the wall, smashing it to pieces. Then, ten years into our marriage, I became pregnant with Sybil. It was a surprise to both of us. We hadn't been trying, and he'd been using protection *most* of the time, but it happened, and that was it. Sometimes, a baby can cure a marriage. But other times, a baby is like a bright light in a dusty, dim room. It exposes the cracks in the walls, the spiderwebs in the corners, the dirt on the floor. In Sybil's case, it was the latter. In many ways, she exposed my marriage for what it was. A dirty, broken thing. For Barry, I think the pressure of being a father, on top of being a bad husband, along with his own perceived inadequacies, drove him a bit mad.

"When I was pregnant with Sybil, he began hitting me," she says stoically. "At first, it was a slap here, a push there. Then, one night, he punched me in the face, knocked out a tooth, and sent me, unconscious, to the floor."

Carlo looks at her with wide, hurt eyes. "Jesus Christ, Rose. I had no idea."

"Please, let me finish," Rose says quietly, politely.

Carlo nods and waits.

"This went on during the entire pregnancy, but thankfully nothing severe enough to keep me from going into a classroom of children, and nothing that hurt the baby, although it was a terror I lived with for nine months, believe me. I was terrified day and night. Not for me, but for the baby growing inside me.

"After Sybil was born, Barry found work, and things settled down a bit. For a year or so, he was almost like his old self. Almost. He loved Sybil, and he doted on her, but I watched him closely when he held her. And I never left him alone with her—something I know he realized and decided to let be.

"For a few years, we lived in relative peace, if not in love. He'd still hit me now and then, but the beatings were not severe, and I lived with it. Sometimes it would be a slap in the face or a little knock to the back of my head. Sometimes he would use a belt. A couple times he'd throw a shoe at me, or a plate, if I said something too snappish for his taste. But worse than the hitting, Carlo, was how he *treated* me. How he *talked* to me. He'd mock me. He'd make fun of my job, my education. He would ask our baby why I was getting so fat, or why my sex was drying up, and then he'd laugh, as if his torment was a joke. Sometimes, he would come up behind me and just . . . *shove* me down. Like a high school bully might do to a smaller, weaker child. Worse than all of that, though, was how he would hardly let me leave the house.

"I could take Sybil to the park, or to school, and I could go to my job, of course. My job is what paid the bills and our health insurance, so he wasn't going to interfere with that, oh no. But if I wanted to see a movie, he'd tell me to watch television. If I wanted to go shopping, he'd berate me about how little money we had, how there were things *he* needed that were more important than what I might need. For years I had no friends outside the teachers at my school, and it was *hard*, Carlo. It was a very hard way to live a life. And then . . . then it began to affect Sybil.

"Around the time she turned five, very close to the age Roy is now, things turned for the worse. Much worse. One night, Sybil spilled a bowl of ice cream on the ugly brown shag carpet in our living room. Barry yelled at her. Sybil started to cry, of course. Then he screamed at her to shut up, you see? To *shut her fucking mouth*, was what he said. Before I could intervene, he grabbed her by the arm and pushed her into the TV set, pushed her so hard he knocked it over, and she—my baby—toppled over along with it. When I yelled at him to stop, he came for me."

Rose takes a deep breath, lets it out. Time is short, and she knows she has to continue. Has to finish.

"I ended up in the hospital. This time, there was no hiding what had happened. No pathetic excuses about falling down the stairs or smacking myself in the face with a door. He'd broken my cheekbone and my arm. I had a concussion from where he'd pushed me into a wall.

"Sybil, thank God, was fine, but she was taken into protective custody while I healed. As much as I hated the idea of it, of knowing how scared she must be, I hated the idea of her being alone with Barry even more.

"I did not press charges against him, and the state had better things to do, so that was the end of it. After I'd healed up enough to be discharged, and had been home for a few days, I was allowed to see a judge, and Sybil was returned to my custody. But we had a weekly visit from Child Protective Services for the next six months, something that really got on Barry's nerves, let me tell you."

Rose begins to recognize the landscape. They're only a handful of minutes away from Autumn Springs. She doesn't know what will happen when she returns, but she can't think about that now.

Not yet.

Not until she's finished.

"What I'm about to tell you is something I've never told anyone, Carlo. But if you're going to marry my daughter, and raise my grandchild, it's something I want you to know. Something I *need* you to know. Okay?"

"Sure, Rose," he says quietly.

"A few months after all this," she continues, talking faster, needing to get it all out. "After life had gone back to relative normality, Barry had another one of his episodes. Screaming at Sybil . . . I don't honestly remember what for, I just remember being terrified. Scared out of my mind for the safety of my baby girl. This time, when I intervened, he got me pretty good with a couple punches and knocked me back into the kitchen.

"I knew, right then, that he was going to kill me. I knew it like you know the sun is going to rise in the morning. So I got to my feet, and I grabbed the knife I'd been cutting carrots with. When he came for me, I rammed it into his throat."

"Jesus Christ—"

"When he tried to pull it out, I grabbed that handle and I pushed it in further. I shoved the knife deep as I could into the neck of my husband until he lay there, bleeding and gurgling, on the kitchen floor. I remember yelling at Sybil to stay out, to stay away. Then I climbed on top of him. I put both my hands on the handle of that blade and I held it there—held it inside him while he slapped at my arms and my head."

Rose touches her neatly set hair, as if feeling for the bloody handprints.

"And then I watched him die, Carlo. I watched the light go out of his eyes, watched his blood pump out of his throat and pool beneath him, and I didn't feel a thing. Not a damned thing."

Carlo, grim-faced and pale, pulls the truck into the Autumn Springs parking lot.

Rose feels a rush of comfort at the sight of it.

Not dread, or fatigue, or despair.

Comfort.

This is home, she thinks, and is surprised at how anxious she is to get back to her life. She scans the parking lot and is disappointed to see no sign of a squad car, the police department apparently having pulled their people away after only a few days.

She can only pray that Hastings got her message.

"You can guess the epilogue," she says quickly, eager to get inside, to find out what comes next. "It was ruled self-defense. Given our history, and my record of hospitalizations, there wasn't too much scrutiny on what had occurred. Later, Barry was cremated. On my way back home from the morgue, I pulled off near an alleyway, and I threw his box of ashes into an old dumpster."

Carlo pulls the truck up to the lobby entrance, puts it into park, and sits back, a stunned look on his face. After a moment of silence, after knowing her story is fully told, he turns to look at her.

"Why are you telling me all this, Rose?"

Rose smiles, but it's a sad, knowing smile. The one you give someone when you know the game is over and nobody has won. "I'm telling you so you know what I'm capable of," Rose says. "I'm telling you so you know . . ."

"Know what, Rose?" he says. But something in his eyes *does* know.

"So you know that if you ever hurt my daughter, or hurt my

grandbaby, that I'll kill you, Carlo. I will kill you in cold blood, and I won't feel a thing," Rose says, hands folded neatly in her lap. "You understand? It won't bother me in the slightest."

To her surprise, Carlo laughs, although without humor. No, none of that. Not here. Not today. But she doesn't hear mockery in that laugh, either. It's the cold, hard laugh of someone who's just been told he's escaped death—as if missing the flight he had a ticket for, the one that crashed into the ocean—while also being made aware of how close death always is, how it lurks in every shadow.

How it just might be waiting for you right around the next corner.

"Jesus, Rose." He looks at her steadily, warily, as if seeing her for the first time. "You're crazy, you know that?"

Rose's smile sweetens. "And now you know."

Carlo shakes his head. "Okay, Rose. Okay. Yeah, now I know. And I hear you, but you don't have to worry, or . . . you know, threaten my life. I love those two more than anything. Believe it."

Rose doesn't respond, but she doesn't reject his avowal, either.

"Tell me something," he says. "How much of this does your daughter know? You said you never told her but, I mean, how much does she know? She's not stupid."

"Sybil knows the bullet points," Rose says. "Beyond that, this is your story now, and you can do with it what you want."

Rose opens the door and steps down from the truck. She shuts her door, then gets her suitcase from the back seat.

"Hey, can I walk you to your room?" Carlo asks, and for the second time in as many minutes, this young man has surprised her. "You're making me a little nervous, here. This is deathbed stuff, Rose."

Good boy.

"I'll be fine," she says. "Get home safe. Kiss your family for me."

After a moment's hesitation, he nods. "You too, Rose," Carlo says. "And I will."

Rose notes that he waits until she's inside the lobby before pulling away and chalks up one more point in his favor.

"Welcome home, Ms. DuBois," the woman at the receptionist desk says, and even though Rose has no recollection of ever seeing her before—and certainly doesn't know her name—she responds with a polite nod and a warm smile.

"Thank you, dear. It's good to be back."

4

At the lobby's rear doors, Rose pauses, debating. *Do I go to the Medical Center and see Miller—assuming he's there at all—or do I go home?*

Rose feels the weight of the suitcase in her hand, the weight of the decision on her heart . . . and decides, finally, to go home. Besides, it's been a couple days, and she wants to see her apartment, make sure everything is where she left it.

To make sure there are no hats on the bed.

She knows she'll have to be careful and, if she's being honest with herself, she's hoping there will be a police officer or security guard around, just in case. It's just now six o'clock (*you're out after curfew, young lady*), and perhaps they've cut things back to nothing but overnight shifts.

Which would mean she's on her own.

Rose turns back to look at the empty lobby and the receptionist, who is now reading a book and sitting quietly at the front desk. The serene view makes her wonder how any of this could have happened or, even more strangely, if it really *did* happen. After all, this is nothing but a quiet retirement home, nestled in the woody confines of upstate New York, amidst trees and babbling creeks.

How could there have been so much murder?

How could there be so much danger?

But there is, and she knows it.

For the first time in decades, Rose stiffens her spine against an incoming storm.

During all the years of her marriage, she'd stood up to her husband as best she could. Sometimes she'd won . . . but most times she'd lost.

But she'd stood up to him.

And she'd stand up again.

Pushing through the doors, back into the cold night, Rose

follows the green tape line toward the Greenview Apartments, toward home.

The first floor of the apartment building is silent—and empty—as
Rose pulls her suitcase across the foyer and waits for the slow elevator to arrive.

After what seems an eternity, the car arrives, the doors shuffle
open, and Rose steps inside. When the doors close, Rose raises
a clenched fist and opens her fingers. She stares at the small silver charm Barbara Baxter had given her; that wide-open eye stares
right back.

If you got a warning to give me, now would be the time, she thinks,
waiting for a vision or a premonition. A sign.

But the charm sits, cold and silent, in her palm.

Rose scoffs as the elevator dings, then closes her fingers around
the charm once more. Right now, she knows she'll need all the help
she can get.

The doors slide open, and Rose steps out into the eerily quiet
foyer, silently cursing herself for not taking Carlo up on the offer to
walk her home.

Stupid pride, she thinks, then looks to her left, toward the hallway where Miller lives. She notes the quiet behind Sandra Freeman's door in unit 28, which always seemed to have some sort of
happy noise coming through it—a party, or some lively music, or
just Sandra's loud, friendly voice as it chatted on the phone. Now it's
as silent as the rest of the building.

Rose turns and heads toward the building's west side, toward
her apartment, Greenview 22, the last door in the corridor, the one
right by a second emergency stairwell leading down.

Twice, Rose stops and looks behind her—just to see if someone
might be walking toward her from the elevators, or to see if a neighbor's door is cracked open—but sees no one. She keeps going—
walking faster now—toward the end of the hall. She keeps one

eye on the door leading to the stairwell, making sure it doesn't pop open, a black-masked killer stepping out, knife in hand.

Finally, she reaches her door, fumbles in her purse for her keys. Breathing fast, heart racing, and hating that she's frightened—*but she can't help feeling exposed, so very exposed*—she fits the key into the lock, twists it hard, and pushes herself inside.

It's dark inside the apartment.

Rose mentally scolds herself for not leaving on a light. Despite the evening still creeping toward the tail end of dusk, the sky hazel but not yet black, there is little light coming through the closed curtains.

Did I close those curtains?

She doesn't know. She doesn't remember.

Perhaps. Perhaps I did, knowing that I'd be gone a while (maybe forever), and so figured it best to keep the sun out until I returned.

Perhaps.

Rose hits the light switch by the door, not letting it close behind her just yet. She wants to hold on to the warm light from the hallway a moment more, keep an escape route open until she's absolutely sure her apartment is empty and secure. That a killer isn't going to leap from a closet, or the bedroom, and run at her, blade raised.

So she stands for a few heartbeats at the open door, listening for sounds of an intruder, studying the apartment—the furniture, the kitchen, the books on the shelves—to see if anything is out of place.

But Rose sees nothing amiss.

No killer sitting at the dining room table, anyway.

She debates calling Hastings again and decides to wait until after she's taken off her coat, used the restroom, and checked the whole apartment thoroughly. She still wants to go to the Medical Center tonight, but will wait for a policeman to walk with her there. Hastings will surely send someone . . . won't he?

Her cell phone rings and she jumps, her fast-beating heart skipping and stumbling as she clutches her chest. She digs the phone from the pocket of her coat, looks at the screen, and is relieved to see—*finally*—that it's Detective Hastings returning her call.

"You're jumping at shadows," she mumbles, and is about to tap the answer icon on the phone when she hears a muffled voice from behind her.

"You should be."

A gloved hand coils around her head and clamps itself over her mouth as she starts to scream. The phone drops, unanswered, from her hand, and thumps dully to the carpet.

There's a bee sting at the side of her neck—the pinch of a needle—and Rose has just enough time to think *STUPID STUPID STUPID* before the light of her world fades slowly to black.

Her limbs go numb and she slides—the last threads of her consciousness clawing and screaming the entire way down—into oblivion.

5

This is the tricky part.

I've got to get her from here, all the way the hell over . . . to *there*.

NOT EASY.

I mean, yeah, it's not like she's heavy. I'd guess 120 pounds soaking wet, and I'm in decent enough shape, but it still sucks carrying a body over your shoulder that distance. We're not talking a few feet, no sir. I've gotta go down a flight of stairs, out the emergency exit (no alarm on that door, thank Christ), and then hump her dead weight across an expanse of weedy grass . . . what? A hundred yards?

The things I do for these people. If only they appreciated how hard I work to make things *interesting*. To kill them in cool and inventive ways.

It's what makes me special.

It's what makes me one of a kind.

Luckily, the police pulled out of here last night. I had to wait for that whole circus to blow over before setting up this last little gem.

Boy, I'm sweating good now. God *damn* this sucks.

I'll say this for you, Rose: it ain't all bad. When you finally do come around, good golly Miss Molly are you gonna be feeling *good*. High and bright as a neon kite.

At least, for a little bit.

Then, well . . . you'll feel not so good.

And then you won't feel anything at all.

Ever.

Almost there, Rose. Almost there.

And then the fun begins.

6

Rose has a vivid, colorful dream that she's in a large, sunlit meadow. All of her friends are there: Tatum, Gopi, Mickey . . . and Miller. They're calling out to her, and she's so excited to see them all, alive and well, that she runs—*runs like a schoolgirl*—toward them, toward the colors, the brilliant colors that make her think of the Judy Garland movie she saw when she was a child—*The Wizard of Oz*—and how she'd gasped when the black-and-white movie flipped into full color, and the whole theater had laughed and applauded for a moment, and then the witch came . . . the *good* witch . . . and then the little people with their strange haircuts, all of them green and red and yellow, and Rose remembers turning to her mother and smiling wildly, thinking: *Can you believe it? Can you believe how wonderful, exciting, terrifying this all is? Can you believe?*

"Rose?"

She shakes her head, wanting to stay in the dream. She focuses on her friends. They're beckoning her, telling her to run faster, faster . . . but then she trips, falls . . . and the meadow isn't sunlit grass . . .

"Rose? Come on, wake up already."

. . . it's hot coals. And she's not in a heavenly meadow and these aren't her friends.

She's in Hell, and the whole world is fire, and the charred demons are cackling, laughing—claws extended, yellow eyes bulging—and then she sees the Baxter sisters, but they're no longer old. They're *young*. Young and naked and dancing around a great shadowy thing and grinning wildly—madly—and Rose shuts her eyes tight and shakes her head *no no no NO NO NO!*

A hand slaps Rose across the face, slaps her so hard that her muscle memory instantly tells her brain to WAKE UP because he's coming for you, and then he's coming for Sybil, and if you don't wake up he's gonna kill her, kill your baby—

Rose opens her eyes . . .

. . . to a shower of stars in a nighttime sky.

The distant white dot of a satellite glides across the dark abyss of space. For a moment, she follows it with her eyes . . . and then realizes she's lying on her back, something cold and hard and sharp beneath her, pressing into her spine, her legs. She turns her head (which feels somehow detached from her body—numb, and fuzzy) and sees someone kneeling next to her. They're not wearing a black ski mask, and it's someone she knows and . . . for the briefest of moments, Rose thinks she's okay.

That she's been saved.

The person kneeling beside her shifts their weight forward so the moonlight catches their face in a wash of silver—their eyes are dancing, sparkling like the stars overhead, and they're smiling down at her, as if truly happy.

Rose looks into those eyes, feels the rub of the bindings at her wrists, the sticky tape sealing her mouth shut, and realizes it's not happiness she sees in those eyes.

It's madness.

"There you are," the woman says. "Welcome back from the dead, Rose. It's good to see you. Are you too cold? I got you a blanket. I'm not a total dick."

Rose wishes she could respond (or even open her mouth to lick her lips), but it's impossible, of course. All she can offer the killer, from deep in her throat, is a grunt of displeasure.

But what she thinks is:

Hello, Nurse.

Mindy Jarvis stares at Rose a few seconds longer, eyes wide, studying her face as if memorizing it. "I can't believe this worked," she says.

Then the young nurse looks off into the distance and her smile slackens, her beaming expression grows dull, as if someone had pulled the plug powering her twisted black brain. "So many variables," she mumbles, then her eyes fall to Rose once more, and the insane grin returns.

"This is the last game, Rose. The very last one. Are you ready?"

Rose rolls her eyes away from that disquieting face, sets her gaze upward, toward the stars, trying to reason . . . but her mind is still muddled, the synapses sluggish and strained as she desperately tries to make sense of what's happening.

Mindy bends down low so that she's whispering directly into Rose's ear.

"Are you ready to die?"

7

Mindy straightens, pulls her head back so her eyes can travel down the length of Rose's body, before returning to look her in the face, that mad grin never wavering. She studies the depths of Rose's frightened eyes, as if searching for something hiding behind them.

"Not sure how fucked up you are. Those drugs I gave you are no joke. The propofol was that little prick you felt before dropping like dead weight. I had plenty left since I didn't even get to use it the first time I tried to grab you." Mindy cocks her head, gives Rose a sly smile. "That was pretty cool, by the way. I mean, yeah, *duh*, I was super pissed at first and nearly broke my damn ankle jumping out your window. These boots are *not* good for such activities."

Mindy swings her leg around, showing Rose a close-up view of one of her boots, which look military grade with their thick, heavy bottoms and laces riding up the shin. But the soles, Rose notices in the dim light, are at least two inches thick. "I like them because they make me look taller than I am," Mindy says, staring at her foot. "But they're tough to run in, and they kind of pinch my toes, if I'm being honest." She shrugs, slides her leg back behind her. "Whatever, I don't need to run much. You old folks aren't exactly Speedy Gonzalez. Ándale! Ándale! YEE-HA!" Mindy half-shrieks this last bit then laughs hysterically, and all Rose can think is that she's in some very deep shit.

"Look, time's a wastin', so I better fill you in. As you may have noticed, Ms. DuBois, you are tied to a railroad track."

Rose's eyes widen as fresh terror surges through her body. She turns her head hard to the left, then to the right, and realizes that what she's been feeling in her back this whole time are the sharp white stones and heavy wooden tracks of the train line that runs past Autumn Springs.

*Twice a day during the week; once on Saturday night, at 8 PM sharp.
Oh, sweet Lord, no.*

"Pretty cool, right? Just like those old-timey movies. A few months ago I snuck into one of those shows your buddy Gopi puts on . . . well, *put* on, past tense. Anyway, he called it 'A Silent Film Retrospective.' At least that's what the flyer said. There were a few that I liked. Some were pretty funny, actually. But the one I really loved was a short movie about some lady chained to train tracks by these wild-eyed bandits." Mindy gazes down at Rose with those bright, startling black eyes, that wide, leering grin. "And I remember thinking: That would be an amazing way to kill someone."

Mindy's gloved hand grips Rose's cheeks, gives her head a shake. "And guess what, Rose? You're the lucky girl I get to do it with! I can't tell you how fucking thrilled I am that it all worked out. Of course, I don't have chain, but this rope cord I stole from the supply room should do the trick. You'll be able to roll around a bit, but I looped the rope under the metal rail here, see? And your feet are tied, of course."

Rose doesn't know if it's her imagination, but she swears she can feel the tracks beneath her . . . *vibrating.*

No, no . . . it can't be. Not yet.

"The train should be getting close now," Mindy says casually, glancing into the distance. "Damn, Rose, why'd you sleep so long? Now you only have—" Mindy looks at her watch. "Twenty minutes to live! But hey, it's good to have some time to reflect, right? At least you're not like your buddy Miller, slowly bleeding out in his apartment."

Rose groans. Tears spill down her face, slide into the dirt and stone of the train tracks beneath her.

"Yeah, I'm not *quite* done with him yet," she says. "You two were real pains in the ass, Rose, no lie. And so I want to keep him dying for a while. But don't you worry; I'll wrap that up as soon as the train comes. And then, when I'm all done, I'm gonna—"

Mindy turns away once more—with urgency this time—her head jerking toward the retirement home. Rose lifts her chin as best she can and notices the buildings are not as far away as she'd imagined. Across the expanse of back lawn, she can even see a few lit windows. She twists her head farther to the left and realizes where she's been taken.

The charred ruins of the old asylum are a stone's throw away, the tall, dense wall of trees leading into the woods just behind.

Then Rose hears what Mindy, with her young ears, must have heard a few seconds prior.

Sirens.

"Shit," Mindy breathes. "They must have found him."

She turns back to Rose, and the smile is wiped from her face. In its place is a deep, hateful scowl, one that is much more in line with Mindy's true nature, Rose thinks.

"I gotta go check that out. But don't you go anywhere, Rose! I'll be back when I can. There's no fucking way I'm missing this." Mindy stands and brushes off the knees of her dark pants. She yanks the ski mask from a pocket of her black hoodie and pulls it down over her face. And just like that, she becomes one with the dark.

As if transformed by the mask, her voice shifts, becomes more high-pitched and unrecognizable. More like the insane monster she truly is.

"By the way, along with the sedative, I crushed the last of my LSD and put it under your tongue while you were out. So, you know, in case you taste something bitter in your mouth. Also, you might start seeing some crazy shit, which is hilarious, right? Have fun, Rose!"

Mindy runs into the night as the sound of sirens grows louder.

Ambulances or police cars? Rose thinks muddily. *Hopefully both.*

Debating what to do—what she *can* do—Rose stares up toward the ceiling of night sky. For the first time she notices the way the stars bend, as if smeared across a painter's canvas instead of outer space, leaving streaks of dull color. She ignores this bizarre effect and focuses instead on her wrists, which are bound tightly to each rail of the track. She tries twisting her body to get a better look at the bindings, but no matter how hard she tries she can't see her hands or the ropes tying them down . . .

She rotates her wrists to get a better idea of how tight, or loose, the knots are . . . and that's when she notices the feel of something strange in her palm, something she'd forgotten about until this moment.

Clutched tightly in one closed hand, she realizes, is the small silver talisman.

A lot of good it's doing, she thinks miserably. *No magic charm is going to help me out of this, and no one even knows I'm out here, trapped in the dark.*

No one will find me quickly enough to beat the train.

Maybe it'll see me and stop, she thinks, a burst of hope springing in her chest. *Yes, it might see me—*

But then Rose realizes something else.

She's not cold.

I got you a blanket. I'm not a total dick.

Rose lifts her head from the wooden track (ignoring the way her vision swims, as if seeing the world through a sheet of water) and realizes she's been covered, chin to toe, in a black wool blanket.

Well, at least I'm not going to freeze to death, she thinks bitterly as she tugs her wrists against the bindings, testing the ropes, but they feel good and tight.

Think, Rose, think!

But what else can she do? Maybe she could loosen them, if she rotates her wrist a certain way . . . if she could only get one free . . .

A whisper comes to her from the dark—someone nearby, speaking words she can't quite make out.

Startled, Rose looks around, wishing she could tear away the tape covering her mouth and yell for help. Instead, her thoughts are left to scream inside her own head.

Is someone here? Hello!?

Like gathering storm clouds, smudges of shadow begin to take form beside her.

And then those smudges coalesce into a shape.

Rose squints at the shadow form as it comes closer, closer. Then it bends down, just like Mindy Jarvis had, and leans in over Rose, who suddenly trembles with horror.

The face of Barbara Baxter—or at least a silver-shadowed likeness of her—stares down.

If Rose didn't know any better, she'd say that the dead woman is smiling.

"Hey there, Rose," the shadow-Barbara says. "Quite a fix you're in here."

Another voice: "She's in trouble, all right." Rose jerks her head toward the other side of the tracks and sees two more shadows.

Bridget and Betsie, I presume, she thinks numbly, wondering if she's losing her mind. *Which would make sense, given that Barbara's ghost is just here on the other side.*

As if any of this makes even the smallest amount of sense.

"You have to *try*, Rose," Barbara says, her voice a wispy, raspy scratching against the air itself, as if stuck just on the other side of an invisible membrane separating reality from the spirit realm. "You have to try and get free. The train is coming. It's close now."

Rose drops her head back to the ground, wishing she could yell, could scream at the spirit: *Good idea! How about some help?*

The silver-tinted shadow chuckles. "I would if I could. We all would. We'd like nothing more than that bitch to get what's coming to her," she says, as if reading Rose's thoughts.

"We're waiting for her," one of the other shadows says. Rose thinks it might be Bridget. "We're saving a spot for her in Hell."

"Please, Rose, try harder," the third voice says.

Hello, Betsie. How's things?

"Try working one wrist in circles," Barbara advises. "That awful woman has tied it around these thick rails, but they're loose in some places."

"I don't think she was planning on leaving you alone," Bridget whispers, her voice the sound of wind whistling through a pipe.

"Definitely not," Betsie adds, like the rustle of dry leaves.

Rose closes her eyes, tries to focus on the feeling of the rope binding her wrists. The logical part of her brain *knows* she's hallucinating, knows that the strange visions are a product of whatever drugs are flooding her system, but it doesn't matter. All that matters is getting free.

Refocusing all her attention on the ropes, she rotates her wrist more and more . . .

And . . . *yes!*

There is a little wiggle room there, isn't there?

Inspired by hope, Rose tugs against the train rail, causing the rope to go taut, then slides her arm *back*, seeing if her hand could possibly slip through.

The rope presses against the meaty bottom of her hand. The rope is thin and smooth. *Cord*, she'd called it. But no matter how hard she pulls, the cord stops tight at the base of her thumb, and her hand will go no further.

In the distance, Rose hears a sound that has become so common, such a part of her everyday life, that at first she hardly notices it. Given her circumstances, however, it now drills a hot spike of terror into her mind.

The *ping-ping-ping* of the railroad crossing at Main Street carries to her through the brittle October air. She can almost visualize the white arms folding down; the flashing orange lights holding up the meager trickle of traffic heading downtown or coming the other way, toward Autumn Springs and beyond; the massive, angry freight train rumbling through at sixty miles per hour, an unstoppable force.

Rose moans and opens her eyes wide, thinking the shadow sisters will be gone—pulled back to her imagination from which they came—but they're still here. Watching her. One of them—Bridget, she thinks—is now floating just above her.

"Let go of the charm, Rose," the spirit rasps. "You're trapped like a raccoon with its hand in a gooseneck jar, palm full of tasty treats you don't want to drop."

"If you let go," Betsie adds, now floating beside her sister, the two of them circling, circling, like a yin-yang symbol with no white half, "maybe you can pull your hand from the jar."

The charm!

Somehow Rose has continued holding on to it after she got stuck with the needle. Her body—possibly with direct orders from her subconscious mind—clutching it tight in one closed fist.

Rose opens her hand, extends her fingers, and feels the cool weight of the silver drop from her palm. Once more, she pulls . . .

The rope pressing against the base of her thumb slides miraculously upward, past her thumb . . . past her knuckles . . . and . . .

Free!

"Good job, Rose!" Barbara says, but the shadow-form is dissolving now, mingling back into the night, the voice growing distant. "But hurry, now. You must hurry . . .

"The train . . . is . . . here."

Once again, Rose feels the vibration of the tracks. But this time, it's no illusion. No trick of her frayed, terrified nerves.

The tracks beneath her are vibrating . . . and the vibrations are growing stronger.

Rose raises her left arm—now gloriously free—and brings it to her face. She finds the edge of the tape stretched across her mouth, all the way to the ear, and picks at one corner with trembling fingers. Slowly, not wanting to rip her lips off, she peels the tape up and across her mouth. When her mouth is free, she gasps with pleasure, sucking in the cold night air, filling her lungs.

Immediately, her body feels stronger, her mind clearer. She tosses the strip of tape away, jerks off the wool blanket, and reaches for her other hand. *I can see this one more easily,* she thinks and—with a jolt of horror—realizes why.

The train has made its turn off of Main Street and is now chugging past the shadowed hulks of the retirement home buildings, heading straight for her at high speed.

Rose doesn't have minutes.

She has *seconds.*

Whimpering, she claws at the knot holding her right hand to the rails.

Can't get it! Can't get it!

She looks up toward the oncoming train. The engine is passing the Greenview building and Rose can't help thinking that the smoking, bellowing engine looks like a mask, an iron mask with two slit eyes that glow a hellish orange, narrowed at their prey, determined to drive forward faster—*faster*—and rip her body to shreds beneath its hungry wheels, feeding her flesh to its monstrous belly. Below those orange-slit eyes are two hard, white headlights that serve very well as nostrils, because just below them is a grinning grill of long metal teeth.

I'M COMING ROSE! the engine screams, smoke chugging out the top of its head like a demon from Hell as it wills itself forward, clawing at the tracks.

I'M COMING TO THE PARTY, AND I HOPE I'M NOT TOO LATE! I'M COMING TO PLAY WITH YOU, ROSE! I WANT TO PLAY THE GAME!

"Oh Lord, please . . ." Rose prays, then turns all her attention to the knot holding her wrist to the shuddering track. *If I can't get it, I'll have to roll out of the way. I'll lose my arm, of course, and I might be dragged a few hundred feet, but I could survive, couldn't I?*

Couldn't I?

A nail breaks off one of her grasping fingers and Rose cries out, the sound lost amid the rumbling of the approaching train, the rails now shaking violently against her arm as she struggles with the rope, the headlights bathing her in the white of looming death.

Then, suddenly . . .

She has it!

One loop comes free, then another, and now she's yanking against the rope.

I can do it. There's still time!

A big strong hand clamps down onto Rose's bound wrist, holds it firmly against the steel rail, keeping her from pulling the last of the knot free.

She looks up in shocked terror.

Directly into the face of her dead husband.

Barry's mouth is stretched into an obscene, toothy snarl, his eyes glowing with that same orange heat of the train's engine.

NO! Impossible!

"What the hell you think you're doing, Rose?" he growls, grinning like a jackal who's just pinned their prey to the desert floor. "You ain't going NOWHERE unless I say so!"

The train bellows, and there's no stopping it now.

"Let me go," she pleads, tears streaming down her face. "Let me go, Barry."

But Barry shakes his head, his hand squeezing her wrist so tight she fears it might break. "No way, no *how*. I'm staying RIGHT HERE. And when I'm done with you, I'm gonna go say hello to our little girl and that bastard she squeezed out from between her legs. You and she are a couple of good-time girls, huh? Can't keep your knees together. Two sluts and a bastard," he says, grinning so wide now that his face *splits*, blood and saliva running down his chin and onto the steel rail of the track, where it hisses like oil on a frying pan. "I'm gonna teach her the same thing I taught you. That *I'm* the one in charge around here. I'm the one calling the shots!"

Rose feels her spine tighten at the thought of this man—ghost or hallucination or demon or whatever he might be—touching her babies. She leans her face close to his, teeth bared, and enjoys seeing the glimpse of doubt in those fire-breathing eyes.

"You let go of me right now," she hisses, "or I will kill your sorry ass all over again."

The orange eyes flicker and dim, the shadow hand relents—pulls back just a couple inches—and Rose yanks the arm free as the train bears down on her.

With an effort that makes her tied ankles scream in agony, she grips one rail with both hands and hurls herself off the tracks, rolling and screaming into the cold wet grass as the engine blasts by her, the squall of soot and smoke and diesel enveloping her in a hot gust of brimstone air.

As it continues to barrel past, she screams and screams—in terror, in triumph—as the train cars slam by just a few feet away, the sound so loud that it vibrates throughout her entire body, presses against her inner ears with fat, hot fingers.

Rose rolls a few more feet, slower now, then stops, face down in the grass, panting, sweating, and shaking so hard her teeth chatter in her thought-muddled head.

After giving herself a few moments to catch her breath, she sits up as best she can and reaches for the ropes binding her ankles. She has to get free, get out of here before—

Mindy's thick-soled boots stop a few inches from Rose's bare feet.

"I'll be goddamned," Mindy says, her voice merging effortlessly with the sounds of the train rumbling past. "Looks like we'll have to do this the easy way."

When Rose looks up, eyes bulging with fear, all she can see through a thick veil of terror is that black ski mask—swallowed in the shadow of a dark hood—and the glint of a large knife coming right at her, the blade already dripping with blood.

8

Rose pulls back as Mindy lunges—but the tip of the knife stops just a few inches from her face, close enough that she can see the slow *drip . . . drip . . .* of someone else's blood falling off its edge.

She feels one cooled drop hit her bared collarbone, where her dress had been pulled away while escaping the train.

Is that Miller's blood?

She feels a sickening wave of nausea, but sucks in another breath of cold air, wills the meager contents of her stomach to stay put. *Too much adrenaline*, she thinks, feeling the *THUMPTHUMPTHUMP* of her poor heart battering against her rib cage.

"It's a mess, I know," Mindy says apologetically.

She pulls the blade back, examines it, then wipes it—once, twice—on her pant leg. "I ran into an officer of the law sneaking out the back door and had to gut him quick. Thankfully he wasn't wearing one of those bulletproof vest thingies, you know what I mean? Dumb luck. Well, not for him, I guess."

Mindy bends her knees, hunches like a gargoyle at Rose's feet. The masked face stares blankly, sunken patches of black where eyes should be. "Hey, how did you get out of that, by the way?" Mindy waggles the point of the knife nonchalantly at the air. "You know what? Forget it; don't even tell me. Us girls need to keep our secrets, am I right? I gotta say, though, you're a great nemesis, Rose. A real badass final girl. Seriously. I'm super impressed. And to be honest, doing it this way is going to be a lot more fun than you just getting smooshed by the train. Way more challenging. How's your trip, by the way? Your eyes are like . . . crazy blown out. You look just like Stan did, right before I pushed him into outer fucking space."

"I'm just an old woman . . ." Rose says, voice choked with despair—not just for her, but for Gopi, and Mickey, and the others.

And for Miller, who is inside one of those buildings right now, likely torn open and bleeding, dying . . . or already dead.

"Don't sell yourself short, Rose," Mindy says. "You're a right pain in the ass! Giving that dumb detective the scoop on the drugs? Convincing him there was a killer when I was just getting warmed up? Goddamn, if I'm being totally honest, I was very uncomfortable with that information being out there. That cramped my style, Rose. It made things *difficult*. And then, of course, you set that trap for me. Man, that was ballsy."

As she speaks, Mindy doesn't get any closer. She stays hunched at Rose's feet, as if waiting for her to make a move so she can run her through and end this.

"Anyhoo," she finally says, as if disappointed. "This place is crawling with cops now. Like fucking ants at a picnic." The masked figure cocks her head, as if finally piecing something together. She points the tip of the knife at Rose's face.

"Did you call them, Rose?" Mindy laughs, as if amused at the idea of almost being caught. "Damn, dude, I think you did! Yeah, I figured you knew I was full of shit when I called about Miller. Man! I screwed that up, didn't I? The diabetes thing was bullshit, right? Ha, that was quick thinking, Rose. You got me all flustered. I was like: Shit, *does* he have diabetes? I know I'm a nurse or whatever, but I don't know jack shit about folks who aren't in the Med Center. So yeah . . . you got me on that one. Hey, good job by you! Another classic nemesis moment."

Rose shakes her head in exhaustion and despair. Part of her just wants this to be over, one way or the other. Her body hurts, her head is cloudy and confused, and she's tired of feeling helpless. Of feeling scared.

I'd rather be dead than feel this way, she thinks sadly. *So come on, bitch. Let's just end this.*

"So what now?" Rose asks, the cold, wet grass seeping through her bottom, her teeth chattering with cold.

Mindy ponders the question for a moment. "Not sure, Rose.

Maybe I should peel the skin off the bottom of your feet or cut off your toes. That'd be fun."

Rose's eyes go wide as Mindy shuffles closer, then lowers the knife to Rose's bound feet . . .

"Please . . ."

. . . and cuts the rope.

"One more game, Rose," the crazed voice says from behind the mask. "But this one you can actually win. Honest."

Rose tucks up her legs, rubs her sore, scraped ankles.

Should I scream? That would end this quick. She'll push that knife into my heart and it will all be over. The end of everything.

"There's a path behind you," Mindy says, aiming the knife toward the woods. "You know, the forest path leading to the old well?"

Rose nods. "I know the path."

"Good," Mindy says, standing. To Rose's shock, she holds out a hand, as if wanting to help Rose up. "Come on, I won't stab you here. Scout's honor."

Rose ignores the hand, but climbs slowly to her feet. It takes effort. Her wrists hurt (she thinks one of them might be fractured), her legs are numb, and she still feels lightheaded . . . *fuzzy.* She doesn't dare look at the stars.

"You run toward that path, you stubborn bitch, and I'm going to stand here and count to ten. Like, really count good, with Mississippi's and everything," Mindy says from behind the mask. "Then I'm gonna come for you."

Rose shakes her head. "Just kill me, Mindy. I'm so damn tired."

Mindy slaps Rose across the face with a gloved hand.

That wakes her up.

This girl slaps me again and I might just fight. I just might.

"Enough of that shit," Mindy snaps, stepping so close to Rose she can smell the sweat and blood coming off of her. For the first time, Mindy's voice isn't singsong, isn't taunting and silly.

She sounds angry, Rose thinks. *She sounds* pissed.

"You've fucked me, Rose," she growls. "Every step of the way

you've tried to ruin my games, and now I'm giving you a fair fucking shot and you're whining like a goddamn baby. So you listen
to me. You hit that trail. I count to ten. If you make it to the well
before I get you, I'll let you live."

"Bullshit," Rose mumbles.

"Not bullshit," Mindy says. "You're my nemesis, Rose! And look,
if it makes you feel any better, let's say you beat me. Let's say you
live, right? I'm still gonna get you down the road. You know, in the
sequel or whatever. But for now, for today, you live. You live, and I
disappear. Those are the rules. That's the game."

Mindy looks quickly back toward the apartments, then refocuses
that dark shadow of a face back onto Rose. "And P.S.: if you run
for the buildings, I'll gut you right here on the back lawn. That's
another rule."

Mindy takes a step back, sheathes the knife.

"A reminder that my boots suck for running, so this could actually
be interesting." Mindy folds her arms across her chest. "Ready . . ."

"I'm not going—"

"Steady . . ."

"Mindy, please—"

"And GO!"

Rose stands there, frozen, unsure what to do.

Do I run? Do I fight?

The masked figure shakes her head slowly. "One Mississippi."

Knowing she's out of options and thinking maybe, just maybe,
there is another way out of this—a way that would break the rules
of Mindy's game—Rose turns her back on the killer and runs.

9

After a few panicked moments, during which she couldn't locate the trailhead, whimpering in fear and frustration, Rose finally sees the small sign, stuck to a dark wood post, indicating the start of the forest trail.

She hits the dirt path as fast as her legs will carry her. She can't remember the last time she'd actually tried to *run*, and she knows she's not moving fast enough—not *nearly* fast enough. Her pace is no more than a light jog for folks half her age.

For someone like Mindy Jarvis.

The path, however, is pitch black, the overhanging branches blocking out any stray scraps of moonlight, which plays perfectly into Rose's last gasp idea for survival.

As she runs deeper and deeper into the trees, she scans to her left and right for a good place to dip into the woods. To hide. If she can somehow hide until morning, maybe the police will come looking for her. Come looking in the woods. And then she could escape—truly escape.

She slows her pace, begins to veer left, and sees Barry standing at the edge of the path, grinning like a wolf, eyes blazing orange fire. "Not this way, sweetheart," he hisses, and swipes at her with an impossibly clawed hand. Rose cries out, stumbles, and falls. Doing her best to keep from crying, from losing her mind to fear, she gets back to her feet and keeps running.

"Keep going, Rose!" the ghostly voice of Barbara Baxter whispers urgently into her ear. Rose shifts her eyes in time to see a flickering, flying shadow keeping pace next to her. "You can do it."

"Here I coooome, Rose!" Mindy sings from the foot of the path.

Did the police hear that? Are they heading this way right now?

The shadow flits into the trees. Rose follows it with her eyes and spots an opening just ahead on the right.

But she also hears pounding footsteps coming from behind. The *clomp, clomp, CLOMP, CLOMP* of those thick-soled boots on packed dirt getting louder, louder.

"Oh, God!" Rose yells and, in a blind panic, cuts hard right into the dark abyss of the trees.

She makes it ten feet before she stumbles, her toes bashing into something hard as stone, but manages not to cry out. She hunches over, slowing down, and extends her arms so she doesn't crash headfirst into a thick branch, or run into a jagged limb and put her eye out.

She doesn't make it much farther, a few feet more perhaps, when she hears Mindy.

"That's cheating, Rose," the young nurse says calmly. "Just remember that I gave you a chance. I gave you a chance and you shat on it. So . . . that's it then."

Footsteps crunch into the undergrowth. Slow, assured footsteps. Coming straight toward her.

"No more games," Mindy sighs. "No more fun."

Rose drops to all fours, climbs behind a tree, clamps her hands over her mouth, and waits. *She'll either find me or she won't,* she thinks. *But Lord knows I'm done. I'm spent.*

After a few seconds, the steady footsteps pass by, just to Rose's left . . . then hesitate.

Rose doesn't dare move an inch.

After a few moments, the steps continue on, past the tree where Rose hides. She debates crawling back toward the path, but the groundcover is littered with brittle leaves and twigs (*and bugs, Rose, don't forget about the bugs*) and she'll make too much noise. Better to stay still—here in the dark—and pray.

Rose slinks lower against the base of the tree.

She no longer hears Mindy's footsteps.

She stopped somewhere.

Don't breathe, Rose. Don't you dare breathe.

Don't make a sound.

Rose closes her eyes and doesn't open them again.

Not even when she clearly hears the crack of a nearby branch, followed by the sound of footsteps coming back toward her, slowing, then stopping just beyond her bare, ice-cold, scratched-up feet.

Not even when she hears the disappointed sigh of the killer.

"Open your eyes, Rose," Mindy says, as if bored.

Rose does, and finds herself staring at a pair of heavy boots. She looks up into the black void of the killer's masked face, the long knife already unsheathed, a ray of moonlight somehow finding the blood-smeared blade, glinting off it like the wink of a star.

"You cheated," Mindy says. "Even so, I'll make this quick."

Crying softly, Rose lifts her hands defensively, as if the gesture would somehow stop the inevitable.

For a moment, time stills.

"What the fuck?"

Rose smells it before she sees it.

A deep, rich, animal smell.

Something brushes past her shoulder, and she turns wide, terrified eyes toward whatever it is moving beside her.

Slinking out from behind the tree . . . is an animal.

It's slung low to the ground, perched on all fours. It has a large head—she makes out a heavy snout and taut, pointed ears—and a slick, heavily muscled coat. At first, Rose thinks it's a dog, but then it turns to look at her—just for a moment—and she sees the golden eyes of a predator.

A mountain lion.

As it passes by, its wide, yellow eyes gaze directly at Rose and—for a split second—they flash a deep, unnatural, hellish red.

And then the animal is striding past her, shoulders bunched, teeth bared.

Its eyes on Mindy.

Blood-covered Mindy.

In a flash, Rose recalls what Betsie Baxter had told her, not so long ago: *If he comes across your path, you'd assume him to be a panther or a cougar. . . .*

Haures.

"Uh . . ." Mindy says, lowering the knife and holding out one placating hand.

Rose doesn't dare move, doesn't dare *flinch*.

"Hey, what is this? What the fuck is this?"

Rose doesn't answer, but instead watches in amazement as Mindy takes a step backward. The animal hisses like only a one-hundred-pound predator can—a sound that strikes pure terror into the heart of anyone within earshot—followed by a deep, rumbling, threatening growl.

Crouching into a defensive posture, Mindy brings the knife back up. She swipes it toward the cougar's head. "Back up!" she screams, arcing the knife through the air again, and again, causing the great cat to bare its long fangs.

"Go on! Beat it! Get out of here!"

A soft voice whispers into Rose's ear.

"Best if you leave now."

Rose—slowly, oh so slowly—pushes her back up the rough bark of the cold tree until she's standing, watching in a sort of awe as Mindy backs up farther and farther into the deep shadows, swiping at the approaching animal, who appears undaunted.

"I said to BACK UP MOTHERFU—"

The animal gives a guttural scream that chills Rose's blood.

And then it leaps.

Mindy cries out as the massive cat crashes into her body, knocking them both to the ground. Rose can do nothing but watch in numb horror as the cougar lets out another one of those hideous, victorious screams, right before sinking its jaws into the flesh of its prey.

Rose doesn't know how long she stands there, watching as a whirlwind of limbs thrash madly against the clawing, biting beast; listening as Mindy's cries of pain and horror turn into gargled whimpers, and then, eventually, silence . . . followed only by the sounds of her body being ripped open and torn apart.

Eaten.

Seconds? Minutes?

In a daze, Rose finally manages to turn away, using the tree as leverage, then makes her way slowly, dazedly, back toward the path. A part of her is waiting for the animal to finish its meal and come for her, leap onto her back with claws extended, teeth digging into her neck, eyes glowing impossibly red.

After a few minutes of bumping into branches and staggering over protruding roots, however, Rose finds the dirt path. Her feet are bleeding, and she's likely broken a couple toes. Her wrist throbs painfully, and she's near frozen with cold, but she makes herself keep moving, one step at a time, back down the path until she reaches the trailhead.

Running on nothing but pure will and instinct, her mind numb with shock, her body beaten and broken, Rose continues on, aiming for the lights, walking across the back lawn of Autumn Springs, toward home.

TWELVE

THE LETTER

Three Days Later.

Rose doesn't like hospitals. Not one bit.

They remind her of the old days—days when she'd spend a night in the hospital with a concussion, or a broken arm and a bruised eye. Those are days she'd like to forget if she could, impossible though it might be.

The night of her escape from Mindy Jarvis, Rose was found—by two police officers who'd been sent to search for her and were happy to see her alive—limping her way back toward the apartments.

Those same two officers had, only minutes earlier, made the recent, gruesome discovery of their friend and colleague, another officer who'd been found stabbed repeatedly before being dumped behind a hedgerow lining the Greenview building.

Once they called in their location, and assured Rose that medical help was on the way, she informed them—in vague, exhausted terms—where they could find the killer.

Or whatever was left of her.

She warned them about the mountain lion, of course, and decided to ignore how they both looked at her like she was a crazy old woman. When they thought they were out of earshot, she heard one of them say to the other: "If she saw a mountain lion, I'm Santa Claus."

But the other officer, the one who'd been studying Rose more carefully while she spoke, seemed to take her warning to heart. "We'll call for backup, ma'am," he'd said, then turned to his partner. "And you better radio Hastings."

After they helped Rose to the nearby service road where a medical crew waited, they laid her down on a gurney and loaded her into the back of an ambulance. Minutes later, Hastings arrived.

For a moment, she just stared at the detective as he stood by the open door, his face ashen, his suit disheveled.

"Tell me," she said.

When she'd called Hastings that afternoon, the message she'd left informed him that the killer had reached out, that it was most likely one of the nurses from the Medical Center, although she wasn't sure which one, and that Miller was in grave danger.

"Please, get someone to check on Miller," she'd told the recording. "I don't know who I can trust, so please get a policeman to check on my friend as soon as you can."

She'd then told him that she was heading back to Autumn Springs and to let her know when he received the message. "A nurse," she said again. "I think it might be the young, pretty one, with the boyish haircut. Mindy something."

Now, standing at the rear door of the ambulance, Hastings informed her that they'd broken down Miller's front door, found him tied to a kitchen chair, gagged, beaten, and horrifically wounded.

"She'd taken her time," he'd said, his eyes sunken, defeated. "She'd been at it for a couple days. I'm sorry it took us so long, Rose. I truly am."

When she arrived at the hospital, Rose was seen by a flurry of doctors and nurses, given an IV drip, and told that she had a badly sprained wrist, three broken toes, a broken finger, abrasions and cuts to her arms and face (one on her left bicep required twelve stitches), and a nasty bump on the head.

She doesn't recall breaking the finger, or the nasty cut on her arm, but she remembers the sheet of pain that consumed her once the adrenaline (and drugs) had worn off, along with the knowledge that her body was damaged far worse than she'd realized while running for her life.

That first night, and for the next couple of days, Sybil stayed at her side, taking care of her, making sure she was comfortable, talking about Roy and Carlo and the future in bright, shining words that cheered Rose's spirits—as much as she could be cheered, at least.

The second day, Hastings stopped by to let her know they'd found the remains of Mindy Jarvis and that it was, in fact, an animal attack.

"Strangest damn thing I ever heard of," he'd said. "Far as I know, there aren't many, if any, mountain lions in this region. A few, maybe . . ."

"She was covered in blood," Rose said, as if in explanation for why the attack had occurred in the first place.

But Rose didn't say what she really thought.

That it wasn't an animal at all.

As Hastings spoke, Rose recalled the night of the asylum fire, asking Miller if he thought the sisters might have conjured their demon.

She still wonders.

"We went back and did autopsies on all her victims, at least those who weren't already ashes," Hastings said. "Found a pharmacy's worth of hallucinogens and narcotics in almost every one, including your friend Mickey, and Stan Swanson. The administrator turned over the letters you'd mentioned to the police a few days after Stan was killed, which supported your story. Poor guy also had a suspicious stab wound that we'd missed. But when someone falls eighty feet, things get messy."

Rose could have told him a few other things that she thought were messy, but held her tongue.

"As far as Mindy Jarvis goes, there's been a domino effect of sorts. Cold cases have been reopened surrounding the murders of nearly ten people who'd spent time at a homeless shelter she worked for in the city." He shrugs, cleared his throat. "No one suspected—"

"I imagine murdered homeless aren't much of a priority," she said evenly. "Similar to us old folks."

"Now, Rose, that's not—"

"Don't be defensive, Detective. I'm just saying she had a certain . . . how do you say? Modus operandi."

Hastings nodded. "That much is true. She was good at making things look like accidents, or overdoses, or suicides. This one liked to play with her food."

Rose shivered at that, but knew he was right.

"Before that, she spent time in a Colorado hospital that had some suspicious deaths of its own. Again, not enough to warrant a full investigation at the time, but in hindsight, yeah. I think that's where it started. If not earlier."

"But now it stops," Rose said.

Hastings smiled, put a gentle hand on her good wrist. "Because of you, Rose," he said. "Because of you, now it stops."

Before Hastings left, he gave her an envelope, her name written across the front in a hand she knew well.

"One last thing," he said, not quite able to meet her eye. "Miller left this in his apartment. I didn't read it, but if there's anything in there I need to know, be a pal and tell me, will you?"

Rose nodded and said she would. Then she set the letter on the table next to her bed and left it there.

She'd read it when the time was right.

Later that same day, Mr. Blackwell came by with flowers. They visited for a long while, and he told her some welcome good news— the first she'd heard in what felt like forever.

"I don't need to go into the why of it all, obviously," he'd said. "And I don't mean to be macabre, but we do we have quite a few openings. If you'll accept it, Rose, I have a lovely unit in the Seaview building, far away from the train tracks, that overlooks the koi pond. I know how much you enjoy that spot. It's the biggest footprint we offer, and I'd upgrade you for free. You'd keep the same payments. And, if it helps in your decision-making," he added sheepishly, "it wasn't a victim. Just someone who broke their lease and fled when this whole nightmare started."

Rose agreed to the move and cried a little at the thought of seeing the empty bench by the pond every day, happy to hold on to those memories of her friend, Tatum Bird.

"One other thing," he continued. "When you're up to it, I'd like to speak with you about a bigger role, one that would be part of administration. You're kind of a celebrity now, Rose, and to be frank, I think Autumn Springs could use an ambassador of sorts, someone to speak of our positives so that any new residents will feel comfortable, feel safe. You'd be compensated, of course."

Rose agreed to that, as well. Although she bargained a bit on the pay.

On the third and last day, Rose is given clearance to leave.

While they wait for the nurse to arrive with the wheelchair and a release form, Rose turns to Sybil, who stands close by holding a duffel bag filled with Rose's personal items, along with a stack of Get Well cards that had come in over the last forty-eight hours.

Downstairs, Roy and Carlo are waiting to take her home.

Back to Autumn Springs.

But first, there's something she must do.

"Hand me that, will you, dear?" Rose says, pointing to the bedside table.

Sybil takes the envelope from the table and hands it to her mother, who sits, fully dressed, on the edge of the hospital bed. Sybil strolls away to the window, giving Rose some privacy as she opens it.

Inside is a folded letter, one filled with Miller's elegant, professorial script.

Dearest Rose,

I don't know what the future holds. I just know that I'm frightened, and I know you must be as well. I hate being scared, don't you?

I'm writing this in case the worst happens. And if these are the words of a dead man, then so be it. But I can't leave this plane of existence without telling you a few things.

First, please know that I'm not upset. Well, not anymore. While it hurt terribly that you thought me capable of such horrid acts, I know deep down it's a defense mechanism for you, a way to protect yourself and protect your heart. And I understand why, Rose. We all have parts of us that are dark, that define who we've become.

That said, while I won't argue against the idea that the past defines us, I also believe that it should not control us.

I suppose that's all there is to say about that, other than I'm sorry for what happened to you, but I don't think you want my pity, or my apologies, so I'll keep those to myself moving forward.

Second, I want you to know that I love you. It might annoy you, dear Rose, to hear such things. But it needs to be said.

I love you, Rose DuBois. In whatever shape, whatever form, that takes. I am of an age where I'll take what I can get and call myself lucky. I'm lucky to have you in my life, and I hope you feel the same about that, anyway, if not the former.

As I said, I have no idea what the future holds, so I best get it all out.

Rose, there are many times I've thought of sharing my true feelings with you, but I knew you didn't want that, and likely still don't, but here we are and it's important to me that you know. So don't give me that look, because I won't apologize. Not for this.

I hope to see you again soon. And I hope you never read this letter, because I fear it would mean that the worst has indeed happened, and I hate the chill that rides up my spine at even writing those words, so let's just move on, shall we?

Lastly, I want you to know that I miss you. You've only been gone a couple days, but it feels like eons. I miss our chats. I miss watching our silly crime movies, and your wonderful desserts, and your smile. I miss it all and will continue to do so until we see each other again, in this life or the next.

Yours always,
Miller

Rose folds up the letter and slides it back into the envelope. She looks to her daughter, who's pretending—quite poorly—that she hadn't been watching closely while she read. "Will you get the nurse, honey? It's time to leave."

"Of course." Sybil smiles at her, then steps into the hall.

Rose gets off the bed and walks to the open door. Her mended toes ache horribly, and she's not supposed to be walking without assistance, but this is something she wants to do alone.

She spots Sybil waiting by the nurse's station, then turns to walk—or limp, rather—in the opposite direction.

At the end of the hall is an elevator. Rose presses the button to go up and waits. It arrives smoothly and quickly, and she smiles, thinking of the crappy elevator from home and how much she misses it.

One floor up, she exits and follows the signs toward intensive care, limping along but happy to be moving. Happy to be free.

As she passes the nurse's station, she waves to the nice woman sitting there, who waves back, recognizing her right away, as it's not Rose's first visit to the ICU this week.

Not by a long shot.

Rose walks over to her friend, who is on a respirator and full of tubes. He looks gaunt, and old, and she hates it. But the prognosis is good, even if the road is long. With a sigh, she sits in the plastic chair at the side of his bed, takes his big hand in both of hers, and squeezes. "I'm here," she says.

To her joyous delight, he squeezes back.

AFTERWORD AND ACKNOWLEDGMENTS

This may seem an odd thing to say about what is, categorically, a slasher novel, but in many ways this book was a very personal, and emotional, project for me.

Both of my parents passed away during the writing of *Autumn Springs*, and in the early stages of working on the novel I found myself changing tack, from what I initially thought the story would be, into something that became much more explorative of themes such as family, and love, and trust. I found myself writing about what it means to reach our later years and how it impacts not only us, but those around us. Our families. Our children.

When I started breathing life into Rose DuBois, I was caught off guard at how rich and volatile and complex she was; how bright and shining her passion for both herself and those she cared for. I was intrigued at how someone could be so strong, and yet so damaged. So determined, and so frightened. How she craved love and companionship while also throwing up emotional walls, terrified of opening herself up once more to someone who might hurt her, or betray her. How she strived for independence while also knowing that independence, inevitably, was fleeting. How she deeply loved and protected her family while also wanting to take care of, and prioritize, her own needs and desires. How she, ultimately, turned so much darkness into light.

In other words, Rose arrived wonderfully whole, and unreservedly human.

More than that, Rose allowed me to explore and process many thoughts and feelings that I'd personally gone through during the writing of her story. As most genre readers know, horror can be cathartic as hell, and this novel, for me, was no exception.

If you've dealt with a loved one stricken with Alzheimer's or suffering from dementia, or faced the gut-wrenching choices that arise when someone you care about needs more help than you can offer, I hope you also found some catharsis in this story, and some strength in knowing you're not alone.

And if you're a veteran of life, reaching the glorious years of advanced age, I hope you found some (admittedly dark) humor in Rose's story, and made a small connection with the folks at Autumn Springs (the ones that lived, anyway). I hope I made you gasp, and possibly chuckle, at the cast of characters and their grim adventures, and that you found a friend in Miller, and in my incredible final girl, Rose DuBois.

Personally, I hope Rose's story will continue. Time will tell.

Please allow me one more moment, dear reader, to thank the many folks who have worked so hard on getting this book into your hands, and who have supported me along the way.

Huge thanks to my literary agent, Elizabeth Copps, who has been a tireless champion of my work going back to my first published novel, and to my Nightfire editor, Kristin Temple—appreciate you going above and beyond for this one.

A big thanks to the folks at Macmillan / Tor Nightfire who worked on this book:

Publicity: Cassidy Sattler

Marketing: Michael Dudding and Valeria Castorena

Art: Esther Kim and Peter Lutjen

Production: Rafal Gibek, Steven Bucsok, and Jeff LaSala

I also want to thank Nadia Saward and all the folks at Hachette / Orbit UK for their hard work and support, and for publishing the UK edition of this novel, and Paul Miller at Earthling Publications for all the beautiful, limited editions he creates for my titles, including this one.

Humor me a quick shout-out to my Sabbath Residents:

Erik Rios, Phil Haagensen, Joan Digney, Mark Hazelden, Jeff Fischer, Thomas Clink, Erik Mann, Zachery Long, Jesse Garcia, Roberto Hull, Michael Runner, Juan Trilleros, Sean Ford, Cristina Mancini, Rob Dolan, Brandon Sharp, JJ Murphy, Jason McDonald,

H Michael Casper, John Fahey, Twan Van Gastel, Frank Scott Valeri, Alexia Simms, Aaron Barnett, Kyle Davis, Hans Curtis, Alex Berman, Kevin Heimann, Shaun Rosel, William Karl Stansell, Noel Badger, David Perry, Andrea Della Gatta, Roger Geis, Scott Griffin, Austin Carroll, Anthony Vincent, Steven Duane Allison Junior, Daniel Benoit, Chase Callaway, James Boyer, Thomas Finnegan, Christine Warwick, Alex Sierra, Paul Miller, Parker McMillan, Shawn Jones, Mike Hughes, David Swisher, Timothy Bedwell.

Thanks to my managers, Zach Cox and Jack Clayman at Circle M+P, and my film agents, Nicole Weinroth and Carolina Beltran at WME, for getting my stories into worlds beyond the page.

Allow me another shout-out for the FF admins: Mitch Hull, Jeff Terry, Steven Duane Allison Junior, and Joshua Poblano. Thanks, dudes.

Thanks to all the Freaks, and all my Patrons. You guys rock.

A raised glass to Josh Malerman and Ron Malfi, for always putting a drink in my hand when I need it most (and for being great pals), and to my friend Laird Barron, for his guidance and friendship.

Big hugs to Dave, Patti, Ernie, Donna, Rod, Jen, Tim, Heather; and to Ernie and Eileen Simard. Love you all.

Lastly, I want to send all my love and gratitude to my son, Dominic, and my wife, Stephanie, for their faith in me and constant support while I live this dream.

And to my readers, I hope you enjoyed your stay at Autumn Springs.

Let's do it again sometime.

PF
Los Angeles
January 2025

ABOUT THE AUTHOR

Stephanie Simard

PHILIP FRACASSI is the Bram Stoker and British Fantasy Award–nominated author of the story collections *Behold the Void*, *Beneath a Pale Sky*, and *No One Is Safe!* His novels include *A Child Alone with Strangers*, *Gothic*, *Boys in the Valley*, and *The Third Rule of Time Travel*. His stories have been published in numerous magazines and anthologies, including *Best Horror of the Year*, *Nightmare Magazine*, *Interzone*, and *Southwest Review*. Fracassi lives in Los Angeles and is represented by Copps Literary Services, Circle M + P, and WME.

pfracassi.com
Bluesky: @pfracassi.bsky.social
Instagram: @pfracassi

ABOUT THE AUTHOR

Stephanie Simard

PHILIP FRACASSI is the Bram Stoker and British Fantasy Award–nominated author of the story collections *Behold the Void, Beneath a Pale Sky,* and *No One Is Safe!* His novels include *A Child Alone with Strangers, Gothic, Boys in the Valley,* and *The Third Rule of Time Travel.* His stories have been published in numerous magazines and anthologies, including *Best Horror of the Year, Nightmare Magazine, Interzone,* and *Southwest Review.* Fracassi lives in Los Angeles and is represented by Copps Literary Services, Circle M + P, and WME.

pfracassi.com
Bluesky: @pfracassi.bsky.social
Instagram: @pfracassi